Rose Madder

STEPHEN KING

Rose Madder

VIKING

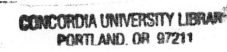

VIKING
Published by the Penguin Group
Penguin Books USA Inc., 375 Hudson Street, New York, New York 10014, U.S.A.
Penguin Books Ltd, 27 Wrights Lane, London W8 5TZ, England
Penguin Books Australia Ltd, Ringwood, Victoria, Australia
Penguin Books Canada Ltd, 10 Alcorn Avenue, Toronto, Ontario, Canada M4V 3B2
Penguin Books (N.Z.) Ltd, 182–190 Wairau Road, Auckland 10, New Zealand

Penguin Books Ltd, Registered Offices: Harmondsworth, Middlesex, England

First published in 1995 by Viking Penguin, a division of Penguin Books USA Inc.

1 3 5 7 9 10 8 6 4 2

Copyright © Stephen King, 1995   All rights reserved

Frontispiece illustration by Mark Geyer. Copyright © Mark Geyer, 1995

Grateful acknowledgment is made for permission to
reprint excerpts from the following copyrighted works:
Lyrics from "Really Rosie" by Maurice Sendak. Copyright © 1975 by
Maurice Sendak. Reprinted by permission of Maurice Sendak.
"Out of the Sea, Early" from The Complete Poems to Solve by May Swenson. Reprinted with
permission of Macmillan Books for Young Readers, an imprint of Simon & Schuster
Children's Publishing Division. Copyright © 1993 by The Literary Estate of May Swenson.
"Ramblin' Rose," words and music by Noel Sherman and Joe Sherman.
Copyright © 1962, renewed 1990 by Erasmus Music, Inc. Administered by the
Songwriter's Guild of America, Weehawken, NJ. Reprinted with permission.
All rights reserved. International copyright secured.
"The Race Is On" by Don Rollins. Copyright © 1964 Tree Publishing Co., Inc./Glad
Music (renewed). All rights administered by Sony Music Publishing, 8 Music Square
West, Nashville, TN 37203. All rights reserved. Used by permission.
"The Name Game," words and music by Lincoln Chase and Shirley Elliston.
© 1964 (renewed 1992) EMI Music Publishing o/b/o Al Gallico Music Corp.
Reprinted by permission of Warner Bros. Publications, Inc.
"Hanky Panky" by Jeff Barry and Ellie Greenwich. © 1962 Trio Music Co., Inc.
& Alley Music Corp. (renewed). All rights reserved. Used by permission.
"Highway 61 Revisited" by Bob Dylan. Copyright © 1965 by Warner Bros. Music.
Copyright renewed 1993 by Special Rider Music. All rights reserved.
International copyright secured. Reprinted by permission.

ISBN 0-670-85869-2

CIP data available

This book is printed on acid-free paper.
∞

Printed in the United States of America by R. R. Donnelley & Sons Company
Set in Simoncini Garamond
Design and rose ornaments by Amy Hill

This book is for
Joan Marks.

I'm really Rosie,
And I'm Rosie Real,
You better believe me,
I'm a great big deal . . .

—Maurice Sendak

A bloody
egg yolk. A burnt hole
spreading in a sheet. An en-
raged rose threatening to bloom.

—May Swenson

Prologue

SINISTER
KISSES

She sits in the corner, trying to draw air out of a room which seemed to have plenty just a few minutes ago and now seems to have none. From what sounds like a great distance she can hear a thin *whoop-whoop* sound, and she knows this is air going down her throat and then sliding back out again in a series of feverish little gasps, but that doesn't change the feeling that she's drowning here in the corner of her living room, looking at the shredded remains of the paperback novel she was reading when her husband came home.

Not that she cares much. The pain is too great for her to worry about such minor matters as respiration, or how there seems to be no air in the air she is breathing. The pain has swallowed her as the whale reputedly swallowed Jonah, that holy draft-dodger. It throbs like a poison sun glowing deep down in the middle of her, in a place where until tonight there was only the quiet sense of a new thing growing.

There has never been any pain like this pain, not that she can remember—not even when she was thirteen and swerved her bike to avoid a pothole and wiped out, bouncing her head off the asphalt and opening up a cut that turned out to be exactly eleven stitches long. What she remembered about that was a silvery jolt of pain followed by starry dark surprise which had actually been a brief faint . . . but that pain had not been this agony. This terrible agony. Her hand on her belly registers flesh that is no longer like flesh at all; it is as if she has been unzipped and her living baby replaced with a hot rock.

Oh God please, she thinks. *Please let the baby be okay.*

But now, as her breath finally begins to ease a little, she realizes that the baby is *not* okay, that he has made sure of that much, anyway. When you're four months pregnant the baby is still more a part of you than of itself, and when you're sitting in a corner with your hair stuck in strings to your sweaty cheeks and it feels as if you've swallowed a hot stone—

Something is putting sinister, slippery little kisses against the insides of her thighs.

"*No,*" she whispers, "*no.* Oh my dear sweet God, *no.* Good God, sweet God, dear God, *no.*"

Let it be sweat, she thinks. *Let it be sweat . . . or maybe I peed myself. Yes, that's probably it. It hurt so bad after he hit me the third time that I peed myself and didn't even know it. That's it.*

Except it isn't sweat and it isn't pee. It's blood. She's sitting here in the corner of the living room, looking at a dismembered paperback lying half on the sofa and half under the coffee-table, and her womb is getting ready to vomit up the baby it has so far carried with no complaint or problem whatsoever.

"*No,*" she moans, "*no,* God, please say no."

She can see her husband's shadow, as twisted and elongated as a cornfield effigy or the shadow of a hanged man, dancing and bobbing on the wall of the archway leading from the living room into the kitchen. She can see shadow-phone pressed to shadow-ear, and the long corkscrew shadow-cord. She can even see his shadow-fingers pulling the kinks out of the cord, holding for a moment and then releasing it back into its former curls again, like a bad habit you just can't get rid of.

Her first thought is that he's calling the police. Ridiculous, of course —he *is* the police.

"Yes, it's an emergency," he's saying. "You're goddam tooting it is, beautiful, she's pregnant." He listens, slipping the cord through his fingers, and when he speaks again his tone is testy. Just that faint irritation in his voice is enough to renew her terror and fill her mouth with a steely taste. Who would cross him, contradict him? Oh, who would be so foolish as to do that? Only someone who didn't know him, of course— someone who didn't know him the way *she* knew him. "Of *course* I won't move her, do you think I'm an idiot?"

Her fingers creep under her dress and up her thigh to the soaked, hot cotton of her panties. *Please,* she thinks. How many times has that word gone through her mind since he tore the book out of her hands? She doesn't know, but here it is again. *Please let the liquid on my fingers be clear. Please, God. Please let it be clear.*

But when she brings her hand out from under her dress the tips of her fingers are red with blood. As she looks at them, a monstrous cramp rips through her like a hacksaw blade. She has to slam her teeth together to stifle a scream. She knows better than to scream in this house.

"Never mind all that bullshit, just get here! Fast!" He slams the phone back into its cradle.

His shadow swells and bobs on the wall and then he's standing in the archway, looking at her out of his flushed and handsome face. The eyes in that face are as expressionless as shards of glass twinkling beside a country road.

"Now look at this," he says, holding out both hands briefly and then letting them drop back to his sides with a soft clap. "Look at this mess."

She holds her own hand out to him, showing him the bloody tips of her fingers—it is as close to accusation as she can get.

"I know," he says, speaking as if his knowing explained everything, put the whole business in a coherent, rational context. He turns and stares fixedly at the dismembered paperback. He picks up the piece on the couch, then bends to get the one under the coffee-table. As he straightens up again, she can see the cover, which shows a woman in a white peasant blouse standing on the prow of a ship. Her hair is blowing back dramatically in the wind, exposing her creamy shoulders. The title, *Misery's Journey,* has been rendered in bright red foil.

"*This* is the trouble," he says, and wags the remains of the book at her like a man shaking a rolled-up newspaper at a puppy that has piddled on the floor. "How many times have I told you how I feel about crap like this?"

The answer, actually, is *never.* She knows she might be sitting here in the corner having a miscarriage if he had come home and found her watching the news on TV or sewing a button on one of his shirts or just napping on the couch. It has been a bad time for him, a woman named Wendy Yarrow has been making trouble for him, and what Norman does with trouble is share the wealth. *How many times have I told you how I feel about that crap?* he would have shouted, no matter what crap it was. And then, just before he started in with his fists: *I want to talk to you, honey. Right up close.*

"Don't you understand?" she whispers. "I'm losing the baby!"

Incredibly, he smiles. "You can have another one," he says. He might be comforting a child who has dropped her ice cream cone. Then he takes the torn-up paperback out to the kitchen, where he will no doubt drop it in the trash.

You bastard, she thinks, without knowing she thinks it. The cramps are coming again, not just one this time but many, swarming into her like terrific insects, and she pushes her head back deep into the corner and moans. *You bastard, how I hate you.*

He comes back through the arch and walks toward her. She pedals with her feet, trying to shove herself into the wall, staring at him with frantic eyes. For a moment she's positive he means to kill her this time, not just hurt her, or rob her of the baby she has wanted for so long, but to really kill her. There is something inhuman about the way he looks as he comes toward her with his head lowered and his hands hanging at his sides and the long muscles in his thighs flexing. Before the kids called people like her husband fuzz they had another word for them, and that's the word that comes to her now as he crosses the room with his head down and his hands swinging at the ends of his arms like meat pendulums, because that's what he looks like—a bull.

Moaning, shaking her head, pedaling with her feet. One loafer coming off and lying on its side. She can feel fresh pain, cramps sinking into her belly like anchors equipped with old rusty teeth, and she can feel more blood flowing, but she can't stop pedaling. What she sees in him when he's like this is nothing at all; a kind of terrible absence.

He stands over her, shaking his head wearily. Then he squats and slides his arms beneath her. "I'm not going to hurt you," he says as he kneels to fully pick her up, "so quit being a goose."

"I'm bleeding," she whispers, remembering he had told the person he'd been talking to on the phone that he wouldn't move her, of course he wouldn't.

"Yeah, I know," he replies, but without interest. He is looking around the room, trying to decide where the accident happened—she knows what he's thinking as surely as if she were inside his head. "That's okay, it'll stop. They'll stop it."

Will they be able to stop the miscarriage? she cries inside her own head, never thinking that if she can do it he can too, or noticing the careful way he's looking at her. And once again she won't let herself overhear the rest of what she is thinking: *I hate you. Hate you.*

He carries her across the room to the stairs. He kneels, then settles her at the foot of them.

"Comfy?" he asks solicitously.

She closes her eyes. She can't look at him anymore, not right now. She feels she'll go mad if she does.

"Good," he says, as if she had replied, and when she opens her eyes she sees the look he gets sometimes—that absence. As if his mind has flown off, leaving his body behind.

If I had a knife I could stab him, she thinks . . . but again, it isn't an idea she will even allow herself to overhear, much less consider. It is only a deep echo, perhaps a reverberation of her husband's madness, as soft as a rustle of batwings in a cave.

Animation floods back into his face all at once and he gets up, his knees popping. He looks down at his shirt to make sure there's no blood on it. It's okay. He looks over into the corner where she collapsed. There *is* blood there, a few little beads and splashes of it. More blood is coming out of her, faster and harder now; she can feel it soaking her with un-healthy, somehow avid warmth. It is *rushing,* as if it has wanted all along to flush the stranger out of its tiny apartment. It is almost as if—oh, horrible thought—her very blood has taken up for her husband's side of it . . . whatever mad side that is.

He goes into the kitchen again and is out there for about five minutes. She can hear him moving around as the actual miscarriage happens and the pain crests and then lets go in a liquid squittering which is felt as much as heard. Suddenly it's as if she is sitting in a sitz bath full of warm, thick liquid. A kind of blood gravy.

His elongate shadow bobs on the archway as the refrigerator opens and closes and then a cabinet (the minute squeak tells her it's the one under the sink) also opens and closes. Water runs in the sink and then he begins to hum something—she thinks it might be "When a Man Loves a Woman"—as her baby runs out of her.

When he comes back through the archway he has a sandwich in one hand—he has not gotten any supper yet, of course, and must be hungry—and a damp rag from the basket under the sink in the other. He squats in the corner to which she staggered after he tore the book from her hands and then administered three hard punches to her belly —*bam, bam, bam,* so long stranger—and begins to wipe up the spatters and drips of blood with the rag; most of the blood and the other mess will be over here at the foot of the stairs, right where he wants it.

He eats his sandwich as he cleans. The stuff between the slices of bread smells to her like the leftover barbecued pork she was going to put together with some noodles for Saturday night—something easy they could eat as they sat in front of the TV, watching the early news.

He looks at the rag, which is stained a faint pink, then into the corner, then at the rag again. He nods, tears a big bite out of his sandwich, and stands up. When he comes back from the kitchen this time, she can hear the faint howl of an approaching siren. Probably the ambulance he called.

He crosses the room, kneels beside her, and takes her hands. He frowns at how cold they are, and begins to chafe them gently as he talks to her.

"I'm sorry," he says. "It's just . . . stuff's been happening . . . that bitch from the motel . . ." He stops, looks away for a moment, then looks back at her. He is wearing a strange, rueful smile. *Look who I'm trying to explain to,* that smile seems to say. *That's how bad it's gotten —sheesh.*

"Baby," she whispers. "Baby."

7

He squeezes her hands, squeezes them hard enough to hurt. "Never mind the baby, just listen to me. They'll be here in a minute or two." Yes—the ambulance is very close now, whooping through the night like an unspeakable hound. "You were coming downstairs and you missed your footing. You fell. Do you understand?"

She looks at him, saying nothing. The pain in her middle is abating a little now, and when he squeezes her hands together this time—harder than ever—she really feels it, and gasps.

"Do you understand?"

She looks into his sunken absent eyes and nods. Around her rises a flat saltwater-and-copper smell. No blood gravy now—now it is as if she were sitting in a spilled chemistry set.

"Good," he says. "Do you know what will happen if you say anything else?"

She nods.

"Say it. It'll be better for you if you do. Safer."

"You'd kill me," she whispers.

He nods, looking pleased. Looking like a teacher who has coaxed a difficult answer from a slow student.

"That's right. And I'd make it last. Before I was done, what happened tonight would look like a cut finger."

Outside, scarlet lights pulse into the driveway.

He chews the last bite of his sandwich and starts to get up. He will go to the door to let them in, the concerned husband whose pregnant wife has suffered an unfortunate accident. Before he can turn away she grasps at the cuff of his shirt. He looks down at her.

"Why?" she whispers. "Why the baby, Norman?"

For a moment she sees an expression on his face she can hardly credit—it looks like fear. But why would he be afraid of her? Or the baby?

"It was an accident," he says. "That's all, just an accident. I didn't have anything to do with it. And that's the way it better come out when you talk to them. So help you God."

So help me God, she thinks.

Doors slam outside; feet run toward the house and there is the toothy metallic clash and rattle of the gurney on which she will be transported to her place beneath the siren. He turns back to her once again, his head lowered in that bullish posture, his eyes opaque.

"You'll have another baby, and this won't happen. The next one'll be fine. A girl. Or maybe a nice little boy. The flavor doesn't matter, does it? If it's a boy, we'll get him a little baseball player's suit. If it's a girl . . ." He gestures vaguely. ". . . a bonnet, or something. You wait and see. It'll happen." He smiles then, and the sight of it makes her feel like screaming. It is like watching a corpse grin in its coffin. "If you mind me, everything will be fine. Take it to the bank, sweetheart."

Then he opens the door to let the ambulance EMTs in, telling them to hurry, telling them there's blood. She closes her eyes as they come toward her, not wanting to give them any opportunity to look into her, and she makes their voices come from far away.

Don't worry, Rose, don't you fret, it's a minor matter, just a baby, you can have another one.

A needle stings her arm, and then she is being lifted. She keeps her eyes closed, thinking *Well all right, yes. I suppose I can have another baby. I can have it and take it beyond his reach. Beyond his murderous reach.*

But time passes and gradually the idea of leaving him—never fully articulated to begin with—slips away as the knowledge of a rational waking world slips away in sleep; gradually there is no world for her but the world of the dream in which she lives, a dream like the ones she had as a girl, where she ran and ran as if in a trackless wood or a shadowy maze, with the hoofbeats of some great animal behind her, a fearful insane creature which drew ever closer and would have her eventually, no matter how many times she twisted or turned or darted or doubled back.

The concept of dreaming is known to the waking mind but to the dreamer there is no waking, no real world, no sanity; there is only the screaming bedlam of sleep. Rose McClendon Daniels slept within her husband's madness for nine more years.

I

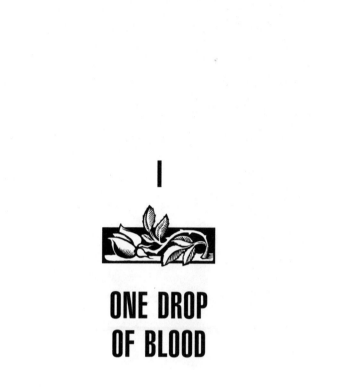

ONE DROP
OF BLOOD

1

It was fourteen years of hell, all told, but she hardly knew it. For most of those years she existed in a daze so deep it was like death, and on more than one occasion she found herself almost certain that her life wasn't really happening, that she would eventually awaken, yawning and stretching as prettily as the heroine in a Walt Disney animated cartoon. This idea came to her most often after he had beaten her so badly that she had to go to bed for awhile in order to recover. He did that three or four times a year. In 1985—the year of Wendy Yarrow, the year of the official reprimand, the year of the "miscarriage"—it had happened almost a dozen times. September of that year had seen her second and last trip to the hospital as a result of Norman's ministrations . . . the last so far, anyway. She'd been coughing up blood. He held off taking her for three days, hoping it would stop, but when it started getting worse instead, he told her just what to say (he *always* told her just what to say) and then took her to St. Mary's. He took her there because the EMTs had taken her to City General following the "miscarriage." It turned out she had a broken rib that was poking at her lung. She told the falling-downstairs story for the second time in three months and didn't think even the intern who'd been there observing the examination and the treatment believed it this time, but no one asked any uncomfortable questions; they just fixed her up and sent her home. Norman knew he had been lucky, however, and after that he was more careful.

Sometimes, when she was lying in bed at night, images would come swarming into her mind like strange comets. The most common was her husband's fist, with blood grimed into the knuckles and smeared across the raised gold of his Police Academy ring. There had been mornings when she had seen the words on that ring—*Service, Loyalty, Community*—stamped into the flesh of her stomach or printed on one of her breasts. This often made her think of the blue FDA stamp you saw on roasts of pork or cuts of steak.

She was always on the verge of dropping off, relaxed and loose-limbed, when these images came. Then she would see the fist floating toward her and jerk fully awake again and lie trembling beside him, hoping he wouldn't turn over, only half-awake himself, and drive a blow into her belly or thigh for disturbing him.

She passed into this hell when she was eighteen and awakened from her daze about a month after her thirty-second birthday, almost half a lifetime later. What woke her up was a single drop of blood, no larger than a dime.

2

She saw it while making the bed. It was on the top sheet, her side, close to where the pillow went when the bed was made. She could, in fact, slide the pillow slightly to the left and hide the spot, which had dried to an ugly maroon color. She saw how easy this would be and was tempted to do it, mostly because she could not just change the top sheet; she had no more clean white bed-linen, and if she put on one of the flower-patterned sheets to replace the plain white one with the spot of blood on it, she would have to put on the other patterned one, as well. If she didn't he was apt to complain.

Look at this, she heard him saying. *Goddam sheets don't even match —you got a white one on the bottom, and one with flowers on it on top. Jesus, why do you have to be so lazy? Come over here—I want to talk to you up close.*

She stood on her side of the bed in a bar of spring sunlight, the lazy slut who spent her days cleaning the little house (a single smeared fingerprint on the corner of the bathroom mirror could bring a blow) and obsessing over what to fix him for his dinner, she stood there looking down at the tiny spot of blood on the sheet, her face so slack and devoid of animation that an observer might well have decided she was mentally retarded. *I thought my damned nose had stopped bleeding,* she told herself. *I was sure it had.*

He didn't hit her in the face often; he knew better. Face-hitting was for the sort of drunken assholes he had arrested by the hundreds in his career as a uniformed policeman and then as a city detective. You hit someone—your wife, for instance—in the face too often, and after awhile the stories about falling down the stairs or running into the bathroom door in the middle of the night or stepping on a rake in the back yard stopped working. People knew. People talked. And eventually you got into trouble, even if the woman kept her mouth shut, because the days when folks knew how to mind their own business were apparently over.

None of that took his temper into account, however. He had a bad one, *very* bad, and sometimes he slipped. That was what had happened last night, when she brought him a second glass of iced tea and spilled some on his hand. Pow, and her nose was gushing like a broken water-main before he even knew what he was doing. She saw the look of disgust on his face as the blood poured down over her mouth and chin, then the look of worried calculation—what if her nose was actually bro-ken? That would mean another trip to the hospital. For a moment she'd thought one of the real beatings was coming, one of the ones that left her huddled in the corner, gasping and crying and trying to get back enough breath so she could vomit. In her apron. Always in her apron. You did not cry out in this house, or argue with the management, and you most certainly did not vomit on the floor—not if you wanted to keep your head screwed on tight, that was.

Then his sharply honed sense of self-preservation had kicked in, and he had gotten her a washcloth filled with ice and led her into the living room, where she had lain on the sofa with the makeshift icepack pressed down between her watering eyes. That was where you had to put it, he told her, if you wanted to stop the bleeding in a hurry and reduce the residual swelling. It was the swelling he was worried about, of course. Tomorrow was her day to go to the market, and you couldn't hide a swollen nose with a pair of Oakleys the way you could hide a black eye.

He had gone back to finish his supper—broiled snapper and roasted new potatoes.

There hadn't been much swelling, as a quick glance in the mirror this morning had shown her (he had already given her a close looking-over and then a dismissive nod before drinking a cup of coffee and leaving for work), and the bleeding had stopped after only fifteen minutes or so with the icepack . . . or so she'd thought. But sometime in the night, while she had been sleeping, one traitor drop of blood had crept out of her nose and left this spot, which meant she was going to have to strip the bed and remake it, in spite of her aching back. Her back always ached these days; even moderate bending and light lifting made it hurt. Her back was one of his favorite targets. Unlike what he called "face-hitting," it was safe to hit someone in the back . . . if the someone in question knew how to keep her mouth shut, that was. Norman had been working on her kidneys for fourteen years, and the traces of blood she saw more and more frequently in her urine no longer surprised or wor-ried her. It was just another unpleasant part of being married, that was all, and there were probably millions of women who had it worse. Thousands right in this town. So she had always seen it, anyway, until now.

She looked at the spot of blood, feeling unaccustomed resentment throbbing in her head, feeling something else, a pins-and-needles tingle, not knowing this was the way you felt when you finally woke up.

There was a small bentwood rocker on her side of the bed which she had always thought of, for no reason she could have explained, as Pooh's Chair. She backed toward it now, never taking her eyes off the small drop of blood glaring off the white sheet, and sat down. She sat in Pooh's Chair for almost five minutes, then jumped when a voice spoke in the room, not realizing at first that it was her own voice.

"If this goes on, he'll kill me," she said, and after she got over her momentary startle, she supposed it was the drop of blood—the little bit of herself that was already dead, that had crept out of her nose and died on the sheet—she was speaking to.

The answer that came back was inside her own head, and it was infinitely more terrible than the possibility she had spoken aloud:

Except he might not. Have you thought of that? He might not.

3

She *hadn't* thought of it. The idea that someday he would hit her too hard, or in the wrong place, had often crossed her mind (although she had never said it out loud, even to herself, until today), but never the possibility that she might *live* . . .

The buzzing in her muscles and joints increased. Usually she only sat in Pooh's Chair with her hands folded in her lap, looking across the bed and through the bathroom door at her own reflection in the mirror, but this morning she began to rock, moving the chair back and forth in short, jerky arcs. She *had* to rock. The buzzing, tingling sensation in her muscles *demanded* that she rock. And the last thing she wanted to do was to look at her own reflection, and never mind that her nose hadn't swollen much.

Come over here, sweetheart, I want to talk to you up close.

Fourteen years of that. A hundred and sixty-eight months of it, beginning with his yanking her by the hair and biting her shoulder for slamming a door on their wedding night. One miscarriage. One scratched lung. The horrible thing he'd done with the tennis racket. The old marks, on parts of her body her clothes covered. Bite-marks, for the

most part. Norman loved to bite. At first she had tried to tell herself
they were lovebites. It was strange to think she had ever been that young,
but she supposed she must have been.

Come over here—I want to talk to you up close.

Suddenly she was able to identify the buzzing, which had now spread
to her entire body. It was anger she was feeling, *rage,* and realization
brought wonder.

Get out of here, that deep part of her said suddenly. *Get out of here
right now, this very minute. Don't even take the time to run a comb
through your hair. Just go.*

"That's ridiculous," she said, rocking back and forth faster than ever.
The spot of blood on the sheet sizzled in her eye. From here, it looked
like the dot under an exclamation point. "That's ridiculous, where would
I go?"

Anywhere he isn't, the voice returned. *But you have to do it right now.
Before . . .*

Before what?

That one was easy. Before she fell asleep again.

A part of her mind—a habituated, cowed part—suddenly realized
that she was seriously entertaining this thought and put up a terrified
clamor. Leave her home of fourteen years? The house where she could
put her hand on anything she wanted? The husband who, if a little short-
tempered and quick to use his fists, had always been a good provider?
The idea was ridiculous. She must forget it, and immediately.

And she might have done so, almost certainly *would* have done so, if
not for that drop on the sheet. That single dark red drop.

Then don't look at it! the part of herself which fancied itself practical
and sensible shouted nervously. *For Christ's sake don't look at it, it's
going to get you into trouble!*

Except she found she could no longer look away. Her eyes remained
fixed upon the spot, and she rocked faster than ever. Her feet, clad in
white lowtop sneakers, patted the floor in a quickening rhythm (the
buzzing was now mostly in her head, rattling her brains, heating her up),
and what she thought was *Fourteen years. Fourteen years of having him
talk to me up close. The miscarriage. The tennis racket. Three teeth, one
of which I swallowed. The broken rib. The punches. The pinches. And the
bites, of course. Plenty of those. Plenty of—*

*Stop it! It's useless, thinking like this, because you're not going any-
where, he'd only come after you and bring you back, he'd find you, he's a
policeman and finding people is one of the things he does, one of the things
he's good at—*

17

"Fourteen years," she murmured, and now it wasn't the last fourteen she was thinking about but the next. Because that other voice, the deep voice, was right. He might *not* kill her. He might *not*. And what would she be like after fourteen more years of having him talk to her up close? Would she be able to bend over? Would she have an hour—fifteen minutes, even—a day when her kidneys didn't feel like hot stones buried in her back? Would he perhaps hit her hard enough to deaden some vital connection, so she could no longer raise one of her arms or legs, or perhaps leave one side of her face hanging slack and expressionless, like poor Mrs. Diamond, who clerked in the Store 24 at the bottom of the hill?

She got up suddenly and with such force that the back of Pooh's Chair hit the wall. She stood there for a moment, breathing hard, wide eyes still fixed on the maroon spot, and then she headed for the door leading into the living room.

Where are you going? Ms. Practical-Sensible screamed inside her head—the part of her which seemed perfectly willing to be maimed or killed for the continued privilege of knowing where the teabags were in the cupboard and where the Scrubbies were kept under the sink. *Just where do you think you're—*

She clapped a lid on the voice, something she'd had no idea she could do until this moment. She took her purse off the table by the sofa and walked across the living room toward the front door. The room suddenly seemed very big, and the walk very long.

I have to take this a step at a time. If I think even one step ahead, I'm going to lose my nerve.

She didn't think that would be a problem, actually. For one thing, what she was doing had taken on a hallucinatory quality—surely she could not simply be walking out of her house and her marriage on the spur of the moment, could she? It had to be a dream, didn't it? And there was something else, too: not thinking ahead had pretty much become a habit with her, one that had started on their wedding night, when he'd bitten her like a dog for slamming a door.

Well, you can't go like this, even if you just make it to the bottom of the block before running out of steam, Practical-Sensible advised. *At the very least change out of those jeans that show how wide your can's getting. And run a comb through your hair.*

She paused, and was for a moment close to giving the whole thing up before she even got to the front door. Then she recognized the advice for what it was—a desperate ploy to keep her in the house. And a shrewd one. It didn't take long to swap a pair of jeans for a skirt or to mousse your hair and then use a comb on it, but for a woman in her position, it would almost certainly have been long enough.

For what? To go back to sleep again, of course. She'd be having serious doubts by the time she'd pulled the zipper up on the side of her skirt, and by the time she'd finished with her comb, she'd have decided she had simply suffered a brief fit of insanity, a transitory fugue state that was probably related to her cycle.

Then she would go back into the bedroom and change the sheets.

"No," she murmured. "I won't do that. I won't."

But with one hand on the doorknob, she paused again.

She shows sense! Practical-Sensible cried, her voice a mixture of relief, jubilation, and—was it possible—faint disappointment. *Hallelujah, the girl shows sense! Better late than never!*

The jubilation and relief in that mental voice turned to wordless horror as she crossed quickly to the mantel above the gas fireplace he had installed two years before. What she was looking for probably wouldn't be there, as a rule he only left it up there toward the end of the month ("So I won't be tempted," he would say), but it couldn't hurt to check. And she knew his pin-number; it was just their telephone number, with the first and last digits reversed.

It WILL hurt! Practical-Sensible screamed. *If you take something that belongs to him, it'll hurt plenty, and you know it! PLENTY!*

"It won't be there anyway," she murmured, but it was—the bright green Merchant's Bank ATM card with his name embossed on it.

Don't you take that! Don't you dare!

But she found she *did* dare—all she had to do was call up the image of that drop of blood. Besides, it was *her* card, too, her *money,* too; wasn't that what the marriage vow meant?

Except it wasn't about the money at all, not really. It was about silencing the voice of Ms. Practical-Sensible; it was about making this sudden, unexpected lunge for freedom a necessity instead of a choice. Part of her knew that if she didn't do that, the bottom of the block *was* as far as she would get before the whole uncertain sweep of the future appeared before her like a fogbank, and she turned around and came back home, hurrying to change the bed so she could still wash the downstairs floors before noon . . . and, hard as it was to believe, that was all she had been thinking about when she got up this morning: washing floors.

Ignoring the clamor of the voice in her head, she plucked the ATM card off the mantel, dropped it into her purse, and quickly headed for the door again.

Don't do it! the voice of Ms. Practical-Sensible wailed. *Oh Rosie, he won't just hurt you for this, for this he'll put you in the hospital, maybe even kill you—don't you know that?*

She supposed she did, but she kept walking just the same, her head down and her shoulders thrust forward, like a woman walking into a strong wind. He probably *would* do those things . . . but he would have to catch her first.

This time when her hand closed on the knob there was no pause— she turned it and opened the door and stepped out. It was a beautiful sunshiny day in mid-April, the branches on the trees beginning to thicken with buds. Her shadow stretched across the stoop and the pale new grass like something cut from black construction paper with a sharp pair of scissors. She stood there breathing deep of the spring air, smelling earth which had been dampened (and perhaps quickened) by a shower that had passed in the night, while she had been lying asleep with one nostril suspended over that drying spot of blood.

The whole world is waking up, she thought. *It isn't just me.*

A man in a jogging suit ran past on the sidewalk as she pulled the door closed behind her. He lifted a hand to her, and she lifted hers in return. She listened for the voice inside to raise its clamor again, but that voice was silent. Perhaps it was stunned to silence by her theft of the ATM card, perhaps it had only been soothed by the tranquil peace of this April morning.

"I'm going," she murmured. "I'm really, really going."

But she stayed where she was a moment longer, like an animal which has been kept in a cage so long it cannot believe in freedom even when it is offered. She reached behind her and touched the knob of the door—the door that led into *her* cage.

"No more," she whispered. She tucked her purse under one arm and took her first dozen steps into the fogbank which was now her future.

4

Those dozen steps took her to the place where the concrete walk merged with the sidewalk—the place where the jogger had passed a minute or so before. She started to turn left, then paused. Norman had told her once that people who thought they were choosing directions at random—people lost in the woods, for example—were almost always simply going in the direction of their dominant hand. It probably wasn't important, but she discovered she didn't even want him to be right about which way she had turned on Westmoreland Street after leaving the house.

Not even that.

She turned right instead of left, in the direction of her stupid hand, and walked down the hill. She went past the Store 24, restraining an urge to raise her hand and cover the side of her face as she passed it. Already she felt like a fugitive, and a terrible thought had begun to gnaw at her mind like a rat gnawing cheese: what if he came home from work early and saw her? What if he saw her walking down the street in her jeans and lowtops, with her purse clamped under her arm and her hair uncombed? He would wonder what the hell she was doing out on the morning she was supposed to be washing the downstairs floors, wouldn't he? And he would want her to come over to him, wouldn't he? Yes. He would want her to come over to where he was so he could talk to her up close.

That's stupid. What reason would he have to come home now? He only left an hour ago. It doesn't make sense.

No . . . but sometimes people did things that didn't make sense. Her, for instance—look at what she was doing right now. And suppose he had a sudden intuition? How many times had he told her that cops developed a sixth sense after awhile, that they knew when something weird was going to happen? *You get this little needle at the base of your spine,* he'd said once. *I don't know how else to describe it. I know most people would laugh, but ask a cop—he won't laugh. That little needle has saved my life a couple of times, sweetheart.*

Suppose he'd been feeling that needle for the last twenty minutes or so? Suppose it had gotten him into his car and headed home? This was just the way he would come, and she cursed herself for having turned right instead of left when leaving their walk. Then an even more unpleasant idea occurred to her, one which had a hideous plausibility . . . not to mention a kind of ironic balance. Suppose he had stopped at the ATM machine two blocks down the street from police headquarters, wanting ten or twenty bucks for lunch? Suppose he had decided, after ascertaining that the card wasn't in his wallet, to come home and get it?

Get hold of yourself. That isn't going to happen. Nothing like that is going to happen.

A car turned onto Westmoreland half a block down. It was red, and what a coincidence *that* was, because *they* had a red car . . . or *he* did; the car was no more hers than the ATM card was, or the money it could access. Their red car was a new Sentra, and—coincidence upon coincidence!—wasn't this car now coming toward her a red Sentra?

No, it's a Honda!

Except it *wasn't* a Honda, that was just what she wanted to believe. It was a *Sentra,* a brand-new red Sentra. *His* red Sentra. Her worst nightmare had come true at almost the very moment she had thought of it.

For a moment her kidneys were incredibly heavy, incredibly painful, incredibly *full,* and she was sure she was going to wet her pants. Had she really thought she could get away from him? She must have been insane.

Too late to worry about that now, Practical-Sensible told her. Its dithery hysteria was gone; now it was the only part of her mind which still seemed capable of thought, and it spoke in the cold, calculating tones of a creature that puts survival ahead of everything else. *You just better think what it is you're going to say to him when he pulls over and asks you what you're doing out here. And you better make it good. You know how quick he is, and how much he sees.*

"The flowers," she muttered. "I came out to take a little walk and see whose flowers were out, that's all." She had stopped with her thighs pressed tightly together, trying to keep the dam from breaking. Would he believe it? She didn't know, but it would have to do. She couldn't think of anything else. "I was just going to walk down to the corner of St. Mark's Avenue and then come back to wash the—"

She broke off, watching with wide, unbelieving eyes as the car—a Honda after all, not new, and really closer to orange than red—rolled slowly past her. The woman behind the wheel gave her a curious glance, and the woman on the sidewalk thought, *If it had been him, no story would have done, no matter how plausible—he would have seen the truth all over your face, underlined and lit in neon.* Now *are you ready to go back? To see sense and go back?*

She couldn't. Her overwhelming need to urinate had passed, but her bladder still felt heavy and overloaded, her kidneys were still throbbing, her legs were shaky, and her heart was pounding so violently in her chest that it frightened her. She would never be able to walk back up the hill, even though the grade was very mild.

Yes, you can. You know you can. You've done harder things than that in your marriage and survived them.

Okay—maybe she *could* climb back up the hill, but now another idea occurred to her. Sometimes he called. Five or six times a month, usually, but sometimes more often than that. Just hi, how are you, do you want me to bring home a carton of Half-n-Half or a pint of ice cream, okay, bye. Only she felt nothing solicitous in these calls, no sense of caring.

He was checking up on her, that was all, and if she didn't answer the telephone, it just rang. They had no answering machine. She had asked him once if getting one might not be a good idea. He had given her a not entirely unfriendly poke and told her to wise up. *You're* the answering machine, he'd said.

What if he called and she wasn't there to answer?

He'll think I went marketing early, that's all.

But he wouldn't. That was the thing. The floors this morning; the market this afternoon. That was the way it had always been, and that was the way he expected it to always be. Spontaneity was not encouraged at 908 Westmoreland. If he called . . .

She began walking again, knowing she had to get off Westmoreland Street at the next corner, even though she wasn't entirely sure where Tremont went in either direction. That wasn't important at this point, anyway; what mattered was that she was on her husband's direct route if he came back from the city by way of I-295, as he usually did, and she felt as if she had been pinned to the bull's-eye of an archery target.

She turned left on Tremont and went walking past more quiet little suburban houses separated from each other by low hedges or lines of decorative trees—Russian olives seemed particularly in vogue down here. A man who looked like Woody Allen with his hornrimmed glasses and freckles and his shapeless blue hat crushed down on top of his head looked up from watering his flowers and gave her a little wave. Everyone wanted to be neighborly today, it seemed. She supposed it was the weather, but she could have done without it. It was all too easy to imagine *him* coming along behind her later on, patiently working her backtrail, asking questions, using his little memory-stimulation tricks, and flashing her picture at every stop.

Wave back at him. You don't want him to register you as an unfriendly, unfriendlies have a way of sticking in the memory, so wave back and just slide along your way.

She waved back and slid along her way. The need to pee had returned, but she would just have to live with it. There was no relief in sight—nothing ahead but more houses, more hedges, more pale green lawns, more Russian olives.

She heard a car behind her and knew it was him. She turned around, eyes wide and dark, and saw a rusty Chevrolet creeping up the center of the street at little more than walking speed. The old man behind the wheel wore a straw hat and a look of terrified determination. She faced forward again before he could register her own look of fright, stumbled, then started walking resolutely with her head lowered. The pulsing ache in her kidneys had returned and her bladder was pounding, too. She guessed she had no more than a minute, possibly two, before everything let go. If that happened, she might as well kiss any chance of unnoticed escape goodbye. People might not remember a pale brownette walking up the sidewalk on a nice spring morning, but she didn't see how they would be able to forget a pale brownette with a large dark stain spreading around the crotch of her jeans. She had to take care of this problem, and right away.

There was a chocolate-colored bungalow two houses up on her side of the street. The shades were pulled; three newspapers lay on the porch. A fourth lay on the walk at the foot of the front steps. Rosie took a quick look around, saw no one observing her, then hurried across the lawn of the bungalow and down along its side. The back yard was empty. A rectangle of paper hung from the knob of the aluminum screen door. She went over, walking in cramped little steps, and read the printed message: *Greetings from Ann Corso, your local Avon Lady! Didn't find you at home this time, but will come again! Thanks! And give me a call at 555-1731 if you want to talk about any of Avon's fine products!* The date scribbled at the bottom was 4/17, two days ago.

Rosie took another look around, saw that she was protected by hedges on one side and Russian olives on the other, unsnapped and unzipped her jeans, and squatted in the niche between the back stoop and the LP gas tanks. It was too late to worry about who, if anyone, might be watching from the upper stories of either neighboring house. And besides, the relief made such questions seem—for the time being, at least—trivial.

You're crazy, you know.

Yes, of course she knew . . . but as the pressure of her bladder decreased and the stream of her urine flowed between the bricks of this back patio in a zigzag streamlet, she felt a crazy joy suddenly fill her heart. In that instant she knew what it must feel like to cross a river into a foreign country, and then set fire to the bridge behind you, and stand on the riverbank, watching and breathing deeply as your only chance of retreat went up in smoke.

5

She walked for nearly two hours, through one unfamiliar neighborhood after another, before coming to a strip mall on the west side of the city. There was a pay phone in front of Paint n Carpet World, and when she used it to call a taxi, she was amazed to discover she was no longer in the city at all, but in the suburb of Mapleton. She had big blisters on both heels, and she supposed it was no wonder—she must have walked over seven miles.

The cab arrived fifteen minutes after her call, and by then she had visited the convenience store at the far end of the strip, where she got a pair of cheap sunglasses and a colorful red rayon kerchief. She remembered Norman saying once that if you wanted to divert attention from your face, the best way was to wear something bright, something which would direct the observer's eye in a different direction.

The cabbie was a fat man with unkempt hair, bloodshot eyes, bad breath. His baggy, faded tee-shirt showed a map of South Vietnam. WHEN I DIE I'LL GO TO HEAVEN 'CAUSE I SERVED MY TIME IN HELL, the words beneath the map read. IRON TRIANGLE, 1969. His beady red eyes scanned her quickly, passing from her lips to her breasts to her hips before appearing to lose interest.

"Where we going, dear?" he asked.

"Can you take me to the Greyhound depot?"

"You mean Portside?"

"Is that the bus terminal?"

"Yep." He looked up and used the rear-view mirror to meet her eyes. "That's on the other side of the city, though. A twenty-buck fare, easy. Can you afford that?"

"Of course," she said, then took a deep breath and added: "Can you find a Merchant's Bank ATM machine along the way, do you think?"

"All life's problems should be so easy," he said, and dropped the flag on his taximeter. $2.50, it read. BASE FARE.

She dated the beginning of her new life from the moment the numbers in the taximeter window clicked from $2.50 to $2.75 and the words BASE FARE disappeared. She would not be Rose Daniels anymore, unless she had to be—not just because Daniels was *his* name, and therefore dangerous, but because she had cast him aside. She would be Rosie McClendon again, the girl who had disappeared into hell at the age of eighteen. There might be times when she would be forced to use her married name, she supposed, but even then she would continue to be Rosie McClendon in her heart and mind.

I'm really Rosie, she thought as the cabbie drove across the Trunkatawny Bridge, and smiled as Maurice Sendak's words and Carole King's voice floated through her mind like a pair of ghosts. *And I'm Rosie Real.*

Was she, though? Was she real?

This is where I start finding out, she thought. *Right here and right now.*

6

The cabbie stopped in Iroquois Square and pointed to a line of cash machines standing in a plaza which came equipped with a fountain and a brushed-chrome sculpture that didn't look like anything in particular. The machine on the far left was bright green.

"That do ya?" he asked.

"Yes, thanks. I'll just be a minute."

But she was a little longer than that. First she couldn't seem to punch in the pin-number correctly, in spite of the machine's large keypads, and when she finally succeeded in that part of the operation, she couldn't decide how much to take. She pressed seven-five-decimal-zero-zero, hesitated over the TRANSACT button, then pulled her hand back. He would beat her up for running away if he caught her—no question about that. If he beat her badly enough to land her in the hospital, though (*or to kill you,* a small voice murmured, *he might actually kill you, Rosie, and you're a fool if you forget that*), it would be because she had dared to steal his ATM card . . . and to use it. Did she want to risk that sort of retribution for a mere seventy-five dollars? Was that enough?

"No," she murmured, and reached out again. This time she tapped three-five-zero-decimal-zero-zero . . . and then hesitated again. She didn't know exactly how much of what he called "the ready" there was in the cash-and-checking account this machine tapped into, but three hundred and fifty dollars had to be a pretty sizeable chunk of it. He was going to be so *angry* . . .

She moved her hand toward the CANCEL/RETRY button, and then asked herself again what difference *that* made. He was going to be angry in any case. There was no going back now.

"Are you going to be much longer, ma'am?" a voice asked from behind her. "Because I'm over my coffee-break right now."

"Oh, sorry!" she said, jumping a little. "No, I was just . . . woolgathering." She hit the TRANSACT button. The words ONE MOMENT PLEASE appeared on the auto-teller's VDT. The wait wasn't long, but it was long enough for her to entertain a vivid fantasy of the machine's suddenly emitting a high, warbling siren and a mechanized voice bellowing *"THIS WOMAN IS A THIEF! STOP HER! THIS WOMAN IS A THIEF!"*

Instead of calling her a thief, the screen flashed a thank-you, wished her a pleasant day, and produced seventeen twenties and a single ten.

Rosie offered the young man standing behind her a nervous, no-eye-contact smile, then hurried back to her cab.

7

Portside was a low, wide building with plain sandstone-colored walls. Buses of all kinds—not just Greyhounds but Trailways, American Pathfinders, Eastern Highways, and Continental Expresses—ringed the terminal with their snouts pushed deep into the loading docks. To Rosie they looked like fat chrome piglets nursing at an exceedingly ugly mother.

She stood outside the main entrance, looking in. The terminal wasn't as crowded as she had half-hoped (safety in numbers) and half-feared (after fourteen years of seeing almost no one but her husband and the colleagues he sometimes brought home for a meal, she had developed more than a touch of agoraphobia), probably because it was the middle of the week and shouting distance from the nearest holiday. Still she guessed there must be a couple of hundred people in there, walking aimlessly around, sitting on the old-fashioned, high-backed wooden benches, playing the video games, drinking coffee in the snackbar, or queuing for tickets. Small children hung onto their mothers' hands, tilted their heads back, and bawled like lost calves at the faded logging mural on the ceiling. A loudspeaker that echoed like the voice of God in a Cecil B. DeMille Bible epic announced destinations: Erie, Pennsylvania; Nashville, Tennessee; Jackson, Mississippi; Miami, Florida (the disembodied, echoing voice pronounced it *Miamuh*); Denver, Colorado.

"Lady," a tired voice said. "Hey, lady, little help here. Little help, what do you say?"

She turned her head and saw a young man with a pale face and a flood of dirty black hair sitting with his back against one side of the terminal entrance. He was holding a cardboard sign in his lap. HOMELESS & HAVE AIDS, it read. PLEASE "AID" ME.

"You got some spare change, don't you? Help me out? You'll be ridin in your speedboat on Saranac Lake long after I'm dead and gone. Whaja say?"

She felt suddenly strange and faint, on the edge of some mental and emotional overload. The terminal appeared to grow before her eyes until it was as large as a cathedral, and there was something horrifying about the tidal movements of the people in its aisles and alcoves. A man with a wrinkled, pulsing bag of flesh hanging from the side of his neck trudged past her with his head down, dragging a duffelbag after him by its string. The bag hissed like a snake as it slid along the dirty tile floor. A Mickey Mouse doll stuck out of the duffel's top, smiling blandly at her. The godlike announcer was telling the assembled travelers that the Trailways express to Omaha would be departing Gate 17 in twenty minutes.

I can't do this, she thought suddenly. *I can't live in this world. It isn't just not knowing where the teabags and Scrubbies are; the door he beat me behind was also the door that kept all this confusion and madness out. And I can never go back through it again.*

For a moment a startlingly vivid image from her childhood Sunday-school class filled her mind—Adam and Eve wearing fig-leaves and identical expressions of shame and misery, walking barefoot down a stony path toward a bitter, sterile future. Behind them was the Garden of Eden, lush and filled with flowers. A winged angel stood before its closed gate, the sword in its hand glowing with terrible light.

"Don't you *dare* think of it that way!" she cried suddenly, and the man sitting in the doorway recoiled so strongly that he almost dropped his sign. "Don't you *dare!*"

"Jesus, I'm *sorry!*" the man with the sign said, and rolled his eyes. "Go on, if that's the way you feel!"

"No, I . . . it wasn't you . . . I was thinking about my—"

The absurdity of what she was doing—trying to explain herself to a beggar sitting in the doorway of the bus terminal—came home to her then. She was still holding two dollars in her hand, her change from the cabbie. She flung them into the cigar-box beside the young man with the sign and fled into the Portside terminal.

8

Another young man—this one with a tiny Errol Flynn moustache and a handsome, unreliable face—had set up a game she recognized from TV shows as three-card monte on top of his suitcase near the back of the terminal.

"Find the ace of spades?" he invited. "Find the ace of spades, lady?"

In her mind she saw a fist floating toward her. Saw a ring on the third finger, a ring with the words *Service, Loyalty,* and *Community* engraved on it.

"No thank you," she said. "I never had a problem with that."

His expression as she passed suggested he thought she had a few bats flying around loose in her belfry, but that was all right. He was not her problem. Neither was the man at the entrance who might or might not have AIDS, or the man with the bag of flesh hanging from his neck and the Mickey Mouse doll poking out of his duffel. Her problem was Rose Daniels—check that, Rosie *McClendon*—and that was her *only* problem.

She started down the center aisle, then stopped as she saw a trash barrel. A curt imperative—DON'T LITTER!—was stenciled across its round green belly. She opened her purse, took out the ATM card, gazed down at it for a moment, then pushed it through the flap on top of the barrel. She hated to let it go, but at the same time she was relieved to see the last of it. If she kept it, using it again might become a temptation she couldn't resist . . . and Norman wasn't stupid. Brutal, yes. Stupid, no. If she gave him a way to trace her, he would. She would do well to keep that in mind.

She took in a deep breath, held it for a second or two, then let it out and headed for the ARRIVALS/DEPARTURES monitors clustered at the center of the building. She didn't look back. If she had, she would have seen the young man with the Errol Flynn moustache already rummaging in the barrel, looking for whatever it was the ditzy lady in the sunglasses and bright red kerchief had eighty-sixed. To the young man it had looked like a credit card. Probably not, but you never knew stuff like that for sure unless you checked. And sometimes a person got lucky. Sometimes? Hell, *often.* They didn't call it the Land of Opportunity for nothing.

9

The next large city to the west was only two hundred and fifty miles away, and that felt too close. She decided on an even bigger one, five hundred and fifty miles farther on. It was a lakeshore city, like this one, but in the next timezone. There was a Continental Express headed there in half an hour. She went to the bank of ticket windows and got into line. Her heart was thumping hard in her chest and her mouth was dry. Just before the person in front of her finished his transaction and moved away from the window, she put the back of her hand to her mouth and stifled a burp that burned coming up and tasted of her morning coffee.

You don't dare use either version of your name here, she cautioned herself. *If they want a name, you have to give another one.*

"Help you, ma'am?" the clerk asked, looking at her over a pair of half-glasses perched precariously on the end of his nose.

"Angela Flyte," she said. It was the name of her best chum in junior high, and the last friend she had ever really made. At Aubreyville High School, Rosie had gone steady with the boy who had married her a week after her graduation, and they had formed a country of two . . . one whose borders were usually closed to tourists.

"Beg your pardon, ma'am?"

She realized she had named a person rather than a place, and how odd

(this guy's probably looking at my wrists and neck, trying to see if the straitjacket left any marks)

it must have sounded. She blushed in confusion and embarrassment, and made an effort to clutch at her thoughts, to put them in some kind of order.

"I'm sorry," she said, and a dismal premonition came to her: whatever else the future might hold, that simple, rueful little phrase was going to follow her like a tin can tied to a stray dog's tail. There had been a closed door between her and most of the world for fourteen years, and right now she felt like a terrified mouse who has misplaced its hole in the kitchen baseboard.

The clerk was still looking at her, and the eyes above the amusing half-glasses were now rather impatient. "Can I help you or not, ma'am?"

"Yes, please. I want to buy a ticket on the eleven-oh-five bus. Are there still some seats on that one?"

"Oh, I guess about forty. One way or round trip?"

"One way," she said, and felt another flush warm her cheeks as the enormity of what she was saying came home to her. She tried to smile and said it again, with a little more force: "One way, please."

"That's fifty-nine dollars and seventy cents," he said, and she felt her knees grow weak with relief. She had been expecting a much higher fare; had even been prepared for the possibility that he would ask for most of what she had.

"Thank you," she said, and he must have heard the honest gratitude in her voice, because he looked up from the form he was drawing to him and smiled at her. The impatient, guarded look had left his eyes.

"A pleasure," he said. "Luggage, ma'am?"

"I . . . I don't have any luggage," she said, and was suddenly afraid of his gaze. She tried to think of an explanation—surely it must sound suspicious to him, an unaccompanied woman headed for a far-off city with no luggage except her purse—but no explanation came. And, she saw, that was all right. He wasn't suspicious, wasn't even curious. He simply nodded and began to write up her ticket. She had a sudden and far from pleasant realization: she was no novelty at Portside. This man saw women like her all the time, women hiding behind dark glasses, women buying tickets to different timezones, women who looked as if they had forgotten who they were somewhere along the way, and what they thought they were doing, and why.

10

Rosie felt a profound sense of relief as the bus lumbered out of the Portside terminal (on time), turned left, re-crossed the Trunkatawny, and then got on I-78 heading west. As they passed the last of the three downtown exits, she saw the triangular glass-sided building that was the new police headquarters. It occurred to her that her husband might be behind one of those big windows right now, that he might even be looking out at this big, shiny bus beetling along the Interstate. She closed her eyes and counted to one hundred. When she opened them again, the building was gone. Gone forever, she hoped.

She had taken a seat three quarters of the way back in the bus, and the diesel engine hummed steadily not far behind her. She closed her eyes again and rested the side of her face on the window. She would not sleep, she was too keyed-up to sleep, but she could rest. She had an idea she was going to need all the rest she could get. She was still amazed at how suddenly this had happened—an event more like a heart attack or a stroke than a change of life. Change? That was putting it mildly. She hadn't just changed it, she had uprooted it, like a woman tearing an African violet out of its pot. Change of life, indeed. No, she would never sleep. Sleep was out of the question.

And so thinking, she slipped not into sleep, but into that umbilical cord which connects sleeping and waking. Here she moved slowly back and forth like a bubble, faintly aware of the diesel engine's steady hum, the sound of the tires on the pavement, of a kid four or five rows up asking his mother when they were going to get to Aunt Norma's. But she was also aware that she had come untethered from herself, and that her mind had opened like a flower (a rose, of course), opened as it does only when one is in neither one place nor the other.

I'm really Rosie . . .

Carole King's voice, singing Maurice Sendak's words. They came floating up the corridor she was in from some distant chamber, echoing, accompanied by the glassy, ghostly notes of a piano.

. . . and I'm Rosie Real . . .

I'm going to sleep after all, she thought. *I think I really am. Imagine that!*

You better believe me . . . I'm a great big deal . . .

She was no longer in the gray corridor but in some dark open space. Her nose, her entire head, was filled with smells of summer so sweet and so strong that they were almost overwhelming. Chief among them was the smell of honeysuckle, drifts of it. She could hear crickets, and when she looked up she saw the polished bone face of the moon, riding high overhead. Its white glow was everywhere, turning the mist rising from the tangled grasses around her bare legs to smoke.

I'm really Rosie . . . and I'm Rosie Real . . .

She raised her hands with the fingers splayed and the thumbs almost touching; she framed the moon like a picture and as the night wind stroked her bare arms she felt her heart first swell with happiness and then contract with fright. She sensed a dozing savagery in this place, as if there might be animals with big teeth loose in the perfumed undergrowth.

Rose. Come over here, sweetheart. I want to talk to you up close.

She turned her head and saw his fist rushing out of the dark. Icy strokes of moonlight gleamed on the raised letters of his Police Academy ring. She saw the stressful grimace of his lips, pulled back in something like a smile—

—and jerked awake in her seat, gasping, her forehead damp with sweat. She must have been breathing hard for some time, because her window was humid with her condensed breath, almost completely fogged in. She swiped a clear patch on the glass with the side of her hand and looked out. The city was almost gone now; they were passing an exurban litter of gas stations and fast-food franchises, but behind them she could see stretches of open field.

I've gotten away from him, she thought. *No matter what happens to me now, I've gotten away from him. Even if I have to sleep in doorways, or under bridges, I've gotten away from him. He'll never hit me again, because I've gotten away from him.*

But she discovered she did not entirely believe it. He would be furious with her, and he would try to find her. She was sure of it.

But how can he? I've covered my trail; I didn't even have to write down my old school chum's name in order to get my ticket. I threw away the bank card, that's the biggest thing. So how can he find me?

She didn't know, exactly . . . but finding people *was* what he did, and she would have to be very, very careful.

I'm really Rosie . . . and I'm Rosie real . . .

Yes, she supposed both sides of that were the truth, but she had never felt less like a great big deal in her whole life. What she felt like was a tiny speck of flotsam in the middle of a trackless ocean. The terror which had filled her near the end of her brief dream was still with her, but so were traces of the exhilaration and happiness; a sense of being, if not powerful, at least free.

She leaned against the high-backed bus seat and watched the last of the fast-food restaurants and muffler shops fall away. Now it was just the countryside—newly opened fields and belts of trees that were turning that fabulous cloudy green that belongs only to April. She watched them roll past with her hands clasped loosely in her lap and let the big silver bus take her on toward whatever lay ahead.

II

THE KINDNESS
OF STRANGERS

1

She had a great many bad moments during the first weeks of her new life, but even at what was very nearly the worst of them all—getting off the bus at three in the morning and entering a terminal four times the size of Portside—she did not regret her decision.

She was, however, terrified.

Rosie stood just inside the doorway of Gate 62, clutching her purse tightly in both hands and looking around with wide eyes as people rushed past in riptides, some dragging suitcases, some balancing string-tied cardboard boxes on their shoulders, some with their arms around the shoulders of their girlfriends or the waists of their boyfriends. As she watched, a man sprinted toward a woman who had just gotten off Rosie's bus, seized her, and spun her around so violently that her feet left the ground. The woman crowed with delight and terror, her cry as bright as a flashgun in the crowded, confused terminal.

There was a bank of video games to Rosie's right, and although it was the darkest hour of the morning, kids—most with their baseball caps turned around backward and at least eighty per cent of their hair buzzed off—were bellied up to all of them. "Try again, Space Cadet!" the one nearest to Rosie invited in a grinding, inhuman voice. "Try again, Space Cadet! Try again, Space Cadet!"

She walked slowly past the video games and into the terminal, sure of only one thing: she didn't dare go out at this hour of the morning. She felt the chances were excellent that she would be raped, killed, and stuffed into the nearest garbage can if she did. She glanced left and saw a pair of uniformed policemen coming down the escalator from the upper level. One was twirling his nightstick in a complex pattern. The other was grinning in a hard, humorless way that made her think of a man eight hundred miles behind her. He grinned, but there was no grin in his constantly moving eyes.

What if their job is to tour the place every hour or so and kick out everyone who doesn't have a ticket? What will you do then?

She'd handle that if it came up, that was what she'd do. For the time being she moved away from the escalator and toward an alcove where a dozen or so travelers were parked in hard plastic contour chairs. Small coin-op TVs were bolted to the arms of these chairs. Rosie kept an eye on the cops as she went and was relieved to see them move across the floor of the terminal and away from her. In two and a half hours, three at the most, it would be daylight. After that they could catch her and kick her out. Until then she wanted to stay right here, where there were lights and lots of people.

She sat down in one of the TV chairs. Two seats away on her left, a girl wearing a faded denim jacket and holding a backpack on her lap was dozing. Her eyes rolled beneath her purple-tinged eyelids, and a long, silvery strand of saliva depended from her lower lip. Four words had been tattooed on the back of her right hand, straggling blue capitals that announced I LOVE MY HUNNEY. *Where's your honey now, sweetheart?* Rosie thought. She looked at the blank screen of the TV, then at the tiled wall on her right. Here someone had scrawled the words SUCK MY AIDS-INFECTED COCK in red Magic Marker. She looked away hastily, as if the words would burn her retinas if she looked at them too long, and gazed across the terminal. On the far wall was a huge lighted clock. It was 3:16 a.m.

Two and a half more hours and I can leave, she thought, and began to wait them through.

2

She'd had a cheeseburger and a lemonade when the bus made a rest-stop around six o'clock the previous evening, nothing since then, and she was hungry. She sat in the TV alcove until the hands of the big clock made it around to four a.m., then decided she'd better get a bite. She crossed to the small cafeteria near the ticket windows, stepping over several sleeping people on her way. Many of them had their arms curled protectively around bulging, tape-mended plastic garbage bags, and by the time Rosie got coffee and juice and a bowl of Special K, she understood that she had been needlessly worried about being kicked out by the cops. These sleepers weren't through-travelers; they were homeless people camping out in the bus terminal. Rosie felt sorry for them, but she also felt perversely comforted—it was good to know there would be a place for *her* tomorrow night, if she really needed one.

And if he comes here, to this city, where do you think he'll check first? What do you think will be his very first stop?

That was silly—he wasn't going to find her, there was absolutely no way he *could* find her—but the thought still sent a cold finger up her back, tracing the curve of her spine.

The food made her feel better, stronger and more awake. When she had finished (lingering over her coffee until she saw the Chicano busboy looking at her with unconcealed impatience), she started slowly back to the TV alcove. On the way, she caught sight of a blue-and-white circle over a booth near the rental-car kiosks. The words bending their way around the circle's blue outer stripe were TRAVELERS AID, and Rosie thought, not without a twinkle of humor, that if there had ever been a traveler in the history of the world who needed aid, it was her.

She took a step toward the lighted circle. There was a man sitting inside the booth under it, she saw—a middle-aged guy with thinning hair and hornrimmed glasses. He was reading a newspaper. She took another step in his direction, then stopped again. She wasn't really going over there, was she? What in God's name would she tell him? That she had left her husband? That she had gone with nothing but her purse, his ATM card, and the clothes she stood up in?

Why not? Practical-Sensible asked, and the total lack of sympathy in her voice struck Rosie like a slap. *If you had the guts to leave him in the first place, don't you have the guts to own up to it?*

She didn't know if she did or not, but she knew that telling a stranger the central fact of her life at four o'clock in the morning would be very difficult. *And probably he'd just tell me to get lost, anyway. Probably his job is helping people to replace their lost tickets, or making lost-children announcements over the loudspeakers.*

But her feet started moving in the direction of the Travelers Aid booth just the same, and she understood that she *did* mean to speak to the stranger with the thinning hair and the hornrimmed glasses, and that she was going to do it for the simplest reason in the universe: she had no other choice. In the days ahead she would probably have to tell a lot of people that she had left her husband, that she had lived in a daze behind a closed door for fourteen years, that she had damned few life-skills and no work-skills at all, that she needed help, that she needed to depend on the kindness of strangers.

But none of that is really my fault, is it? she thought, and her own calmness surprised her, almost stunned her.

She came to the booth and put the hand not currently clutching the strap of her purse on the counter. She looked hopefully and fearfully down at the bent head of the man in the hornrimmed glasses, looking at his brown, freckled skull through the strands of hair laid across it in neat thin rows. She waited for him to look up, but he was absorbed in his paper, which was written in a foreign language that looked like either Greek or Russian. He carefully turned a page and frowned at a picture of two soccer players tussling over a ball.

"Excuse me?" she asked in a small voice, and the man in the booth raised his head.

Please let his eyes be kind, she thought suddenly. *Even if he can't do anything, please let his eyes be kind . . . and let them see me,* me, *the real person who is standing here with nothing but the strap of this Kmart purse to hold onto.*

And, she saw, his eyes *were* kind. Weak and swimmy behind the thick lenses of his glasses . . . but kind.

"I'm sorry, but can you help me?" she asked.

3

The Travelers Aid volunteer introduced himself as Peter Slowik, and he listened to Rosie's story in attentive silence. She told as much as she could, having already come to the conclusion that she could not depend on the kindness of strangers if she held what was true about her in reserve, out of either pride or shame. The only important thing she didn't tell him—because she couldn't think of a way to express it—was how *unarmed* she felt, how totally unprepared for the world. Until the last eighteen hours or so, she'd had no conception of how much of the world she knew only from TV, or from the daily paper her husband brought home.

"I understand that you left on the spur of the moment," Mr. Slowik said, "but while you were riding the bus did you have any ideas about what you should do or where you should go when you got here? Any ideas at all?"

"I thought I might be able to find a women's hotel, to start with," she said. "Are there still such places?"

"Yes, at least three that I know of, but the cheapest has rates that would probably leave you broke in a week. They're hotels for well-to-do ladies, for the most part—ladies who've come to spend a week in the city touring the shops, or visiting relatives who don't have room to put them up."

"Oh," she said. "Well, then, what about the YWCA?"

Mr. Slowik shook his head. "They closed down the last of their boarding facilities in 1990. They were being overrun by crazy people and drug addicts."

She felt a touch of panic, then made herself think of the people who slept here on the floor, with their arms around their taped garbage bags of possessions. *There's always that,* she thought.

"Do *you* have any ideas?" she asked.

He looked at her for a moment, tapping his lower lip with the barrel of a ballpoint pen, a plain-faced little man with watery eyes who had nevertheless seen her and spoken to her—who hadn't just told her to get lost. *And, of course, he didn't tell me to lean forward so he could talk to me up close,* she thought.

Slowik seemed to come to a decision. He opened his coat (an off-the-rack polyester that had seen better days), felt around in his inside pocket, and brought out a business card. On the side where his name and the Travelers Aid logo were displayed, he carefully printed an address. Then he turned the card over and signed the blank side, writing in letters that struck her as comically large. His oversized signature made her think of something her American History teacher had told her class back in high school, about why John Hancock had written his name in especially large letters on the Declaration of Independence. "So King George can read it without his spectacles," Hancock was supposed to have said.

"Can you make out the address?" he asked, handing her the card.

"Yes," she said. "251 Durham Avenue."

"Good. Put the card in your purse and don't lose it. Someone will probably want a look at it when you get there. I'm sending you to a place called Daughters and Sisters. It's a shelter for battered women. Rather unique. Based on your story, I'd say you qualify."

"How long will they let me stay?"

He shrugged. "I believe that varies from case to case."

So that's what I am now, she thought. *A case.*

He seemed to read her thought, because he smiled. There was nothing very lovely about the teeth the smile revealed, but it looked honest enough. He patted her hand. It was a quick touch, awkward and a bit timid. "If your husband beat you as badly as you say, Ms. McClendon, you've bettered your situation wherever you end up."

"Yes," she said. "I think so, too. And if all else fails, there's always the floor here, isn't there?"

He looked taken aback. "Oh, I don't think it will come to that."

"It might. It could." She nodded at two of the homeless people, sleeping side by side on their spread coats at the end of a bench. One of them had a dirty orange cap pulled down over his face to block out the relentless light.

Slowik looked at them for a moment, then back at her. "It won't come to that," he repeated, this time sounding more sure of himself. "The city buses stop right outside the main doors; turn to your left and you'll see where. Various parts of the curb are painted to correspond with the various bus routes. You want an Orange Line bus, so you'll stand on the orange part of the curb. Understand?"

"Yes."

"It costs a buck, and the driver will want exact change. He's apt to be impatient with you if you don't have it."

"I've got plenty of change."

"Good. Get off at the corner of Dearborn and Elk, then walk up Elk two blocks . . . or maybe it's three, I can't remember for sure. Anyway, you'll come to Durham Avenue. You'll want to make a left. It's about four blocks up, but they're short blocks. A big white frame house. I'd tell you it looks like it needs to be painted, but they might have gotten around to that by now. Can you remember all that?"

"Yes."

"One more thing. Stay in the bus terminal until it's daylight. Don't go out anywhere—not even to the city bus stop—until then."

"I wasn't planning to," she said.

4

She had gotten only two or three hours' worth of broken sleep on the Continental Express which had brought her here, and so what happened after she stepped off the Orange Line bus really wasn't surprising: she got lost. Rosie decided later that she must have started by going the wrong way on Elk Street, but the result—almost three hours of wandering in a strange neighborhood—was much more important than the reason. She trudged around block after block, looking for Durham Avenue and not finding it. Her feet hurt. Her lower back throbbed. She began to get a headache. And there were certainly no Peter Slowiks in this neighborhood; the faces which did not ignore her completely regarded her with mistrust, suspicion, or outright disdain.

Not long after getting off the bus she passed a dirty, secretive-looking bar called The Wee Nip. The shades were down, the beer signs were dark, and a grate had been pulled across the door. When she came back to the same bar some twenty minutes later (not realizing she was re-covering ground she'd already walked until she saw it; the houses all looked the same), the shades were still down but the beer signs were on and the grate had been rolled back. A man in chino workclothes leaned in the doorway with a half-empty beer-stein in his hand. She looked at her watch and saw it was not quite six-thirty in the morning.

Rosie lowered her head until she could see the man only from the corner of one eye, held the strap of her purse a little tighter, and walked a little faster. She guessed the man in the doorway would know where Durham Avenue was, but she had no intention of asking him for directions. He had the look of a guy who liked to talk to people—women, especially—up close.

"Hey baby hey baby," he said as she passed The Wee Nip. His voice was absolutely uninflected, almost the voice of a robot. And although she didn't want to look at him, she couldn't help shooting a single terrified glance back at him over her shoulder. He had a receding hairline, pale skin on which a number of blemishes stood out like partially healed burns, and a dark red walrus moustache that made her think of David Crosby. There were little dots of beer-foam in it. "Hey baby wanna get it on you don't look too bad priddy good in fact nice tits whaddaya say wanna get it on do some low ridin wanna get it on wanna do the dog whaddaya say?"

She turned away from him and forced herself to walk at a steady pace, her head now bent, like a Muslim woman on her way to market; forced herself not to acknowledge him further in any way. If she did that, he might come after her.

"Hey baby let's put all four on the floor whaddaya say? Let's get down let's do the dog let's get it on get it on get it *on*."

She turned the corner and let out a long breath that pulsed like a living thing with the frantic, frightened beat of her heart. Until that moment she hadn't missed her old town or neighborhood in the slightest, but now her fear of the man in the bar doorway and her disorientation—*why* did all the houses have to look so much the same, *why?*—combined in a feeling that was close to homesickness. She had never felt so horribly alone, or so convinced that things were going to turn out badly. It occurred to her that perhaps she would never escape this nightmare, that perhaps this was just a preview of what the rest of her life was going to be like. She even began to speculate that there *was* no Durham Avenue; that Mr. Slowik in Travelers Aid, who had seemed so nice, was actually a sadistic sicko who delighted in turning people who were already lost even further around.

At quarter past eight by her watch—long after the sun had come up on what promised to be an unseasonably hot day—she approached a fat woman in a housedress who was at the foot of her driveway, loading empty garbage cans onto a dolly with slow, stylized movements.

Rosie took off her sunglasses. "Beg pardon?"

The woman wheeled around at once. Her head was lowered and she wore the truculent expression of a lady who has frequently been called fatty-fatty-two-by-four from across the street or perhaps from passing cars. "Whatchoo want?"

"I'm looking for 251 Durham Avenue," Rosie said. "It's a place called Daughters and Sisters. I had directions, but I guess—"

"What, the welfare lesbians? You ast the wrong chicken, baby girl. I got no use for crack-snackers. Get lost. The fuck outta here." With that she turned back to her dolly and began to push the rattling cans up the driveway in the same slow, ceremonial manner, holding them on with one plump white hand. Her buttocks jiggled freely beneath her faded housedress. When she reached the steps she turned and looked back at the sidewalk. "Didn't you hear me? Get the fuck *outta* here. 'Fore I call the cops."

That last word felt like a sharp pinch in a sensitive place. Rosie put her sunglasses back on and walked quickly away. Cops? No thank you. She wanted nothing to do with the cops. *Any* cops. But after she had put a little distance between herself and the fat lady, Rosie realized she actually felt a little better. She had at least made sure that Daughters and Sisters (known in some quarters as the welfare lesbians) actually existed, and that was a step in the right direction.

Two blocks farther down, she came to a mom-and-pop store with a bike rack in front and a sign reading OVEN-FRESH ROLLS in the window. She went in, bought a roll—it was still warm and made Rosie think of her mother—and asked the old man behind the counter if he could direct her to Durham Avenue.

"You come a little out of your way," he said.

"Oh? How much?"

"Two mile or so. C'mere."

He settled a bony hand on her shoulder, led her back to the door, and pointed to a busy intersection only a block away. "That there's Dearborn Avenue."

"Oh God, is it?" Rosie wasn't sure if she needed to laugh or cry.

"Yessum. Only trouble with findin things by way of Big D is that she run mostway across the city. You see that shutdown movie tee-ayter?"

"Yes."

"You want to turn right onto Dearborn there. You have to go sixteen–eighteen blocks. It's a bit of a heel n toe. You'd best take the bus."

"I suppose," Rosie said, knowing she wouldn't. Her quarters were gone, and if a bus driver gave her a hard time about breaking a dollar bill, she would burst into tears. (The thought that the man she was talking to would have happily given her change for a buck never crossed her tired, confused mind.)

"Eventually you'll come to—"

"—Elk Street."

He gave her a look of exasperation. "Lady! If you knew how to go, why'd you ask?"

"I *didn't* know how to go," she said, and although there had been nothing particularly unkind in the old man's voice, she could feel the tears threatening. "I don't know *anything!* I've been wandering around for hours, I'm *tired,* and—"

"Okay, okay," he said, "that's all right, don't get your water hot, you'll be just fine. Get off the bus at Elk. Durham is just two or three blocks up. Easy as pie. You got a street address?"

She nodded her head.

"All right, there you go," he said. "Should be no problem."

"Thank you."

He pulled a wrinkled but clean handkerchief from his back pocket. He held it out to her with one gnarled hand. "Wipe you face a li'l bit, dear," he said. "You leakin."

5

She walked slowly up Dearborn Avenue, barely noticing the buses that snored past her, resting every block or two on bus stop benches. Her headache, which had come mostly from the stress of being lost, was gone, but her feet and back hurt worse than ever. It took her an hour to get to Elk Street. She turned right on it and asked the first person she saw—a young pregnant woman—if she was headed toward Durham Avenue.

"Buzz off," the young pregnant woman said, her face so instantly wrathful that Rosie took two quick steps backward.

"I'm sorry," Rosie said.

"Sorry, schmorry. Who ast you to speak to me in the first place, that's what *I'd* like to know! Get outta my way!" And she pushed by Rosie so violently she almost knocked her into the gutter. Rosie watched her go with a kind of stupefied amazement, then turned and went on her way.

6

She walked more slowly than ever up Elk, a street of small shops—dry-cleaning establishments, florists, delis with fruit displays out front on the sidewalk, stationers'. She was now so tired she didn't know how long she would be able to remain on her feet, let alone keep walking. She felt a lift when she came to Durham Avenue, but it was only temporary. Had Mr. Slowik told her to turn right or left on Durham? She couldn't remember. She tried right and found the numbers going up from the mid–four hundreds.

"Par for the course," she muttered, and turned around again. Ten minutes later she was standing in front of a very large white frame house (which was indeed in serious need of paint), three stories high and set back behind a big, well-kept lawn. The shades were pulled. There were wicker chairs on the porch, almost a dozen of them, but none was currently occupied. There was no sign reading Daughters and Sisters, but the street-number on the column to the left of the steps leading to the porch was 251. She made her way slowly up the flagged walk and then the steps, her purse now hanging at her side.

They're going to send you away, a voice whispered. *They'll send you away, then you can head on back to the bus station. You'll want to get there early, so you can stake out a nice piece of floor.*

The doorbell had been covered over with layers of electrician's tape, and the keyhole had been plugged with metal. To the left of the door was a keycard slot that looked brand-new, and an intercom box above it. Below the box was a small sign which read VISITORS PRESS AND SPEAK.

Rosie pressed. In the course of her long morning's tramp she had rehearsed several things she might say, several ways she might introduce herself, but now that she was actually here, even the least clever and most straightforward of her possible opening gambits had gone out of her head. Her mind was a total blank. She simply let go of the button and waited. The seconds passed, each one like a little chunk of lead. She was reaching for the button again when a woman's voice came out of the speaker. It sounded tinny and emotionless.

"Can I help you?"

Although the man with the moustache outside The Wee Nip had frightened her and the pregnant woman had amazed her, neither had made her cry. Now, at the sound of this voice, the tears came—there was nothing at all she could do to stop them.

"I hope someone can," Rosie said, wiping at her cheeks with her free hand. "I'm sorry, but I'm in the city all by myself, I don't know anyone, and I need a place to stay. If you're all full I understand, but could I at least come in and sit for awhile and maybe have a glass of water?"

There was more silence. Rosie was reaching for the button again when the tinny voice asked who had sent her.

"The man in the Travelers Aid booth at the bus station. David Slowik." She thought that over, then shook her head. "No, that's wrong. *Peter.* His name was Peter, not David."

"Did he give you a business card?" the tinny voice asked.

"Yes."

"Please find it."

She opened her purse and rummaged for what felt like hours. Just as fresh tears began to prick at her eyes and double her vision, she happened on the card. It had been hiding beneath a wad of Kleenex.

"I have it," she said. "Do you want me to put it through the letter-slot?"

"No," the voice said. "There's a camera right over your head."

She looked up, startled. There was indeed a camera mounted over the door and looking down at her with its round black eye.

"Hold it up to the camera, please. Not the front but the back."

As she did so, she remembered the way Slowik had signed the business card, making his signature as large as he possibly could. Now she understood why.

"Okay," the voice said. "I'm going to buzz you inside."

"Thanks," Rosie said. She used the Kleenex to wipe at her cheeks but it did no good; she was crying harder than ever, and she couldn't seem to stop.

7

That evening, as Norman Daniels lay on the sofa in his living room, looking up at the ceiling and already thinking of how he might begin the job of finding the bitch (*a break,* he thought, *I need a break to start with, just a little one would probably be enough*), his wife was being taken to meet Anna Stevenson. By then Rosie felt a strange but welcome calm—the sort of calm one might feel in a recognized dream. She half-believed she *was* dreaming.

She had been given a late breakfast (or perhaps it had been an early lunch) and then taken to one of the downstairs bedrooms, where she had slept like a stone for six hours. Then, before being shown into Anna's study, she had been fed again—roast chicken, mashed potatoes, peas. She had eaten guiltily but hugely, unable to shake the idea that it was non-caloric dreamfood she was stuffing herself with. She finished with a goblet of Jell-O in which bits of canned fruit floated like bugs in amber. She was aware that the other women at the table were looking at her, but their curiosity seemed friendly. They talked, but Rosie could not follow their conversations. Somebody mentioned the Indigo Girls, and she at least knew who they were—she had seen them once on *Austin City Limits* while waiting for Norman to come home from work.

While they ate their Jell-O desserts, one of the women put on a Little Richard record and two other women danced the jitterbug, popping their hips and twirling. There was laughter and applause. Rosie looked at the dancers with a numb absence of interest, wondering if they *were* welfare lesbians. Later, when the table was cleared, Rosie tried to help but they wouldn't let her.

"Come on," one of the women said. Rosie thought her name was Consuelo. She had a wide, disfiguring scar under her left eye and down her left cheek. "Anna wants to meet you."

"Who's Anna?"

"Anna Stevenson," Consuelo said as she led Rosie down a short hall which opened off the kitchen. "Boss-lady."

"What's she like?"

"You'll see." Consuelo opened the door of a room which had probably once been the pantry, but made no move to go in.

The room was dominated by the most fabulously cluttered desk Rosie had ever seen. The woman who sat behind it was a bit stout but undeniably handsome. With her short but carefully dressed white hair, she reminded Rosie of Beatrice Arthur, who had played Maude on the old TV sitcom. The severe white blouse/black jumper combination accentuated the resemblance even further, and Rosie approached the desk timidly. She was more than half convinced that, now that she had been fed and allowed a few hours' sleep, she would be turned out onto the street again. She told herself not to argue or plead if that happened; it was their place, after all, and she was already two meals to the good. She wouldn't have to stake out a piece of bus station floor, either, at least not yet—she still had money enough for several nights in a cheap hotel or motel. Things could be worse. A *lot* worse.

She knew that was true, but the woman's crisp demeanor and direct blue eyes—eyes that must have seen hundreds of Rosies come and go over the years—still intimidated her.

"Sit down," Anna invited, and when Rosie was seated in the room's only other chair (she had to remove a stack of papers from the seat and put them on the floor beside her—the nearest shelf was full), Anna introduced herself and then asked Rosie for her name.

"I guess it's actually Rose Daniels," she said, "but I've gone back to McClendon—my maiden name. I suppose that isn't legal, but I don't want to use my husband's name anymore. He beat me, and so I left him." She realized that sounded as if she'd left him the first time he'd done it and her hand went to her nose, which was still a little tender up where the bridge ended. "We were married a long time before I got up the courage, though."

"How long a time are we talking about?"

"Fourteen years." Rosie discovered she could no longer meet Anna Stevenson's direct blue gaze. She dropped her eyes to her hands, which were knotted so tightly together in her lap that the knuckles were white.

Now she'll ask why it took me so long to wake up, she thought. *She won't ask if maybe some sick part of me* liked *getting beaten up, but she'll think it.*

Instead of asking why about anything, the woman asked how long Rosie had been gone.

It was a question she found she had to consider carefully, and not just because she was now on Central Standard Time. The hours on the bus combined with the unaccustomed stretch of sleep in the middle of the day had disoriented her time-sense. "About thirty-six hours," she said after a bit of mental calculation. "Give or take."

"Uh-huh." Rosie kept expecting forms which Anna would either hand to Rosie or start filling in herself, but the woman only went on looking at her over the strenuous topography of her desk. It was unnerving. "Now tell me about it. Tell me everything."

Rosie drew a deep breath and told Anna about the drop of blood on the sheet. She didn't want to give Anna the idea that she was so lazy— or so crazy—that she had left her husband of fourteen years because she didn't want to change the bed-linen, but she was terribly afraid that was how it must sound. She wasn't able to explain the complex feelings that spot had aroused in her, and she wasn't able to admit to the anger she had felt—anger which had seemed simultaneously new and like an old friend—but she *did* tell Anna that she had rocked so hard she had been afraid she might break Pooh's Chair.

"That's what I call my rocker," she said, blushing so hard that her cheeks felt as if they might be on the verge of smoking. "I know it's stupid—"

Anna Stevenson waved it off. "What did you do after you made your mind up to go? Tell me that."

Rosie told her about the ATM card, and how she had been sure that Norman would have a hunch about what she was doing and either call or come home. She couldn't bring herself to tell this severely handsome woman that she had been so scared she'd gone into someone's back yard to pee, but she told about using the ATM card, and how much she'd drawn out, and how she'd come to this city because it seemed far enough away and the bus would be leaving soon. The words came out of her in bursts surrounded by periods of silence in which she tried to think of what to say next and contemplated with amazement and near-disbelief what she had done. She finished by telling Anna about how she'd gotten lost that morning, and showing her Peter Slowik's card. Anna handed it back after a single quick glance.

"Do you know him very well?" Rosie asked. "Mr. Slowik?"

Anna smiled—to Rosie it looked like it had a bitter edge. "Oh yes," she said. "He is a friend of mine. An *old* friend. Indeed he is. And a friend of women like you, as well."

"Anyway, I finally got here," Rosie finished. "I don't know what comes next, but at least I got this far."

A ghost of a smile touched the corners of Anna Stevenson's mouth. "Yes. And made a good job of it, too."

Gathering all her remaining courage—the last thirty-six hours had taken a great deal of it—Rosie asked if she could spend the night at Daughters and Sisters.

"Quite a bit longer than that, if you need to," Anna replied. "Technically speaking, this is a shelter—a privately endowed halfway house. You can stay up to eight weeks, and even that is an arbitrary number. We are quite flexible here at Daughters and Sisters." She preened slightly (and probably unconsciously) as she said this, and Rosie found herself remembering something she had learned about a thousand years ago, in French II: *L'état, c'est moi.* Then the thought was swept away by amazement as she really realized what the woman was saying.

"Eight . . . eight . . ."

She thought of the pale young man who had been sitting outside the entrance to the Portside terminal, the one with the sign in his lap reading HOMELESS & HAVE AIDS, and suddenly knew how he would feel if a passing stranger for some reason dropped a hundred-dollar bill into his cigar-box.

"Pardon me, did you say up to eight *weeks?*"

Dig out your ears, little lady, Anna Stevenson would say briskly. *Days, I said—eight* days. *Do you think we'd let the likes of you stay here for eight weeks? Let's be sensible, shall we?*

Instead, Anna nodded. "Although very few of the women who come to us end up having to stay so long. That's a point of pride with us. And you'll eventually pay for your room and board, although we like to think the prices here are very reasonable." She smiled that brief, preening smile again. "You should be aware that the accommodations are a long way from fancy. Most of the second floor has been turned into a dormitory. There are thirty beds—well, cots—and one of them just happens to be vacant, which is why we are able to take you in. The room you slept in today belongs to one of the live-in counsellors. We have three."

"Don't you have to ask someone?" Rosie whispered. "Put my name up before a committee, or something?"

"*I'm* the committee," Anna replied, and Rosie later thought that it had probably been years since the woman had heard the faint arrogance in her own voice. "Daughters and Sisters was set up by my parents, who were well-to-do. There's a very helpful endowed trust. I choose who's invited to stay, and who isn't invited to stay . . . although the reactions of the other women to potential D and S candidates are important. Crucial, maybe. Their reaction to you was favorable."

"That's good, isn't it?" Rosie asked faintly.

"Yes indeed." Anna rummaged on her desk, moved documents, and finally found what she wanted behind the PowerBook computer sitting to her left. She flapped a sheet of paper with a blue Daughters and Sisters letterhead at Rosie. "Here. Read this and sign it. Basically it says that you agree to pay sixteen dollars a night, room and board, payment to be deferred if necessary. It's not even really legal; just a promise. We like it if you can pay half as you go, at least for awhile."

"I can," Rosie said. "I still have some money. I don't know how to thank you for this, Mrs. Stevenson."

"It's Ms. to my business associates and Anna to you," she said, watching Rosie scribble her name on the bottom of the sheet. "And you don't need to thank me, or Peter Slowik, either. It was Providence that brought you here—Providence with a capital *P,* just like in a Charles

Dickens novel. I really believe that. I've seen too many women crawl in here broken and walk out whole not to believe it. Peter is one of two dozen people in the city who refer women to me, but the force that brought you to him, Rose . . . that was Providence."

"With a capital *P*."

"Correct." Anna glanced at Rosie's signature, then placed the paper on a shelf to her right, where, Rosie felt sure, it would disappear into the general clutter before another twenty-four hours had passed.

"Now," Anna said, speaking with the air of someone who has finished with the boring formalities and may now get down to what she really likes. "What can you do?"

"Do?" Rosie echoed. She suddenly felt faint again. She knew what was coming.

"Yes, *do*, what can you do? Any shorthand skills, for instance?"

"I . . ." She swallowed. She had taken Shorthand I and II back at Aubreyville High, and she had gotten A's in both, but these days she wouldn't know a pothook from a boathook. She shook her head. "No. No shorthand. Once, but no more."

"Any other secretarial skills?"

She shook her head. Warm prickles stung at her eyes. She blinked them back savagely. The knuckles of her interlocked hands were gleaming white again.

"Clerical skills? Typing, maybe?"

"No."

"Math? Accounting? Banking?"

"No!"

Anna Stevenson happened on a pencil amid the heaps of paper, extracted it, and tapped the eraser end against her clean white teeth. "Can you waitress?"

Rosie desperately wanted to say yes, but she thought about the large trays waitresses had to balance all day long . . . and then she thought about her back and her kidneys.

"No," she whispered. She was losing her battle with the tears; the little room and the woman on the other side of the desk began to blur and soften. "Not yet, anyway. Maybe in a month or two. My back . . . right now it's not strong." And oh, it sounded like a lie. It was the kind of thing that, when he heard someone say it on TV, made Norman laugh cynically and talk about welfare Cadillacs and foodstamp millionaires.

Anna Stevenson did not seem particularly perturbed, however. "What skills *do* you have, Rose? Any at all?"

"Yes!" she said, appalled by the harsh, angry edge she heard in her voice but unable to make it go away or even mute it. "Yes indeed! I can dust, I can wash dishes, I can make beds, I can vacuum the floor, I can cook meals for two, I can sleep with my husband once a week. And I can take a punch. That's another skill I have. Do you suppose any of the local gyms have openings for sparring partners?"

Then she *did* burst into tears. She wept into her cupped hands as she had so often during the years since she had married him, wept and waited for Anna to tell her to get out, that they could fill that empty cot upstairs with someone who wasn't a smartass.

Something bumped the back of her left hand. She lowered it and saw a box of Kleenex. Anna Stevenson was holding it out to her. And, incredibly, Anna Stevenson was smiling.

"I don't think you'll have to be anyone's sparring partner," she said. "Things are going to work out for you, I think—they almost always do. Here, dry your eyes."

And, as Rosie dried them, Anna explained about the Whitestone Hotel, with which Daughters and Sisters had had a long and useful relationship. The Whitestone was owned by a corporation on whose board Anna's well-to-do father had once sat, and a great many women had relearned the satisfactions of working for pay there. Anna told Rosie that she would have to work only as hard as her back allowed her to work, and that if her overall physical condition didn't begin to improve in twenty-one days, she would be hauled off the job and taken to a hospital for tests.

"Also, you'll be paired with a woman who knows the ropes. A sort of counsellor who lives here full time. She'll teach you, and she'll be responsible for you. If you steal something, it'll be her who gets in trouble, not you . . . but you're not a thief, are you?"

Rosie shook her head. "Just my husband's bank card, that's all, and I only used it once. To make sure I could get away."

"You'll work at the Whitestone until you find something that suits you better, as you almost certainly will—Providence, remember."

"With a capital *P*."

"Yes. While you're at the Whitestone, we ask only that you do your best—in order to protect the jobs of all the women who'll come after you, if for no other reason. Do you follow me?"

Rosie nodded. "Don't spoil it for the next person."

"Don't spoil it for the next person, just so. It's good to have you here, Rose McClendon." Anna stood up and extended both hands in a gesture which held more than a little of the unconscious arrogance Rosie had already sensed in her. Rosie hesitated, then stood and took the offered hands. Now their fingers were linked above the clutter of the desk. "I have three more things to tell you," Anna said. "They're important, so I want you to clear your mind and listen carefully. Will you do that?"

"Yes," Rosie said. She was fascinated by Anna Stevenson's clear blue gaze.

"First, taking the bank card doesn't make you a thief. That was your money as well as his. Second, there's nothing illegal about resuming your maiden name—it will belong to you your whole life. Third, you can be free if you want to."

She paused, looking at Rosie with her remarkable blue eyes from above their clasped hands.

"Do you understand me? *You can be free if you want to.* Free of his hands, free of his ideas, free of *him.* Do you want that? To be free?"

"Yes," Rosie said in a low, wavering voice. "I want that more than anything in the world."

Anna Stevenson bent across the desk and kissed Rosie softly on the cheek. At the same time she squeezed Rosie's hands. "Then you've come to the right place. Welcome home, dear."

8

It was early May, real spring, the time when a young man's fancy is supposed to lightly turn to thoughts of love, a wonderful season and un- doubtedly a great emotion, but Norman Daniels had other things on his mind. He had wanted a break, one little break, and now it had come. It had taken too long—almost three goddam weeks—but it had finally come.

He sat on a park bench eight hundred miles from the place where his wife was currently changing hotel sheets, a big man in a red polo shirt and gray gabardine slacks. In one hand he held a fluorescent green tennis ball. The muscles of his forearm flexed rhythmically as he squeezed it.

A second man came across the street, stood at the edge of the sidewalk looking into the park, then spotted the man on the bench and began walk- ing toward him. He ducked as a Frisbee sailed close by, then stopped short as a large German Shepherd charged past him, chasing it. This second man was both younger and slighter than the man on the bench. He had a handsome, unreliable face and a tiny Errol Flynn moustache. He stopped in front of the man with the tennis ball in his right hand and looked at him uncertainly.

"Help you, bro?" the man with the tennis ball asked.

"Is your name Daniels?"

The man with the tennis ball nodded that it was.

The man with the Errol Flynn moustache pointed across the street at a new highrise loaded with glass and angles. "Guy in there told me to come over here and see you. He said maybe you could help me with my problem."

"Was it Lieutenant Morelli?" the man with the tennis ball asked.

"Yeah. That was his name."

"And what problem do you have?"

"You know," the man with the Errol Flynn moustache said.

"Tell you what, bro—maybe I do and maybe I don't. Either way, I'm the man and you're just a greasy little halfbreed cockgobbler with a very troubled life. I think you better tell me what I want to hear, don't you? And what I want to hear right now is what kind of problem you've got. Say it right out loud."

"I'm up on a dope charge," the man with the Errol Flynn moustache said. He looked sullenly at Daniels. "Sold an eightball to a narc."

"Ooops," the man with the tennis ball said. "That's a felony. It can be a felony, anyway. But it gets worse, doesn't it? They found something of mine in your wallet, didn't they?"

"Yeah. Your fuckin bank card. Just my luck. Find an ATM card in the trash, it belongs to a fuckin cop."

"Sit down," Daniels said genially, but when the man with the Errol Flynn moustache started to move to the right side of the bench, the cop shook his head impatiently. "Other side, dickweed, other side."

The man with the moustache backtracked, then sat gingerly down on Daniels's left side. He watched as the right hand squeezed the tennis ball in a steady, quick rhythm. Squeeze . . . squeeze . . . squeeze. Thick blue veins wriggled up the white underside of the cop's arm like watersnakes.

The Frisbee floated by. The two men watched the German Shepherd chase after, its long legs galloping like the legs of a horse.

"Beautiful dog," Daniels said. "Shepherds are beautiful dogs. I always like a Shepherd, don't you?"

"Sure, great," the man with the moustache said, although he actually thought the dog was butt-ugly and looked like it would happily chew you a new asshole if you gave it half a chance.

"We've got a lot to talk about," the cop with the tennis ball said. "In fact, I think this is going to be one of the most important conversations of your young life, my friend. Are you ready for that?"

The man with the moustache swallowed past some sort of blockage in his throat and wished—for about the eight hundredth time that day—that he had gotten rid of the goddam bank card. Why hadn't he? Why had he been such a total goddamned idiot?

Except he knew why he had been such a total goddamned idiot—because he'd kept thinking that eventually he might figure out a way to use it. Because he was an optimist. This was America, after all, the Land of Opportunity. Also because (and this was a lot closer to the nub of the truth) he had sort of forgotten it was there in his wallet, tucked in behind a bunch of the business cards he was always picking up. Coke had that effect on you—it kept you running, but you couldn't fuckin remember why you were running.

The cop was looking at him, and he was smiling, but there was no smile in his eyes. The eyes looked . . . famished. All at once the man with the moustache felt like one of the three little pigs sitting on a park bench next to the big bad wolf.

"Listen, man, I never used your bank card. Let's just get that up front. They told you that, didn't they? I never fuckin used it once."

"Of course you didn't," the cop said, half-laughing. "You couldn't get the pin-number. It's based on my home phone number, and my number's unlisted . . . like most cops'. But I bet you already know that, right? I bet you checked."

"No!" the man with the moustache said. "No, I didn't!" He had, of course. He had checked the phone book after trying several different combinations of the street address on the card, and the zip-code, with no luck. He had punched ATM buttons all over the city at first. He had punched buttons until his fingers were sore and he felt like an asshole playing the world's most miserly slot machine.

"So what's gonna happen when we check the computer runs on Merchant's Bank ATM machines?" the cop asked. "We're not going to find my card in the CANCEL/RETRY *column about a billion times? Hey, if we don't, I'll buy you a steak dinner. What do you think about that, bro?"*

The man with the moustache didn't know what to think about it, or anything else. He was getting a very bad feeling. A bitch of a bad feeling. Meanwhile, the cop's fingers went on working the tennis ball—in and out, in and out, in and out. It was creepy how he never stopped doing that.

"Your name's Ramon Sanders," the cop named Daniels said. "You got a rap sheet long as my arm. Theft, con, dope, vice. Everything but assault, battery, crimes of that nature. No mixing it up for you, right? You fags don't like getting hit, do you? Even the ones that look like Schwarzenegger. Oh, they don't mind wearing a security tee-shirt and flexing their pecs for the limousines in front of some homo club, but if anyone actually starts hitting, you guys go flat in a hurry. Don't you?"

Ramon Sanders said nothing. It seemed by far the wisest course.

"I don't mind hitting," the cop named Daniels said. "Kicking, either.

Even biting." He spoke almost reflectively. He seemed to be looking both at and beyond the German Shepherd, which was now trotting back in their direction with the Frisbee in its mouth. "What do you think of that, angel eyes?"

Ramon went on saying nothing, and he tried to keep a poker face, but a lot of little lights inside his head were turning red, and a dismaying tingle had begun to shake its way through his nerve-tree. His heart was picking up speed like a train leaving the station and heading into open country. He kept snatching little glances of the big man in the red polo shirt, and liking less and less what he saw. The guy's right forearm was totally flexed now, veins fat with blood, muscles popped like freshly risen breadrolls.

Daniels didn't seem to mind Ramon's failure to answer. The face he turned toward the smaller man was smiling . . . or appeared to be smiling, if you ignored the eyes. The eyes were as blank and shiny as two new quarters.

"I got good news for you, little hero. You can do the stroll on the dope charge. Give me a little help and you're as free as a bird. Now what do you think about that?"

What he thought was that he wanted to go right on keeping his mouth shut, but that no longer seemed like an option. This time the cop wasn't just rolling on; this time he was waiting for an answer.

"That's great," Ramon said, hoping he was giving the right one. "That's great, really excellent, thanks for giving me a break."

"Well, maybe I like you, Ramon," the cop said, and then he did an astounding thing, something Ramon never would have expected from a screwhead ex-gyrene like this guy: he plopped his left hand into Ramon's crotch and began giving him a rubdown, right out in front of God, the kids on the playground, and anybody who cared to take a look. He slid his hand in a gentle clockwise motion, his palm moving back and forth and up and down over the little patch of flesh which had more or less run Ramon's life ever since two of his father's buddies—men Ramon was supposed to call Uncle Bill and Uncle Carlo—had taken turns blowing him when he was nine years old. And what happened next was probably not very extraordinary, although it seemed very fucking bizarre right then: he began to get hard.

"Yeah, maybe I like you, maybe I like you a lot, greasy little cocksucker in shiny black pants and pointy shoes, what's not to like?" The cop kept on giving his cock a shoeshine while he talked. He varied his stroke every now and then, applying a little squeeze that caused Ramon to gasp. "And it's a good thing I like you, Ramon, you better believe it, because they *really nailed you this time. Felony bust. But you know what bothers me? Leffingwell and Brewster—the cops who busted you—were laughing in the squadroom this morning. They were laughing about you, and that was okay, but I also have this feeling that they were laughing about* me, *and that's not okay. I don't like for people to laugh about me, and I generally don't put up with it. But this morning I had to, and this afternoon I'm going to be your best friend, I'm going to lose some pretty serious drug charges even though you had my fucking bank card. Can you guess why?"*

The Frisbee floated by again with the German Shepherd in close pursuit, but this time Ramon Sanders barely saw it. He was stiff as a railspike under the cop's hand, and as scared as a mouse under the claws of a cat.

The hand squeezed harder this time, and Ramon uttered a hoarse little howl. His café-au-lait skin was running with sweat; his moustache looked like a dead earthworm after a hard rain.

"Can you guess, Ramon?"

"No," Ramon said.

"Because the woman who ditched the card was my wife," Daniels said. "That's mostly why Leffingwell and Brewster were laughing, that's my deduction. She takes my bank card, she uses it to draw a few hundred bucks out of the bank—money I earned—and when the card turns up again, it's in the possession of a greasy little spick cocksucker named Ramon. No wonder they're laughing."

Please, *Ramon wanted to say,* please don't hurt me, I'll tell you anything but please don't hurt me. *He wanted to say those things, but he couldn't say a word. Not one. His asshole had contracted until it felt roughly the size of an inner-tube valve.*

The big cop leaned closer to him, close enough so that Ramon could smell cigarettes and Scotch on his breath.

"Now that I've shared with you, I want you to share with me." The rubbing stopped, and strong fingers curled around Ramon's testes through the thin fabric of his slacks. The shape of his erect penis was clear above the cop's hand; it looked like one of those toy bats you could buy at a baseball park souvenir stand. Ramon could feel the strength in that hand. "And you better share the right thing, Ramon. Do you know why?"

Ramon shook his head numbly. He felt as if someone had turned on a warm water tap somewhere in his body and his entire skin was leaking.

Daniels extended his right hand, the one with the tennis ball, until it was under Ramon's nose. Then he closed his hand with a sudden, vicious snap. There was a pop and a brief harsh whisper—fwahhhh—as his fingers punched through the ball's furry fluorescent skin. The ball collapsed inward, then turned halfway inside-out.

"I can do that with my left hand, too," Daniels said. "Do you believe that?"

Ramon tried to say he did and found he still couldn't talk. He nodded instead.

"Will you keep it in mind?"

Ramon nodded again.

"Okeydoke. So now here's what I want you to tell me, Ramon. I know you're just a stinking little spick rump-wrangler who doesn't know much about women, except maybe for fucking your mother up the ass in your younger years—you've just got that motherfucker look about you, somehow—but you go on and use your imagination. How do you think it feels to come home and find out that your wife, the woman who promised to love, honor, and fucking obey *you—has run off with your bank card? How do you think it feels to find out she used it to pay for her fucking vacation, and then she stuffed it in a bus-terminal garbage can for a greasy little penis-vacuum like you to find?"*

"Not too good," Ramon whispered. "I bet it don't feel too good, please don't hurt me, officer, please don't—"

Daniels slowly tightened his hand; tightened it until the tendons in his wrist stood out like the strings on a guitar. A wave of pain, heavy as liquid lead, rolled into Ramon's belly and he tried to scream. Nothing came out but a hoarse exhalation.

"Not too good?" Daniels whispered in his face. His breath was warm and steamy and boozy and cigarettey. "Is that the best you can do? What a fucking numbnuts you are! Still . . . I guess it's not an entirely wrong answer, either."

The hand loosened, but only a little. Ramon's lower belly was a lake of agony, but his penis was as hard as ever. He had never been into pain, whatever drove the bondage freaks was totally beyond him, and he could only suppose he still had a hardon because the blood in his cock was trapped there by the heel of the cop's hand. He swore to himself that if he got out of this alive, he would go directly to St. Patrick's and say fifty Hail Marys. Fifty? A hundred and fifty.

"They're laughing at me in there," the cop said, lifting his chin in the direction of the brand-new cop-shop across the street. "They're laughing all right, oh yeah. Big tough Norman Daniels, and guess what? His wife ran out on him . . . but she took time to clean out most of the ready before she went."

Daniels made an inarticulate growling sound, the sort of sound that a person should only have to hear while visiting the zoo, and gave Ramon's balls another squeeze. The pain was unbearable. He leaned forward and vomited between his knees—white chunks of curd laced with brown streaks that was probably the remains of the quesadilla *he'd eaten for lunch. Daniels did not seem to notice. He was gazing into the sky above the jungle gym, lost in his own world.*

"I should let them dance you around so even more people can laugh?" *he asked. "So that they can yuck it up at the courthouse as well as at the police station? I don't think so."*

He turned and looked into Ramon's eyes. He smiled. The smile made Ramon want to scream.

"Here comes the big question," the cop said. "And if you lie, little hero, I'm going to rip your scrote off and feed it to you."

Daniels squeezed Ramon's crotch again, and now folds of darkness began to fall across Ramon's vision. He fought them desperately. If he passed out, the cop was apt to kill him just for spite.

"Do you understand what I'm saying?"

"Yes!" Ramon wept. "I unnerstand! I unnerstand!"

"You were at the bus station and you saw her stick the card in the trash. That much I know. What I need to know is where she went next."

Ramon could have wept with relief because, although there was no reason why he should be able to answer this question, it just so happened he could. He had looked after the woman once to make sure she wasn't looking back at him . . . and then, five minutes later, long after he had slid the green plastic card into his wallet, he had spotted her again. She had been hard to miss, with that red thing over her hair; it was as bright as the side of a freshly painted barn.

"She was at the ticket-windows!" Ramon cried out of the darkness that was relentlessly enveloping him. "At the windows!"

This effort was rewarded by another ruthless squeeze. Ramon began to feel as if his balls had been torn open, doused with lighter fluid, and then set on fire.

"I know she was at the windows!" Daniels half-laughed, half-screamed at him. "What else would she be doing at Portside if she wasn't going someplace on a bus? Doing a sociological study on scumbuckets like you? Which ticket-window, that's what I want to know—which fucking window and what fucking time?"

And oh thank God, thank Jesus and Mother Mary, he knew the answers to both of those questions, too.

"Continental Express!" he cried, now separated from his own voice by what felt like miles. "I seen her at the Continental Express window, ten-thirty, quarter of eleven!"

"Continental? You're sure?"

Ramon Sanders didn't answer. He collapsed sideways on the bench, one hand dangling, slim fingers outstretched. His face was dead white except for two small purplish patches high on his cheeks. A young man and a young woman walked by, looked at the man lying on the bench, then looked at Daniels, who had by now removed his hand from Ramon's crotch.

"Don't worry," Daniels said, giving the couple a large smile. "He's epileptic." He paused and let his smile widen. "I'll take care of him. I'm a cop."

They walked on a little faster and didn't look back.

Daniels got an arm around Ramon's shoulders. The bones in there felt as fragile as bird's wings. "Upsa-daisy, big boy," he said, and hauled Ramon up to a sitting position. Ramon's head lolled like the head of a flower on a broken stalk. He started to slide back down immediately, making little thick grunts in his throat. Daniels hauled him up again, and this time Ramon balanced.

Daniels sat there beside him, watching the German Shepherd race joyfully after the Frisbee. He envied dogs, he really did. They had no responsibilities, no need to work—not in this country, anyhow—all food was provided for them, plus a place to sleep, and they didn't even have to worry about heaven or hell when the ride was over. He had once asked Father O'Brian back in Aubreyville about that and Father had told him that pets had no souls—when they died they just winked out like Fourth of July sparklers. It was true that the Shep had probably lost his balls not even six months after he was born, but . . .

"But in a way that's a blessing, too," Daniels murmured. He patted Ramon's crotch, where the penis was now deflating even as the testicles began to swell. "Right, big boy?"

Ramon muttered deep in his throat. It was the sound of a man having a terrible dream.

Still, Daniels thought, what you got was what you got, and so you might as well be content with it. He might be lucky enough to be a German Shepherd in his next life, with nothing to do but chase Frisbees in the park and stick his head out the back window of the car on his way home to a nice big supper of Purina Dog Chow, but in this one he was a man, with a man's problems.

At least he was *a man, unlike his little buddy.*

Continental Express. Ramon had seen her at the Continental Express ticket-window at ten-thirty or quarter to eleven, and she wouldn't have waited long—she was too scared of him to wait for long, he'd bet his life on that. So he was looking for a bus that had left Portside between, say, eleven in the morning and one in the afternoon. Probably headed for a large city where she felt she could lose herself.

"But you can't do that," Daniels said. He watched the Shep jump and snatch the Frisbee out of the air with its long white teeth. *No, she couldn't do that. She might* think *she could, but she was wrong. He would work it on weekends to start with, mostly using the phone. He would have to do it that way; there was a lot going on at the company store, a big bust coming down* (his *bust, if he was lucky). But that was all right. He'd be ready to turn his full attention to Rose soon enough, and before long she was going to regret what she had done. Yes. She was going to regret it for the rest of her life, a period of time which might be short but which would be extremely . . . well . . .*

"Extremely intense," he said out loud, and yes—*that was the right* word. Exactly *the right word.*

He got up and walked briskly back toward the street and the police station on the other side, not wasting a second glance on the semiconscious young man sitting on the bench with his head down and his hands laced limply together in his crotch. In Detective Inspector 2/Gr Norman Daniels's mind, Ramon had ceased to exist. Daniels was thinking about his wife, and all the things she had to learn. About all the things they had to talk about. And they would *talk about them, just as soon as he tracked her down. All sorts of things—ships and sails and sealing wax, not to mention what should happen to wives who promised to love, honor, and obey, and then took a powder with their husbands' bank cards in their purses. All those things.*

They would talk about them up close.

9

She was making another bed, but this time it was all right. It was a different bed, in a different room, in a different city. Best of all, this was a bed she had never slept in and never would.

A month had passed since she had left the house eight hundred miles east of here, and things were a lot better. Currently her worst problem was her back, and even that was getting better; she was sure of it. Right now the ache around her kidneys was strong and unpleasant, true enough, but this was her eighteenth room of the day, and when she'd begun at the Whitestone she had been close to fainting after a dozen rooms and unable to go on after fourteen—she'd had to ask Pam for help. Four weeks could make a hell of a difference in a person's outlook,

Rosie was discovering, especially if it was four weeks without any hard shots to the kidneys or the pit of the stomach.

Still, for now it was enough.

She went to the hall door, poked her head out, and looked in both directions. She saw nothing but a few room-service trays left over from breakfast, Pam's trolley down by the Lake Michigan Suite at the end of the hall, and her own trolley out here in front of 624.

Rosie lifted a pile of fresh washcloths stacked on the end of the trolley, exposing a banana. She took it, walked back across the room to the overstuffed chair by 624's window, and sat down. She peeled the piece of fruit and began to eat it slowly, looking out at the lake, which glimmered like a mirror on this still, rainy afternoon in May. Her heart and mind were filled with a huge, simple emotion—gratitude. Her life wasn't perfect, at least not yet, but it was better than she ever would have believed on that day in mid-April when she had stood on the porch of Daughters and Sisters, looking at the intercom box and the keyhole that had been filled with metal. At that moment, she had seen nothing in the future but darkness and misery. Now her kidneys hurt, and her feet hurt, and she was very aware that she did not want to spend the rest of her life as an off-the-books chambermaid in the Whitestone Hotel, but the banana tasted good and the chair felt wonderful beneath her. At that moment she would not have traded her place in the scheme of things for anyone's. In the weeks since she had left Norman, Rosie had become exquisitely aware of small pleasures: reading for half an hour before bed, talking with some of the other women about movies or TV shows as they did the supper dishes together, or taking five minutes off to sit down and eat a banana.

It was also wonderful *to know what was coming next,* and to feel sure it wasn't going to include something sudden and painful. To know, for instance, that there were only two more rooms to go, and then she and Pam could go down in the service elevator and out the back door. On the way to the bus stop (she was now able to differentiate easily between Orange, Red, and Blue Line buses) they would probably pop into the Hot Pot for coffee. Simple things. Simple pleasures. The world could be good. She supposed she had known that as a child, but she had forgotten. Now she was learning it over again, and it was a sweet lesson. She didn't have all she wanted, not by any means, but she had enough for now . . . especially since she didn't know what the rest might be. That would have to wait until she was out of Daughters and Sisters, but she had a feeling she would be moving soon, probably the next time a room turned up vacant on what the residents at D & S called Anna's List.

A shadow fell across the open hotel doorway, and before she could even think where she might hide her half-eaten banana, let alone get to her feet, Pam poked her head in. "Peek, baby," she said, and giggled when Rosie jumped.

"Don't *ever* do that, Pammy! You almost gave me a heart attack."

"Aww, they'd never fire you for sitting down and eating a banana," Pam said. "You should see some of the stuff that goes on in this place. What have you got left, Twenty-two and Twenty?"

"Yes."

"Want some help?"

"Oh, you don't have to—"

"I don't mind," Pam said. "Really. With two of us on the case, we can turn those two rooms in fifteen minutes. What do you say?"

"I say yes," Rosie told her gratefully. "And I'm buying at the Hot Pot after work—pie as well as coffee, if you want."

Pam grinned. "If they've got any of that chocolate cream, I want, believe me."

10

Good days—four weeks of good days, give or take.

That night, as she lay on her cot with her hands laced behind her head, looking into the darkness and listening to the woman who had come in the previous evening sobbing quietly two or three cots down on her left, Rosie thought that the days were mostly good for a negative reason: there was no Norman in them. She sensed, however, that it would soon take more than his absence to satisfy and fulfill her.

Not quite yet, though, she thought, and closed her eyes. *For now, what I've got is still plenty. These simple days of work, food, sleep . . . and no Norman Daniels.*

She began to drift, to come untethered from her conscious mind, and in her head Carole King once again started to sing the lullaby that sent her off to sleep most nights: *I'm really Rosie . . . and I'm Rosie Real . . . you better believe me . . . I'm a great big deal . . .*

Then there was darkness, and a night—they were becoming more frequent—when there were no bad dreams.

III

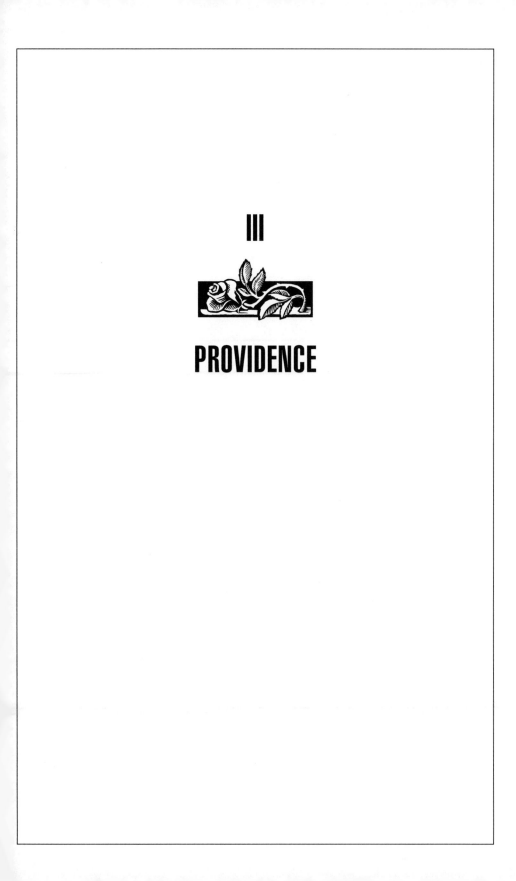

PROVIDENCE

1

Whaen Rosie and Pam Haverford came down in the service elevator after work on the following Wednesday, Pam looked pale and unwell. "It's my period," she said when Rosie expressed concern. "I'm having cramps like a bastard."

"Do you want to stop for a coffee?"

Pam thought about it, then shook her head. "You go on without me. All I want to do right now is go back to D and S and find an empty bedroom before everyone shows up from work and starts yakking. Gobble some Midol and sleep for a couple of hours. If I do that, maybe I'll feel like a human being again."

"I'll come with you," Rosie said as the elevator doors opened and they stepped out.

Pam shook her head. "No you don't," she said, and her face lit in a brief smile. "I can make it on my own just fine, and you're old enough to have a cup of coffee without a chaperone. Who knows—you might even meet someone interesting."

Rosie sighed. To Pam, *someone interesting* always meant a man, usually the kind with muscles that stood out under their form-fitting tee-shirts like geological landmarks, and as far as Rosie was concerned, she could do without that kind of man for the rest of her life.

Besides, she was married.

She glanced down at her wedding band and diamond engagement ring inside it as they stepped out onto the street. How much that glance had to do with what happened a short time later was something of which she was never sure, but it did place the engagement ring, which in the ordinary course of things she hardly ever thought of at all, somewhere toward the front of her mind. It was a little over a carat, by far the most expensive thing her husband had ever given her, and until that day the idea that it belonged to *her*, and she could dispose of it if she wanted to (and in any way she wanted to), had never crossed her mind.

Rosie waited at the bus stop around the corner from the hotel with

Pam in spite of Pam's protestations that it was totally unnecessary. She really didn't like the way Pam looked, with all the color gone from her cheeks and dark smudges under her eyes and little pain-lines running down from the corners of her mouth. Besides, it felt good to be looking out for someone else, instead of the other way around. She actually came quite close to getting on the bus with Pam just to make sure she got back all right, but in the end, the call of fresh hot coffee (and maybe a piece of pie) was just too strong.

She stood on the curb and waved at Pam when Pam sat down beside one of the bus windows. Pam waved back as the bus pulled away. Rosie stood where she was for a moment, then turned and started walking down Hitchens Boulevard toward the Hot Pot. Her mind turned, naturally enough, back to her first walk in this city. She couldn't recall very much of those hours—what she remembered most was being afraid and disoriented—but at least two figures stood out like rocks in a billowing mist: the pregnant woman and the man with the David Crosby moustache. Him, particularly. Leaning in the tavern doorway with a beer-stein in his hand and looking at her. Talking

(hey baby hey baby)

to her. Or at her. These recollections possessed her mind wholly for a little while, as only our worst recollections can—memories of times when we have felt lost and helpless, utterly unable to exert any control over our own lives—and she walked past the Hot Pot without even seeing it, her heedless eyes blank and full of dismay. She was still thinking about the man in the tavern doorway, thinking about how much he had frightened her and how much he had reminded her of Norman. It wasn't anything in his face; mostly it had been a matter of posture. The way he'd stood there, as if every muscle was ready to flex and leap, and it would take only a single glance of acknowledgement from her to set him off—

A hand seized her upper arm and Rosie nearly shrieked. She looked around, expecting either Norman or the man with the dark red moustache. Instead she saw a young fellow in a conservative summer-weight suit. "Sorry if I startled you," he said, "but for a second there I was sure you were going to step right out into the traffic."

She looked around and saw that she was standing on the corner of Hitchens and Watertower Drive, one of the busiest intersections in the city and at least three full blocks past the Hot Pot, maybe four. Traffic raced by like a metal river. It suddenly occurred to her that the young man beside her might have saved her life.

"Th-Thank you. A lot."

"Not a problem," he said, and on the far side of Watertower, WALK flashed out in white letters. The young man gave Rosie a final curious glance and then stepped off the curb and into the crosswalk with the rest of the pedestrians and was borne away.

Rosie stayed where she was, feeling the momentary dislocation and deep relief of someone who wakes from a really bad dream. *And that's exactly what I was having,* she thought. *I was awake and walking down the street, but I was still having a bad dream. Or a flashback.* She looked down and saw she was holding her purse clamped tightly against her midsection in both hands, as she had held it during that long, bewildering tramp in search of Durham Avenue five weeks ago. She slipped the strap over her shoulder, turned around, and began retracing her steps.

The city's fashionable shopping section started beyond Watertower Drive; the area she was now passing through as she left Watertower behind consisted of much smaller shops. Many of them looked a little seedy, a trifle desperate around the edges. Rosie walked slowly, looking in the windows of secondhand clothing stores trying to pass themselves off as grunge boutiques, shoe stores with signs reading BUY AMERICAN and CLEARANCE SALE in the windows, a discount place called No More Than 5, its window heaped with dollbabies made in Mexico or Manila, a leathergoods place called Motorcycle Mama, and a store called Avec Plaisir with a startling array of goods—dildos, handcuffs, and crotchless underwear—displayed on black velvet. She looked in here for quite awhile, marvelling at this stuff which had been put out for anyone passing to see, and at last crossed the street. Half a block farther up she could see the Hot Pot, but she had decided to forgo the coffee and pie, after all; she would simply catch the bus and go on back to D & S. Enough adventures for one day.

Except that wasn't what happened. On the far corner of the intersection she had just crossed was a nondescript storefront with a neon sign in the window reading PAWNS   LOANS   FINE JEWELRY BOUGHT AND SOLD. It was the last service which caught Rosie's attention. She looked down at her engagement ring again, and remembered something Norman had told her not long before they were married—*If you wear that on the street, wear it with the stone turned in toward your palm, Rose. That's a helluva big rock and you're just a little girl.*

She had asked him once (this was before he had begun teaching her that it was safer not to ask questions) how much it had cost. He had answered with a headshake and a small indulgent smile—the smile of a parent whose child wants to know why the sky is blue or how much snow there is at the North Pole. *Never mind,* he said. *Content yourself with knowing it was either the rock or a new Buick. I decided on the rock. Because I love you, Rose.*

Now, standing here on this streetcorner, she could still remember how that had made her feel—afraid, because you *had* to be afraid of a man capable of such extravagance, a man who could choose a ring over a new car, but a little breathless and sexy, too. Because it was romantic. He had bought her a diamond so big that it wasn't safe to flash it on the street. A diamond as big as the Ritz. *Because I love you, Rose.*

And perhaps he had . . . but that had been fourteen years ago, and the girl he'd loved had possessed clear eyes and high breasts and a flat stomach and long, strong thighs. There had been no blood in that girl's urine when she went to the bathroom.

Rosie stood on the corner near the storefront with the neon in the window and looked down at her diamond engagement ring. She waited to see what she would feel—an echo of fear or perhaps even romance —and when she felt nothing at all, she turned toward the pawnshop's door. She would be leaving Daughters and Sisters soon, and if there was someone inside this place who would give her a reasonable sum of money for her ring, she could leave clean, owing nothing for her room and board, and maybe even with a few hundred dollars left over.

Or maybe I just want to be rid of it, she thought. *Maybe I don't want to spend even another day carting around the Buick he never bought.*

The sign on the door read LIBERTY CITY LOAN & PAWN. That struck her as momentarily strange—she had heard several nicknames for this city, but all of them had to do either with the lake or the weather. Then she dismissed the thought, opened the door, and went inside.

2

She had expected it to be dark, and it *was* dark, but it was also unexpectedly golden inside the Liberty City Loan & Pawn. The sun was low in the sky now, shining straight down Hitchens, and it fell through the pawnshop's west-facing windows in long, warm beams. One of them turned a hanging saxophone into an instrument which looked as if it were made of fire.

That's not accidental, either, Rosie thought. *Someone hung that sax there on purpose. Someone smart.* Probably true, but she still felt a little enchanted. Even the smell of the place added to that sense of enchantment—a smell of dust and age and secrets. Very faintly, off to her left, she could hear many clocks ticking softly.

She walked slowly up the center aisle, past ranks of acoustic guitars strung up by their necks on one side and glass cases filled with appliances and stereo equipment on the other. There seemed to be a great many of those oversized, multi-function sound-systems that were called "boomboxes" on the TV shows.

At the far end of this aisle was a long counter with another neon sign bent in an arc overhead. GOLD   SILVER   FINE JEWELRY, it said in blue. Then, below it, in red: WE BUY   WE SELL   WE TRADE.

Yes, but do you crawl on your belly like a reptile? Rosie thought with a small ghost of a smile, and approached the counter. A man was sitting on a stool behind it. There was a jeweller's loupe in his eye. He was using it to look at something which lay on a pad in front of him. When she got a little closer, Rosie saw that the item under examination was a pocket-watch with its back off. The man behind the counter was poking into it with a steel probe so thin she could barely see it. He was young, she thought, maybe not even thirty yet. His hair was long, almost to his shoulders, and he was wearing a blue silk vest over a plain white undershirt. She thought the combination unconventional but rather dashing.

There was movement off to her left. She turned in that direction and saw an older gentleman squatting on the floor and going through piles of paperbacks stacked under a sign reading THE GOOD OLD STUFF. His topcoat was spread out around him in a fan, and his briefcase—black, old-fashioned, and starting to come unsprung at the seams—stood patiently beside him, like a faithful dog.

"Help you, ma'am?"

She returned her attention to the man behind the counter, who had removed the loupe and was now looking at her with a friendly grin. His eyes were hazel with a greenish undertint, very pretty, and she wondered briefly if Pam might classify him as *someone interesting.* She guessed not. Not enough tectonic plates sliding around under the shirt.

"Maybe you can," she said.

She slipped off her wedding ring and her engagement ring, then put the plain gold band into her pocket. It felt strange not to be wearing it, but she supposed she could get used to that. A woman capable of walking out of her own house for good without even a change of underwear could probably get used to quite a lot. She laid the diamond down on the velvet pad beside the old watch the jeweller had been working on.

"How much would you say that's worth?" she asked him. Then, as an afterthought, she added: "And how much could you give me for it?"

He slipped the ring over the end of his thumb, then held it up into the dusty sunbeam slanting in over his shoulder through the third of the west-facing windows. The stone sent back sparks of multicolored fire into her eyes, and for just a moment she felt a pang of regret. Then the jeweller gave her a quick look, just a glance, really, but it was long enough for her to see something in his hazel eyes she didn't immediately understand—a look that seemed to say *Are you joking?*

"What?" she asked. "What is it?"

"Nothing," he said. "Just a mo'." He screwed the loupe back into his eye and took a good long look at the stone in her engagement ring. When he looked up the second time, his eyes were surer and easier to read. Impossible not to read, really. Suddenly Rosie knew everything, but she felt no surprise, no anger, and no real regret. The best she could do was a weary sort of embarrassment: why had she never realized before? How could she have been such a chump?

You weren't, that deep voice answered her. *You really weren't, Rosie. If you hadn't known on some level that the ring was a fake—known it almost from the start—you would have come into a place like this a lot sooner. Did you ever really believe, once you got past your twenty-second birthday, that is, that Norman Daniels would have given you a ring worth not just hundreds but thousands of dollars? Did you really?*

No, she supposed not. She'd never been worth it to him, for one thing. For another, a man who had three locks on the front door, three on the back, motion-sensor lights in the yard, and a touch-alarm on his new Sentra automobile would never have let his wife do the marketing with a diamond as big as the Ritz on her finger.

"It's a fake, isn't it?" she asked the jeweller.

"Well," he said, "it's a perfectly real *zirconia,* but it's certainly not a diamond, if that's what you mean."

"Of *course* it's what I mean," she said. "What else would I mean?"

"Are you okay?" the jeweller asked. He looked genuinely concerned, and she had an idea, now that she was seeing him up close, that he was closer to twenty-five than thirty.

"Hell," she said, "I don't know. Probably."

She took a Kleenex out of her purse, though, just in case of a tearful outburst—these days she never knew when one was coming. Or maybe a good laughing jag; she'd had several of those, as well. It would be nice if she could avoid both extremes, at least for the time being. Nice to leave this place with at least a few shreds of dignity.

"I hope so," he said, "because you're in good company. Believe me, you are. You'd be surprised how many ladies, ladies just like you—"

"Oh, stop," she told him. "When I need something uplifting, I'll buy a support bra." She had never in her life said anything remotely like that to a man—it was downright suggestive—but she had never *felt* like this in her whole life . . . as if she were spacewalking, or running giddily across a tightrope with no net beneath. And wasn't it perfect, in a way? Wasn't it the only fitting epilogue to her marriage? *I decided on the rock,* she heard him say in her mind; his voice had been shaking with sentiment, his gray eyes actually a little moist. *Because I love you, Rose.*

For a moment the laughing jag was very close. She held it at arm's length by sheer force of will.

"Is it worth *anything?*" she asked. "Anything at all? Or is it just something he got out of a gum-machine somewhere?"

He didn't bother with the loupe this time, just held the ring up into the sunbeam again. "Actually, it *is* worth a bit," he said, sounding relieved to be able to pass on a little good news. "The stone's a ten-buck item, but the setting . . . that might have gone as much as two hundred bucks, retail. 'Course, I couldn't give you that," he added hurriedly. "My dad'd read me the riot act. Wouldn't he, Robbie?"

"Your dad always reads you the riot act," said the old man squatting by the paperbacks. "That's what kids are for." He didn't look up.

The jeweller glanced at him, glanced back at Rosie, and stuck a finger into his half-open mouth, miming a retch. Rosie hadn't seen that one since high school, and it made her smile. The man in the vest smiled back. "I could give you fifty for it," he said. "Interested?"

"No, thanks." She picked up the ring, looked at it thoughtfully, then wrapped it in the unused Kleenex she was holding.

"You check any of the other shops along here," he said. "If anyone says they'll give you more, I'll match the best offer. That's Dad's policy, and it's a good one."

She dropped the Kleenex into her purse and snapped it shut. "Thanks, but I guess not," she said. "I'll hang onto it."

She was aware that the man who'd been checking out the paperbacks—the one the jeweller had called Robbie—was now looking at her, and with an odd expression of concentration on his face, but Rosie decided she didn't care. Let him look. It was a free country.

"The man who gave me that ring said it was worth as much as a brand-new car," she said. "Do you believe that?"

"Yes." He replied with no hesitation, and she remembered his telling her she was in good company, that lots of ladies came in here and learned unpleasant truths about their treasures. She guessed this man, although still young, must already have heard a great many variations on the same basic theme.

"I suppose you do," she said. "Well then, you should understand why I want to keep the ring. If I ever start getting woozy about someone else—or even *think* I am—I can dig it out and look at it while I wait for the fever to pass."

She was thinking of Pam Haverford, who had long, twisting scars on both forearms. In the summer of '92 her husband had thrown her through a storm door while he was drunk. Pam had raised her arms to protect her face as she went through the glass, and the result had been sixty stitches in one arm and a hundred and five in the other. Yet she still almost melted with happiness if a construction worker or house-painter whistled at her legs when she walked by, and what did you call that? Endurance or stupidity? Resilience or amnesia? Rose had come to think of it as Haverford's Syndrome, and only hoped that she herself could avoid it.

"Whatever you say, ma'am," the jeweller replied. "I'm sorry to be the bearer of bad news, though. Myself, I think it's why pawnshops have such a bad rep. We almost always get the job of telling people that things aren't what they're cracked up to be. Nobody likes that."

"No," she agreed. "Nobody likes that, Mr.—"

"Steiner," he said. "Bill Steiner. My dad's Abe Steiner. Here's our card."

He held one out, but she shook her head, smiling. "I'd have no use for it. Have a nice day, Mr. Steiner."

She started back toward the door, this time taking the third aisle because the elderly gentleman had advanced a few steps toward her with his briefcase in one hand and a few of the old paperbacks in the other. She wasn't sure he wanted to talk to her, but she was *very* sure that she didn't want to talk to him. All she wanted right now was to make a quick exit from Liberty City Loan & Pawn; to climb aboard a bus and get busy forgetting she had ever been here.

She was only vaguely aware that she was passing through an area of the pawnshop where clusters of small statuary and pictures, both framed and unframed, had been gathered together on the dusty shelves. Her head was up, but she was looking at nothing; she was not in the mood to appreciate art, fine or otherwise. So her sudden, almost skidding stop was all the more remarkable. It was as if she never saw the picture at all, at least on that first occasion.

It was as if the picture saw *her.*

3

Its powerful attraction was without precedent in her life, but this did not strike Rosie as extraordinary—she had been living an unprecedented life for over a month now. Nor did that attraction strike her (at first, anyway) as abnormal. The reason for this was simple: after fourteen years of marriage to Norman Daniels, years when she had been all but cut off from the rest of the world, she had no tools for judging the normal from the abnormal. Her yardstick for measuring how the world behaved in given situations mostly consisted of TV dramas and the occasional movie he had taken her to (Norman Daniels would go see anything starring Clint Eastwood). Within the framework provided by those media, her reaction to the picture seemed almost normal. In the movies and on TV, people were always getting swept off their feet.

And really, none of that mattered. What did was how the picture called to her, making her forget what she had just found out about her ring, making her forget that she wanted to get away from the pawnshop, making her forget how glad her sore feet were going to be when she saw the Blue Line bus pulling up in front of the Hot Pot, making her forget *everything*. She only thought: *Look at that! Isn't that the most wonderful picture!*

It was an oil painting in a wooden frame, about three feet long and two feet high, leaning against a stopped clock on the left end and a small naked cherub on the right end. There were pictures all around it (an old tinted photograph of St. Paul's Cathedral, a watercolor of fruit in a bowl, gondolas at dawn on the Grand Canal, a hunting print which showed a pack of the unspeakable chasing a pair of the uneatable across a misty English moor), but she hardly gave them a glance. It was the picture of the woman on the hill she was interested in, and only that. In both subject and execution it was not much different from pictures moldering away in pawnshops, curio shops, and roadside bargain barns all over the country (all over the world, for that matter), but it filled her eyes and her mind with the sort of clean, revelatory excitement that belongs only to the works of art that deeply move us—the song that made us cry, the story that made us see the world clearly from another's perspective, at least for awhile, the poem that made us glad to be alive, the dance that made us forget for a few minutes that someday we will not be.

Her emotional reaction was so sudden, so hot, and so completely without connection to her real, practical life that at first her mind simply floundered, with no idea at all of how to cope with this unexpected burst of fireworks. For that moment or two she was like a transmission that has suddenly popped out of gear and into neutral—although the engine was revving like crazy, nothing was happening. Then the clutch engaged and the transmission slipped smoothly back into place.

It's what I want for my new place, that's why I'm excited, she thought. *It's exactly what I want to make it mine.*

She seized on this thought eagerly and gratefully. It would only be a single room, true enough, but she had been promised it would be a *large* room, with a little kitchen alcove and an attached bathroom. In any case it would be the first place in her whole life that was hers and hers alone. That made it important, and that made the things she chose for it important, too . . . and the first would be the most important of all, because it would set the tone for everything that followed.

Yes. No matter how nice it might be, the room would be a place where dozens of single, low-income people had lived before her and more dozens would live after her. But it was going to be an important place, all the same. These last five weeks had been an interim period, a hiatus between the old life and the new. When she moved into the room she had been promised, her new life—her *single* life—would really begin . . . and this picture, one Norman had never seen and passed judgement on, one that was just *hers,* could be the symbol of that new life.

This was how her mind—sane, reasonable, and quite unprepared to admit or even recognize anything which smacked of the supernatural or paranormal—simultaneously explained, rationalized, and justified her sudden spike reaction to the picture of the woman on the hill.

4

It was the only painting in the aisle that was covered with glass (Rosie had an idea that oil paintings usually weren't glassed in, maybe because they had to breathe, or something), and there was a small yellow sticker in the lower lefthand corner. $75 OR ? it said.

She reached out with hands that trembled slightly and took hold of the frame's sides. She lifted the picture carefully off the shelf and carried it back up the aisle. The old man with the battered briefcase was still there, and still watching her, but Rosie hardly saw him. She went directly to the counter and put the picture carefully down in front of Bill Steiner.

"Found something you fancy?" he asked her.

"Yes." She tapped the price-sticker in the corner of the frame. "Seventy-five dollars or question-mark, it says. You told me you could give me fifty for my engagement ring. Would you be willing to trade, even-Steven? My ring for this picture?"

Steiner walked down his side of the counter, flipped up the pass-through at the end, and came around to Rosie's side. He looked at the picture as carefully as he had looked at her ring . . . but this time he looked with a certain amusement.

"I don't remember this. I don't think I've ever seen it before. Must be something the old man picked up. He's the art-lover of the family; I'm just a glorified Mr. Fixit."

"Does that mean you can't—"

"Dicker? Bite your tongue! I'll dicker until the cows come home, if you let me. But this time I don't have to. I'm happy to do it your way —even swapsies. Then I don't have to watch you walk out of here with your face practically dragging on the floor."

And here was another first; before she knew what she was doing, Rosie had wrapped her arms around Bill Steiner's neck and given him a brief, enthusiastic hug. "Thank you!" she cried. "Thanks so much!"

Steiner laughed. "Oh boy, you're welcome," he said. "I think that's the first time I've ever been hugged by a customer in these hallowed halls. See any other pictures you really want, lady?"

The old fellow in the topcoat—the one Steiner had called Robbie— walked over to look at the picture. "Considering what most pawnshop patrons are like, that's probably a blessing," he said.

Bill Steiner nodded. "You have a point."

She barely heard them. She was rooting through her purse, hunting for the twist of Kleenex with the ring in it. Finding it took her longer than it needed to, because her eyes kept wandering back to the picture on the counter. *Her* picture. For the first time she thought of the room she would be going to with real impatience. Her own place, not just one cot among many. Her own place, and her own picture to hang on the wall. *It's the first thing I'll do,* she thought as her fingers closed over the bundle of tissue. *The very first.* She unwrapped the ring and held it out to Steiner, but he ignored it for the time being; he was studying the picture.

"It's an original oil, not a print," he said, "and I don't think it's very good. Probably that's why it's covered with glass—somebody's idea of dolling it up. What's that building at the bottom of the hill supposed to be? A burned-out plantation-house?"

"I believe it's supposed to be the ruins of a temple," the old guy with the mangy briefcase said quietly. "A Greek temple, perhaps. Although it's difficult to say, isn't it?"

It *was* difficult to say, because the building in question was buried almost to the roof in underbrush. Vines were growing up the five columns in front. A sixth lay in segments. Near the fallen pillar was a fallen statue, so overgrown that all that could be glimpsed above the green was a smooth white stone face looking up at the thunderheads with which the painter had enthusiastically filled the sky.

"Yeah," Steiner said. "Anyway, it looks to me like the building's out of perspective—it's too big for where it is."

The old man nodded. "But it's a necessary cheat. Otherwise nothing would show but the roof. As for the fallen pillar and statue, forget them—they wouldn't be visible at all."

She didn't care about the background; all of her attention was fixed upon the painting's central figure. At the top of the hill, turned to look down at the ruins of the temple so anyone viewing the picture could only see her back, was a woman. Her hair was blonde, and hung down her back in a plait. Around one of her shapely upper arms—the right —was a broad circle of gold. Her left hand was raised, and although you couldn't see for sure, it looked as if she was shading her eyes. It was odd, given the thundery, sunless sky, but that was what she appeared to be doing, just the same. She was wearing a short dress—a toga, Rosie supposed—which left one creamy shoulder bare. The garment's color was a vibrant red-purple. It was impossible to tell what, if anything, she was wearing on her feet; the grass that she was standing in came almost up to her knees, where the toga ended.

"What do you call it?" Steiner asked. He was speaking to Robbie. "Classical? Neo-classical?"

"I call it bad art," Robbie said with a grin, "but at the same time I think I understand why this woman wants it. It has an emotional quality to it that's quite striking. The *elements* may be classical—the sort of thing one might see in old steel engravings—but the *feel* is gothic. And then there's the fact that the principal figure has her back turned. I find that *very* odd. On the whole . . . well, one can't say this young lady has chosen the *best* picture in the joint, but I'm sure she's chosen the most *peculiar* one."

Rosie was still barely hearing them. She kept finding new things in the picture to engage her attention. The dark violet cord around the woman's waist, for instance, which matched her robe's trim, and the barest hint of a left breast, revealed by the raised arm. The two men were only nattering. It was a *wonderful* picture. She felt she could look at it for hours on end, and when she had her new place, she would probably do just that.

"No title, no signature," Steiner said. "Unless—"

He turned the picture around. Printed in soft, slightly blurred charcoal strokes on the paper backing were the words ROSE MADDER.

"Well," he said doubtfully, "here's the artist's name. I guess. Funny name, though. Maybe it's a pseudonym."

Robbie shook his head, opened his mouth to speak, then saw that the woman who had chosen the picture also knew better.

"It's the name of the *picture,*" she said, and then added, for some reason she could never have explained, "Rose is *my* name."

Steiner looked at her, completely bewildered.

"Never mind, that's just a coincidence." But was it? she wondered. Was it really? "Look." She gently turned the picture around again. She tapped the glass over the toga the woman in the foreground was wearing. "That color—that purply-red—is called rose madder."

"She's right," Robbie said. "Either the artist—or more likely the last person to own the picture, since charcoal rubs away fairly rapidly—has named the painting after the color of the woman's chiton."

"Please," Rose said to Steiner, "could we do our business? I'm anxious to be on my way. I'm late as it is."

Steiner started to ask once more if she was sure, but he saw that she was. He saw something else, as well—she had a fine-drawn look about her, one that suggested she'd had a difficult go of it just lately. It was the face of a woman who might regard honest interest and concern as teasing, or possibly as an effort to alter the terms of the deal in his own favor. He simply nodded. "The ring for the picture, straight trade. And we both go away happy."

"Yes," Rosie said, and gave him a smile of dazzling brilliance. It was the first real smile she had given anyone in fourteen years, and in the moment of its fullness, his heart opened to her. "And we both go away happy."

5

She stood outside for a moment, blinking stupidly at the cars rushing past, feeling the way she had as a small child after leaving the movies with her father—dazed, caught with half of her brain in the world of real things and half of it still in the world of make-believe. But the picture was real enough; she only had to look down at the parcel she held under her left arm if she doubted that.

The door opened behind her, and the elderly man came out. Now she even felt good about him, and she gave him the sort of smile people reserve for those with whom they have shared strange or marvellous experiences.

"Madam," he said, "would you consider doing me a small favor?"

Her smile was replaced with a look of caution. "It depends on what it is, but I'm not in the habit of doing favors for strangers." That, of course, was an understatement. She wasn't even used to *talking* to strangers.

He looked almost embarrassed, and this had a reassuring effect on her. "Yes, well, I suppose it'll sound odd, but it might benefit both of us. My name is Lefferts, by the way. Rob Lefferts."

"Rosie McClendon," she said. She thought about holding out her hand and rejected the idea. Probably she shouldn't even have given him her name. "I really don't think I have time to do any favors, Mr. Lefferts—I'm running a little late, and—"

"Please." He put down his weary briefcase, reached into the small brown bag he was holding in his other hand, and brought out one of the old paperbacks he'd found inside the pawnshop. On the cover was a stylized picture of a man in a black-and-white-striped prison outfit stepping into what might have been a cave or the mouth of a tunnel. "All I want is for you to read the first paragraph of this book. Out loud."

"Here?" She looked around. "Right here on the street? In heaven's name, why?"

He only repeated "Please," and she took the book, thinking that if she did as he asked, she might be able to get away from him without any further foolishness. That would be fine, because she was starting to think he was a little nuts. Maybe not dangerous, but nuts, all the same. And if he *did* turn out to be dangerous, she wanted to find out while the Liberty City Loan & Pawn—and Bill Steiner—was still within dashing distance.

The name of the book was *Dark Passage*, the author David Goodis. As she paged past the copyright notice, Rosie decided it wasn't surprising she'd never heard of him (although the title of the novel rang a faint bell); *Dark Passage* had been published in 1946, sixteen years before she was born.

She looked up at Rob Lefferts. He nodded eagerly at her, almost vibrating with anticipation . . . and hope? How could that be? But it certainly *looked* like hope.

Feeling a little excited herself now (like calls to like, her mother had often said), Rosie began to read. The first paragraph was short, at least.

"It was a tough break. Parry was innocent. On top of that he was a decent sort of guy who never bothered people and wanted to lead a quiet life. But there was too much on the other side and on his side of it there was practically nothing. The jury decided he was guilty. The judge handed him a life sentence and he was taken to San Quentin."

She looked up, closed the book, held it out to him.

"Okay?"

He was smiling, clearly delighted. "Very much okay, Ms. McClendon. Now wait . . . just one more . . . humor me . . ." He went paging rapidly through the book, then handed it back to her. "Just the dialogue, please. The scene is between Parry and a cab-driver. From 'Well, it's funny.' Do you see it?"

She saw, and this time she didn't demur. She had decided Lefferts wasn't dangerous, and that maybe he wasn't crazy, either. Also, she still felt that queer sense of excitement, as if something really interesting was going to happen . . . or was happening already.

Yes, sure, you bet, the voice inside told her happily. *The picture, Rosie—remember?*

Sure, of course. The picture. Just thinking of it lifted her heart and made her feel lucky.

"This is very peculiar," she said, but she was smiling. She couldn't help herself.

He nodded, and she had an idea that he would have nodded in exactly the same way if she'd told him her name was Madame Bovary. "Yes, yes, I'm sure it seems that way, but . . . *do* you see where I want you to start?"

"Uh-huh."

She scanned the dialogue quickly, trying to get a sense of who these people were from what they were saying. The cab-driver was easy; she quickly formed a mental picture of Jackie Gleason as Ralph Kramden in the *Honeymooners* reruns they showed on Channel 18 in the afternoons. Parry was a little harder—generic hero, she supposed, comes in a white can. Oh, well; it was no big deal either way. She cleared her throat and began, quickly forgetting that she was standing on a busy streetcorner with a wrapped painting under her arm, unaware of the curious glances she and Lefferts were drawing.

" 'Well, it's funny,' the driver said. 'From faces I can tell what people think. I can tell what they do. Sometimes I can even tell who they are . . . you, for instance.'

" 'All right, me. What about me?'

" 'You're a guy with troubles.'

" 'I don't have a trouble in the world,' Parry said.

" 'Don't tell me, brother,' the driver said. 'I know. I know people. I'll tell you something else. Your trouble is women.'

" 'Strike one. I'm happily married.'

Suddenly, just like that, she had a voice for Parry: he was James Woods, nervous and high-strung, but with a brittle sense of humor. This delighted her and she went on, warming to the story now, seeing a scene from a movie that had never been made inside her head—Jackie Gleason and James Woods sparring in a cab that was racing through the streets of some anonymous city after dark.

" 'Call it a two-base hit. You're not married. But you used to be, and it wasn't happy.'

" 'Oh, I get it. You were there. You were hiding in the closet all the time.'

"The driver said, 'I'll tell you about her. She wasn't easy to get along with. She wanted things. The more she got, the more she wanted. And she always got what she wanted. That's the picture.' "

Rosie had reached the bottom of the page. Feeling a strange chill up her back, she silently handed the book back to Lefferts, who now looked happy enough to hug himself.

"Your voice is absolutely wonderful!" he told her. "Low but not drony, melodious and very clear, with no definable accent—I knew all that at once, but voice alone means very little. You can read, though! You can actually *read!*"

"Of *course* I can read," Rosie said. She didn't know whether to be amused or exasperated. "Do I look like I was raised by wolves?"

"No, of course not, but often even very good readers aren't able to read aloud—even if they don't actually stumble over the words, they have very little in the way of expression. And dialogue is *much* tougher than narration . . . the acid test, one might say. But I heard two different people. I actually *heard* them!"

"Yes, so did I. Mr. Lefferts, I really have to go now. I—"

He reached out and touched her lightly on the shoulder as she started to turn away. A woman with a bit more experience of the world would have known an audition, even one on a streetcorner, for what it was and consequently would not have been entirely surprised by what Lefferts said next. Rosie, however, was stunned to temporary silence when he cleared his throat and offered her a job.

6

*A*t the moment Rob Lefferts was listening to his fugitive wife read on a *streetcorner, Norman Daniels was sitting in his small office cubicle on the fourth floor of police headquarters with his feet up on his desk and his hands laced behind his head. It was the first time in years that it had been possible for him to put his feet up; under ordinary circumstances, his desk was heaped high with forms, fast-food wrappers, half-written reports, departmental circulars, memos, and other assorted trash. Norman was not the sort of man who picks up after himself without thinking about it (in just five weeks the house which Rosie kept pin-neat across all the years had come to look quite a bit like Miami after Hurricane Andrew), and usually his office reflected this, but now it looked positively austere. He had spent most of the day cleaning it out, taking three large plastic garbage bags full of swill down to the waste-disposal site in the basement, not wanting to leave the job to the nigger women who came in to clean between midnight and six on weekday mornings. What was left to niggers didn't get done—this was a lesson Norman's father had taught him, and it was a true lesson. There was one basic fact which the politicians and the do-gooders either could not or would not understand: niggers didn't understand work. It was their African temperament.*

Norman ran his gaze slowly across the top of his desk, upon which nothing now rested but his feet and his phone, then shifted his eyes to the wall on his right. For years this had been papered with want-sheets, hot-sheets, lab results, and takeout menus—not to mention his calendar with pending court-dates noted in red—but now it was completely bare. He finished his visual tour by noting the stack of cardboard liquor cartons by the door. As he did so, he reflected how unpredictable life was. He had a temper, and he would have been the first to admit it. That his temper had a way of getting him in trouble and keeping him in trouble was also something he would have freely admitted. And if, a year ago, he had been granted a vision of his office as it was today, he would have drawn a simple conclusion from it: his temper had finally gotten him into a jam he couldn't wiggle out of, and he had been canned. Either he had finally piled up enough reprimands in his jacket to warrant dismissal under departmental rules, or he had been caught really hurting someone, as he supposed he had really hurt the little spick, Ramon Sanders. The idea that it mattered if a queerboy like Ramon got hurt a little was ridiculous, of course—Saint Anthony he was not—but you had to abide by the rules of the game . . . or at least not be caught breaking them. It was like not saying out loud that niggers didn't understand the concept of work, although everybody (everybody white, at least) knew it.

But he was not *being canned. He was moving, that was all. Moving from this shitty little cubicle which had been home since the first year of the Bush Presidency. Moving into a real office, where the walls went all the way up to the ceiling and came all the way down to the floor. Not canned;* promoted. *It made him think of a Chuck Berry song, one that went* C'est la vie, *it goes to show you never can tell.*

The bust had happened, the big one, and things couldn't have gone better for him if he'd written the script himself. An almost unbelievable transmutation had taken place: his ass had turned to gold, at least around here.

It had been a city-wide crack ring, the sort of combine you never get whole and complete . . . except this time he had. Everything had fallen into place; it had been like rolling a dozen straight sevens at a crap-table in Atlantic City and doubling your money every time. His team had ended up arresting over twenty people, half a dozen of them really big bugs, and the busts were righteous—not so much as a whiff of entrapment. The D.A. was probably reaching heights of orgasm unmatched since cornholing his cocker spaniel back in junior high school. Norman, who had once believed he might end up being prosecuted by that geeky little fuck if he couldn't manage to put a checkrein on his temper, had become the D.A.'s fair-haired boy. Chuck Berry had been right: you never could tell.

"The Coolerator was jammed with TV dinners and ginger ale," *Norman sang, and smiled. It was a cheerful smile, one that made most people want to smile back at him, but it would have chilled Rosie's skin and made her frantically wish to be invisible. She thought of it as Norman's biting smile.*

A very good spring on top, a very good spring indeed, but underneath it had been a very bad spring. A totally shitty *spring, to be exact, and Rose was the reason why. He had expected to settle her hash long before now, but he hadn't. Somehow Rose was still out there. Still out there somewhere.*

He had gone to Portside on the very same day he had interrogated his good friend Ramon in the park across from the station. He had gone with a picture of Rose, but it hadn't been much help. When he mentioned the sunglasses and the bright red scarf (valuable details he had found in the transcript of Ramon Sanders's original interrogation), one of Continental's two daytime ticket-sellers had hollered Bingo. The only problem was that the ticket-seller couldn't remember what her destination had been, and there was no way to check the records, because there were no records. She had paid cash for her ticket and checked no baggage.

Continental's schedule had offered three possibilities, but Norman thought the third—a bus which had departed on the southern route at 1:45 p.m.—was unlikely. She wouldn't have wanted to hang around that long. That left two other choices: a city two hundred and fifty miles away and another, larger city in the heart of the midwest.

He had then made what he was slowly coming to believe had been a mistake, one which had cost him at least two weeks: he had assumed that she wouldn't want to go too far from home, from the area where she'd grown up—not a scared little mouse like her. But now—

Norman's palms were covered with a faint lacework of semicircular white scars. They had been made by his fingernails, but their real source was deep inside his head, an oven which had been running at broil for most of his life.

"You better *be scared," he murmured. "And if you're not now, I guarantee you will be soon."*

Yes. He had to have her. Without Rose, everything that had happened this spring—the glamour bust, the good press, the reporters who had stunned him by asking respectful questions for a change, even the promotion—meant nothing. The women he had slept with since Rose had left meant nothing, either. What mattered was *she had left him.* What mattered more was *he hadn't had the slightest clue she meant to do it. And what mattered most was she had taken his bank card. She had only used it once, and for a paltry three hundred and fifty dollars, but that wasn't the point. The point was that she had taken what was his, she had forgotten who was the meanest motherfucker in the jungle, and for that she would have to pay. The price would be high, too.*

High.

He'd strangled one of the women he'd been with since Rose left. Choked her, then dumped her behind a grain-storage tower on the west side of the lake. Was he supposed to blame that one on his temper, too? He didn't know, how was that for nuts? For right out to lunch? All he knew was he had picked the woman out of the strolling meat-market down on Fremont Street, a little brunette honey in fawn-colored hotpants with these big Daisy Mae tits poking out the front of her halter. He didn't really see how much she looked like Rose (or so he told himself now, and so he perhaps really believed) until he was shagging her in the back of his current duty-car, an anonymous four-year-old Chevy. What had happened was she turned her head and the lights around the top of the nearest grain-storage tower had shone on her face for a moment, shone on it in a certain way, and in that moment the whore was Rose, the bitch who had walked out on him without even leaving a note, without leaving so much as one fucking word, *and before he knew what he was doing he had the halter wrapped around the whore's neck and the whore's tongue was sticking out of her mouth and the whore's eyes were bulging out of their sockets like glass marbles. And the worst thing about it was that once she was dead, the whore hadn't looked like Rose at all.*

Well, he hadn't panicked . . . but then, why would he? It hadn't been the first time, after all.

Had Rose known that? Sensed that?

Was that why she had run? Because she was afraid he might—

"Don't be an asshole," *he muttered, and closed his eyes.*

A bad idea. What he saw was what he all too often saw in his dreams lately: the green ATM card from Merchant's Bank, grown to an enormous size and floating in the blackness like a currency-colored dirigible. He opened his eyes again in a hurry. His hands hurt. He unrolled his fingers and observed the welling cuts in his palms with no surprise. He was accustomed to the stigmata of his temper, and he knew how to deal with it: by reestablishing control. That meant thinking and planning, and those things began with review.

He had called the police in the closer of the two cities, had identified himself, and then had identified Rose as the prime suspect in a big-money bank-card scam (the card was the worst thing of all, and it never really left his mind anymore). He gave her name as Rose McClendon, feeling sure she would have gone back to her maiden name. If it turned out she hadn't, he would simply pass off as coincidence the fact that the suspect and the investigating officer shared the same name. It had been known to happen. And it was Daniels they were talking about, not Trzewski or Beauschatz.

He had also faxed the cops side-by-side pictures of Rose. One was a photo of her sitting on the back steps, taken by Roy Foster, a cop friend of his, last August. It wasn't very good—it showed how much lard she'd put on since hitting the big three-oh, for one thing—but it was black and white and showed her facial features with reasonable clarity. The other was a police artist's conception (Al Kelly, one talented sonofabitch, had done it on his own time, at Norman's request) of the same woman, only with a scarf over her head.

The cops in that other city, the closer city, had asked all the right questions and gone to all the right places—the homeless shelters, the transient hotels, the halfway houses where you could sometimes get a look at the current guest-list, if you knew who and how to ask—with no result. Norman himself had made as many calls as he'd had time for, hunting with ever-increasing frustration for some sort of paper trail. He even paid for a faxed list of the city's newest driver's license applicants, with no result.

The idea that she might escape him entirely, escape her just punishment for what she had done (especially for daring to take the bank card), still hadn't crossed his mind, but he now reluctantly came to the conclusion that she could have gone to that other city after all, that she could have been so afraid of him that two hundred and fifty miles just wasn't far enough.

Not that eight hundred miles would be, a fact she would soon learn.

In the meantime, he had been sitting here long enough. It was time to find a dolly or a janitor's cart and start moving his crap into his new office two floors up. He swung his feet off the desk, and as he did, the telephone rang. He picked it up.

"Is this Inspector Daniels?" the voice on the other end asked.

"Yes it is," he replied, thinking (with no great pleasure) Detective Inspector First Grade Daniels, as a matter of fact.

"Oliver Robbins here."

Robbins. Robbins. The name was familiar, but—

"From Continental Express? I sold a bus ticket to a woman you're looking for."

Daniels sat up straighter in his seat. "Yes, Mr. Robbins, I remember you very well."

"I saw you on television," Robbins said. "It's wonderful that you caught those people. That crack is awful stuff. We see people using it in the bus station all the time, you know."

"Yes," Daniels said, allowing no trace of impatience to show in his voice. "I'm sure you do."

"Will those people actually go to jail?"

"I think most of them will. How can I help you today?"

"Actually I'm hoping that I can help you," Robbins said. "Do you remember telling me to call you if I remembered anything else? About the woman in the dark glasses and red scarf, I mean."

"Yes," Norman said. His voice was still calm and friendly, but the hand not holding the phone had rolled into a tight fist again, and the nails were digging, digging.

"Well, I didn't think I would, but something came to me this morning while I was in the shower. I've been thinking about it all day, and I'm sure I'm right. She really did say it that way."

"Say what what way?" he asked. *His voice was still reasonable, calm —pleasant, even—but now blood was brightly visible in the creases of his closed fist. Norman opened one of the drawers of his empty desk and hung the fist over it. A little baptism on behalf of the next man to use this shitty little closet.*

"You see, she didn't tell me where she wanted to go; I told her. *That's probably why I couldn't remember when you asked me, Inspector Daniels, although my head for that sort of thing is usually quite good."*

"I'm not getting you."

"People buying tickets usually give you their destination," *Robbins said. " 'Give me a round trip to Nashville,' or 'One way to Lansing, please.' Follow me?"*

"Yes."

"This woman didn't do it that way. She didn't say the name of the place; *she said the time she wanted to go. That's what I remembered this morning in the shower. She said, 'I want to buy a ticket on the eleven-oh-five bus. Are there still some seats on that one?' As if the place she was going didn't matter, as if it only mattered that—"*

"—that she go as quick as she could and get as far away as she could!" Norman exclaimed. "Yes! Yes, of course! Thanks, Mr. Robbins!"

"I'm glad I could help." Robbins sounded a bit taken aback by the burst of emotion from the other end of the line. "This woman, you guys must really want her."

"We do," Norman said. He was once more smiling the smile which had always chilled Rosie's skin and made her want to back up against a wall to protect her kidneys. "You bet we do. That eleven-oh-five bus, Mr. Robbins—where does it go?"

Robbins told him, then asked: "Was she part of the crack-ring? The woman you're looking for?"

"No, it's a credit-card scam," Norman said, and Robbins started to reply to that—he was apparently ready to settle into a comfy little chat—but Norman dropped the phone back into the cradle, cutting him off in midrap. He put his feet up on the desk again. Finding a dolly and moving his crap could wait. He leaned back in the desk chair and looked at the ceiling. "A credit-card scam, you bet," he said. "But you know what they say about the long arm of the law."

He reached out with his left hand and opened his fist, exposing the blood-smeared palm. He flexed the fingers, which were also bloody.

"Long arm of the law, bitch," he said, and suddenly began to laugh. "Long fucking arm of the law, coming for you. You best believe it." He

*kept flexing his fingers, watching small drops of blood patter down to the
surface of his desk, not caring, laughing, feeling fine.*

Things were back on track again.

7

When she got back to D & S, Rosie found Pam sitting in a folding
chair in the basement rec room. She had a paperback in her lap, but
she was watching Gert Kinshaw and a skinny little thing who had come
in about ten days before—Cynthia something. Cynthia had a gaudy punk
hairdo—half green, half orange—and looked as if she might weigh all
of ninety pounds. There was a bulky bandage over her left ear, which
her boyfriend had tried, with a fair amount of success, to tear off. She
was wearing a tank-top with Peter Tosh at the center of a swirling blue-
green psychedelic sunburst. NOT GONNA GIVE IT UP! the shirt proclaimed. Every time she moved, the oversized armholes of the shirt
disclosed her teacup-sized breasts and small strawberry-colored nipples.
She was panting and her face streamed with sweat, but she looked almost
daffily pleased to be where she was and who she was.

Gert Kinshaw was as different from Cynthia as dark from day. Rosie
had never gotten it completely clear in her mind if Gert was a counsellor,
a long-time resident of D & S, or just a friend of the court, so to speak.
She showed up, stayed a few days, and then disappeared again. She often sat in the circle during therapy sessions (these ran twice a day at
D & S, with attendance at four a week a mandatory condition for residents), but Rosie had never heard her say anything. She was tall, six feet
one at least, and big—her shoulders were wide and soft and dark brown,
her breasts the size of melons, and her belly a large, pendulous pod that
pooched out her size XXXL tee-shirts and hung over the sweatpants she
always wore. Her hair was a jumble of frizzy braids (it was *very* kinky).
She looked so much like one of those women you saw sitting in the
laundromat, eating Twinkies and reading the latest issue of the *National
Enquirer,* that it was easy to miss the hard flex of her biceps, the toned
look of her thighs under the old gray sweatpants, and the way her big
ass did *not* jiggle when she walked. The only time Rosie ever heard her
talk much was during these rec-room seminars.

Gert taught the fine art of self-defense to any and all D & S residents
who wanted to learn. Rosie had taken a few lessons herself, and still
tried to practice what Gert called Six Great Ways to Fuck Up an Asshole
at least once a day. She wasn't very good at them, and couldn't imagine

actually trying them on a real man—the guy with the David Crosby moustache leaning in the doorway of The Wee Nip, for instance—but she liked Gert. She particularly liked the way Gert's broad dark face changed when she was teaching, breaking out of its customary claylike immobility and taking on animation and intelligence. Becoming pretty, in fact. Rosie had once asked her what, exactly, she was teaching—was it tae kwon do, or jujitsu, or karate? Some other discipline, perhaps? Gert had just shrugged. "A little of this and a little of that," she had said. "Leftovers."

Now the Ping-Pong table had been moved aside and the middle of the rec-room floor had been covered with gray mats. Eight or nine folding chairs had been set up along one pine-panelled wall, between the ancient stereo and the prehistoric color TV, where everything looked either pale green or pale pink. The only chair currently occupied was the one Pam was sitting on. With her book in her lap, her hair tied back with a piece of blue yarn, and her knees primly together, she looked like a wallflower at a high-school dance. Rosie sat down next to her, propping her wrapped picture against her shins.

Gert, easily two hundred and seventy pounds, and Cynthia, who probably could have tipped the scales over a hundred only by wearing Georgia Giants and a fully loaded backpack, circled each other. Cynthia was panting and smiling hugely. Gert was calm and silent, slightly bent at her nonwaist, her arms held out in front of her. Rosie looked at them, both amused and uneasy. It was like watching a squirrel, or maybe a chipmunk, stalk a bear.

"I was getting worried about you," Pam said. "The thought of a search-party had crossed my mind, actually."

"I had the most *amazing* afternoon. How 'bout you, though? How you feeling?"

"Better. In my opinion, Midol is the answer to all the world's problems. Never mind that, what happened to you? You're glowing!"

"Really?"

"Really. So give. How come?"

"Well, let's see," Rosie said. She began to tick things off on her fingers. "I found out my engagement ring was a fake, I swapped it for a picture—I'm going to hang it in my new place when I get it—I got offered a job . . ." She paused—a calculating pause—and then added, ". . . And I met *someone interesting.*"

Pam looked at her with round eyes. "You're making it up!"

"Nope. Swear to God. Don't get your water hot, though, he's sixty-five if he's a day." She was speaking of Robbie Lefferts, but the image her mind briefly presented to her was Bill Steiner, he of the blue silk vest and interesting eyes. But that was ridiculous. At this point in her life she needed love-interest like she needed lip-cancer. And besides, hadn't she decided that Steiner had to be at least seven years younger than she? Just a baby, really. "He's the one who offered me the job. His name is Robbie Lefferts. But never mind him right now—want to see my new picture?"

"Aw, come on an do it!" Gert said from the middle of the room. She sounded both amiable and irritated. "This ain't the school dance, sugar." The last word came out *sugah*.

Cynthia rushed her, the tail of her oversized tank-top flapping. Gert turned sideways, took the slender girl with the tu-tone hair by the forearms, and flipped her. Cynthia went over with her heels in the air and landed on her back. *"Wheeee!"* she said, and bounced back to her feet like a rubber ball.

"No, I don't want to see your *picture*," Pam said. "Not unless it's of the *guy*. Is he really sixty-five? I *doubt* it!"

"Maybe older," Rosie said. "There *was* another one, though. He was the one who told me that the diamond in my engagement ring was only a zirconia. Then he traded me for the picture." She paused. *"He* wasn't sixty-five."

"What did he look like?"

"Hazel eyes," Rosie said, and bent over her picture. "No more until you tell me what you think of this."

"Rosie, don't be a *booger!*"

Rosie grinned—she had almost forgotten the pleasures of a little harmless teasing—and continued to strip off the wrapping paper with which Bill Steiner had carefully covered the first meaningful purchase of her new life.

"Okay," Gert told Cynthia, who was once more circling her. Gert bounced slowly up and down on her large brown feet. Her breasts rose and subsided like ocean waves beneath the white tee-shirt she was wearing. "You see how it's done, now do it. Remember, you can't flip me— a pipsqueak like you'd wind up in traction, trying to flip a truck like me—but you can help me to flip myself. You ready?"

"Ready-ready-Teddy," Cynthia said. Her grin widened, revealing tiny wicked white teeth. To Rosie they looked like the teeth of some small but dangerous animal: a mongoose, perhaps. *"Gertrude Kinshaw, come on down!"*

Gert rushed. Cynthia seized her meaty forearms, turned a flat, boyish hip into the swell of Gert's flank with a confidence Rosie knew she herself would never be able to match . . . and suddenly Gert was airborne, flipping over in midair, a hallucination in a white shirt and gray sweatpants. The shirt slid up to reveal the largest bra Rosie had ever seen; the beige Lycra cups looked like World War I artillery shells. When Gert hit the mats, the room shuddered.

"Yesss!" Cynthia screamed, dancing nimbly around and shaking her clasped hands over her head. *"Big mama goes down! Yessss! YESSSS! Down for the count! Down for the fucking cou—"*

Smiling—a rare expression that turned her face into something rather gruesome—Gert picked Cynthia up, held her over her head for a moment with her treelike legs spread, and then began to spin her like an airplane propeller.

"Ouggghhh, I'm gonna puke!" Cynthia screamed, but she was laughing, too. She went around in a speedy blur of green-orange hair and psychedelic tank-top. *"Ouggghhhh, I'm gonna EEEEJECT!"*

"Gert, that's enough," a voice said quietly. It was Anna Stevenson, standing at the foot of the stairs. She was once again dressed in black and white (Rosie had seen her in other combinations, but not many), this time tapered black pants and a white silk blouse with long sleeves and a high neck. Rosie envied her elegance. She *always* envied Anna's elegance.

Looking slightly ashamed of herself, Gert set Cynthia gently back on her feet.

"I'm okay, Anna," Cynthia said. She wobbled four zigzag steps across the mat, stumbled, sat down, and began to giggle.

"I see you are," Anna said dryly.

"I flipped Gert," she said. "You should have seen it. I think it was the thrill of my life. Honestly."

"I'm sure it was, but Gert would tell you she flipped herself," Anna said. "You just helped her do what her body wanted to do already."

"Yeah, I guess so," Cynthia said. She got cautiously to her feet, then promptly plumped back down on her fanny (what there was of it) and giggled some more. "God, it's like someone put the whole room on a record-player."

Anna came across the room to where Rosie and Pam were sitting. "What have you got there?" she asked Rosie.

"A picture. I bought it this afternoon. It's for my new place, when I get it. My room." And then, a little fearfully, she added: "What do you think?"

"I don't know—let's get it into the light."

Anna picked the picture up by the sides of the frame, carried it across the room, and set it on the Ping-Pong table. The five women gathered around it in a semicircle. No, Rosie saw, glancing around, now they were seven. Robin St. James and Consuelo Delgado had come downstairs and joined them—they were standing behind Cynthia, looking over her narrow, bird-boned shoulders. Rosie waited for someone to break the silence—she was betting on Cynthia—and when nobody did and it began to spin out, she started feeling nervous.

"Well?" she asked at last. "What do you think? Somebody say something."

"It's an odd picture," Anna said.

"Yeah," Cynthia agreed. "Weird. I think I seen one like it before, though."

Anna was looking at Rosie. "Why did you buy it, Rosie?"

Rosie shrugged, feeling more nervous than ever. "I don't know that I can explain, really. It was like it called to me."

Anna surprised her—and eased her considerably—by smiling and nodding. "Yes. That's really all art is about, I think, and not just pictures—it's the same with books and stories and sculpture and even castles in the sand. Some things call to us, that's all. It's as if the people who made them were speaking inside our heads. But this particular painting . . . is it beautiful to you, Rosie?"

Rosie looked at it, trying to see it as she had in the Liberty City Loan & Pawn, when its silent tongue had spoken to her with such force that she had been stopped cold, all other thoughts driven from her mind. She looked at the blonde woman in the rose madder toga (or chiton—that was what Mr. Lefferts had called it) standing in the high grass at the top of the hill, again noting the plait which hung straight down the middle of her back and the gold armlet above her right elbow. Then she let her gaze move to the ruined temple and the tumbled

(god)

statue at the foot of the hill. The things the woman in the toga was looking at.

How do you know that's what she's looking at? How can you know? You can't see her face!

That was true, of course . . . but what else *was* there to look at?

"No," Rosie said. "I didn't buy it because it was beautiful to me. I bought it because it seemed *powerful* to me. The way it stopped me in my tracks was powerful. Does a picture have to be beautiful to be good, do you think?"

"Nope," Consuelo said. "Think about Jackson Pollock. His stuff wasn't about beauty, it was about energy. Or Diane Arbus, how about her?"

"Who's she?" Cynthia asked.

"A photographer who got famous taking pictures of women with beards and dwarves smoking cigarettes."

"Oh." Cynthia thought this over, and her face suddenly brightened with recollection. "I saw this picture once, at a catered party back when I was cocktailing. In an art gallery, this was. It was by some guy named Applethorpe, Robert Applethorpe, and you want to know what it was? One guy gobbling another guy's crank! Seriously! And it wasn't any fake job like in a skin magazine, either. I mean that guy was making an *effort,* he was taking care of business and working overtime. You wouldn't think a guy could get that much of the old broomhandle down his—"

"Mapplethorpe," Anna said dryly.

"Huh?"

*"Mapple*thorpe, not *Apple*thorpe."

"Oh yeah. I guess that's right."

"He's dead now."

"Oh yeah?" Cynthia asked. "What got him?"

"AIDS." Anna was still looking at Rosie's picture and spoke absently. "Known as broomhandle disease in some quarters."

"You said you saw a picture like Rosie's before," Gert rumbled. "Where was that, squirt? Same art gallery?"

"No." While discussing the Mapplethorpe, Cynthia had only looked interested; now color pinked her cheeks and the corners of her mouth dimpled in a defensive little smile. "And it wasn't, you know, really the *same,* but . . ."

"Go on, tell," Rosie said.

"Well, my dad was a Methodist minister back in Bakersfield," Cynthia said. "This is Bakersfield, California, where I came from. We lived in the parsonage, and there were all these old pictures in the little meeting-rooms downstairs. Some were Presidents, and some were flowers, and some were dogs. They didn't matter. They were just things to hang on the walls so they wouldn't look too bare."

Rosie nodded, thinking of the pictures which had surrounded hers on those dusty pawnshop shelves—gondolas in Venice, fruit in bowls, dogs and foxes. Just things to hang on the walls so they wouldn't look too bare. Mouths without tongues.

"But there was this one . . . it was called . . ." She frowned, trying to remember. "I think it was called *De Soto Looks West.* It showed this explorer in tin pants and a saucepan hat standing on top of a cliff with these Indians around him. And he was lookin over all these miles of woods toward a great big river. The Mississippi, I guess. But see . . . the thing was . . ."

She looked at them uncertainly. Her cheeks were pinker than ever and her smile was gone. The bulky bandage over her ear seemed very white, very much *there,* like some sort of peculiar accessory which had been grafted onto the side of her head, and Rosie found time to wonder— not for the first time since she had come to D & S—why so many men were so unkind. What was wrong with them? Was it something that had been left out, or something nasty which had been unaccountably built in, like a bad circuit in a computer?

"Go on, Cynthia," Anna said. "We won't laugh. Will we?"

The women shook their heads.

Cynthia stuck her hands behind her back like a little girl who has been called upon to recite in front of the entire class. "Well," she said, speaking in a much smaller voice than her usual one, "it was like the river was *moving,* that was the thing that fascinated me. The picture was in the room where my father had his Thursday-night Bible school classes, and I'd go in there and sometimes I'd sit in front of that picture for an hour or more, looking at it like it was television. I was watching the river move . . . or waiting to see if it *would* move. Now I can't remember which, but I was only nine or ten. One thing I do remember is thinking that if it *was* moving, a raft or a boat or an Indian canoe would go by sooner or later and then I'd know for sure. Except one day I went in and the picture was gone. Poof. I think my mother must have looked in and seen me just sitting there in front of it, you know, and—"

"She got worried and took it away," Robin said.

"Yeah, probably threw it in the trash," Cynthia said. "I was just a kid. But your picture reminds me of it, Rosie."

Pam peered at it closely. "Yep," she said, "no wonder. I can see the woman breathing."

They all laughed then, and Rosie laughed with them.

"No, it's not *that,*" Cynthia said. "It's just . . . it looks a little old-fashioned, you know . . . like a schoolroom picture . . . and it's pale. Except for the clouds and her dress, the colors are pale. In my De Soto picture everything was pale except for the river. The river was bright silver. It looked more *there* than the rest of the picture."

Gert turned to Rosie. "Tell us about your job. I heard you say you got a job."

"Tell us *everything,*" Pam said.

"Yes," Anna said. "Tell us everything, and then I wonder if you could step into my office for a few minutes."

"Is it . . . is it what I've been waiting for?"

Anna smiled. "As a matter of fact, I think it is."

8

"It's an optimum room, one of the best on our list, and I hope you'll be as delighted as I am," Anna said. There was a stack of fliers perched precariously on the corner of her desk, announcing the forthcoming Daughters and Sisters Swing into Summer Picnic and Concert, an event which was part fundraiser, part community relations, and part celebration. Anna took one, turned it over, and sketched quickly. "Kitchen here, hide-a-bed here, and a little living-room area here. This is the bathroom. It's hardly big enough to turn around in, and in order to sit on the commode you'll practically have to put your feet in the shower, but it's *yours.*"

"Yes," Rosie murmured. "Mine." A feeling that she hadn't had in weeks—that all this was a wonderful dream and at any moment she would wake up beside Norman again—was creeping over her.

"The view is nice—it's not Lake Drive, of course, but Bryant Park is very pretty, especially in the summer. Second floor. The neighborhood got a little ragged in the eighties, but it's pulling itself together again now."

"It's as if you've stayed there yourself," Rosie said.

Anna shrugged—a slender, pretty gesture—and drew the hall in front of the room, then a flight of stairs. She sketched with the no-frills economy of a draftsman. She spoke without looking up. "I've been there on a good many occasions," she said, "but of course that's not what you mean, is it?"

"No."

"A little of me goes out with every woman when she leaves. I suppose that sounds corny, but I don't care. It's true, and that's all that really matters. So what do you think?"

Rosie hugged her impulsively, and instantly regretted it when she felt Anna stiffen. *I shouldn't have done it,* she thought as she let go. *I knew better.* And she had. Anna Stevenson was kind, there was no doubt about that in Rosie's mind—maybe even saintly—but there was that strange arrogance, and there was this, too: Anna didn't like people in her space. Anna especially didn't like to be touched.

"I'm sorry," she said, drawing back.

"Don't be silly," Anna said brusquely. "What do you think?"

"I love it," Rosie said.

Anna smiled and the small awkwardness was behind them. She drew an *X* on the wall of the living-room area, near a tiny rectangle which represented the room's only window. "Your new picture . . . I'll bet you decide it belongs right here."

"I'll bet I do, too."

Anna put the pencil down. "I'm delighted to be able to help you, Rosie, and I'm so glad you came to us. Here, you're leaking." It was the Kleenex again, but Rosie doubted it was the same box Anna had offered her during their first interview in this room; she had an idea that a lot of Kleenex got used in here.

She took one and wiped her eyes. "You saved my life, you know," she said hoarsely. "You saved my life and I'll never, ever forget it."

"Flattering but inaccurate," Anna said in her dry, calm voice. "I saved your life no more than Cynthia flipped Gert downstairs in the rec room. You saved your own life when you took a chance and walked out on the man who was hurting you."

"Just the same, thank you. Just for being here."

"You're very welcome," Anna said, and for the only time during her stay at D & S, Rosie saw tears standing in Anna Stevenson's eyes. She handed the box of Kleenex back across the desk with a little smile.

"Here," she said. "Looks like you've sprung a leak yourself."

Anna laughed, took a Kleenex, used it, and tossed it into the waste-basket. "I hate to cry. It's my deepest, darkest secret. Every now and then I think I'm done with it, that I *must* be done with it, and then I do it again. It's sort of the way I feel about men."

For another brief moment, Rosie found herself thinking about Bill Steiner and his hazel eyes.

Anna took the pencil again and scratched something below the rough floor-plan she'd drawn. Then she handed the sheet to Rosie. It was an address she'd jotted down: 897 Trenton Street.

"That's where you live," Anna said. "It's most of the way across the city from here, but you can use the buses now, can't you?"

Smiling—and still crying a little—Rosie nodded.

"You may give that address to some of the friends you've made here, and eventually to friends you make beyond here, but right now nobody knows but the two of us." What she was saying felt like a set-piece to Rosie—a goodbye speech. "People who show up at your place will not have found out how to get there at *this* place. It's just how we do things at D and S. After twenty years of working with abused women, I'm convinced it's the only way to do things."

Pam had explained all this to Rosie; so had Consuelo Delgado and Robin St. James. These explanations had taken place during Big Fun Hour, which was what the residents called evening chores at D & S, but Rosie hadn't really needed them; it only took three or four therapy sessions in the front room for a person of reasonable intelligence to learn most of what she needed to know about the protocols of the house. There was Anna's List, and there were also Anna's Rules.

"How worried are you about him?" Anna asked.

Rosie's attention had wandered a little; now it snapped back in a hurry. At first she wasn't even sure who Anna was talking about.

"Your husband—how worried are you? I know that in your first two or three weeks here, you expressed fears that he would come after you . . . that he'd 'track you down,' in your words. How do you feel about that now?"

Rosie considered the question carefully. First of all, *fear* was an inadequate word to express her feelings about Norman during her first week or two at D & S; even terror didn't completely serve, because the core of her feelings concerning him was lapped about—and to some degree altered—by other emotions: shame at having failed in her marriage, homesickness for a few possessions she had cared deeply about (Pooh's Chair, for instance), a sensation of euphoric freedom which seemed to renew itself at some point each day, and a relief so cold it was somehow horrible; the sort of relief a wire-walker might feel after tottering at the furthest edge of balance while crossing a deep canyon . . . and then recovering.

Fear had been the keychord, though; there was no doubt about that. During those first two weeks at D & S she'd had the same dream over and over: she was sitting in one of the wicker chairs on the porch when a brand-new red Sentra pulled up to the curb in front. The driver's door opened and Norman got out. He was wearing a black tee-shirt with a map of South Vietnam on it. Sometimes the words beneath the map said HOME IS WHERE THE HEART IS; sometimes they said HOMELESS & HAVE AIDS. His pants were splattered with blood. Tiny bones—finger-bones, they looked like—dangled from his earlobes. In one hand he held some sort of mask which was splattered with blood and dark clots of meat. She tried to get up from the chair she was in and couldn't; it was as if she were paralyzed. She could only sit and watch him come slowly up the walk toward her with his bone earrings bobbing. Could only sit there as he told her he wanted to talk to her up close. He smiled and she saw his teeth were also covered with blood.

"Rosie?" Anna asked softly. "Are you here?"

"Yes," she said, speaking in a little breathless rush. "I'm here, and yes, I'm still afraid of him."

"That's not exactly surprising, you know. On some level I suppose you'll always be afraid of him. But you'll be all right as long as you remember that you're going to have longer and longer periods when you're not afraid of anything . . . and when you don't even *think* of him. But that isn't exactly what I asked, either. I asked if you're still afraid that he'll come after you."

Yes, she was still afraid. No, not *as* afraid. She had heard a lot of his business-related telephone conversations over the last fourteen years, and she'd heard him and his colleagues discuss a lot of cases, sometimes in the rec room downstairs, sometimes out on the patio. They barely noticed her when she brought them warm-ups for their coffee or fresh bottles of beer. It was almost always Norman who led these discussions, his voice quick and impatient as he leaned over the table with a beer bottle half-buried in one big fist, hurrying the others along, overriding their doubts, refusing to entertain their speculations. On rare occasions he had even discussed cases with her. He wasn't interested in her ideas, of course, but she was a handy wall against which to bounce his own. He was quick, a man who wanted results yesterday, and he had a tendency to lose interest in cases once they were three weeks old. He called them what Gert had called her self-defense moves: leftovers.

Was *she* a leftover to him now?

How much she wanted to believe that. How hard she had tried. And yet, she couldn't . . . quite . . . do it.

"I don't know," she said. "A part of me thinks that if he was going to show up, he would have already. But there's another part that thinks he's probably still looking. And he's not a truck-driver or a plumber; he's a cop. He knows *how* to look for people."

Anna nodded. "Yes, I know. That makes him especially dangerous, and that means you'll have to be especially careful. It's also important for you to remember *you're not alone.* The days when you were are over for you, Rosie. Will you remember that?"

"Yes."

"Are you sure?"

"Yes."

"And if he *does* show up, what will you do?"

"Slam the door in his face and lock it."

"And then?"

"Call 911."

"With no hesitation?"

"None at all," she said, and that was the truth, but she would be afraid. Why? Because Norman was a cop and *they* would be cops, the people she called. Because she knew Norman had a way of getting his way—he was an alpha-dog. Because of what Norman had told her, again and again and again: that all cops were brothers.

"And after you called 911? What would you do then?"

"I'd call you."

Anna nodded. "You're going to be fine. Absolutely fine."

"I know." She spoke with confidence, but part of her still wondered . . . would *always* wonder, she supposed, unless he showed up and took the matter out of the realm of speculation. If that happened, would all of this life she had lived over the last month and a half—D & S, the Whitestone Hotel, Anna, her new friends—fade like a dream on waking the moment she opened her door to an evening knock and found Norman standing there? Was that possible?

Rosie's eyes shifted to her picture, leaning against the wall beside the door to the office, and knew it was not. The picture was facing inward so only the backing showed, but she found she could see it anyway; already the image of the woman on the hill with the thundery sky above and the half-buried temple below was crystal clear in her mind, not the least dreamlike. She didn't think *anything* could turn her picture into a dream.

And with luck, these questions of mine will never have to be answered, she thought, and smiled a little.

"What about the rent, Anna? How much?"

"Three hundred and twenty dollars a month. Will you be all right for at least two months?"

"Yes." Anna knew that, of course; if Rosie hadn't had enough runway to assure her of a safe take-off, they would not have been having this discussion. "That seems very reasonable. As far as the room-rent goes, I'll be fine to start with."

"To start with," Anna repeated. She steepled her fingers under her chin and directed a keen look across the cluttered desk at Rosie. "Which brings me to the subject of your new job. It sounds absolutely wonderful, and yet at the same time it sounds . . ."

"Iffy? Impermanent?" These were words which had occurred to her on her walk home . . . along with the fact that, despite Robbie Lefferts's enthusiasm, she didn't really know if she could *do* this job yet, and wouldn't—not for sure—until next Monday morning.

Anna nodded. "They aren't the words I would have chosen myself—I don't know what words *would* be, exactly—but they'll do. The point is, if you leave the Whitestone, I can't absolutely *guarantee* I could get you back in, especially on short notice. There are always new girls here at D and S, as you know very well, and they have to be my first priority."

"Of course. I understand that."

"I'd do what I could, naturally, but—"

"If the job Mr. Lefferts offered me doesn't pan out, I'll look for work waitressing," Rosie said quietly. "My back is much better now, and I think I could do it. Thanks to Dawn, I can probably get a late-shift job in a Seven-Eleven or a Piggly-Wiggly, if it comes to that." Dawn was Dawn Verecker, who gave rudimentary clerking lessons on a cash register that was kept in one of the back rooms. Rosie had been an attentive student.

Anna was still looking at Rosie keenly. "But you don't think it will come to that, do you?"

"No." She directed another glance down at her picture. "I think it will work out. In the meantime, I owe you so much . . ."

"You know what to do about that, don't you?"

"Pass it on."

Anna nodded. "That's right. If you should see a version of yourself walking down the street someday—a woman who looks lost and afraid of her own shadow—just pass it on."

"Can I ask you something, Anna?"

"Anything at all."

"You said your parents founded Daughters and Sisters. Why? And why do you carry it on? Or pass it on, if you like that better?"

Anna opened one of her desk drawers, rummaged, and brought out a thick paperback book. She tossed it across the desk to Rosie, who picked it up, stared at it, and experienced a moment of recall so vivid it was like one of the flashbacks combat veterans sometimes suffered. In that instant she did not just remember the wetness on the insides of her thighs, a sensation like small, sinister kisses, but seemed to re-experience it. She could see Norman's shadow as he stood in the kitchen, talking on the phone. She could see his shadow-fingers pulling restlessly at a shadow-cord. She could hear him telling the person on the other end that of *course* it was an emergency, his wife was pregnant. And then she saw him come back into the room and start picking up the pieces of the paperback he had torn out of her hands before beginning to hit her.

The same redhead was on the cover of the book Anna had tossed her. This time she was dressed in a ballgown and caught up in the arms of a handsome gypsy who had flashing eyes and—apparently—a pair of rolled-up socks in the front of his breeches.

This is the trouble, Norman had said. *How many times have I told you how I feel about crap like this?*

"Rose?" It was Anna, sounding concerned. She also sounded very far away, like the voices you sometimes heard in dreams. "Rose, are you all right?"

She looked up from the book (*Misery's Lover,* the title proclaimed in that same red foil, and, below it, *Paul Sheldon's Most Torrid Novel!*) and forced a smile. "Yes, I'm fine. This looks hot."

"Bodice-rippers are one of my secret vices," Anna said. "Better than chocolate because they don't make you fat and the men in them are better than real men because they don't call you at four in the morning, drunk and whining for a second chance. But they're trash, and do you know why?"

Rosie shook her head.

"Because the whole round world is explained in them. There are reasons for *everything.* They may be as farfetched as the stories in the supermarket tabloids and they may run counter to everything a halfway intelligent person understands about how people behave in real life, but they're *there,* by God. In a book like *Misery's Lover,* Anna Stevenson would undoubtedly run Daughters and Sisters because she had been an abused woman herself . . . or because her mother had been. But I was never abused, and so far as I know, my mother never was, either. I was often *ignored* by my husband—we've been divorced for twenty years, in case Pam or Gert hasn't told you—but never abused. In life, Rosie, people sometimes do things, both bad and good, *just-because.* Do you believe that?"

Rosie nodded her head slowly. She was thinking of all the times Norman had hit her, hurt her, made her cry . . . and then one night, for no reason at all, he might bring her half a dozen roses and take her out to dinner. If she asked why, what the occasion was, he usually just shrugged and said he "felt like treating her." *Just-because,* in other words. Mommy, why do I have to go to bed at eight even in the summertime, when the sky is still light outside? *Just-because.* Daddy, why did Grandpa have to die? *Just-because.* Norman undoubtedly thought these occasional treats and whirlwind dates made up for a lot, that they must offset what he probably thought of as his "bad temper." He would never know (and never understand even if she told him) that they terrified her even more than his anger and his bouts of rage. Those, at least, she knew how to deal with.

"I *hate* the idea that everything we do gets done because of the things people have done to us," Anna said moodily. "It takes everything out of our hands, it doesn't account *in the least* for the occasional saints and devils we glimpse among us, and most important of all, it doesn't ring true to my heart. It's good in books like Paul Sheldon's, though. It's comforting. Lets you believe, at least for a little while, that God is sane and nothing bad will happen to the people that you like in the story. May I have my book back? I'm going to finish it tonight. With lots of hot tea. *Gallons*."

Rosie smiled, and Anna smiled back.

"You'll come for the picnic, won't you, Rosie? It's going to be at Ettinger's Pier. We'll need all the help we can get. We always do."

"Oh, you bet," Rosie said. "Unless Mr. Lefferts decides I'm a prodigy and wants me to work on Saturdays, that is."

"I doubt that." Anna got up and came around the desk; Rosie also stood. And now that their talk was almost over, the most elementary question of all occurred to her.

"When can I move in, Anna?"

"Tomorrow, if you want." Anna bent and picked up the picture. She looked thoughtfully at the words charcoaled on the backing, then turned it around.

"You said it was odd," Rosie said. "Why?"

Anna tapped the glass fronting with one nail. "Because the woman is at the center, and yet her back is turned. That seems an extremely peculiar approach to this sort of painting, which has been otherwise quite conventionally executed." Now she glanced over at Rosie, and when she went on, her tone was a bit apologetic. "The building at the bottom of the hill is out of perspective, by the way."

"Yes. The man who sold me the picture mentioned that. Mr. Lefferts said it was probably done on purpose. Or some of the elements would be lost."

"I suppose that's true." She looked at it for several moments longer. "It does have *something,* doesn't it? A *fraught* quality."

"I don't understand what you mean."

Anna laughed. "Neither do I . . . except that there's something about it that makes me think of my romance novels. Strong men, lusty women, gushing hormones. *Fraught*'s the only word I can think of that comes close to describing what I mean. A calm-before-the-storm thing. Probably it's just the sky." She turned the frame around again and restudied the words charcoaled on the backing. "Is this what caught your eye to start with? Your own name?"

"Nope," Rosie said, "by the time I saw *Rose Madder* on the back, I already knew I wanted the painting." She smiled. "It was just a coincidence, I guess—the kind that isn't allowed in the romance novels you like."

"I see." But Anna didn't look as if she did, quite. She ran the ball of her thumb across the printed letters. They smudged easily.

"Yes," Rose said. Suddenly, for no reason at all, she felt very uneasy. It was as if, somewhere off in that other timezone where evening had already begun, a man was thinking of her. "After all, Rose is a fairly common name—not like Evangeline or Petronella."

"I suppose you're right." Anna handed the picture over to her. "But it's funny about the charcoal it's written in, just the same."

"Funny how?"

"Charcoal smudges so easily. If it isn't protected—and the words on the backing of your picture haven't been—it turns into nothing but a smear in no time. The words *Rose Madder* must have been printed on the backing recently. But why? The picture *itself* doesn't look recent; it must be at least forty years old, and it might be eighty or a hundred. There's something else odd about it, too."

"What?"

"No artist's signature," Anna said.

IV

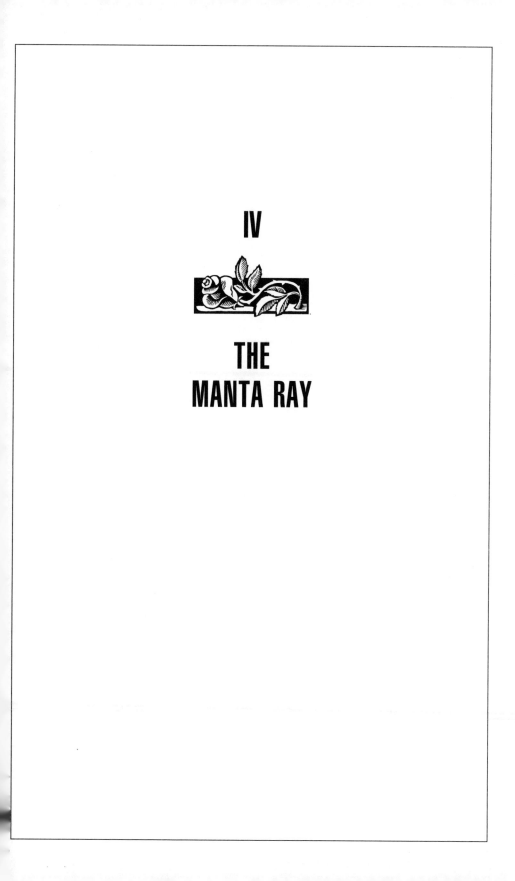

THE
MANTA RAY

1

Norman left his hometown on Sunday, the day before Rosie was sched-
uled to start her new job . . . the job she was still not entirely sure she
could do. He left on the 11:05 Continental Express bus. This wasn't a
matter of economy; it was a matter—a vital matter—of slipping back inside Rose's head. Norman was still not able to admit how badly her totally
unexpected flight had rocked him. He tried to tell himself he was upset
because of the bank card—only that and nothing more—but his heart
knew better. It was about how he'd never had a clue. Not so much as a
premonition.

There had been a long time in their marriage when he had known her
every waking thought and most of her dreams. The fact that that had
changed was driving him nuts. His biggest fear—unacknowledged but not
entirely hidden from the deeper run of his thoughts—was that she had
been planning her escape for weeks, months, possibly even a year. If he
had known the truth of how and why she had left (if he had known about
the single drop of blood, in other words), he would perhaps have been
comforted. Or perhaps he would have been more unsettled than ever.

Regardless, he realized that his first impulse—to take off his husband's
hat and put on his detective's hat—had been a bad idea. In the wake of
Oliver Robbins's phone-call, he had realized that he needed to take off
both of his hats and put on one of hers. He would have to think like her,
and riding the bus she had ridden was a way of starting to do that.

He climbed up the bus steps with his overnight bag in his hand and
stood by the driver's seat, looking down the aisle.

"You want to move it, buddy?" a man asked from behind him.

"You want to find out how getting your nose broken feels?" Norman
replied without missing a beat. The guy behind him didn't have anything
to say to that.

He took a moment or two longer, deciding which seat
(she)
he wanted, then made his way down the aisle to it. She wouldn't have

gone all the way to the back of the bus; his fastidious Rose would never have taken a seat near the toilet cubicle unless all the other seats were full, and Norman's good friend Oliver Robbins (from whom he had bought his ticket, just as she had) had assured him that the 11:05 was hardly ever full. Nor would she want to sit over the wheels (too bumpy) or too close to the front (too conspicuous). Nope, just about halfway down would suit her, and on the left side of the bus, because she was left-handed, and people who thought they were choosing at random were in many cases simply going in the direction of their dominant hands.

In his years as a cop, Norman had come to believe that telepathy was perfectly possible, but it was hard work . . . impossible work, if you were wearing the wrong hat. You had to find your way into the head of the person you were after like some kind of tiny burrowing animal, and you had to keep listening for something that wasn't a beat but a brainwave: not a thought, precisely, but a way of thinking. And when you finally had that, you could take a shortcut—you could go racing across the curve of your quarry's thoughts and some night, when he or she least expected it, there you'd be, stepping out from behind the door . . . or lying under the bed with a knife in your hand, ready to ram it upward through the mattress the moment the springs squeaked and the poor sap (sapette, in this case) lay down.

"When you least expect it," Norman murmured as he sat in what he hoped had been her seat. He liked the sound of it and so he said it again as the bus backed out of its slot, ready to head west: "When you least expect it."

It was a long trip, but he rather enjoyed it. Twice he got off to use the toilet at rest-stops when he didn't really need to go because he knew she would have needed to go, and she wouldn't have wanted to use the bus toilet. Rose was fastidious but Rose also had weak kidneys. Probably a little genetic gift from her late mother, who had always looked to Norman like the sort of bitch who couldn't trot past a lilac bush without a pause to squat and piddle.

At the second of these rest-stops he saw half a dozen people clustered around a butt-can at one corner of the building. He watched longingly for a moment, then went past them and inside. He was dying for a smoke, but Rose wouldn't have been; she didn't have the habit. Instead he paused to handle a number of fuzzy stuffed animals because Rose liked crap like that, and then purchased a paperback mystery from the rack by the door because she sometimes read that shit. He had told her a billion times that real police work was nothing like the crap in those books, and she always agreed with him—if he said it, it must be true—but she went on reading them just the same. He wouldn't have been too surprised to learn that Rosie had turned this same rack, had picked a book from it . . . and then put it reluctantly back again, not wanting to spend five dollars on three hours' entertainment when she had so little money and so many unanswered questions.

He ate a salad, forcing himself to read the book as he did, and then went back to his seat on the bus. In a little while they were off again, Norman sitting still with his book in his lap, watching the fields open out more and more as the East gave up its hold. He turned his watch back when the driver announced it was time to do so, not because he gave a shit about timezones (he was on his own clock for the next thirty days or so) but because that was what Rose would have done. He picked the book up, read about a vicar finding a body in a garden, and put it down again, bored. Yet that was only on the surface. Deeper down, he wasn't bored at all. Deeper down he felt strangely like Goldilocks in the old kids' story. He was sitting in Baby Bear's chair, he had Baby Bear's book in his lap, and he was going to find Baby Bear's little housie. Before long, if all went well, he would be hiding underneath Baby Bear's little beddie.

"When you least expect it," he said. "When you least expect it."

He got off the bus in the early hours of the following morning and stood just inside the door from the loading-gate, surveying the echoing, high-ceilinged terminal, trying to put aside his cop's assessment of the pimps and the whores, the buttboys and the beggars, trying to see it as she must have seen it, getting off this same bus and walking into this same terminal and seeing it at this same hour, when human nature is always at low tide.

He stood there and let this echoing world flood in on him: its look and smell and taste and feel.

Who am I? he asked himself.

Rose Daniels, *he answered.*

How do I feel?

Small. Lost. And terrified. That's the bottom line, right there. I'm utterly terrified.

For a moment he was overwhelmed by an awful idea: what if, in her fear and panic, Rose had approached the wrong person? It was certainly possible; for a certain type of bad guy, places like this were feeding-pools. What if that wrong person had led her off into the dark, then robbed and murdered her? It was no good telling himself it was unlikely; he was a cop and knew it wasn't. If a crackhead saw that stupid gumball-machine ring of hers, for instance—

He took several deep breaths, regrouping, refocusing the part of his mind that was trying to be Rose. What else was there to do? If she'd been murdered, she'd been murdered. There was nothing he could do about it, so it was best not to think of it . . . and besides, he couldn't bear the thought that she might have escaped him that way, that some coked-up boogie might have taken what belonged to Norman Daniels.

Never mind, *he told himself.* Never mind, just do your job. And right now your job is to walk like Rosie, talk like Rosie, think like Rosie.

He moved slowly out into the terminal, holding his wallet in one hand (it was his substitute for her purse), looking at the people who rushed past in riptides, some dragging suitcases, some balancing string-tied cardboard boxes on their shoulders, some with their arms around the shoulders of their girlfriends or the waists of their boyfriends. As he watched, a man sprinted toward a woman and a little boy who had just gotten off Norman's bus. The man kissed the woman, then seized the little boy and tossed him high into the air. The little boy shrieked with fear and delight.

I'm scared—everything's new, everything's different, and I'm scared to death, *Norman told himself.* Is there anything I feel sure about? Anything I feel I can trust? Anything at all?

He walked across the wide tile floor, but slowly, slowly, listening to his feet echo and trying to look at everything through Rose's eyes, trying to feel everything through her skin. A quick peek at the glassy-eyed kids (with some it was just three-in-the-morning tiredness; with some it was Nebraska Red) in the video alcove, then back into the terminal itself. She looks at the bank of pay phones, but who is she going to call? She has no friends, she has no family—not even the providential old aunt in the Texas Panhandle or the mountains of Tennessee. She looks at the doors to the street, perhaps thinking of leaving, of finding a room for the night, a door to put between her and the whole wide confusing indifferent dangerous world— she has money enough for a room, thanks to his ATM card—but does she do it?

Norman stopped by the foot of the escalator, frowning, changing the shape of the question: Do I do it?

No, *he decided,* I don't. I don't want to check into a motel at three-thirty and be kicked out at noon, for one thing; it's bad value for my money. I can stay up a little longer, run on my nerves a little longer, if I have to. But there's something else keeping me here, as well: I'm in a strange city, and dawn is still at least two hours away. I've seen a lot of TV crime-shows, I've read a lot of paperback mysteries, and I'm married to a cop. I know what can happen to a woman who goes out into the darkness by herself, and I think I'll wait for sunrise.

So what do I do? How do I pass the time?

His stomach answered the question for him, rumbling.

Yes, I have something to eat. The last rest-stop was at six in the evening, and I'm pretty hungry.

There was a cafeteria not far from the ticket-windows and Norman went that way, stepping over the bag-bums and restraining the urge to kick a few ugly, lice-ridden heads into the nearest steel chair-leg. This was an urge he had to restrain more and more often these days. He hated homeless people; thought of them as dog turds with legs. He hated their whining excuses and their inept pretenses at insanity. When one who was only semi-comatose stumbled over to him and asked if he had any spare change, Norman was barely able to resist an impulse to grab the bum's arm and heat him up with an old-fashioned Indian Burn. Instead he said, "Leave me alone, please," in a soft voice, because that's what she *would have said and how she would have said it.*

He started to grab bacon and scrambled eggs from the steam-table, then remembered she didn't eat that stuff unless he insisted, which he sometimes did (what she ate wasn't important to him, but her not forgetting who was boss of the shooting match was *important,* very *important). He ordered cold cereal instead, along with a foul cup of coffee and half a grapefruit that looked as if it might have come over on the* Mayflower. *The food made him feel better, more awake. When he was done he grabbed automatically for a cigarette, briefly touched the pack in his shirt pocket, then let his hand drop away. Rose didn't smoke, therefore Rose wouldn't be subject to the craving he now felt. After a moment or two of meditation on this subject, the craving retreated, as he had known it would.*

The first thing he saw as he came out of the cafeteria and stood there, tucking in the back of his shirt with the hand that wasn't holding his wallet, was a large lighted blue-and-white circle with the words TRAVELERS AID *printed on the outer stripe.*

Inside Norman's head, a bright light suddenly went on.

Do I go there? Do I go to the booth under that big, comforting sign? Do I see if there's anything there for me?

Of course I do—where else?

He walked over there, but on a slant, first sliding past the booth and then hooking back toward it again, getting a good look at the booth's occupant from both sides. He was a pencil-necked Jewboy who looked about fifty and about as dangerous as Bambi's friend Thumper. He was reading a newspaper Norman recognized as Pravda, *and every now and then he would raise his head from it and shoot a meaningless, random glance out into the terminal. If Norman had still been doing Rose, Thumper would undoubtedly have spotted him, but Norman was doing Norman again, Detective Inspector Daniels on stakeout, and that meant he blended into the scene. Mostly he kept moving back and forth in a gentle arc behind the booth (keeping in motion was the important part; in places like this you didn't run much risk of being noticed unless you stood still), staying out of Thumper's view but within earshot of Thumper's conversations.*

Around quarter past four, a crying woman came up to the Travelers Aid booth. She told Thumper that she'd been on the Greyhound from New York City and someone had stolen her wallet out of her purse while she was sleeping. There was a lot of blah-de-blah, the woman used several of Thumper's Kleenexes, and he ended up finding a hotel that would trust her for a couple of nights, until her husband could send her some more money.

If I was your husband, lady, I'd bring you the money myself, *Norman thought, still describing his drifting little back-and-forth pendulum movement behind the booth.* I'd also bring you a swift kick in the ass for doing such a dumbass thing in the first place.

In the course of his telephone conversation with the hotel, Thumper gave his name as Peter Slowik. It was enough for Norman. As the Jewboy began talking with the woman again, giving her directions, Norman quit the vicinity of the booth and returned to the pay phones, where there were actually two telephone books which hadn't yet been torched, torn to pieces, or carried away. He could get the information he needed later in the day, by calling his own police department, but he preferred not to do it that way. Depending on how things went with the Pravda-*reading Jewboy, calling people could be dangerous, the kind of thing that might come back to haunt a person later. And it turned out not to be necessary. There were just three Slowiks and one Slowick in the city directory. Only one of them was a Peter.*

Daniels jotted down Thumperstein's address, left the station, and walked over to the cab-stand. The guy in the lead cab was white—a break—and Norman asked him if there was a hotel left in this city where a person could get a room for cash and not have to listen to the cockroach races once the lights were off. The driver thought it over, then nodded. "The Whitestone. Good, cheap, cash accepted, no questions."

Norman opened the back door of the cab and got in. "Let's do it," he said.

2

Robbie Lefferts was there, just as he'd promised, when Rosie followed the gorgeous redhead with the long fashion-model legs into Studio C of Tape Engine on Monday morning, and he was as nice to her as he had been on the streetcorner, when he'd persuaded her to read aloud from one of the paperbacks he had just bought. Rhoda Simons, the fortyish woman who was to be her director, was also nice to her, but . . . *director!* Such a strange word to think of in connection with Rosie McClendon, who hadn't even tried out for her senior class play. Curtis Hamilton, the recording engineer, was also nice, although he was at first too busy with his controls to do more than give her hand a quick, abstracted shake. Rosie joined Robbie and Ms. Simons for a cup of coffee before setting sail (which was how Robbie put it), and she was able to manage her cup normally, without spilling a single drop. Yet when she stepped through the double doors and into the small glass-sided recording booth, she was seized with an attack of such overwhelming panic that she almost dropped the sheaf of Xeroxed pages which Rhoda called "the sides." She felt much as she had when she had seen the red car coming up Westmoreland Street toward her and thought it was Norman's Sentra.

She saw them staring at her from the other side of the glass—even serious young Curtis Hamilton was looking at her now—and their faces looked distorted and wavery, as if she were seeing them through water instead of air. *This is the way goldfish see people who bend down to look in through the side of the tank,* she thought, and on the heels of that: *I can't do this. What in the name of God ever made me think I could?*

There was a loud click that made her jump.

"Ms. McClendon?" It was the recording engineer's voice. "Could you sit down in front of the mike so I can get a level?"

She wasn't sure she could. She wasn't sure she could even move. She was rooted to the spot, looking across the room to where the head of the mike was pointing at her like the head of some dangerous, futuristic snake. Even if she *did* manage to cross the room, nothing would come out of her mouth once she sat down, not so much as a single dry squeak.

In that moment Rosie saw the collapse of everything she had built up—it flashed past her mind's eye with the nightmarish speed of an old Keystone Kops short. She saw herself turned out of the pleasant little room she'd lived in for only four days when her small supply of cash ran out, saw herself getting the cold shoulder from everyone at Daughters and Sisters, even Anna herself.

I can't very well give you your old place back, can I? she heard Anna say inside her head. *There are always new girls here at D and S, as you know very well, and they have to be my first priority. Why were you so foolish, Rosie? What ever made you think you could be a* performance artist, *even at such a humble level as this?* She saw herself being turned away from the waitress jobs in the downtown coffee shops, not because of how she looked but because of how she *smelled*—of defeat, shame, and lost expectations.

"Rosie?" That was Rob Lefferts. "Would you sit down so Curt can get a level?"

He didn't know, neither of the men knew, but Rhoda Simons did . . . or suspected, at least. She had taken the pencil which had been sticking out of her hair and was doodling on a pad in front of her. She wasn't looking at what she was doodling, though; she was looking at Rosie, and her eyebrows were drawn together in a frown.

Suddenly, like a drowning woman flailing for any piece of floating detritus which might support her for a little while longer, Rosie found herself thinking of her picture. She had hung it exactly where Anna had suggested, beside the window in the living-room area—there had even been a picture-hook there, left over from a previous tenant. It was the perfect place, especially in the evening; you could look out the window for awhile, at the sun going down over the forested greeny-black of Bryant Park, then back at the picture, then out at the park again. The two things seemed perfect together, the window and the picture, the picture and the window. She didn't know why it was so, but it was. If she lost the room, though, the picture would have to come down . . .

No, it's got to stay there, she thought. *It's* supposed *to stay there!*

That got her moving, at least. She walked slowly across to the table, put her sides (they were photo-enlargements of the pages of a paperback novel published in 1951) in front of her, and sat down. Except it felt more like *falling* down, as if her knees were locked in position by pins and someone had just pulled them.

You can do this, Rosie, the deep voice assured her, but its authority now sounded false. *You did it on the streetcorner outside the pawnshop, and you can do it here.*

She wasn't terribly surprised to find herself unconvinced. What *did* surprise her was the thought which followed: *The woman in the picture wouldn't be afraid of this; the woman in the rose madder chiton wouldn't be afraid of* this *piddle at all.*

The idea was ridiculous, of course; if the woman in the picture were real, she would have existed in an ancient world where comets were considered harbingers of doom, gods were thought to dally on the tops of mountains, and most folks lived and died without ever seeing a book. If a woman from that time were transported into a room like this, a room with glass walls and cold lights and a steel snake's head poking out of the only table, she would either run screaming for the door or faint dead away.

Except Rosie had an idea that the blonde woman in the rose madder chiton had never fainted dead away in her entire life, and it would take a lot more than a recording studio to make her scream.

You're thinking about her as if she's real, the deep voice said. It sounded nervous. *Are you sure that's wise?*

If it gets me through this, you bet, she thought back at it.

"Rosie?" It was Rhoda Simons's voice coming through the speakers. "Are you all right?"

"Yes," she said, and was relieved to find that her voice was still there, only a little croaky. "I'm thirsty, that's all. And scared to death."

"There's a cooler filled with Evian water and fruit juices under the left side of the table," Rhoda said. "As for being afraid, that's natural. And it will pass."

"Give me a little more, Rosie," Curtis invited. He had a pair of earphones on now, and was tweaking a row of dials.

The panic *was* passing, thanks to the woman in the rose madder gown. As a calmative, thinking of her even beat fifteen minutes of rocking in Pooh's Chair.

No, it's not her, it's you, the deep voice told her. *You're on top of it, kiddo, at least for the time being, but you did it yourself. And would you do me a favor, no matter how the rest of this turns out? Try to keep remembering who's really Rosie around here, and who's Rosie Real.*

"Talk about anything," Curtis was telling her. "It doesn't matter what."

For a moment she was utterly at a loss. Her eyes dropped to the sides in front of her. The first was a cover reproduction. It showed a scantily clad woman being menaced by a hulking, unshaven man with a knife. The man had a moustache, and a thought almost too fleeting to be recognizable

(wanna get it on wanna do the dog)

brushed past her consciousness like a breath of bad air.

"I'm going to read a book called *The Manta Ray,*" she said in what she hoped was a normal speaking voice. "It was published in 1951 by Lion Books, a little paperback company. Although it says on the cover that the author's name is . . . have you got enough?"

"I'm fine on the reel-to-reel," Curtis said, foot-powering himself from one end of his board to the other in his wheeled chair. "Just give me a little more for the DAT. But you're sounding good."

"Yes, wonderful," Rhoda said, and Rosie didn't think she was imagining the relief in the director's voice.

Feeling encouraged, Rosie addressed the mike again.

"It says on the cover that the book was written by Richard Racine, but Mr. Lefferts—Rob—says it was actually written by a woman named Christina Bell. It's part of an unabridged audio series called 'Women in Disguise,' and I got this job because the woman who was supposed to read the Christina Bell novels got a part in a—"

"I'm fine," Curtis Hamilton said.

"My God, she sounds like Liz Taylor in *Butterfield 8*," Rhoda Simons said, and actually clapped her hands.

Robbie nodded. He was grinning, obviously delighted. "Rhoda will help you along, but if you do it just like you did *Dark Passage* for me outside the Liberty City, we're all going to be very happy."

Rosie leaned over, just avoided whamming her head on the side of the table, and got a bottle of Evian water from the cooler. When she twisted the cap, she saw that her hands were shaking. "I'll do my best. I promise you that."

"I know you will," he said.

Think of the woman on the hill, Rosie told herself. *Think of how she's standing there right now, not afraid of anything coming toward her in her world or coming up behind her from mine. She doesn't have a single weapon, but she's not afraid—you don't need to see her face to know that, you can see it in the set of her back. She's . . .*

". . . ready for *anything*," Rosie murmured, and smiled.

Robbie leaned forward on his side of the glass. "Pardon? I didn't get that."

"I said I'm ready to go," she said.

"Level's good," Curtis said, and turned to Rhoda, who had set out her own Xeroxed copy of the novel next to her pad of paper. "Ready when you are, Professor."

"Okay, Rosie, let's show 'em how it's done," Rhoda said. "This is *The Manta Ray*, by Christina Bell. The client is Audio Concepts, the director is Rhoda Simons, and the reader is Rose McClendon. Tape is rolling. Take one on my mark, and . . . *mark*."

Oh God I can't, Rosie thought once more, and then she narrowed her mind's vision down to a single powerfully bright image: the gold circlet the woman in the picture wore on her upper right arm. As it came clear to her, this fresh cramp of panic also began to pass.

"*Chapter One.*

"*Nella didn't realize she was being followed by the man in the ragged gray topcoat until she was between streetlights and a garbage-strewn alley yawned open on her left like the jaws of an old man who has died with food in his mouth. By then it was too late. She heard the sound of shoes with steel taps on their heels closing in behind her, and a big, dirt-grimed hand shot out of the dark . . ."*

3

Rosie pushed her key into the lock of her second-floor room on Trenton Street that evening at quarter past seven. She was tired and hot—summer had come early to the city this year—but she was also very happy. Curled in one arm was a little bag of groceries. Poking out of the top was a sheaf of yellow fliers, announcing the Daughters and Sisters Swing into Summer Picnic and Concert. Rosie had gone by D & S to tell them how her first day at work had gone (she was all but bursting with it), and as she was leaving, Robin St. James had asked her if she would take a handful of fliers and try to place them with the storekeepers in her neighborhood. Rosie, trying hard not to show how thrilled she was just to *have* a neighborhood, agreed to get as many up as she could.

"You're a lifesaver," Robin said. She was in charge of ticket sales this year, and had made no secret of the fact that so far they weren't going very well. "And if anybody asks you, Rosie, tell them there are no teenage runaways here, and that *we're not dykes*. Those stories're half the problem with sales. Will you do that?"

"Sure," Rosie had replied, knowing she'd do no such thing. She couldn't imagine giving a storekeeper she had never met before a lecture on what Daughters and Sisters was all about . . . and what it *wasn't* all about.

But I can say they're nice women, she thought, turning on the fan in the corner and then opening the fridge to put away her few things. Then, out loud: "No, I'll say *ladies.* Nice *ladies.*"

Sure, that was probably a better idea. Men—especially those past forty—for some reason felt more comfortable with that word than they did with *women.* It was silly (and the way some women fussed and clucked over the semantics was even sillier, in Rose's opinion), but thinking about it called up a sudden memory: how Norman talked about the prostitutes he sometimes busted. He never called them ladies (that was the word he used when talking about the wives of his colleagues, as in "Bill Jessup's wife's a real nice lady"); he never called them women, either. He called them the gals. The gals this and the gals that. She had never realized until this moment how much she had hated that hard little back-of-the-throat word. *Gals.* Like a sound you might make when you were trying hard not to vomit.

Forget him, Rosie, he's not here. He's not going to be here.

As always, this simple thought filled her with joy, amazement, and gratitude. She had been told—mostly in the Therapy Circle at D & S —that these euphoric feelings would pass, but she found that hard to believe. She was on her own. She had escaped the monster. She was free.

Rosie closed the refrigerator door, turned around, and looked across her room. The furnishings were minimal and the decorations—except for her picture—were nonexistent, but she still saw nothing which did not make her want to crow with delight. There were pretty cream-colored walls that Norman Daniels had never seen, there was a chair from which Norman Daniels had never pushed her for "being smart," there was a TV Norman Daniels had never watched, sneering at the news or laughing along with reruns of *All in the Family* and *Cheers*. Best of all, there was not a single corner where she'd sat crying and reminding herself to vomit into her apron if she got sick to her stomach. Because he wasn't here. He wasn't going to *be* here.

"I'm on my own," Rosie murmured . . . and then actually hugged herself with joy.

She walked across the room to the picture. The blonde woman's chiton seemed almost to glow in the late-spring light. And *she* was a woman, Rosie thought. Not a lady, and most certainly not a *gal*. She stood up there on her hill, looking fearlessly down at the ruined temple and the tumbled gods . . .

Gods? But there's only one . . . isn't there?

No, she saw, there were actually two—the one peering serenely up at the thunderheads from its place near the fallen pillar, and another one, way over to the right. This one was gazing sideways through the tall grass. You could just see the white curve of stone brow, the orbit of one eye, and the lobe of an ear; the rest was hidden. She hadn't noticed this one until now, but what of that? There were probably *lots* of things in the picture she hadn't noticed yet, lots of little details—it was like one of those *Where's Waldo* pictures, full of things you didn't see at first, and . . .

. . . and that was bullshit. The picture was very simple, actually.

"Well," Rosie whispered, "it *was*."

She found herself thinking of Cynthia's story about the picture in the parsonage where she had grown up . . . *De Soto Looks West*. How she'd sat in front of it for hours, watching it like television, watching the river move.

"*Pretending* to watch it move," Rosie said, and ran up the window, hoping to catch a breeze and fill the room with it. The thin voices of little kids in the park playground and bigger kids playing baseball drifted in. *"Pretending,* that's all. That's what kids do. I did it myself."

She put a stick in the window to prop it open—it would stay where it was for a little bit, then come down with a crash if you didn't—and turned to look at the picture again. A sudden dismaying thought, an idea so strong it was almost a certainty, had come to her. The folds and creases in the rose madder gown were not the same. They had changed position. They had changed position because the woman wearing the toga, or chiton, or whatever it was, had changed position.

"You're crazy if you think that," Rosie whispered. Her heart was thumping. "I mean totally *bonkers.* You know that, don't you?"

She did. Nevertheless, she leaned close to the picture, peering into it. She stayed in that position, with her eyes less than two inches from the painted woman on top of the hill, for almost thirty seconds, holding her breath so as not to fog the glass which overlaid the image. At last she pulled back and let the air out of her lungs in a sigh that was mostly relief. The creases and folds in the chiton hadn't changed a bit. She was sure of it. (Well, *almost* sure.) It was just her imagination, playing tricks on her after her long day—a day which had been both wonderful and terribly stressful.

"Yeah, but I got through it," she told the woman in the chiton. Talking out loud to the woman in the painting already seemed perfectly okay to her. A little eccentric, maybe, but so what? Who did it hurt? Who even knew? And the fact that the blonde's back was turned somehow made it easier to believe she was really listening.

Rosie went to the window, propped the heels of her hands on the sill, and looked out. Across the street, laughing children ran the bases and pumped on the swings. Directly below her, a car was pulling in at the curb. There had been a time when the sight of a car pulling in like that would have terrified her, filled her with visions of Norman's fist and Norman's ring riding on it, riding toward her, the words *Service, Loyalty,* and *Community* getting bigger and bigger until they seemed to fill the whole world . . . but that time had passed. Thank God.

"Actually, I think I did a little more than just get through it," she told the picture. "I think I did a really good job. Robbie thought so, I know, but the one I *really* had to convince was Rhoda. I think she was prepared not to like me when I came in, because I was *Robbie's* find, you know?" She turned toward the picture once more, turned as a woman will turn to a friend, wanting to judge from her face how some idea or statement strikes her, but of course the woman in the picture just went on looking down the hill toward the ruined temple, giving Rosie nothing but her back to judge from.

"You know how bitchy us *gals* can be," Rosie said, and laughed. "Except I really think I won her over. We only got through fifty pages, but I was a lot better toward the end, and besides, all those old paperbacks are short. I'll bet I can finish by Wednesday afternoon, and do you know the best thing? I'm making almost a hundred and twenty dollars a day—not a *week,* a *day*—and there are *three more* Christina Bell novels. If Robbie and Rhoda give me those, I—"

She broke off, staring at the picture with wide eyes, not hearing the thin cries from the playground anymore, not even hearing the footsteps which were now climbing the stairs from the first floor. She was looking at the shape on the far right side of the picture again—curve of brow, curve of bland, pupilless eye, curve of ear. A sudden insight came to her. She had been both right and wrong—right about that second crashed statue's not being visible before, wrong in her impression that the stone head had somehow just materialized in the picture while she'd been off recording *The Manta Ray.* Her idea that the folds in the woman's dress had changed position might have been her subconscious mind's effort to bolster that first erroneous impression by creating a kind of hallucination. It did, after all, make slightly more sense than what she was seeing now.

"The picture is *bigger,*" Rosie said.

No. That wasn't quite it.

She lifted her hands, sizing the air in front of the hung picture and confirming the fact that it was still covering the same three-feet-by-two-feet area of wall. She was also seeing the same amount of white matting inside the frame, so what was the big deal?

That second stone head wasn't there before, and that's *the big deal,* she thought. *Maybe . . .*

Rosie suddenly felt dizzy and a little sick to her stomach. She closed her eyes tightly and began rubbing at her temples, where a headache was trying to be born. When she opened her eyes and looked at the picture again, it burst upon her as it had the first time, not as separate elements—the temple, the fallen statues, the rose madder chiton, the raised left hand—but as an integrated whole, something which called to her in its own voice.

There was more to look at now. She was nearly positive that this impression wasn't hallucination but simple fact. The picture wasn't *really* bigger, but she could see more on both sides . . . and on the top and bottom, as well. It was as if a movie projectionist had just realized he was using the wrong lens and switched, turning boxy thirty-five milli-meter into wide-screen Cinerama 70. Now you could see not just Clint, but the cowboys on both sides of him, as well.

You're nuts, Rosie. Pictures don't get bigger.

No? Then how did you explain the second god? She was sure it had been there all the time, and she was only seeing it now because . . .

"Because there's more *right* in the picture now," she murmured. Her eyes were very wide, although it would have been difficult to say if the expression in them was dismay or wonder. "Also more *left,* and more *up,* and more *d*—"

There was a sudden flurry of knocks on the door behind her, so fast and light they almost seemed to collide with each other. Rosie whirled around, feeling as if she were moving in slow motion or underwater.

She hadn't locked the door.

The knocks came again. She remembered the car she'd seen pulling up at the curb below—a small car, the kind of car a man travelling alone would be apt to rent from Hertz or Avis—and all thoughts of her picture were overwhelmed by another thought, one edged about in dark tones of resignation and despair: Norman had found her after all. It had taken him awhile, but somehow he had done it.

Part of her last conversation with Anna recurred—Anna asking what she'd do if Norman *did* show up. Lock the door and dial 911, she'd said, but she had forgotten to lock the door and there was no phone. That last was the most hideous irony of all, because there was a jack in the corner of the living-room area, and the jack was live—she'd gone to the phone company on her lunch hour today and paid a deposit. The woman who waited on her had given her her new telephone number on a little white card, Rosie had tucked it into her purse, and then out the door she'd marched. Right past the display of phones for sale she had marched. Thinking she could get one at least ten dollars cheaper by marching out to the Lakeview Mall when she got a chance. And now, just because she'd wanted to save a lousy ten dollars . . .

Silence from the other side of the door, but when she dropped her eyes to the crack at the bottom, she could see the shapes of his shoes. Big black shiny shoes, they would be. He no longer wore the uniform, but he still wore those black shoes. They were hard shoes. She could testify to that, because she had worn their marks on her legs and belly and buttocks many times over her years with him.

The knocking was repeated, three quick series of three: *rapraprap* pause, *rapraprap* pause, *rapraprap*.

Once again, as during her terrible breathless panic that morning in the recording booth, Rosie's mind turned to the woman in the picture, standing there on top of the overgrown hill, not afraid of the coming thunderstorm, not afraid that the ruins slumped below her might be haunted by ghosts or trolls or just some wandering band of thugs, not afraid of *anything*. You could tell by the set of her back, by the way her hand was so nonchalantly raised, even (so Rosie really believed) by the shape of that one barely glimpsed breast.

I'm not her, I am *afraid—so afraid I'm almost wetting my pants—but I'm not going to let you just take me, Norman. I swear to God I won't do that.*

For a moment or two she tried to remember the throw Gert Kinshaw had shown her, the one where you seized the forearms of your onrushing opponent and then turned sideways. It was no good—when she tried to visualize the crucial move, all she could see was Norman coming at her, his lips drawn back to show his teeth (drawn back in what she thought of as his biting smile), wanting to talk to her up close.

Right up close.

Her grocery bag was still standing on the kitchen counter with the yellow picnic-announcement fliers beside it. She'd taken out the perishables and stuck them in the refrigerator, but the few canned goods she'd picked up were still in the bag. She walked across to the counter on legs which seemed as devoid of feeling as wooden planks, and reached in.

Three more quick knocks: *rapraprap.*

"Coming," Rosie said. Her voice sounded amazingly calm to her own ears. She pulled out the biggest thing left in the bag, a two-pound can of fruit cocktail. She closed her hand around it as best she could and started toward the door on her numb woodplank legs. "I'm coming, just a second, be right there."

4

*W*hile Rosie was marketing, Norman Daniels was lying on a Whitestone Hotel bed in his underwear, smoking a cigarette and staring up at the ceiling.

He had picked up the smoking habit as many boys do, hooking cigarettes from his dad's packs of Pall Malls, resigning himself to a beating if he got caught, thinking that possibility a fair trade for the status you gained by being seen downtown on the corner of State and Route 49, leaning against a phone pole outside the Aubreyville Drugstore and Post Office, perfectly at home with the collar of your jacket turned up and that cigarette dripping down from your lower lip: *crazy, baby, I'm just a real cool breeze.* When your friends passed in their old cars, how could they know you'd hawked the butt from the pack on your old man's dresser, or that the one time you'd gotten up courage enough to try and buy a pack of your own in the drug, old man Gregory had snorted and told you to come back when you could grow a moustache?

Smoking had been a big deal at fifteen, a very big deal, something that had made up for all the stuff he hadn't been able to have (a car, for instance, even an old jalop' like the ones his friends drove—cars with primer on the rocker panels and white "plastic steel" around the headlights and bumpers held on with twists of haywire), and by the time he was sixteen he was hooked—two packs a day and a bona fide *smoker's hack* in the morning.

Three years after he married Rose, her entire family—father, mother, sixteen-year-old brother—had been killed on that same Route 49. They had been coming back from an afternoon of swimming at Philo's Quarry when a gravel truck veered across the road and wiped them out like flies on a windowpane. Old man McClendon's severed head had been found in a ditch thirty yards from the crash, with the mouth open and a generous splash of crowshit in one eye (by then Daniels was a cop, and cops heard such things). These facts hadn't disturbed Daniels in the least; he had, in fact, been delighted by the accident. As far as he was concerned, the nosy old bastard had gotten exactly what he had coming to him. McClendon had been prone to asking his daughter questions he had no business asking. Rose wasn't McClendon's daughter anymore, after all—not in the eyes of the law, at least. In the eyes of the law she had become Norman Daniels's wife.

He dragged deep on his cigarette, blew three smoke rings, and watched them float slowly toward the ceiling in a stack. Outside, traffic beeped and honked. He had only been here half a day, and already he hated this city. It was too big. It had too many hiding places. Not that it mattered. Because things were right on track, and soon a very hard and very heavy brick wall was going to drop onto Craig McClendon's wayward little daughter, Rosie.

At the McClendon funeral—a tripleheader with just about everyone in Aubreyville in attendance—Daniels had started coughing and had been unable to stop. People were turning around to look at him, and he hated that kind of staring worse than practically anything. Red-faced, furious with embarrassment (but still unable to stop coughing), Daniels pushed past his sobbing young wife and hurried out of the church with one hand pressed uselessly over his mouth.

He stood outside, coughing so hard at first he had to bend over and put *his hands on his knees to keep from actually passing out, looking through his watery eyes at several others who had stepped out for cigarettes, three men and two women who weren't able to go cold turkey even for a lousy half-hour funeral service, and suddenly he decided he was done smoking. Just like that. He knew that the coughing-fit might have been brought on by his usual summer allergies, but that didn't matter. It was a dumb fucking habit, maybe the dumbest fucking habit on the planet, and he was damned if some County Coroner was going to write* Pall Malls *on the cause-of-death line of his death certificate.*

On the day he had come home and found Rosie gone—that night, actually, after he discovered the ATM card was missing and could no longer put off facing what had to be faced—he had gone down to the Store 24 at the bottom of the hill and bought his first pack of cigarettes in eleven years. He had gone back to his old brand like a murderer returning to the scene of his crime. In hoc signo vinces *was what it said on each blood-red pack,* in this sign shalt thou conquer, *according to his old man, who had conquered Daniels's mother in a lot of kitchen brawls but not much else, so far as Norman had ever seen.*

The initial drag had made him feel dizzy, and by the time he'd finished the first cigarette, smoking it all the way down to a roach, he'd been sure he was going to puke, faint, or have a heart attack. Maybe all three at once. But now here he was, back up to two packs a day and hacking out that same old way-down-in-the-bottom-of-your-lungs cough when he rolled out of bed in the morning. It was like he'd never been away.

That was all right, though; he was going through a stressful life experience, as the psychology pukes liked to say, and when people went through stressful life experiences, they often went back to their old habits. Habits —especially bad ones like smoking and drinking—were crutches, people said. So what? If you had a limp, what was wrong with using a crutch? Once he'd taken care of Rosie (made sure that if there was going to be an informal divorce, it would be on his terms, you might say), he would throw all his crutches away.

This time for good.

Norman turned his head and looked out the window. Not dark yet, but getting there. Close enough to get going, anyway. He didn't want to be late for his appointment. He mashed out his cigarette in the overflowing ashtray on the nighttable beside the telephone, swung his feet off the bed, and began to dress.

There was no hurry, that was the nicest thing; he'd had all those accumulated off-days coming, and Captain Hardaway hadn't been the slightest bit chintzy about giving them to him when he asked. There were two reasons for that, Norman reckoned. First, the newspapers and TV stations had made him the flavor of the month; second, Captain Hardaway didn't like him, had twice sicced the IA shooflies on him because of excessive-force allegations, and had undoubtedly been glad to get rid of him for awhile.

"Tonight, bitch," Norman murmured as he rode down in the elevator, alone except for his reflection in the tired old mirror at the back of the car. "Tonight, if I get lucky. And I feel lucky."

There was a line of cabs drawn up at the curb, but Daniels bypassed them. Cab-drivers kept records, and sometimes they remembered faces. No, he would ride the bus again. A city bus, this time. He walked briskly toward the bus stop on the corner, wondering if he had been kidding himself about feeling lucky and deciding he had not been. He was close, he knew it. He knew it because he had found his way back into her head.

The bus—one that ran the Green Line route—came around the corner and rolled up to where Norman was standing. He got on, paid his four bits, sat in back—he didn't have to be Rose tonight, what a relief—and looked out the window as the streets rolled by. Bar signs. Restaurant signs. DELI. BEER. PIZZA BY THE SLICE. SEXEE TOPLESS GIRLZ.

You don't belong here, Rose, *he thought as the bus went past the window of a restaurant named Pop's Kitchen—"Strictly Kansas City Beef," said the blood-red neon sign in the window.* You don't belong here, but that's all right, because I'm here now. I've come to take you home. To take you *somewhere,* anyway.

The tangles of neon and the darkening velvet sky made him think of the good old days when life hadn't seemed so weird and somehow claustrophobic, like the walls of a room that keeps getting smaller, slowly closing in on you. When the neon came on the fun started—that was how it had been, anyway, back then in the relatively uncomplicated years of his twenties. You found a place where the neon was bright and you slipped in. Those days were gone, but most cops—most good cops—remembered how to slip around after dark. How to slip around behind the neon, and how to ride the streetgrease. A cop who couldn't do those things didn't last very long.

He had been watching the signs march past and judged that he should be approaching Carolina Street now. He got to his feet, walked to the front of the bus, and stood there holding the pole. When the bus pulled up at the corner and the doors flapped open, he walked down the steps and slipped into the darkness without saying a word.

He'd bought a city street-map in the hotel newsstand, six dollars and fifty cents, outrageous, but the cost of asking directions could be even higher. People had a way of remembering the people who asked them directions; sometimes they remembered even five years later, amazing but true. So it was better not to ask. In case something happened. Something bad. Probably nothing would, but TCB and CYA were always the best rules to live by.

According to his map, Carolina Street connected with Beaudry Place about four blocks west of the bus stop. A nice little walk on a warm evening. Beaudry Place was where the Travelers Aid Jewboy lived.

Daniels walked slowly, really just sauntering, with his hands in his pockets. His expression was bemused and slightly dopey, giving no clue that all his senses were on yellow alert. He catalogued each passing car, each passing pedestrian, looking especially for anyone who appeared to be looking especially at him. To be seeing *him. There was no one, and that was good.*

When he reached Thumper's house—and that's what it was, a house, not an apartment, another break—he walked past it twice, observing the car in the driveway and the light in the lower front window. Living-room window. The drapes were open but the sheers were drawn. Through them he could see a soft colored blur that had to be the television. Thumper was up, Thumper was home, Thumper was watching a little tube and maybe munching a carrot or two before heading down to the bus station, where he would try to help more women too stupid to deserve help. Or too bad.

Thumper hadn't been wearing a wedding ring and had the look of a closet queer to Norman anyway, but better safe than sorry. He drifted up the driveway and peeked into Thumper's four- or five-year-old Ford, looking for anything that would suggest the man didn't live alone. He saw nothing that set off any warning bells.

Satisfied, he looked up and down the residential street again and saw no one.

You don't have a mask, *he thought.* You don't even have a nylon stocking you can pull over your face, Normie, do you?

No, he didn't.

You forgot, didn't you?

Well . . . actually, no. He hadn't. He had an idea that when the sun came up tomorrow, there was going to be one less urban Jewboy in the world. Because sometimes bad stuff happened even in nice residential neighborhoods like this. Sometimes people broke in—jigs and junkies for the most part, of course—and there went the old ballgame. Tough but true. Shit happens, as the teeshirts and bumperstickers said. And sometimes, hard as it was to believe, shit happened to the right people instead of the wrong ones. Pravda-*reading Jewboys who helped wives get away from husbands, for instance. You couldn't just put up with stuff like that; it was no way to run a society. If everyone acted like that, there wouldn't even* be *a society.*

It was pretty much rampant behavior, though, because most of the bleeding hearts got away with it. Most of the bleeding hearts hadn't made the mistake of helping his wife, however . . . and this man *had. Norman knew that as well as he knew his own name. This* man had *helped her.*

He mounted the steps, took one more quick look around, and rang the doorbell. He waited, then rang again. Now his ears, already attuned to catch the slightest noise, picked up the sound of approaching feet, not clack-clack-clack *but* hish-hish-hish, *Thumper in his stocking feet, how cozy.*

"Coming, coming," Thumper called.

The door opened. Thumper looked out at him, big eyes swimming behind his hornrimmed glasses. "Can I help you?" he asked. His outer shirt was unbuttoned and untucked, hanging over a strap-style teeshirt, the same style of teeshirt Norman himself wore, and suddenly it was too much, suddenly it was the last straw, the one that fractured the old dromedary's spinal column, and he was insane with rage. That a man like this should wear an undershirt like his! A white man's *undershirt!*

"I think you can," Norman said, and something in his face or his voice—perhaps it was both—must have alarmed Slowik, because his brown eyes widened and he started to draw back, his hand going to the door, probably meaning to slam it in Norman's face. If so, he was too late. Norman moved fast, seizing the sides of Slowik's outer shirt and driving him back into the house. Norman raised one foot and kicked the door shut behind him, feeling as graceful as Gene Kelly in an MGM musical.

"Yeah, I think so," he said again. "I hope for your sake you can. I'm going to ask you some questions, Thumper, good *questions, and you better pray to your bignose Jewboy God that you're able to come up with some good answers."*

"Get out of here!" Slowik cried. "Or I'll call the police!"

Norman Daniels had a good chuckle at that, and then he whirled Slowik around, twisting Slowik's left fist up until it touched his scrawny right shoulderblade. Slowik began to scream. Norman reached between his legs and cupped his testicles.

"Stop," he said. "Stop it right now or I'll pop your balls like grapes. You'll hear them go."

Thumper stopped. He was gasping and letting out an occasional choked whimper, but Norman could live with that. He herded Thumper back into the living room, where he used the remote control he found sitting on an endtable to turn up the television.

He frogmarched his new pal into the kitchen and let go of him. "Stand against the refrigerator," he said. "I want to see your ass and shoulderblades squashed right up against that baby, and if you move so much as an inch away from it, I'll rip your lips off. Got it?"

"Y-Y-Yes," Thumper said. "Who-Who-Who are you?" He still looked like Bambi's friend Thumper, but now he was starting to sound like Woodsy Fucking Owl.

"Irving R. Levine, NBC News," Norman said. "This is how I spend my day off." He began pulling open the drawers along the counter, keeping an eye on Thumper as he did so. He didn't think old Thump was going to run, but he might. Once people got beyond a certain level of fright, they became as unpredictable as tornadoes.

"What . . . I don't know what—"

"You don't have to know what," Norman said. "That's the beauty of this, Thump. You don't have to know a goddam thing except the answers to a few very simple questions. Everything else can be left to me. I'm a professional. Think of me as one of the Good Hands People."

He found what he was looking for in the fifth and last drawer down the line: two oven gloves with flower patterns. How cute. Just what the well-dressed Jewboy would want to wear when taking his wittle kosher cassewoles out of his wittle kosher oven. Norman pulled them on, then went quickly back down the drawerpulls, rubbing out any prints he might have left. Then he marched Thumper back into the living room, where he picked up the remote control and wiped it briskly on the front of his shirt.

"We're going to have us a little face-to-face here, Thumper," Norman said as he did this. His throat had thickened; the voice which came out of it sounded barely human, even to its owner. Norman wasn't very surprised to find he had a raging hardon. He tossed the remote control onto the sofa and turned to Slowik, who was standing there with his shoulders slumped and tears oozing out from beneath his thick hornrimmed glasses. Standing there in that white man's undershirt. "I'm going to talk to you up close. Right up close. Do you believe that? You better, Thump. You just fucking better."

"Please," Slowik moaned. He held his shaking hands out to Norman. "Please don't hurt me. You've got the wrong man—whoever you want it's not me. I can't help you."

But in the end, Slowik helped quite a bit. By then they were down cellar, because Norman had begun to bite, and not even the TV turned all the way to top volume would have completely stifled the man's screams. But, screams or no screams, he helped quite a bit.

When the festivities were over, Norman found the garbage bags under the kitchen sink. Into one of these he put the oven gloves and his own shirt, which could not now be worn in public. He would take the bag with him and get rid of it later.

Upstairs, in Thumper's bedroom, he found only one item of clothing that would come even close to covering his own much broader upper body: a baggy, faded Chicago Bulls sweatshirt. Norman laid this on the bed, then went into Thumper's bathroom and turned on Thumper's shower. While he waited for the water to run hot, he looked in Thumper's medicine cabinet, found a bottle of Advil, and took four. His teeth hurt and his jaws ached. The entire lower half of his face was covered with blood and hair and little tags of skin.

He stepped into the shower and grabbed Thump's bar of Irish Spring, reminding himself to dump that into the bag, too. He actually didn't know how much good any of these precautions were going to be, because he had no idea how much forensic evidence he might have left downstairs in the basement. He had kind of grayed out there for awhile.

As he washed his hair he began to sing: "Raaamblin' Rose . . . Raaamblin' Rose . . . where you raaamble . . . no one knows . . . wild and windblown . . . that's how you've grown . . . who can cling to . . . a Ramblin' Rose?"

He turned off the shower, stepped out, and looked at his own faint, ghostly image in the steamy mirror over the sink.

"I can," he said flatly. "I can, that's who."

5

Bill Steiner was raising his free hand to knock yet again, mentally cursing his nervousness—he was a man who wasn't ordinarily nervous about women—when she answered. "Coming! I'm coming, just a second, be right there." She didn't sound pissed, thank God, so maybe he hadn't rousted her out of the bathroom.

What in hell am I doing here, anyway? he asked himself again as the footsteps approached the door. *This is like a scene in some half-baked romantic comedy, the kind of thing not even Tom Hanks can do much with.*

That might be true, but it didn't change the fact that the woman who had come into the shop last week had lodged firmly in his mind. And, rather than fading as the days went by, her effect on him seemed to be cumulative. Two things were certain: this was the first time in his life he'd ever brought flowers to a woman he didn't know, and he hadn't felt this nervous about asking for a date since he'd been sixteen years old.

As the footsteps reached the other side of the door, Bill saw that one of the big daisies was on the verge of doing a header out of the bouquet. He made a hurried adjustment as the door opened, and when he looked up he saw the woman who'd traded her fake diamond ring for a piece of bad art standing there with murder in her eyes and a can of what looked like fruit cocktail raised over her head. She appeared frozen between her desire to make a pre-emptive strike and her mind's struggling realization that this wasn't the person she'd expected. It was, Bill thought later, one of the most exotic moments of his life.

The two of them stood looking at each other across the doorjamb of Rosie's second-floor room on Tremont Street, he with his bouquet of spring flowers from the shop two doors down on Hitchens Avenue, she with her two-pound can of fruit cocktail raised over her head, and although the pause could not have lasted more than two or three seconds, it seemed very long to him. It was certainly long enough for him to realize something that was distressing, dismaying, annoying, amazing, and rather wonderful. Seeing her did not change things, as he had rather expected it would; it made them worse, instead. She wasn't beautiful, not the media version of beauty, anyhow, but she was beautiful to him. The look of her lips and the line of her jaw for some reason just about stopped his heart, and the catlike tilt of her bluish-gray eyes made him feel weak. His blood felt too high and his cheeks too hot. He knew perfectly well what these feelings signalled, and he resented them even as they made him captive.

He held out the flowers to her, smiling hopefully but keeping tabs on the upraised can.

"Truce?" he said.

6

His invitation to go out to dinner with him followed so quickly on her realization that he wasn't Norman that she was surprised into accepting. She supposed simple relief played a part, too. It wasn't until she was in the passenger seat of his car that Practical-Sensible, who had been pretty much left in the dust, caught up and asked her what she was doing, going out with a man (a *much younger* man) she didn't know, was she insane? There was real terror in these questions, but Rosie recognized the questions themselves for what they were—mere camouflage. The important question was so horrifying Practical-Sensible didn't dare ask it, even from her place inside Rosie's head.

What if Norman catches you? That was the important question. What if Norman caught her eating dinner with another man? A younger, good-looking man? The fact that Norman was eight hundred miles east of here didn't matter to Practical-Sensible, who really wasn't Practical and Sensible at all, but only Frightened and Confused.

Norman wasn't the *only* issue, however. She hadn't been alone with any man but her husband in her entire life as a woman, and right now her emotions were a gorgeous stew. Eat dinner with him? Oh, sure. Right. Her throat had narrowed down to a pinhole and her stomach was sudsing like a washing machine.

If he had been wearing anything dressier than clean, faded jeans and an oxford shirt, or if he'd given the faintest look of doubt to her own unpretentious skirt-and-sweater combination, she would have said no, and if the place he took her to had looked too difficult (it was the only word she could think of), she didn't believe she would have been able even to get out of his Buick. But the restaurant looked welcoming rather than threatening, a brightly lighted storefront called Pop's Kitchen, with paddle-fans overhead and red-and-white-checked tablecloths spread across butcherblock tables. According to the neon sign in the window, Pop's Kitchen served Strictly Kansas City Beef. The waiters were all older gentlemen who wore black shoes and long aprons tied up under their armpits. To Rosie they looked like white dresses with Empire waists. The people eating at the tables looked like her and Bill—well, like Bill, anyway: middle-class, middle-income folks wearing informal clothes. To Rosie the restaurant felt cheerful and open, the kind of place where you could breathe.

Maybe, but they don't *look like you,* her mind whispered, *and don't you go thinking that they do, Rosie. They look confident, they look happy, and most of all they look like they belong here. You don't and you never will. There were too many years with Norman, too many times when you sat in the corner vomiting into your apron. You've forgotten how people are, and what they talk about . . . if you ever knew to begin with. If you try to be like these people, if you even* dream *you can be like these people, you are going to earn yourself a broken heart.*

Was that true? It was terrifying to think it might be, because part of her *was* happy—happy that Bill Steiner had come to see her, happy that he had brought flowers, happy that he had asked her to dinner. She didn't have the slightest idea how she felt about him, but that she had been asked out on a date . . . that made her feel young and full of magic. She couldn't help it.

Go on, feel happy, Norman said. He whispered the words into her ear as she and Bill stepped through the door of Pop's Kitchen, words so close and so real that it was almost as if he were passing by. *Enjoy it while you can, because later on he's going to take you back out into the dark, and then he's going to want to talk to you up close. Or maybe he won't bother with the talking part. Maybe he'll just drag you into the nearest alley and do you against the wall.*

No, she thought. Suddenly the bright lights inside the restaurant were *too* bright and she could hear everything, *everything,* even the big sloppy gasps of the overhead paddle-fans walloping the air. *No, that's a lie— he's nice and that's a lie!*

The answer was immediate and inexorable, the Gospel According to Norman: *No one's nice, sweetheart—how many times have I told you that? Down deep, everyone's streetgrease. You, me, everyone.*

"Rose?" Bill asked. "You okay? You look pale."

No, she wasn't okay. She knew the voice in her head was a lying voice, one which came from a part of her that was still blighted by Norman's poison, but what she knew and what she felt were very different things. She couldn't sit in the midst of all these people, that was all, smelling their soaps and colognes and shampoos, listening to the bright inter-weavings of their chatter. She couldn't deal with the waiter who would come bending into her space with a list of specials, some perhaps in a foreign language. Most of all she couldn't deal with Bill Steiner—talking to him, answering his questions, and all the time wondering how his hair would feel under her palm.

She opened her mouth to tell him she *wasn't* okay, that she felt sick to her stomach and he'd better take her home, perhaps another time. Then, as she had in the recording studio, she thought of the woman in the rose madder chiton, standing there on top of the overgrown hill with her hand upraised and one bare shoulder gleaming in the strange, cloudy light of that place. Standing there, completely unafraid, above a ruined temple that looked more haunted than any house Rosie had ever seen in her life. As she visualized the blonde hair in its plait, the gold armlet, and the barely glimpsed upswell of breast, the flutters in Rosie's stomach quieted.

I can get through this, she thought. *I don't know if I can actually eat, but surely I can find enough courage to sit down with him for awhile in this well-lighted place. And am I going to worry about him raping me later on? I think rape is the last thing on this man's mind. That's just one of Norman's ideas—Norman, who believes no black man ever owned a portable radio that wasn't stolen from a white man.*

The simple truth of this made her sag a little with relief, and she smiled at Bill. It was weak and a little trembly at the corners, but better than no smile at all. "I'm all right," she said. "A tiny bit scared, that's all. You'll have to bear with me."

"Not scared of me?"

Damned right scared of you, Norman said from the place in her head where he lived like a vicious tumor.

"No, not exactly." She raised her eyes to his face. It was an effort, and she could feel her cheeks flushing, but she managed. "It's just that you're only the second guy I've ever gone out with in my whole life, and if this is a date, it's the first real one I've been on since my high-school senior prom. That was back in 1980."

"Holy God," he said. He spoke softly, and without a trace of facetiousness. "Now *I'm* getting a little scared."

The host—Rosie wasn't sure if you called him a *maître d'* or if that was someone else—came up and asked if they wanted smoking or nonsmoking.

"Do you smoke?" Bill asked her, and Rosie quickly shook her head. "Somewhere out of the mainstream would be great," Bill said to the man in the tuxedo, and Rosie caught a gray-green flicker—she thought it was a five-dollar bill—passing from Bill's hand to the host's. "A corner, maybe?"

"Certainly, sir." He led them through the brightly lighted room and beneath the lazily turning paddle-fans.

When they were seated, Rosie asked Bill how he had found her, although she supposed she already knew. What she was really curious about was *why* he had found her.

"It was Robbie Lefferts," he said. "Robbie comes in every few days to see if I've gotten any new paperbacks—well, *old* paperbacks, actually; you know what I mean—"

She remembered David Goodis—*It was a tough break, Parry was innocent*—and smiled.

"I knew he hired you to read the Christina Bell novels, because he came in special to tell me. He was *very* excited."

"Was he really?"

"He said you were the best voice he'd heard since Kathy Bates's recording of *Silence of the Lambs,* and that means a lot—Robbie *worships* that recording, along with Robert Frost reading 'The Death of the Hired Man.' He's got that on an old thirty-three-and-a-third Caedmon LP. It's scratchy, but it's amazing."

Rosie was silent. She felt overwhelmed.

"So I asked him for your address. Well, that's maybe a little too glossy. The ugly truth is I pestered him into it. Robbie's one of those people who happen to be very vulnerable to pestering. And to do him full credit, Rosie . . ."

But the rest drifted away from her. *Rosie,* she was thinking. *He called me Rosie. I didn't ask him to; he just did it.*

"Would either of you folks care for a drink?" A waiter had appeared at Bill's elbow. Elderly, dignified, handsome, he looked like a college literature professor. *One with a penchant for Empire-waist dresses,* Rosie thought, and felt like giggling.

"I'd like iced tea," Bill said. "How 'bout you, Rosie?"

And again. He did it again. How does he know I was never really a Rose, that I've always been really Rosie?

"That sounds fine."

"Two iced teas, excellent," the waiter said, and then recited a short list of specials. To Rosie's relief, all were in English, and at the words *London broil,* she actually felt a thin thread of hunger.

"We'll think it over, tell you in a minute," Bill said.

The waiter left, and Bill turned back to Rosie.

"Two other things in Robbie's favor," he said. "He suggested I stop by the studio . . . you're in the Corn Building, aren't you?"

"Yes, Tape Engine is the name of the studio."

"Uh-huh. Anyway, he suggested I stop by the studio, that all three of us could maybe go out for a drink after wrap one afternoon. Very protective, almost fatherly. When I told him I couldn't do that, he made me absolutely *promise* that I'd call you first. And I tried, Rosie, but I couldn't get your number from directory assistance. Are you unlisted?"

"I don't actually have a phone yet," she said, sidestepping a little. She *was* unlisted, of course; it had cost an extra thirty dollars, money she could ill afford, but she could afford even less to have her number pop up on a police computer back home. She knew from Norman's bitching that the police couldn't conduct random sweeps of unlisted phone numbers the way they could sweep the ones in the phone books. It was illegal, an invasion of the privacy people voluntarily gave up when they allowed the phone company to list their numbers. So the courts had ruled, and like most of the cops she had met during the course of her marriage, Norman had a virulent hatred for all courts and all their works.

"Why couldn't you come by the studio? Were you out of town?"

He picked up his napkin, unfolded it, and put it carefully down on his lap. When he looked up again she saw his face had changed somehow, but it took several moments more for her to grasp the obvious—he was blushing.

"Well, I guess I didn't want to go out with you in a gang," he said. "You don't really get to talk to a person that way. I just sort of wanted to . . . well . . . get to know you."

"And here we are," she said softly.

"Yes, that's right. Here we are."

"But *why* did you want to get to know me? To go out with me?" She paused for a moment, then said the rest. "I mean, I'm sort of old for you, aren't I?"

He looked incredulous for a moment, then decided it was a joke and laughed. "Yeah," he said. "How old are you, anyway, granny? Twenty-seven? Twenty-eight?"

At first she thought *he* was making a joke—not a very good one, either—and then realized he was serious enough underneath the light tone. Not even trying to flatter her, only stating the obvious. What was obvious to *him,* anyway. The realization shocked her, and her thoughts went flying in all directions again. Only one came through with any sort of clarity: the changes in her life had not ended with finding a job and a place of her own to live; they had only begun. It was as if everything that had happened up to this point had just been a series of preshocks, and this was the onset of the actual quake. Not an earthquake but a lifequake, and suddenly she was hungry for it, and excited in a way she did not understand.

Bill started to speak, and then the waiter came with their iced teas. Bill ordered a steak, and Rosie asked for the London broil. When the waiter asked her how she wanted it, she started to say medium-well—that was how she ate beef because that was how Norman ate beef—and then she took it back.

"Rare," she said. "Very."

"Excellent!" the waiter said, speaking as if he really meant it, and as he walked away Rosie thought what a wonderful place a waiter's utopia would be—a place where every choice was excellent, very good, marvellous.

When she looked back at Bill she saw his eyes still on her—those disquieting eyes with their dim green undertint. Sexy eyes.

"How bad was it?" he asked her. "Your marriage?"

"What do you mean?" she asked awkwardly.

"You know what. I meet this woman in my dad's Swap n Loan, I talk to her for maybe ten minutes, and the goddamnedest thing happens to me—I can't forget her. This is something I've seen in the movies and occasionally read about in the kind of magazines you always find in the doctor's waiting room, but I never really believed it. Now, boom, here it is. I see her face in the dark when I turn out the light. I think about her when I eat my lunch. I—" He paused, giving her a considering, worried look. "I hope I'm not scaring you."

He was scaring her a *lot,* but at the same time she thought she had never heard anything so wonderful. She was hot all over (except for her feet, which were cold as ice), and she could still hear the fans churning the air overhead. There seemed to be a thousand of them at least, a battalion of fans.

"This lady comes in to sell me her engagement ring, which she thinks is a diamond . . . except way down deep, where she knows better. Then, when I find out where she lives and go to see her—with a bouquet in my hand and my heart in my mouth, you might say—she comes this far from braining me with a can of fruit cocktail." He held up his right hand with the thumb and the forefinger half an inch apart.

Rosie held her own hand up—the left—with the thumb and forefinger an inch apart. "Actually, it was more like this," she said. "And I'm like Roger Clemens—I have *excellent* control."

He laughed hard at that. It was a good sound, honest and from the belly. After a moment, she joined him.

"In any case, the lady doesn't exactly fire the missile, just makes this scary little downward twitch with it, then hides it behind her back like a kid with a copy of *Playboy* he stole out of his dad's bureau drawer. She says, 'Oh my God, I'm sorry,' and I wonder who the enemy is, since it's not me. And *then* I wonder how ex the husband can be, when the lady came into my dad's pawnshop with her rings still on. You know?"

"Yes," she said. "I suppose I do."

"It's important to me. If it seems like I'm being nosy, okay, probably I am, but . . . on very short notice I'm very taken with this woman, and I don't want her to be very attached. On the other hand, I don't want her to be so scared she has to go to the door with a jumbo-sized can of fruit cocktail in her hand every time someone knocks. Is any of this making any sense to you?"

"Yes," she said. "The husband is pretty ex." And then, for no reason at all, she added: "His name is Norman."

Bill nodded solemnly. "I see why you left him."

Rosie began to giggle and clapped her hands to her mouth. Her face felt hotter than ever. At last she got it under control, but by then she had to wipe her eyes with the corner of her napkin.

"Okay?" he asked.

"Yes. I think so."

"Want to tell me about it?"

An image suddenly arose in her mind, one with all the clarity of something seen in a vivid nightmare. It was Norman's old tennis racket, the Prince with the black tape wound around the handle. It was still hanging by the foot of the cellar stairs back home, as far as she knew. He had spanked her with it several times during the first years of their marriage. Then, about six months after her miscarriage, he had anally raped her with it. She had shared a lot of things about her marriage (that was what they called it, *sharing,* a word she found simultaneously hideous and apt) in Therapy Circle at D & S, but that was one little nugget she'd kept to herself—how it felt to have the taped handle of a Prince tennis racket jammed up your ass by a man who sat straddling you, with his knees on the outsides of your thighs; how it felt to have him lean over and tell you that if you fought, he would break the water-glass on the table beside the bed and cut your throat with it. How it felt to lie there, smelling the Dentyne on his breath and wondering how bad he was ripping you up.

"No," she said, and was grateful that her voice didn't tremble. "I don't want to talk about Norman. He was abusive and I left him. End of story."

"Fair enough," Bill said. "And he's out of your life for good?"

"For good."

"Does *he* know that? I only ask because of, you know, the way you came to the door. You sure weren't expecting a representative from the Church of Latter-Day Saints."

"I don't know if he knows it or not," she said, after a moment or two to think it over—certainly it was a fair enough question.

"Are you afraid of him?"

"Oh, yes. You bet. But that doesn't necessarily mean a lot. I'm afraid of *everything.* It's all new to me. My friends at . . . my friends say I'll grow out of it, but I don't know."

"You weren't afraid to come out to dinner with me."

"Oh yes I was. I was *terrified.*"

"Why did you, then?"

She opened her mouth to say what she had been thinking earlier— that he had surprised her into it—and then closed it again. That was the truth, but it wasn't the truth *inside* the truth, and this was an area where she didn't want to do any sidestepping. She had no idea if the two of them had any sort of future beyond this one meal in Pop's Kitchen, but if they did, fancy footwork would be a bad way to begin the trip.

"Because I wanted to," she said. Her voice was low but clear.

"All right. No more about that."

"And no more about Norman, either."

"That's his for-real no-fooling name?"

"Yes."

"As in Bates."

"As in Bates."

"Can I ask you about something else, Rosie?"

She smiled a little. "As long as I don't have to promise to answer."

"Fair enough. You thought you were older than me, didn't you?"

"Yes," she said. "Yes, I did. How old *are* you, Bill?"

"Thirty. Which has got to make us something like next-door neighbors in the age sweepstakes . . . same street, anyway. But you made an almost automatic assumption that you weren't just older, you were a lot older. So here comes the question. Are you ready?"

Rosie shrugged uneasily.

He leaned toward her, those eyes with their fascinating greenish undertint fixed on hers. "Do you know you're beautiful?" he asked. "That's not a come-on or a line, it's plain old curiosity. *Do* you know you're beautiful? You don't, do you?"

She opened her mouth. Nothing emerged but one tiny breath-noise from the back of her throat. It was closer to a whistle than a sigh.

He put his hand over hers and squeezed it gently. His touch was brief, but it still lit up her nerves like an electric shock, and for a moment he was the only thing she could see—his hair, his mouth, and most of all his eyes. The rest of the world was gone, as if the two of them were on a stage where all the lights except for one bright, burning spot had been turned out.

"Don't make fun of me," she said. Her voice trembled. "Please don't make fun. I can't stand it if you do."

"No, I'd never do that." He spoke absently, as if this were a subject beyond discussion, case closed. "But I'll tell you what I see." He smiled and stretched out his hand to touch hers again. "I'll *always* tell you what I see. That's a promise."

7

She said he needn't bother escorting her up the stairs, but he insisted and she was glad. Their conversation had passed on to less personal things when their meals came—he was delighted to find out the Roger Clemens reference hadn't been a fluke, that she had a knowledgeable fan's understanding of baseball, and they had talked a lot about the city's teams as they ate, passing naturally enough from baseball to basketball. She'd hardly thought of Norman at all until the ride back, when she began imagining how she would feel if she opened the door of her room and there he was, Norman, sitting on her bed, drinking a cup of coffee, maybe, and contemplating her picture of the ruined temple and the woman on the hill.

Then, as they mounted the narrow stairs, Rosie in the lead and Bill a step or two behind, she found something else to worry about: What if he wanted to kiss her goodnight? And what if, after a kiss, he asked if he could come in?

Of course *he'll want to come in,* Norman told her, speaking in the heavily patient voice he employed when he was trying not to be angry with her but was getting angry anyway. *In fact, he'll insist on it. Why else would he spring for a fifty-dollar meal? Jesus, you ought to be flattered—there are gals on the street prettier than you who don't get fifty for half-and-half. He'll want to come in and he'll want to fuck you, and maybe that's good—maybe that's what you need to get your head out of the clouds.*

She was able to get her key out of her bag without dropping it, but the tip chattered all the way around the slot in the center of the metal disk without going in. He closed his hand over hers and guided it home. She felt that electric shock again when he touched her, and was helpless not to think of what the key sliding into the lock called to her mind.

She opened the door. No Norman, unless he was hiding in the shower or the closet. Just her pleasant room with the cream-colored walls and the picture hanging by the window and the light on over the sink. Not home, not yet, but a little closer than the dorm at D & S.

"This is not bad, you know," he said thoughtfully. "No duplex in the suburbs, but not at all bad."

"Would you like to come in?" she asked through lips that felt completely numb—it was as if someone had slipped her a shot of Novocain. "I could give you a cup of coffee . . ."

Good! Norman exulted from his stronghold inside her head. *Might as well get it overwith, right, hon? You give him the coffee, and he'll give you the cream. Such a deal!*

Bill appeared to think it over very carefully before shaking his head. "It might not be such a good idea," he said. "Not tonight, at least. I don't think you have the slightest idea of how you affect me." He laughed a little nervously. "I don't think *I* have the slightest idea of how you affect me." He looked over her shoulder and saw something that made him smile and offer her a pair of thumbs-up. "You were right about the picture—I never would have believed it at the time, but you were. I guess you must have had this place in mind, though, huh?"

She shook her head, now smiling herself. "When I bought the picture, I didn't even know this room existed."

"You must be psychic, then. I bet it looks especially good there where you've hung it in the late afternoon and early evening. The sun must sidelight it."

"Yes, it's nice then," Rosie said, not adding that she thought the picture looked good—perfectly right and perfectly in place—at all times of the day.

"You're not bored with it yet, I take it?"

"No, not at all."

She thought of adding, *And it's got some very funny tricks. Step over and take a closer look, why don't you? Maybe you'll see something even more surprising than a lady getting ready to brain you with a can of fruit cocktail. You tell me, Bill—has that picture somehow gone from ordinary screen size to Cinerama 70, or is that just my imagination?*

She said none of this, of course.

Bill put his hands on her shoulders and she looked up at him solemnly, like a child being put to bed, as he leaned forward and kissed her forehead on the smooth place between her eyebrows.

"Thank you for coming out with me," he said.

"Thank you for asking." She felt a tear go sliding down her left cheek and wiped it away with her knuckle. She was not ashamed or afraid for him to see it; she felt she could trust him with at least one tear, and that was nice.

"Listen," he said. "I've got a motorcycle—an old butch Harley softail. It's big and loud and sometimes it stalls at long red lights, but it's comfortable . . . and I'm a remarkably safe cyclist, if I do say so myself. One of the six Harley owners in America who wears a helmet. If Saturday's nice, I could come over and pick you up in the morning. There's a place I know about thirty miles up the lake. Beautiful. It's still too cold to swim, but we could bring a picnic."

At first she was incapable of any sort of answer—she was simply flattened by the fact that he was asking her out *again*. And then there was the idea of riding on his motorcycle . . . how would that be? For a moment all Rosie could think of was how it might feel to be behind him on two wheels cutting through space at fifty or sixty miles an hour. To have her arms around him. A totally unexpected heat rushed through her, something like a fever, and she did not recognize it for what it was, although she thought she remembered feeling something like it, a very long time ago.

"Rosie? What do you say?"

"I . . . Well . . ."

What *did* she say? Rosie touched her tongue nervously to her upper lip, glanced away from him in an effort to clear her mind, and saw the pile of yellow fliers sitting on the counter. She felt both disappointment and relief as she looked back at Bill.

"I can't. Saturday's the Daughters and Sisters picnic. Those are the people who helped me when I came here—my friends. There's a softball game, races, horseshoes, craft booths—things like that. And then a concert that night, which is supposed to be the real moneymaker. This year we're having the Indigo Girls. I promised I'd work the teeshirt concession from five o'clock on, and I ought to do it. I owe them such a lot."

"I could have you back by five no sweat," he said. "Four, if you wanted."

She *did* want to . . . but she had a lot more to be afraid of than just showing up late to sell teeshirts. Would he understand that if she told him? If she said, *I'd love to put my arms around you while you drive fast, and I'd love for you to wear a leather jacket so I could put my face against the shoulder and smell that good smell and hear the little creaking sounds it makes when you move. I'd love that, but I think I'm afraid of what I might find out later on, when the ride was over . . . that the Norman inside my head was right all along about the things you really want. What scares me the most is having to investigate the most basic premise of my husband's life, the one thing he never said out loud because he never had to: that the way he treated me was perfectly okay, perfectly normal. It's not pain I'm afraid of; I know about pain. What I'm afraid of is the end of this small, sweet dream. I've had so few of them, you see.*

She realized what she needed to say, and realized in the next moment that she couldn't say it, perhaps because she'd heard it in so many movies, where it always came out sounding like a whine: *Don't hurt me.* That was what she needed to say. *Please don't hurt me. The best part of me that's left will die if you hurt me.*

But he was still waiting for her answer. Waiting for her to say *something.*

Rose opened her mouth to say no, she really ought to be there for the picnic as well as the concert, maybe another time. Then she looked at the picture hanging on the wall beside the window. *She* wouldn't hesitate, Rosie thought; she would count the hours until Saturday, and when she was finally mounted behind him on that iron horse, she would spend most of the ride thumping him on the back and urging him to make it gallop faster. For a moment Rosie could almost see her sitting there, the hem of her rose madder chiton hiked high, her bare thighs firmly clasping his hips.

That hot flash swept through her again, stronger this time. Sweeter.

"Okay," she said, "I'll do it. On one condition."

"Name it," he said. He was grinning, obviously delighted.

"Bring me back to Ettinger's Pier—that's where the D and S thing is happening—and stay for the concert. I'll buy the tickets. It's my treat."

"Deal," he said instantly. "Can I pick you up at eight-thirty, or is that too early?"

"No, it's fine."

"You'll want to wear a coat and maybe a sweater, too," he said. "You might be able to stow em in the saddlebags coming back in the afternoon, but going out's going to be chilly."

"All right," she said, already thinking that she would have to borrow those items from Pam Haverford, who was about the same size. Rosie's entire outerwear wardrobe at this point consisted of one light jacket, and the budget wouldn't stand any further purchases in that department, at least for awhile.

"I'll see you, then. And thanks again for tonight." He seemed briefly to consider kissing her again, then simply took her hand and squeezed it for a moment.

"You're welcome."

He turned and ran quickly down the stairs, like a boy. She couldn't help contrasting this to Norman's way of moving—either at a head-down plod or with a kind of spooky, darting speed. She watched his elongated shadow on the wall until it disappeared, then she closed the door, secured both locks, and leaned against it, looking across the room at her picture.

It had changed again. She was almost sure of it.

Rosie walked across the room and stood in front of it with her hands clasped behind her back and her head thrust slightly forward, the position making her look comically like a *New Yorker* caricature of an art gallery patron or museum *habitué.*

Yes, she saw, although the picture's dimensions remained the same, she was all but positive that it had widened again somehow. On the right, beyond the second stone face—the one peering blindly sideways through the tall grass—she could now see what looked like the beginnings of a forest glade. On the left, beyond the woman on the hill, she could now see the head and shoulders of a small shaggy pony. It was wearing blinders, was cropping at the high grass, and appeared to be harnessed to some sort of a rig—perhaps a cart, perhaps a shay or a surrey. That part Rosie couldn't see; it was out of the picture (so far, at least). She could see some of its shadow, however, and another shadow as well, growing out of it. She thought this second shadow was probably the head and shoulders of a person. Someone standing beside the vehicle to which the pony was harnessed, maybe. Or maybe—

Or maybe you've gone out of your mind, Rosie. You don't really think this picture is getting bigger, do you? Or showing more stuff, if you like that better?

But the truth was she *did* believe that, she *saw* that, and she found herself more excited than scared by the idea. She wished she had asked Bill for his opinion; she would have liked to know if he saw anything like what she was seeing . . . or *thought* she was seeing.

Saturday, she promised herself. *Maybe I'll do it Saturday.*

She began to undress, and by the time she was in the tiny bathroom, brushing her teeth, she had forgotten all about Rose Madder, the woman on the hill. She had forgotten all about Norman, too, and Anna, and Pam, and the Indigo Girls on Saturday night. She was thinking about her dinner with Bill Steiner, replaying her date with him minute by minute, second by second.

8

She lay in bed, slipping toward sleep, listening to the sound of crickets coming from Bryant Park.

As she drifted she found herself remembering—without pain and seemingly from a great distance—the year 1985 and her daughter, Caroline. As far as Norman was concerned, there never had been a Caroline, and the fact that he had agreed with Rosie's hesitant suggestion that Caroline was a nice name for a girl didn't change that. To Norman there had been only a tadpole that ended early. If it happened to be a girl-tadpole according to some nutty headtrip his wife was on, so what? Eight hundred million Red Chinese didn't give a shit, in Normanspeak.

1985—what a year that had been. What a year from hell. She had lost
(*Caroline*)
the baby, Norman had nearly lost his job (had come close to being arrested, she had an idea), she had gone to the hospital with a broken rib
that had lacerated and almost punctured her lung, and, as a small extra
added attraction, she had been cornholed with the handle of a tennis
racket. That was also the year her mind, remarkably stable until then, began to slip a little, but in the midst of all those other festivities, she barely
noticed that half an hour in Pooh's Chair sometimes felt like five minutes,
and that there were days when she took eight or nine showers between the
time Norman left for work and the time he came back home.

She must have caught pregnant in January, because that was when she
started to be sick in the mornings, and she missed her first period in
February. The case which prompted Norman's "official reprimand"—
one that would be carried in his jacket until the day he retired—had
come in March.

What was his name? she asked herself, still drifting in her bed, somewhere between sleep and waking, but for the time being still closer to
the latter. *The man who started all the trouble, what was his name?*

For a moment it wouldn't come, only the memory that he had been
a black man . . . a jiggedy-jig, in Normanspeak. Then she got it.

"Bender," she murmured in the dark, listening to the low creak of
the crickets. "Richie Bender. That was his name."

1985, a hell of a year. A hell of a *life.* And now there was this life.
This room. This bed. And the sound of crickets.

Rosie closed her eyes and drifted.

9

Less than three miles from his wife now, Norman lay in his own bed,
slipping toward sleep, slipping into darkness and listening to the steady
rumble of traffic on Lakefront Avenue, nine floors below him. His teeth
and jaws still ached, but the pain was distant now, unimportant, hidden
behind a mixture of aspirin and Scotch.

As he drifted, he also found himself thinking about Richie Bender; it
was as if, unknown to either of them, Norman and Rosie had shared a
brief telepathic kiss.

"Richie," he murmured into the shadows of his hotel room, and then
put his forearm over his closed eyes. "Richie Bender, you puke. You fucking puke."

A Saturday, it had been—the first Saturday in March of 1985. Nine years ago, give or take. Around eleven a.m. on that day, a jiggedy-jig had walked into the Payless store on the corner of 60th and Saranac, put two bullets in the clerk's head, looted the register, and walked out again. While Norman and his partner were questioning the clerk in the bottle-redemption center next door, they were approached by another jig, this one wearing a Buffalo Bills jersey.

"I know that nigger," he said.

"What nigger is that, bro?" Norman asked.

"Nigger rob that Payless," the jig had replied. "I was standin right over there by that mailbox when he come out. Name Richie Bender. He a bad nigger. Sell crack out of his motel room down there." He had pointed vaguely east, toward the train station.

"What motel might that be?" Harley Bissington asked. Harley had been partnered with Norman on that unfortunate day.

"Ray'road Motel," the black man said.

"I don't suppose you happen to know which room?" Harley had asked. "Does your knowledge of the purported miscreant stretch that far, my brown-skinned friend?"

Harley had almost always talked that way. Sometimes it cracked Norman up. More often it'd made him want to grab the man by one of his narrow little knit ties and choke the Kokomo out of him.

Their brown-skinned friend knew, all right, of course he did. He was undoubtedly in there himself two or three times a week—maybe five or six, if his current cash-flow situation was good—buying rock from that bad nigger Richie Bender. Their brown-skinned friend and all his brown-skinned jiggedy-jig pals. Probably this fellow currently had some sort of down on Richie Bender, but that was nothing to Norman and Harley; all Norman and Harley wanted was to know where the shooter was so they could bust his ass right over to County and clear this case before cocktail hour.

The jig in the Bills jersey hadn't been able to recall the number of Bender's room, but he'd been able to tell them where it was, just the same: first floor, main wing, right in between the Coke machine and the newspaper boxes.

Norman and Harley had bopped on down to the Railroad Motel, clearly one of the city's finer dives, and knocked on the door between the Coke machine and the newspaper dispensers. The door had been opened by a slutty high-yellow gal in a filmy red dress that let you get a good look at her bra and panties, and she was obviously one stoned American, and the two cops could see what looked like three empty crack vials standing on top of the motel television, and when Norman asked her where Richie

Bender was, she made the mistake of laughing at him. "I don't own no Waring Blender," she said. "You go on now, boys, n get your honky asses out of here."

All of that was pretty straightforward, but then the various accounts had gotten a little confusing. Norman and Harley said that Ms. Wendy Yarrow (known more familiarly in the Daniels kitchen that spring and summer as "the slutty high-yellow gal") had taken a nailfile from her purse and slashed Norman Daniels with it twice. Certainly he had long, shallow cuts across his forehead and the back of his right hand, but Ms. Yarrow claimed that Norman had made the cut across his hand himself and his partner had done the one over his eyebrows for him. They had done this, she said, after pushing her back into Unit 12 of the Railroad Motel, breaking her nose and four of her fingers, fracturing nine bones in her left foot by stamping on it repeatedly (they took turns, she said), pulling out wads of her hair, and punching her repeatedly in the abdomen. The short one then raped her, she told the IA shooflies. The broad-shouldered one had tried to rape her, but hadn't been able to get it up at first. He bit her several times on the breasts and face, and then he was able to get an erection, she told them, "but he squirted all over my leg before he could get it in. Then he hit me some more. He tole me he want to talk to me up close, but he did mos of his talkin with his fists."

Now, lying in bed at the Whitestone, lying on sheets his wife had had in her hands, Norman rolled onto his side and tried to push 1985 away. It didn't want to go. No surprise there; once it came, it never did. 1985 was a hanger-arounder, like some blabby asshole gasbag neighbor you just can't get rid of.

We made a mistake, *Norman thought.* We believed that goddam jig in the football jersey.

Yes, that had been a mistake, all right, a rather big one. And they had believed that a woman who looked so much as if she belonged with a Richie Bender must be in Richie Bender's room, and that was either a second mistake or an extension of the first one, and it didn't really matter which, because the results were the same. Ms. Wendy Yarrow was a part-time waitress, a part-time hooker, and a full-time drug addict, but she had not been in Richie Bender's room, did not in fact know there was such a creature as Richie Bender on the planet. Richie Bender had turned out to be the man who had robbed the Payless and wasted the clerk, but his room wasn't between the soda machine and the newspaper boxes; that was Wendy Yarrow's room and Wendy Yarrow had been all by herself, at least on that particular day.

Richie Bender's room had been on the other side of the Coke machine.

That mistake had almost cost Norman Daniels and Harley Bissington their jobs, but in the end the IA people had believed the nailfile story and there had been no sperm to support Ms. Yarrow's claims of rape. Her assertion that the older of the two—the one who had actually gotten it into her— had used a condom and then flushed it down the toilet was not provable.

There had been other problems, though. Even their greatest partisans in the department had to admit that Inspectors Daniels and Bissington might have gone a little overboard in their efforts to subdue this one-hundred-and-ten-pound wildcat with the nailfile; she did have quite a few broken fingers, for instance. Hence the official reprimand. Nor had that been the end of it. The uppity bitch had found that kike . . . that little baldheaded kike . . .

But the world was full of uppity, troublemaking bitches. His wife, for instance. But she was one uppity bitch he could do something about . . . always supposing, that was, he could get a little sleep.

Norman rolled over onto his other side, and 1985 at last began to fade away. "When you least expect it, Rose," he murmured. "That's when I'll come for you."

Five minutes later he was asleep.

10

That *slutty gal, he called her,* Rose thought in her own bed. She was close to sleep herself now, but not there quite yet; she could still hear the crickets in the park. *That slutty high-yellow gal. How he hated her!*

Yes, of course he had. There had been a mess with the Internal Affairs investigators, for one thing. Norman and Harley Bissington had escaped from that with their skins intact—barely—only to discover that the slutty high-yellow gal had found herself a lawyer (a baldheaded kike ambulance-chaser, in Normanspeak) who had filed a huge civil suit on her behalf. It named Norman, Harley, the entire police department. Then, not long before Rosie's miscarriage, Wendy Yarrow had been murdered. She was found behind one of the grain elevators on the west side of the lake. She had been stabbed over a hundred times, and her breasts had been hacked off.

Some sicko, Norman had told Rosie, and although he had not been smiling after he put the telephone down—someone at the cop-shop must have been really excited, to have called him at home—there had been undeniable satisfaction in his voice. *She sat in at the game once too often and a wildcard came out of the deck. Hazard of the job.* He had touched her hair then, very gently, stroking it, and had smiled at her. Not his biting smile, the one that made her feel like screaming, but she'd felt like screaming anyway, because she had known, just like that, what had happened to Wendy Yarrow, the slutty high-yellow gal.

See how lucky you are? he'd asked her, now stroking the back of her neck with his big hard hands, now her shoulders, now the swells of her breasts. *See how lucky you are not to be out on the street, Rose?*

Then—maybe it had been a month later, maybe six weeks—he had come in from the garage, found Rosie reading a romance novel, and decided he needed to talk to her about her entertainment tastes. Needed to talk to her about them right up close, in fact.

1985, a hell of a year.

Rosie lay in bed with her hands under her pillow, slipping toward sleep and listening to the sound of the crickets coming in through the window, so close they sounded as if her room had been magically transported onto the bandstand in the park, and she thought of a woman who had sat in the corner with her hair plastered against her sweaty cheeks and her belly as hard as a stone and her eyes rolling in their shock-darkened sockets as the sinister kisses began to tickle at her thighs, that woman who was still years from seeing the drop of blood on the sheet, that woman who had not known places like Daughters and Sisters or men like Bill Steiner existed, that woman who had crossed her arms and gripped the points of her shoulders and prayed to a God she no longer believed in that it not be a miscarriage, that it not be the end of her small sweet dream, and then thinking, as she felt it happening, that maybe it was better. She knew how Norman fulfilled his responsibilities as a husband; how might he fulfill them as a father?

The soft hum of the crickets, lulling her to sleep. And she could even smell grass—a husky-sweet aroma that seemed out of place in May. This was a smell she associated with August hayfields.

I never smelled grass from the park before, she thought sleepily. *Is this what love—infatuation, at least—does to you? Does it sharpen your senses at the same time it's making you crazy?*

Very distantly, she heard a rumble that could have been thunder. That was strange, too, because the sky had been clear when Bill brought her home—she had looked up and marvelled at how many stars she could see, even with all the orange hi-intensity streetlights.

She drifted, sliding away, sliding into the last dreamless sleep she would have for some time, and her final thought before the darkness claimed her was *How can I hear crickets or smell grass? The window's not open; I closed it before I got into bed. Closed it and locked it.*

V

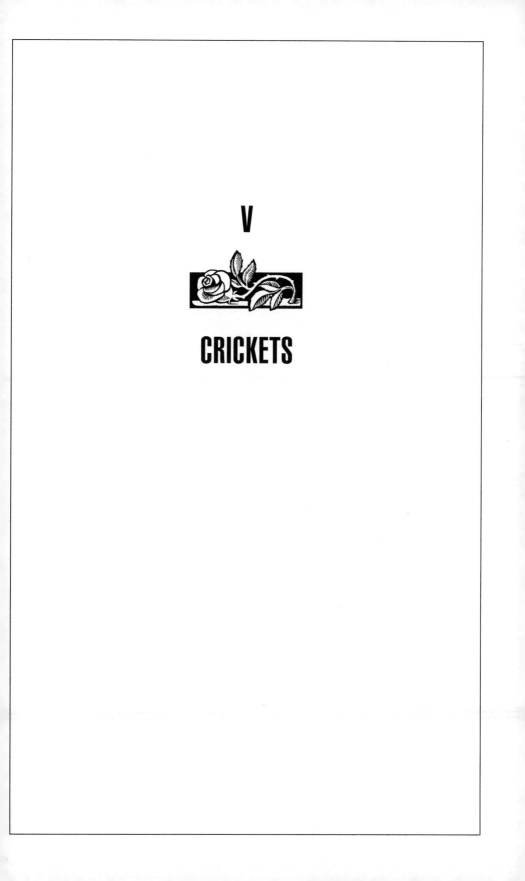

CRICKETS

1

Late that Wednesday afternoon, Rosie almost floated into the Hot Pot. She ordered a cup of tea and a pastry and sat by the window, slowly eating and drinking as she watched the endless river of pedestrians outside—most of them office-workers at this hour, headed home for the day. The Hot Pot was actually out of her way now that she was no longer working at the Whitestone, but she'd come here unhesitatingly just the same, perhaps because she had had so many pleasant after-work cups of tea here with Pam, perhaps because she wasn't much of an explorer—not yet, at least—and this was a place she knew and trusted.

She had finished reading *The Manta Ray* around two o'clock, and had been reaching under the table for her purse when Rhoda Simons had clicked through on the speaker. "Do you want a little break before we start the next one, Rosie?" she had asked, and there it was, as simple as that. She had hoped she would get the other three Bell/Racine novels, had *believed* she would, but the relief of actually *knowing* could not be matched.

Nor was that all. When they'd broken at four, already two chapters into a lurid little slash-and-stalk thriller called *Kill All My Tomorrows,* Rhoda had asked Rosie if she would mind stepping down to the ladies' bathroom with her for a few minutes.

"I know it sounds weird," she said, "but I'm dying for a smoke and it's the only place in the whole damned building I dare to sneak one. Modern life's a bitch, Rosie."

In the bathroom, Rhoda had lit a Capri and perched on the sink-ledge between the two basins with an ease that bespoke long familiarity. She crossed her legs, hooked her right foot behind her left calf, and looked at Rosie speculatively.

"Love your hair," she said.

Rosie touched it self-consciously. It was a spur-of-the-moment thing she'd had done in a beauty-shop the previous evening, fifty dollars she could not afford . . . and had been unable not to spend. "Thanks," she said.

"Robbie's going to offer you a contract, you know."

Rosie frowned and shook her head. "No—I *don't* know. What are you talking about?"

"He may look like Mr. Pennybags on the Monopoly Community Chest cards, but Robbie's been in the audio-book biz since 1975, and he knows how good you are. He knows better than you do. You think you owe him a lot, don't you?"

"I *know* I do," Rosie replied stiffly. She didn't like the way this conversation was going; it made her think of those Shakespearian plays where people stabbed their friends in the back and then reeled off long, sanctimonious soliloquies explaining how unavoidable it had been.

"Don't let your gratitude get in the way of your self-interest," Rhoda said, tapping cigarette ash neatly into the basin and chasing it with a squirt of cold water. "I don't know the story of your life and I don't particularly *want* to know it, but I know you did *The Manta Ray* in just a hundred and four takes, which is fucking phenomenal, and I know you sound like the young Elizabeth Taylor. I also know—because it's just about taped to your forehead—that you're on your own and not used to it. You're so *tabula rasa* it's scary. Do you know what that means?"

Rosie wasn't entirely sure—something about being naive, she thought—but she wasn't going to let on to Rhoda. "Yes, of course."

"Good. And don't get me wrong, for Christ's sake—I'm not trying to cut in on Robbie, or cut my own piece out of your cake. I'm *rooting* for you. So's Rob, and so's Curtis. It's just that Rob's also rooting for his wallet. Audio-books is still a brand-new field. If this were the movie business, we'd be halfway through the Age of the Silents. Do you understand what I'm trying to say?"

"Sort of."

"When Robbie listens to you reading *The Manta Ray,* he's thinking of an audio version of Mary Pickford. I know that sounds crazy, but it's true. Even the *way* he met you adds to that. There's a legend about Lana Turner being discovered in Schwab's Drugstore. Well, Robbie's already making a legend in his own mind about how he discovered you in his friend Steiner's pawnshop, looking at antique postcards."

"Is that what he told you I was doing?" she asked, feeling a surge of warmth for Robbie Lefferts that was almost love.

"Uh-huh, but where he found you and what you were doing there doesn't really matter. The fact is that you're *good,* Rosie, you're really,

really talented. It's almost as if you were born to this job. Rob discovered you, but that doesn't give him a right to your pipes for the rest of your life. Don't let him own you."

"He'd never want to do that," Rosie said. She was frightened and excited at the same time, and also a little angry at Rhoda for being so cynical, but all of these feelings had been suppressed beneath a bright layer of joy and relief: she was going to be all right for a little longer. And if Robbie really *did* offer her a contract, she might be all right for even longer than that. It was all very well for Rhoda Simons to preach caution; Rhoda wasn't living in a single room three blocks from an area of town where you didn't park your car at the curb if you wanted to keep your radio and your hubcaps; Rhoda had an accountant husband, a house in the suburbs, and a 1994 silver Nissan. Rhoda had a VISA and an American Express card. Better yet, Rhoda had a Blue Cross card, and savings she could draw on if she got sick and couldn't work. For people who had those things, Rosie imagined, advising caution in business affairs was probably as natural as breathing.

"Maybe not," Rhoda said, "but you could be a small goldmine, Rosie, and sometimes people change when they discover goldmines. Even nice people like Robbie Lefferts."

Now, drinking her tea and looking out the window of the Hot Pot, Rosie remembered Rhoda dousing her cigarette under the cold tap, dropping it in the trash, and then coming over to her. "I know you're in a situation where job security is very important to you, and I'm not saying Robbie's a bad man—I've been working with him off and on since 1982 and I know he's not—but I'm telling you to keep an eye on the birds in the bush while you're making sure the one in your hand doesn't fly away. Do you follow me?"

"Not entirely, no."

"Agree to do six books to start with, no more. Eight in the morning to four in the afternoon, right here at Tape Engine. A thousand a week."

Rosie goggled at her, feeling as if someone had stuck a vacuum-cleaner hose down her throat and sucked the air out of her lungs. "A *thousand* dollars a *week,* are you *crazy?*"

"Ask Curt Hamilton if *he* thinks I'm crazy," Rhoda said calmly. "Remember, it's not just the voice, it's the *takes.* You did *The Manta Ray* in a hundred and four. No one else I work with could have done it in less than two hundred. You have great voice management, but the absolutely incredible thing is your breath control. If you don't sing, how in God's name did you get such great control?"

A nightmarish image had occurred to Rosie then: sitting in the corner with her kidneys swelling and throbbing like bloated bags filled with hot water, sitting there with her apron held in her hands, praying to God she wouldn't have to fill it because it hurt to throw up, it made her kidneys feel as if they were being stabbed with long, splintery sticks. Sitting there, breathing in long, flat inhales and slow, soft exhales because that was what worked best, trying to make the runaway beat of her heart match the calmer rhythm of her respiration, sitting there and listening to Norman making himself a sandwich in the kitchen and singing "Daniel" or "Take a Letter, Maria" in his surprisingly good barroom tenor.

"I don't know," she had told Rhoda, "I didn't even know what breath control was until I met you. I guess it's just a gift."

"Well, count your blessings, keed," Rhoda said. "We better get back; Curt'll think we're practicing weird female rituals in here."

Robbie had called from his office downtown to congratulate her on finishing *The Manta Ray*—just as she was getting ready to leave for the day, this had been—and although he hadn't specifically mentioned a contract, he had asked if she would have lunch with him on Friday to discuss what he called "a business arrangement." Rosie had agreed and hung up, feeling bemused. She remembered thinking that Rhoda's description of him was perfect; Robbie Lefferts *did* look like the little man on the Monopoly cards.

When she put down the telephone in Curtis's private office—a cluttery little closet with hundreds of business cards stuck to the cork walls on pushpins—and went back out into the studio to collect her purse, Rhoda was gone, presumably for a final smoke in the ladies'. Curt was marking boxes of reel-to-reel tape. He looked up and gave her a grin. "Great work today, Rosie."

"Thanks."

"Rhoda says Robbie's going to offer you a contract."

"That's what she says," Rosie agreed. "And I actually think she might be right. Knock on wood."

"Well, you ought to remember one thing while you're dickering," Curtis said, putting the tape boxes on a high shelf where dozens of similar boxes were ranged like thin white books. "If you made five hundred bucks for *The Manta Ray*, Robbie's already ahead of the game . . . because you saved maybe seven hundred in studio time. Get it?"

She'd gotten it, all right, and now she sat here in the Hot Pot with the future looking unexpectedly bright. She had friends, a place to live, a job, and the promise of more work when she had finished with Christina Bell. A contract that might mean as much as a thousand dollars a week, more money than Norman made. It was crazy, but it was true. *Might* be true, she amended.

Oh, and one other thing. She had a date for Saturday . . . *all* of Saturday, if you counted in the Indigo Girls concert that night.

Rosie's face, usually so solemn, broke into a brilliant smile, and she felt a totally inappropriate desire to hug herself. She took the last bite of her pastry and looked out the window again, wondering if all these things could possibly be happening to her, if there could actually be a real life where real people walked out of their prisons, turned right . . . and walked into heaven.

2

Half a block away, DON'T WALK went out and WALK came on. Pam Haverford, now changed out of her white chambermaid's uniform and into a pair of trim red slacks, crossed the street with two dozen other people. She had worked an extra hour tonight and had no reason on earth to think Rosie would be in the Hot Pot . . . but she did think it, just the same. Call it woman's intuition, if you wanted.

She glanced briefly at the big lug crossing beside her, who she thought she had seen at the Whitestone newsstand a few minutes ago. He might have qualified as *someone interesting* if not for the look in his eyes . . . which was no look at all. He glanced briefly at her as they stepped up on the far curb, and the lack of expression in those eyes—the feeling of some *absence* behind them—actually chilled her.

3

Inside the Hot Pot, Rosie abruptly decided she wanted a second cup of tea. She had no earthly reason to think Pam might drop in—it was a full hour past their usual time—but she did, just the same. Maybe it was woman's intuition. She got up and turned toward the counter.

4

The little bitch beside him was sort of cute, Norman thought, tight red slacks, nice little ass. He dropped back a couple of steps—the better to enjoy the view, my dear—but almost as soon as he did, she turned into a *little restaurant. Norman glanced in the window as he went by, but saw nothing interesting, just a bunch of old bags eating gooey shit and slopping up coffee and tea, plus a few waiters rushing around in that mincing, faggy way they had.*

The old ladies must like it, *Norman thought.* Fag-walking like that must pay off in tips. *It* had *to; why else would grown men walk that way? They couldn't* all *be fags . . . could they?*

His gaze into the Hot Pot—brief and disinterested—touched on one lady considerably younger than the blue-rinsed, pants-suited types sitting at most of the tables. She was walking away from the window and toward the cafeteria-style serving counter at the far end of the tearoom (at least he supposed that was what you called places like this). He took a quick look at her ass, simply because that was where his eyes always went first *when it was a woman younger than forty, judged it not too bad but nothing to write home to Mother about.*

Rose's ass used to look like that, *he thought.* Back in the days before she let herself go and it got as big as a goddam footstool, that is.

The woman he glimpsed through the window also had great hair, much better than her fanny, actually, but her hair didn't make him think of Rosie. Rosie was what Norman's mother had always called a "brownette," and she rarely took any pains with her hair (given its lackluster mousehide color, Norman didn't blame her). Pulling it back in a ponytail and securing it with a rubber band was her usual way of wearing it; if they were going out to dinner or a movie, she might thread it through one of those elastic scrunch things they sold in the drugstore.

The woman upon whom Norman's gaze touched briefly when he looked into the Hot Pot was not a brownette but a slim-hipped blonde, and her hair was not in a ponytail or a scrunch. It hung down to the middle of her back in a carefully made plait.

5

Perhaps the best thing to happen all day, even better than Rhoda's stunning news that she might be worth a thousand dollars a week to Robbie Lefferts, was the look on Pam Haverford's face when Rosie turned away from the Hot Pot cash register with her fresh cup of tea. At first Pam's eyes slid over her with absolutely no recognition at all . . . and then they snapped back, widening as they did so. Pam started to grin and then actually *shrieked,* probably pushing at least half a dozen pacemakers in the ferny little room dangerously close to overload.

"Rosie? Is that you? Oh . . . my . . . *God!*"

"It's me," Rosie said, laughing and blushing. She was aware that people were turning to look at them, and discovered—wonder of wonders —that she did not exactly mind.

They took their tea to their old table by the window, and Rosie even allowed Pam to talk her into another pastry, although she had lost fifteen pounds since coming to the city and had no intention of putting it back on if she could help it.

Pam kept telling her that she couldn't *beleeve* it, simply couldn't *beleeeve* it, a remark Rosie might have been tempted to chalk up to flattery, except for the way Pam's eyes kept moving from her face to her hair, as if she was trying to get the truth of it straight in her mind.

"It makes you look five years younger," she said. "Hell, Rosie, it makes you look like jailbait!"

"For fifty dollars, it ought to make me look like Marilyn Monroe," Rosie replied, smiling . . . but since her talk with Rhoda, she felt a lot easier in her mind about the amount she'd spent on her hair.

"Where did you—" Pam began, then stopped. "It's the picture you bought, isn't it? You had your hair done the same as the woman in the picture."

Rosie thought she would blush at this, but no blush came. She simply nodded. "I loved that style, so I thought I'd try it." She hesitated, then added: "As for changing the color, I still can't believe I did it. It's the first time in my whole life that I've changed the color of my hair."

"The first—! I don't believe it!"

"It's true."

Pam leaned across the table, and when she spoke it was in a throaty, conspiratorial whisper: "It's happened, hasn't it?"

"What are you talking about? What's happened?"

"You've met *someone interesting!*"

Rosie opened her mouth. Closed it. Opened it again without the slightest idea of what she intended to say. It turned out to be nothing; what came out instead of words was laughter. She laughed until she cried, and before she was done, Pam had joined in.

6

Rosie didn't need her key to open the street door at 897 Trenton Street—that one was left unlocked until eight or so on weeknights—but she needed the small one to open her mailbox (R. McCLENDON taped to the front of it, boldly asserting that she belonged here, yes she did), which was empty except for a Wal-Mart circular. As she started up the stairs to the second floor, she shook out another key. This one opened the door to her room, and except for the building super, she had the only one. Like the mailbox, it was hers. Her feet were tired—she had walked the entire three miles from downtown, feeling too restless and too happy to sit on a bus, also wanting more time than a bus would give her to think and dream. She was hungry in spite of two Hot Pot pastries, but her stomach's low growling added rather than detracted from her happiness. Had she ever in her life felt such gladness? She thought not. It had spilled over from her mind into her entire body, and although her feet were tired, they still felt light. And her kidneys didn't hurt a bit, in spite of the long walk.

Now, letting herself into her room (and remembering to lock the door behind her this time), Rosie began to giggle again. Pam and her *someone interesting*s. She had been forced to admit a few things—she was, after all, planning to bring Bill to the Indigo Girls concert on Saturday night and the women from D & S would meet him then—but when she protested that she hadn't colored her hair and plaited it simply on Bill's account (this felt true to her, actually), she got only comically rolling eyeballs and a burlesque wink from Pam. It was irritating . . . but also rather sweet.

She opened the window, letting in the mild late-spring air and the sounds of the park, then crossed to her small kitchen table, where a paperback lay beside the flowers Bill had brought her on Monday night. The flowers were fading now, but she didn't think she could bring herself to throw them out. Not, at least, until after Saturday. Last night she had dreamed of him, had dreamed of riding behind him on his motorcycle. He kept driving faster and faster, and at some point a terrible, wonderful word had occurred to her. A magic word. She couldn't remember exactly what it had been now, something nonsensical like *deffle* or *feffle,* but in the dream it had seemed like a beautiful word . . . powerful, too. *Don't say it unless you really, really mean it,* she remembered thinking as they flashed along some country highway with hills on the left and the lake winking blue and gold sunflashes through the firs on their right. Up ahead was an overgrown hill, and she knew that there was a ruined temple on the far side of it. *Don't say it unless you mean to commit yourself, body and soul.*

She had said the word; it came out of her mouth like a bolt of electricity. The wheels of Bill's Harley had left the road—for just a moment she had seen the front one, still spinning but now six inches above the pavement—and she had seen their shadow not beside them but some-how *beneath* them. Bill had twisted the hand-throttle and suddenly they were bolting up toward the bright blue sky, emerging from the lane the road made in the trees like a submarine coming to the surface of the ocean, and she had awakened in her bed with the covers balled up all around her, shivering and yet gasping in the hold of some deep heat which seemed hidden in the center of her, unseen but powerful, like the sun in eclipse.

She doubted very much if they would fly like that no matter how many magic words she tried, but she thought she would keep the flowers awhile longer, anyway. Perhaps even press a couple of them between the pages of this very book.

She had bought the book in Elaine's Dreams, the place where she had gotten her hair done. The title was *Simple but Elegant: Ten Hairstyles You Can Do at Home.* "These are good," Elaine had told her. "Of course you should always get your hair done by a professional, that's my view, but if you can't afford it every week, timewise or moneywise, and the thought of actually dialing the 800 number and ordering the Topsy Tail makes you feel like shooting yourself, this is a decent compromise. Just for Jesus' sake promise me that if some guy invites you to a country club dance in Westwood, you'll come see me first."

Rosie sat down and turned to Style #3, the Classic Plait . . . which, the opening paragraph informed her, was also known as the Classic French Braid. She went through the black-and-white photographs which showed a woman first separating and then plaiting her hair, and when she reached the end, she began to work her way backward, undoing the plait. Unmaking it in the evening turned out to be a lot simpler than making it in the morning; it had taken her forty-five minutes and one good round of cursing to get it looking more or less the way it had when she'd left Elaine's Dreams the night before. It had been worth it, how-ever; Pam's unabashed shriek of amazement in the Hot Pot was worth all of that and more.

As she finished her work, her mind turned to Bill Steiner (it had never been very far away from him), and she wondered if he would like her hair plaited. If he would like her hair *blonde.* Or if he would, in fact, notice either of these changes at all. She wondered if she would be unhappy if he didn't notice, then sighed and wrinkled her nose. Of course she would be. On the other hand, what if he not only noticed but reacted as Pam had (minus the squeal, of course)? He might even sweep her into his arms, as they said in the romance novels . . .

She was reaching for her purse, wanting the comb inside, and beginning to slide into a harmless little fantasy of Saturday morning—of Bill tying the end of the plait with a piece of velvet ribbon, in fact (why he would happen to have a piece of velvet ribbon on his person could go completely unexplained; that was the nice thing about kitchen table daydreams)—when her thoughts were interrupted by a small sound from the far side of the room.

Reep. Reep-reep.

A cricket. The sound wasn't coming through the open window from Bryant Park, either. It was a lot closer than that.

Reep-reep. Reep-reep.

She swept her eyes along the baseboard and saw something jump. She got up, opened the cupboard to the left of the sink, and took down a glass mixing bowl. She walked across the room, pausing to pluck the Wal-Mart circular from the seat of the chair in the living-room area. Then she knelt by the insect, which had made its way almost into the unadorned south corner where she supposed she would put her TV, if she actually got around to buying one before moving out of here. After today, moving to a bigger place—and soon—seemed like more than just a daydream.

It *was* a cricket. How it had gotten up here to the second floor was a bit of a mystery, but it was definitely a cricket. Then the answer occurred to her, and it included the reason why she'd heard it when she was falling asleep. The cricket must have come up with Bill, probably in the cuff of his pants. A little extra present to go along with the flowers.

You didn't hear just one *cricket the other night,* Practical-Sensible spoke up suddenly. That particular voice hadn't gotten much use lately. It sounded rusty and a little hoarse. *You heard a whole* fieldful *of crickets. Or a whole parkful.*

Bullshit, she replied comfortably as she lowered the bowl over the insect and then slid the advertising circular under the lip, poking the bug with the corner of it until he hopped, letting her slide the paper entirely over the inverted mouth of the bowl. *My mind just turned one cricket into a chorus, that's all. I was going to sleep, remember. I was probably half in a dream already.*

She picked the bowl up and turned it over, holding the circular over the top so the cricket couldn't escape before she was ready for it to. It jumped energetically up and down meanwhile, its armored back ticking off a picture of the new John Grisham novel, which could be purchased at Wal-Mart for only sixteen dollars, plus tax. Humming "When You Wish Upon a Star," Rosie took the cricket over to the open window, removed the circular, and held the bowl out into space. Insects could fall from much greater heights than this and walk away unhurt (hop away, her mind amended) when they landed. She was sure she had read that somewhere, or perhaps seen it on some TV nature program.

"Go on, Jiminy," she said. "Be a good boy and hop. See the park over there? Tall grass, plenty of dew to drink, lots of girl crick—"

She broke off. The bug hadn't come upstairs in Bill's cuffs, because he'd been wearing jeans on Monday night, when he'd taken her out to dinner. She questioned her memory on that, wanting to be sure, and the same information came back quickly, and with no shade of doubt. Oxford shirt and Levi's with no cuffs. She remembered being comforted by his clothes; they were insurance that he wasn't going to try taking her to some fancy place where she would be stared at.

Bluejeans, no cuffs.

So where had Jiminy come from?

What did it matter? If the cricket hadn't come upstairs in one of Bill's pantscuffs, it had probably come up in someone else's, that was all, hopping out on the second-floor landing when it got a little restless— hey, t'anks for the ride, bud. Then it had simply slipped under her door, and what of that? She could think of less pleasant uninvited guests.

As if to express agreement with this, the cricket suddenly sprang out of the bowl and took the plunge.

"Have a nice day," Rosie said. "Stop by anytime. Really."

As she brought the bowl back inside, a minor gust of wind blew the Wal-Mart circular out from beneath her thumb and sent it seesawing lazily to the floor. She bent over to pick it up, then froze with her outstretched fingers still an inch away from it. Two more crickets, both dead, lay against the baseboard, one on its side and the other on its back with its little legs sticking up.

One cricket she could understand and accept, but three? In a second-floor room? How, exactly, did you explain that?

Now Rosie saw something else, something lying in the crack between two boards close to the dead crickets. She knelt, fished it out of the crack, and held it up to her eyes.

It was a clover flower. A tiny pink clover flower.

She looked down at the crack from which she had plucked it; she looked again at the pair of dead crickets; then she let her eyes climb slowly up the cream-colored wall . . . to her picture, hanging there by the window. To Rose Madder (it was as good a name as any) standing on her hill, with the newly discovered pony cropping grass behind her.

Conscious of her heartbeat—a big slow muffled drum in her ears—

Rosie leaned forward toward the picture, toward the pony's snout, watching the image dissolve into layered shades of old paint, beginning to see the brush-strokes. Below the muzzle were the forest-green and olive-green hues of the grass, which appeared to have been done in quick, layered downstrokes of the artist's brush. Dotted among them were small pink blobs. Clover.

Rose looked at the tiny pink flower in the palm of her hand, then held it out to the painting. The color matched exactly. Suddenly, and with no forethought at all, she raised her hand to the level of her lips and puffed the tiny flower toward the picture. She half-expected (no, it was more than that, actually; for a moment she was utterly positive) the tiny pink ball would float through the surface of the painting and enter that world which had been created by some unknown artist sixty, eighty, perhaps even a hundred years ago.

It didn't happen, of course. The pink flower struck the glass covering the painting (unusual for an oil to be covered with glass, Robbie had said on the day she met him), bounced off, and fluttered to the floor like a tiny shred of balled-up tissue-paper. Maybe the painting was magic, but the glass covering it clearly wasn't.

Then how did the crickets get out? You do *think that's what happened, don't you? That the crickets and the clover flower somehow got out of the painting?*

God help her, that *was* what she thought. She had an idea that when she was out of this room and with other people, the notion would seem ridiculous or fade away completely, but for now that was what she thought: the crickets had hopped out of the grass under the feet of the blonde woman in the rose madder chiton. They had somehow hopped from the world of Rose Madder and into that of Rosie McClendon.

How? Did they just sort of ooze through the glass?

No, of course not. That was stupid, but—

She reached out with hands that trembled slightly and lifted the painting off its hook. She took it into the kitchen area, set it on the counter, and then turned it around. The charcoaled words on the paper backing were more blurred than ever; she wouldn't have known for sure that they said ROSE MADDER if she hadn't seen them earlier.

Hesitantly, feeling afraid now (or perhaps she'd been afraid all along and was just now beginning to realize it), she touched the backing. It crackled when she poked it. Crackled too much. And when she poked at it lower down, where the brown paper disappeared into the frame, she felt something . . . some *things* . . .

She swallowed, and the back of her throat was so dry it hurt. She opened one of the counter drawers with a hand that didn't feel like her own, picked up a paring knife, and brought its blade slowly toward the brown paper backing.

Don't do it! Practical-Sensible shrieked. *Don't do it, Rosie, you don't know* what *might come out of there!*

She held the tip of the knife poised against the brown paper for a moment, then laid it aside for the time being. She lifted the picture and looked at the bottom of the frame, noting with some distant part of her mind that her hands were shaking very badly now. What she saw running through the wood—a crack at least a quarter-inch across at its widest point—didn't really surprise her. She set the picture back down on the counter, holding it up with her right hand and using her left—her smart hand—to bring the tip of the paring knife against the paper backing again.

Don't, Rosie. Practical-Sensible wasn't shrieking this time; she was moaning. *Please don't do this, please leave well enough alone.* Except that was ridiculous advice, when you thought about it; if she had followed it the first time Ms. P-S had given it, she would still be living with Norman. Or dying with him.

She used the knife to slit the backing, down low where she felt those bulges. Half a dozen crickets tumbled out onto the counter, four of them dead, one twitching feebly, the sixth frisky enough to hop off down the counter before tumbling into the sink. Along with the crickets came a few more pink clover-puffs, a few grass-cuttings . . . and part of a brown dead leaf. Rosie picked this last up and looked at it curiously. It was an oak-leaf. She was almost sure of it.

Working carefully (and ignoring the voice of Practical-Sensible), Rosie used the paring knife to cut all the way around the paper backing. When she removed it, more rustic treasures fell out: ants (most dead but three or four still able to crawl), the plump corpse of a honeybee, several daisy-petals of the sort you were supposed to pluck from the central flower while chanting he-loves-me, he-loves-me-not . . . and a few filmy white hairs. She held these up to the light, gripping the turned-around painting tighter with her right hand as a shudder went up her back like big feet climbing a set of stairs. If she took these hairs to a veterinarian and asked him to look at them under a microscope, Rosie knew what he'd tell her: they were horse-hairs. Or, more accurately, they were hairs from a small, shaggy pony. A pony that was currently cropping grass in another world.

I'm losing my mind, she thought calmly, and that wasn't the voice of Practical-Sensible; that was her own voice, the one which spoke for the central, integrated core of her thoughts and her self. It wasn't hysterical or goosey; it spoke rationally, calmly, and with a touch of wonder. It was, she suspected, the same tone in which her mind would acknowledge the inevitability of death, in the days or weeks when its approach could no longer be denied.

Except she didn't really *believe* she was losing her mind, not the way she would be forced to believe in the finality of, say, cancer, once it had progressed to a certain stage. She had opened the back of her picture and a bunch of grass, hair, and insects—some still alive—had fallen out. Was that so impossible to believe? She had read a story in the newspaper a few years back about a woman who had discovered a small fortune in perfectly good stock certificates hidden in the backing of an old family portrait; compared to that, a few bugs seemed mundane.

But still alive, Rosie? And what about the clover, still fresh, and the grass, still green? The leaf was dead, but you know what you're thinking about that—

She was thinking that it had blown through dead. It was summer in the picture, but you found dead leaves in the grass even in June.

So I repeat: I'm losing my mind.

Except the stuff was *here,* scattered all over her kitchen counter, a litter of bugs and grass.

Stuff.

Not dreams or hallucinations but *real stuff.*

And there was something else, the one thing she did not really want to approach head-on. This picture had talked to her. No, not out loud, but from the first moment she'd seen it, it had spoken to her, just the same. It had her name on the back—a version of it, anyway—and yesterday she had spent much more than she could afford to make her hair look like the hair of the woman in the picture.

Moving with sudden decisiveness, she inserted the flat of the paring knife's blade under the top part of the frame and levered upward. She would have stopped immediately if she'd sensed strong resistance—this was the only paring knife she had, and she didn't want to snap the blade off—but the nails holding the frame together gave easily. She pulled off the top, now using her free hand to keep the glass front from falling to the counter and shattering, and laid it aside. Another dead cricket clicked to the counter. A moment later she held the bare canvas in her hands. It was about thirty inches long and eighteen inches high, with the frame and the matting removed. Gently, Rose ran her finger across the long-dried oil paints, feeling layers of minutely different heights, feeling even the fine-combed tracks left by the artist's brush. It was an interesting, slightly eerie sensation, but there was nothing supernatural about it; her finger did not slip through the surface and into that other world.

The phone, which she had bought and plugged into the wall-jack yesterday, rang for the first time. The volume was turned up all the way, and its sudden, shrill warble made Rosie jump and voice her own cry. Her hand tensed, and her outstretched finger almost poked through the painted canvas.

She laid the picture down on the kitchen table and hurried to the phone, hoping it was Bill. If it was, she thought she might invite him over—invite him to take a good look at her painting. And show him the assorted detritus that had fallen out of it. The *stuff*.

"Hello?"

"Hello, Rosie?" Not Bill. A woman. "It's Anna Stevenson."

"Oh, Anna! Hello! How are you?"

From the sink came a persistent *reep-reep*.

"I'm not doing too well," Anna said. "Not too well at all. Something very unpleasant has happened, and I need to tell you about it. It may not have anything to do with you—I hope with all my heart it doesn't —but it might."

Rosie sat down, frightened now in a way she hadn't been even when she had felt the shapes of dead insects hiding behind the backing of her picture. "What, Anna? What's wrong?"

Rosie listened with growing horror as Anna told her. When she had finished, she asked if Rosie wanted to come over to Daughters and Sisters, perhaps spend the night.

"I don't know," Rosie said numbly. "I'll have to think. I . . . Anna, I have to call someone else now. I'll get back to you."

She hung up before Anna could reply, dialed 411, asked for a number, got it, dialed it.

"Liberty City," an older man's voice said.

"Yes, may I speak to Mr. Steiner?"

"This *is* Mr. Steiner," the slightly hoarse voice replied, sounding amused. Rosie was confused for a moment, then remembered that he was in business with his dad.

"Bill," she said. Her throat was dry and painful again. "Bill, I mean . . . is he there?"

"Hold on, miss." A rustle and a clunk as the phone was laid down, and, distant: *"Billy! It's a lady forya!"*

Rosie closed her eyes. Very distantly, she heard the cricket in the sink: *Reep-reep.*

A long, unbearable pause. A tear slipped out from beneath the lashes of her left eye and started down her cheek. It was followed by one from her right, and a snatch of some old country song drifted through her mind: "Well, the race is on and here comes Pride up the back-stretch . . . Heartache is goin' to the inside . . ." She wiped them away. So many tears she had wiped away in this life of hers. If the Hindus were right about reincarnation, she hated to think what she must have been in her last one.

The telephone was picked up. "Hello?" A voice she now heard in her dreams.

"Hello, Bill." It wasn't her normal speaking voice, not even a whisper, not really. It was more like the husk of a whisper.

"I can't hear you," Bill said. "Can you speak up, ma'am?"

She didn't want to speak up; she wanted to *hang* up. She couldn't, though. Because if Anna was right, Bill could be in trouble, too—very bad trouble. If, that was, he was perceived by a certain someone as being a little too close to her. She cleared her throat and tried again. "Bill? It's Rosie."

"Rosie!" he cried, sounding delighted. "Hey, how are you?"

His unaffected, undisguised delight only made it worse; all of a sudden it felt as if someone were twisting a knife in her guts. "I can't go out with you on Saturday," she said, speaking rapidly. The tears were coming faster now, oozing from beneath her eyelids like some nasty hot grease. "I can't go out with you at all. I was crazy to think I could."

"Of course you can! Jesus, Rosie! What are you talking about?"

The panic in his voice—not the anger she had half-expected, but real panic—was bad, but somehow the bewilderment was worse. She couldn't stand it.

"Don't call me and don't come over," she told him, and suddenly she could see Norman with horrible clarity, standing across from her build-ing in the pouring rain with the collar of his overcoat turned up and a streetlight faintly illuminating the lower half of his face—standing there like one of the hellish, brutal villains in a novel by "Richard Racine."

"Rosie, I don't understand—"

"I know, and that's actually for the best," she said. Her voice was wavering, starting to break apart. "Just stay away from me, Bill."

She hung the telephone up quickly, stared at it a moment, then voiced a loud, agonized cry. She turned the phone out of her lap with the backs of her hands. The handset flew to the end of its cord and lay on the floor, its open-line hum sounding strangely like the hum of the crickets which had sent her off to sleep on Monday night. Suddenly she couldn't stand the sound, felt that if she had to listen to it for even another thirty seconds, it would split her head in two. She got up, went to the wall, squatted, and pulled the phone-jack. When she tried to get up again, her trembling legs would not support her. She sat on the floor, covered her face with her hands, and let the tears have their way with her. There was really no choice.

Anna had kept saying over and over again that she wasn't sure, that Rosie couldn't be sure, either, whatever she might suspect. But Rosie *was* sure. It was Norman. Norman was here, Norman had lost whatever remained of his sanity, Norman had killed Anna's ex-husband, Peter Slowik, and Norman was looking for her.

7

*F*ive *blocks beyond the Hot Pot, where he had come within four seconds of meeting his wife's eyes through the plate-glass window, Norman turned into a discount store called No More Than 5. "Everything in the Store Priced Under $5.00!" the store's motto read. It was printed below a wretchedly executed drawing of Abraham Lincoln. There was a broad grin on Lincoln's bearded face, he was dropping a wink, and to Norman Daniels he looked quite a bit like a man he had once arrested for strangling his wife and all four of his children. In this store, which was literally within shouting distance of Liberty City Loan & Pawn, Norman bought all the disguise he intended to wear today: a pair of sunglasses and a cap with* CHISOX *printed above the bill.*

As a man with just over ten years' experience as a detective inspector, Norman had come to believe that disguises only belonged in three places: spy movies, Sherlock Holmes stories, and Halloween parties. They were especially useless in the daytime, when the only thing makeup looked like was makeup and the only thing a disguise looked like was a disguise. And the gals in Daughters and Sisters, the New Age whorehouse where his pal Peter Slowik had finally admitted sending his rambling Rose, were apt to be particularly sensitive to predators slinking around their waterhole. For gals like these, paranoia was a lot more than a way of life; it was full state-of-the-art.

The cap and dark glasses would serve his purpose; all he had planned for this early evening was what Gordon Satterwaite, his first detective partner, would have called "a little rekky." Gordon had also been fond of grabbing his young associate and telling him it was time to do a little of what he called "the old gumshoe." Gordon had been a fat, smelly, tobacco-

chewing slob with brown teeth, and Norman had despised him almost from the first moment he had seen him. Gordon had been a cop for twenty-six years and an inspector for nineteen, but he had no feel for the work. Norman did. He didn't like it, and he hated the jizzbags he had to talk to (and sometimes even associate with, if the job was undercover), but he had a feel for it, and that feel had been invaluable over the years. It had helped bring him through the case which had resulted in his promotion, the case which had turned him—however briefly—into a media golden boy. In that investigation, as in most that involved organized crime, there came a point where the path the investigators had been following disappeared into a bewildering maze of diverging paths, and the straight way was lost. The difference in the drug case was that Norman Daniels was—for the first time in his career—in charge, and when logic failed, he did without hesitation what most cops could not or would not do: he had switched over to intuition and then trusted his entire future to what it told him, plunging forward aggressively and fearlessly.

To Norman there was no such thing as "a little rekky"; to Norman there was only trolling. When you were stumped, you went somewhere that had a bearing on the case, you looked at it with your mind perfectly open, not junked up with a lot of worthless ideas and half-baked suppositions, and when you did that you were like a guy sitting in a slow-moving boat, casting your line out and reeling it in, casting out and reeling in, waiting for something to grab hold. Sometimes nothing did. Sometimes you got nothing but a submerged tree-limb or an old rubber boot or the kind of fish not even a hungry raccoon would eat.

Sometimes, though, you hooked a tasty one.

He put on the hat and the sunglasses, then turned left onto Harrison Street, now on his way to Durham Avenue. It was easily a three-mile hike to the neighborhood where Daughters and Sisters was located, but Norman didn't mind; he could use the walk to empty out his head. By the time he reached 251, he would be like a blank sheet of photographic paper, ready to receive whatever images and ideas might come, without trying to change them so they would fit his own preconceptions. If you didn't have any preconceptions, you couldn't do that.

His overpriced map was in his back pocket, but he only stopped to consult it once. He had been in the city less than a week, but he already had its geography much more clearly fixed in his mind than Rosie did, and again, this was not so much training as it was a gift.

When he had awakened yesterday morning with his hands and shoulders and groin aching, with his jaws too sore to open his mouth more than halfway (the first attempt at a wakeup yawn as he swung his feet out of *bed had been agony), he had done so with the dismaying realization that what he had done to Peter Slowik—aka Thumperstein, aka The Amazing Urban Jewboy—had probably been a mistake. Just how bad a mistake was hard to say, because a lot of what had happened at Slowik's house was only a blur to him, but it had been a mistake, all right; by the time he had reached the hotel newsstand, he'd decided there was no probably about it. Probably was for the dinks of the world, anyway—this had been an unspoken but fiercely held tenet of his life's code ever since his early teens, when his mother had left and his father had really started to crank up the beatings.*

He had bought a paper at the newsstand and leafed through it rapidly in the elevator as he went back up to his room. There was nothing in it about Peter Slowik, but Norman had found that only a minor relief. Thumper's body might not have been discovered in time for the news to make the early editions; might, in fact, still be lying where Norman had left it (where he thought *he had left it, he amended; it was all pretty hazy), crammed in behind the basement water-heater. But guys like Thumper, guys who did lots of public-service work and had lots of bleeding-heart friends, didn't go undiscovered for long. Someone would get worried, other someones would come around looking for him at his cozy little rabbit-hole on Beaudry Place, and eventually some someone would make an exceptionally unpleasant discovery behind the water-heater.*

And sure enough, what had not been in the paper yesterday morning was there today, on page one of the Metro section: CITY SOCIAL WORKER SLAIN IN HOME. *According to the piece, Travelers Aid had been only one of Thumper's after-hours activities . . . and he hadn't exactly been poor, either. According to the paper, his family—of which Thump had been the last—had been worth a pretty good chunk of change. The fact that he had been working in a bus station at three in the morning, sending runaway wives to the whores at Daughters and Sisters, only proved to Norman that the man was either short a few screws or sexually bent. Anyway, he had been your typical do-gooding shitbug, trundling here and there, too busy trying to save the world most days to change his underpants. Travelers Aid, Salvation Army, Dial* HELP, *Bosnian Relief, Russian Relief (you'd have thought a Jewboy like Thump would have had at least enough sense to skip that one, but nope), and two or three "women's causes" as well. The paper didn't identify these last, but Norman already knew one of them: Daughters and Sisters, also known as Lesbo Babes in Toyland. There was going to be a memorial service for Thumper on Saturday, except the paper called it a "remembrance circle." Dear bleeding Jesus.*

He also knew that Slowik's death could have had to do with any of the

STEPHEN KING

causes the man worked for . . . or none of them. The cops would be checking into his personal life as well (always assuming a walking Room to Rent like Thumper had a personal life), and they would not neglect the possibility that it had been the ever more popular "motiveless crime," committed by some psycho who maybe just happened to walk in. A guy looking for a bite, you could say.

None of these things, however, were going to matter much to the whores at Daughters and Sisters; Norman knew that as well as he knew his own name. He'd had a fair amount of experience with women's halfway houses and shelters in the course of his job, more as the years went by and the people Norman thought of as New Age Fern-Sniffers really started to have an effect on the way people thought and behaved. According to the New Age Fern-Sniffers, everyone came from a dysfunctional family, everyone was sublimating the child inside, and everyone had to watch out for all the mean, nasty people out there who had the nerve to try going through life without whining and crying and running off to some Twelve-Step program every night. The Fern-Sniffers were assholes, but some of them —and the women in places like this Daughters and Sisters were often prime examples—could be extremely cautious *assholes.* Cautious? Shit. *They gave an entirely new dimension to the term* bunker mentality.

Norman had spent most of yesterday in the library, and he had found out a number of interesting things about Daughters and Sisters. The most hilarious was that the woman who ran the place, Anna Stevenson, had been Mrs. Thumper until 1973, when she had apparently divorced him and taken her maiden name back. It seemed like a wild coincidence only if you were unfamiliar with the mating rites and rituals of the Fern Folks. They ran in pairs, but were hardly ever able to run in harness, not for the long haul. One always ended up wanting to gee while the other wanted to haw. They were unable to see the simple truth: politically correct marriages didn't work.

Thumper's ex-wife didn't run her place along the lines of most battered-women shelters, where the motto was "only women know, only women tell." In a Sunday-supplement article about the place which had been published a little over a year ago, the Stevenson woman (Norman was struck by how much she looked like that cunt Maude on the old TV show) had dismissed that idea as "not only sexist, but stupid as well." A woman named Gert Kinshaw was also quoted on this subject. "Men aren't our enemies unless they prove they're our enemies," she said. "But if they hit, we hit back." There was a picture of her, a big old nigger bitch who reminded Norman vaguely of that Chicago football player William "Re-

170

frigerator" Perry. *"You ever try to hit me, sweetheart, I'll use you for a trampoline,"* he had murmured.

But that stuff, interesting as it might be, was really beside the point. There might be men as well as women in this city who knew where the place was and were allowed to make referrals, and it might be run by just one New Age Fern-Sniffer instead of a committee of them, but in one respect he was sure they would be exactly the same as their more traditional counterparts: the death of Peter Slowik would have them on red alert. They wouldn't make the assumptions the cops would make; unless and until proved otherwise, they would assume Slowik's murder had to do with them . . . specifically with one of the referrals Slowik had made during the last six or eight months of his life. Rosie's name might already have surfaced in that respect.

So why did you do it? *he asked himself.* Why in God's name did you do it? There were other ways of getting to where you are now, and you know what they are. You're a cop, for Christ's sake, of course you do! So why did you put their wind up? That fat slob in the newspaper article, Dirty Gertie What's-Her-Face, is probably standing in the parlor window of the goddam place, using binoculars to examine every swinging dick who goes by. If she hasn't dropped dead of a Twinkie-assisted stroke by now, that is. So why did you do it? Why?

The answer was there, but he turned away from it before it could do more than begin to surface in his conscious mind; turned away because the implications were too grim to look at. He had done Thumper for the same reason he had strangled the redheaded whore in the fawn-colored hotpants—because something had crawled up from the bottom of his mind and made *him* do it. That thing was there more and more now, and he wouldn't think of it. It was better not to. Safer.

Meantime, here he was; Pussy Palace dead ahead.

Norman crossed to the even-numbered side of Durham Avenue at a leisurely amble, knowing that any watchers would feel less threatened by a guy on the far side of the street. The specific watcher he kept imagining was the darkie tubbo whose picture had been in the paper, a giant economy-sized bag of works with a pair of hi-resolution field glasses in one hand and a melting clump of Mallow Cremes in the other. He slowed down a little more, but not much—red alert, he reminded himself, they'll be on red alert.

It was a big white frame house, not quite Victorian, one of those turn-of-the-century dowagers that's three full stories of ugly. It looked narrow from the front, but Norman had grown up in a house not so different from *this and was willing to bet it went almost all the way back to the street on the far side of the block.*

And with a whore-whore here and a whore-whore there, *Norman thought, being careful not to change his walk from its current slow amble, and being careful to swallow the house not in one long stare but in small sips.* Here a whore, there a whore, everywhere a whore-whore.

Yes indeed. Everywhere a whore-whore.

He felt the familiar rage begin to pulse at his temples now, and with it came a familiar image, the one which stood for all the things he could not express: the bank card. The green bank card she had dared to steal. The image of that card was always close now, and it had come to stand for all the terrors and compulsions of his life—the forces he raged against, the faces (his mother's, for instance, so white and doughy and somehow sly) that sometimes slipped into his mind while he was lying in bed at night and trying to sleep, the voices that came in his dreams. His father's, for instance. "Come on over here, Normie. I've got something to tell you, and I want to tell you up close." Sometimes that meant a blow. Sometimes, if you were lucky and he was drunk, it meant a hand creeping in between your legs.

But that didn't matter now; only the house across the street mattered. He wouldn't get another look this good at it, and if he wasted these precious seconds thinking about the past, who was the monkey then?

He was directly opposite the place. Nice lawn, narrow but deep. Pretty flowerbeds, flushed with spring blooms, flanked the long front porch. There were metal posts dressed in ivy standing in the center of each bed. The ivy had been pruned away from the black plastic cylinders at the tops of the posts, though, and Norman knew why: there were TV cameras inside those dark pods, giving overlapping views up and down the street. If anyone was looking at the monitors inside right now, they would be seeing a little black-and-white man in a baseball hat and sunglasses moving from screen to screen, walking hunched and slightly bent-kneed so that his six-feet-three would look quite a bit shorter to the casual observer.

There was another camera mounted over a front door for which there would be no keyhole; keys were too easy to duplicate, tumblers too easy to tickle, if you were handy with a set of picks. No, there would be a keycard slot, a numerical keypad console, or maybe both. And more cameras in the back yard, of course.

As he walked past the house, Norman risked one final look into the side yard. Here was a vegetable garden, and two whores in shorts sliding long sticks—tomato-stakes, he supposed—into the ground. One looked like a taco-bender: olive skin and long dark hair tied back in a ponytail.

Dynamite body, looked about twenty-five. The other was younger, maybe not even out of her teens yet, one of these punky-grungy scumbuckets with her hair dyed two different colors. There was a bandage covering her left ear. She was wearing a sleeveless psychedelic shirt, and Norman could see a tattoo on her left bicep. His eyes weren't quite good enough to make out what it was, but he had been a cop long enough to know it was probably either the name of a rock group or a badly executed drawing of a marijuana plant.

Norman saw himself suddenly rushing across the street, ignoring the cameras; saw himself grabbing Little Miss Hot Snatch with the rock-star hair; saw himself sliding one of his big hands around her thin neck and running it up until it was stopped by the shelf of her jaw. "Rose Daniels," he would say to the other one, the taco-bender with the dark hair and the dynamite bod. "Get her out here right now or I'll snap this spermbucket's neck like a chicken-bone."

That would be great, but he was almost positive Rosie was no longer here. His library research told him that almost three thousand women had availed themselves of the services offered by Daughters and Sisters since Leo and Jessica Stevenson had opened the place in 1974, and the average length of stay was four weeks. They moved them out into the community at a pretty good pace, breeders and disease-spreaders, pretty mosquitoes. Probably gave them dildos instead of diplomas when they graduated.

No, Rose was almost surely gone, working at some menial job her lesbo pals had found her and going home at night to a scurgy room they'd also found her. The bitches across the street would know where she was, though—the Stevenson woman would have her address in her files, and probably the ones over there in the garden had already been up to her little roachtrap for tea and Girl Scout cookies. Those who hadn't would have been told all about it by those who had, too, because that was the way women were made. You had to kill them to shut them up.

The younger of the gardeners, the one with the rock-star hair, startled him horribly by raising her head, seeing him . . . and waving. For one awful moment he was sure she was laughing at him, that they were all laughing, that they were lined up at the windows inside Castle Lesbo and laughing at him, at Inspector Norman Daniels, who had been able to bust half a dozen coke-barons but couldn't keep his own wife from stealing his motherfucking ATM card.

His hands snapped into fists.

Get hold of yourself! *the Norman Daniels version of Practical-Sensible screamed inside him.* She probably waves at everybody! She probably waves at stray dogs! It's what twats like her do!

Yes. Yes, of course it was. Norman unrolled his hands, raised one of them, and chopped the air in a brief return wave. He even managed a little smile, which reawoke the ache of muscles and tendon—even of bone—at the back of his mouth. Then, as Little Miss Hot Snatch turned back to her gardening, the smile faded and he hurried on with his heart thumping.

He tried to return his thoughts to his current problem—how he was going to isolate one of those bitches (the Head Bitch, preferably; that way he wouldn't have to risk coming up with one who didn't know what he needed to find out) and get her to talk—but his ability to work rationally at this problem seemed to be gone, at least for the time being.

He raised his hands to the sides of his face and massaged the hinges of his jaws. He had hurt himself this way before, but never this badly—what had *he done to Thumper? The paper hadn't said, but this ache in his jaws—and in his teeth, it was in his teeth, too—suggested that it had been plenty.*

I'm in trouble if they catch me, *he told himself.* They'll have photographs of the marks I left on him. They'll have samples of my saliva and . . . well . . . any other fluids I might have left. They have a whole array of exotic tests these days, they test *everything,* and I don't even know if I'm a secretor.

Yes, true, but they weren't going to catch him. He was registered at the Whitestone as Alvin Dodd from New Haven, and if he was pressed, he could even produce a driver's license—a photo *driver's license—that would back that up. If the cops here called the cops back home, they would be told that Norman Daniels was a thousand miles from the midwest, camping in Utah's Zion National Park and taking a well-deserved vacation. They might even tell the cops here not to be stupid, that Norman Daniels was a* bona fide *golden boy. Surely they wouldn't pass on the story of Wendy Yarrow . . . would they?*

No, probably they wouldn't. But sooner or later—

The thing was, he no longer cared about later. These days he only cared about sooner. About finding Rose and having a serious discussion with her. About giving her a present. His bank card, in fact. And it would never be recovered from another trash barrel or from some greasy little fag's wallet, either. He was going to make sure she never lost it or threw it away again. He was going to put it in a safe place. And if he could see only darkness beyond the . . . the insertion of that final gift . . . well, maybe that was a blessing.

Now that his mind had returned to the bank card it dwelled there, as it almost always did these days, in his sleep as well as when he was awake. It was as if that piece of plastic had become a weird green river (the Merchant's instead of the Mississippi) and the run of his thoughts was a stream which flowed into it. All thoughts ran downhill now, eventually losing their identity as they merged into the green current of his obsession. The enormous, unanswerable question surfaced again: How could she have dared? How could she have possibly dared to take it? That she should have left, run away from him, that he supposed he could understand, even if he could not condone it, and even if he knew that she would have to die just for fooling him so completely, for hiding the treachery in her stinking woman's heart so well. But that she should have dared to take his bank card, to take what was his, like the kid who had snuck up the beanstalk and stolen the sleeping giant's golden hen . . .

Without realizing what he was doing, Norman put the first finger of his left hand into his mouth and began to bite down on it. There was pain— quite a lot of it—but this time he didn't feel it; he was deep in his own thoughts. There was a thick pad of callus high up on the first fingers of both hands, because this biting in moments of stress was an old, old habit of his, one that went back to childhood. At first the callus held, but as he continued to think about the bank card, as its green began to deepen in his mind until it had become the near-black of a fir-tree seen at dusk (a color quite unlike the card's actual lime color), it gave way and blood began to flow down his hand and over his lips. He dug his teeth into his finger, relishing the pain, grinding at the flesh, tasting his blood, so salty and so thick, like the taste of Thumper's blood when he had bitten through the cord at the base of his—

"Mommy? Why's that man doing that to his hand?"

"Never mind, come on."

That brought him around. He looked sluggishly over his shoulder, like a man waking from a nap which has been short but deep, and saw a young woman and a little boy of perhaps three walking away from him—she was moving the kid along so fast he was almost running, and when the woman took her own look back, Norman saw she was terrified.

What, exactly, had he been doing?

He looked down at his finger and saw deep, bleeding crescents on either side of it. One of these days he was apt to bite the damned thing right off, bite it off and swallow it. Not that it would be the first time he'd bitten something off. Or swallowed it, either.

That was a bad street to go down, though. He took the handkerchief out of his back pocket and wrapped it around his bleeding finger. Then he *raised his head and looked around. He was surprised to see it was well on the way to being dark; there were lights on in some of the houses. How far had he come? Where, exactly, was he?*

He squinted at the street-sign on the corner of the next intersection and read the words Dearborn Avenue. *On his right was a little mom-and-pop store with a bike rack in front and a sign reading* OVEN-FRESH ROLLS *in the window. Norman's stomach growled. He realized that he was really hungry for the first time since getting off the Continental Express bus and eating cold cereal in the terminal cafeteria, eating it because it was what she would have eaten.*

A few rolls were suddenly just what he wanted, the only thing in the world he wanted . . . but not just *rolls. He wanted* oven-fresh *rolls, like the kind his mother used to make. She was a fat slob who never stopped yelling, but she could cook, all right. No doubt about that. And she had been her own best customer.*

They better be fresh, *Norman thought as he mounted the steps. Inside, he could see an old man pottering around behind the counter.* They better be fresh, *pal, or God help you.*

He was reaching for the doorhandle when one of the posters in the window caught his eye. It was bright yellow, and although he had no way of knowing that Rosie had placed this particular flier herself, he felt something stir inside him even before he saw the words Daughters and Sisters.

He bent forward to read it, eyes suddenly very small and very intent, his heart picking up speed in his chest.

COME OUT AND PLAY WITH US
AT BEAUTIFUL *ETTINGER'S PIER*
AS WE CELEBRATE
CLEAR SKIES AND WARM DAYS WITH

THE 9TH ANNUAL DAUGHTERS AND SISTERS "SWING INTO SUMMER" PICNIC AND CONCERT

SATURDAY, JUNE 4TH

BOOTHS * CRAFTS * GAMES OF CHANCE *
GAMES OF SKILL * RAP DJ FOR THE KIDDIES
! ! ! PLUS ! ! !
THE INDIGO GIRLS, LIVE AND IN CONCERT, 8 P.M.

SINGLE PARENTS, THERE *WILL* BE CHILD-MINDING!

"COME ONE, COME ALL!"

ALL PROCEEDS BENEFIT DAUGHTERS AND SISTERS,
WHO REMIND YOU THAT
VIOLENCE AGAINST *ONE* WOMAN
IS A CRIME AGAINST *ALL* WOMEN

Saturday the fourth. This *Saturday. And would she be there, his rambling Rose? Of course she would be, she and all her new lesbo friends. Cunts of a feather flocked together.*

Norman traced the fifth line up from the bottom of the poster with the finger he had bitten. Bright poppies of blood were already soaking through the handkerchief wrapped around it.

Come one, come all.

That was what it said, and Norman thought he just might take them up on it.

8

Thursday morning, almost eleven-thirty. Rosie took a sip of Evian, rolled it around in her mouth, swallowed, and picked up the sides again.

"*She was coming, all right; this time his ears weren't just playing tricks on him. Peterson could hear the staccato rap of her high heels moving up the hallway. He could imagine her with her purse already open, rummaging in there for her key, worrying about the devil who might be coming along behind when she should have been worried about the one lying in wait. He checked quickly to make sure he still had his knife, then pulled the nylon stroking down over his head. As her key rattled in the lock, Peterson pulled the knife out and—*"

"Cut-cut-*cut!*" Rhoda cried impatiently through the speakers.

Rosie looked up and through the glass wall. She didn't like the way Curt Hamilton was just sitting there by his DAT deck and looking at her with his earphones resting on his collarbones, but what alarmed her was the fact that Rhoda was smoking one of her slim cigarettes right in the control room, ignoring the NO PUFFIN sign on the wall. Rhoda looked like she was having a terrible morning, but she wasn't the only one.

"Rhoda? Did I do something wrong?"

"Not if you wear nylon strokings, I guess," Rhoda said, and tapped ash into a styrofoam cup sitting on the control panel in front of her. "I've had a few guys stroke mine over the years, now that I think about it, but mostly I call them nylon *stockings.*"

For a moment Rosie didn't have the slightest idea what she was talking about, then she mentally replayed the last few sentences she'd read and groaned. "Jeepers, Rhoda, I'm sorry."

Curt slipped his cans back over his ears and pushed a button. *"Kill All My Tomorrows,* take seventy-thr—"

Rhoda put a hand on his arm and said something which filled Rosie's stomach with icewater: "Don't bother." Then she glanced through the window, saw Rosie's stricken face, and offered her a smile which was wan but game. "All's cool, Rosie, I'm just calling lunch half an hour early, that's all. Come on out."

Rosie got up too fast, bumping her left thigh a good one on the bottom of the table and almost overturning the plastic bottle of Evian water. She hurried out of the booth.

Rhoda and Curt were standing just outside, and for a moment Rosie was sure—no, she *knew*—that they had been talking about her.

If you really believe that, Rosie, you probably ought to go see a doctor, Practical-Sensible spoke up sharply. *The kind that shows you inkblots and asks about your potty training.* Rosie usually had very little use for that voice, but this time she welcomed it.

"I can do better," she told Rhoda. "And I will, this afternoon. Honest to God."

Was that true? The hell of it was, she just didn't know. She had tried all morning to submerge herself in *Kill All My Tomorrows* as she had in *The Manta Ray,* but with small success. She would begin to slip into that world where Alma St. George was being pursued by her psychotic admirer, Peterson, and then be hauled out of it by one of the voices from last night: Anna's telling her that her ex-husband, the man who had sent her to Daughters and Sisters, had been murdered, or Bill's, sounding panicky and bewildered as he asked her what was wrong, or, worst of all, her own, telling him to stay away. To just stay away.

Curt patted her on the shoulder. "You're having a bad voice day," he said. "It's like a bad hair day, only worse. We see a lot of it here in the Audio Chamber of Horrors, don't we, Rho?"

"You bet," Rhoda said, but her eyes never paused in their inspection of Rosie's face, and Rosie had a pretty good idea of what Rhoda was seeing. She'd gotten only two or three hours' worth of sleep last night, and she didn't have the sort of high-powered cosmetics that would hide that kind of damage.

And wouldn't know how to use them if I did, she thought.

She'd had a few of the basic makeup items in high school (the time of life, ironically, when she had needed such helps the least), but since marrying Norman she'd gotten along with nothing but a little powder and two or three lipsticks in the most natural shades. If I'd wanted to look at a hooker I would have married one, Norman had told her once.

She thought it was probably her eyes that Rhoda was studying the most carefully: the red lids, the bloodshot whites, the dark circles underneath. After she'd turned out the light she had cried helplessly for over an hour, but she hadn't cried herself to sleep—that would actually have been a blessing. The tears had dried up and she had simply lain there in the darkness, trying not to think and thinking anyway. As midnight passed and slowly receded, a really terrible idea had come to her: that she had been wrong to call Bill, that she had been wrong to deny herself his comfort—and possibly his protection—when she most desperately needed it.

Protection? she thought. *Oh boy, that's a laugh. I know you like him, sweetie, and there's nothing wrong with that, but let's face it: Norman would eat him for lunch.*

Except she had no way of knowing that Norman was in town—that was what Anna had kept emphasizing over and over again. Peter Slowik had espoused a number of causes, not all of them popular. Something else might have gotten him in trouble . . . gotten him killed.

Except Rosie knew. Her *heart* knew. It was Norman.

Still that voice had continued to whisper as the long hours passed. *Did* her heart know? Or was the part of her that was not Practical and Sensible but only Shaky and Terrified just hiding behind that idea? Had it perhaps seized on Anna's call as an excuse to choke off her friendship with Bill before it could develop any further?

She didn't know, but she *did* know the thought she might not see him anymore made her feel miserable . . . and frightened, as well, as if she had lost some vital piece of operating equipment. It was impossible for one person to become dependent on another so quickly, of course, but as one o'clock came and went, and two (and three), the idea began to seem less and less ridiculous. If such instant dependency was impossible, why did she feel so panicky and oddly drained at the thought of never seeing him again?

When she finally *had* fallen asleep, she'd dreamed of riding on his motorcycle again; of wearing the rose madder gown and squeezing him with her bare thighs. When the alarm had wakened her—much too soon after she finally fell asleep—she had been breathing hard and was hot all over, as if with a fever.

"Rosie, *are* you all right?" Rhoda asked.

"Yes," she said. "Just . . ." She glanced at Curtis, then back at Rhoda.

She shrugged and hoisted the corners of her mouth in a lame little smile. "It's just, you know, a bad time of the month for me."

"Uh-huh," Rhoda said. She didn't look convinced. "Well, come on down to the caff with us. We'll drown our sorrows in tuna salad and strawberry milkshakes."

"You bet," Curt said. "My treat."

Rosie's smile was a trifle more genuine this time, but she shook her head. "I'm going to pass. What I want is a good walk, with my face right into the wind. Blow some of the dust out."

"If you don't eat, you'll probably faint dead away around three o'clock," Rhoda said.

"I'll grab a salad. Promise." Rosie was already heading for the creaky old elevator. "Anything more than that and I ruin half a dozen perfectly good takes by burping, anyway."

"It wouldn't make much difference today," Rhoda said. "Twelve-fifteen, okay?"

"You bet," she said, but as the elevator lumbered down the four floors to the lobby, Rhoda's last comment kept clanging in her head: *It wouldn't make much difference today.* What if she *wasn't* any better this afternoon? What if they went from take seventy-three to take eighty to take a-hundred-and-who-knew-how-many? What if, when she met with Mr. Lefferts tomorrow, he decided to give her her notice instead of a contract? What then?

She felt a sudden surge of hatred for Norman. It hit her between the eyes like some dull, heavy object—a doorstop, perhaps, or the blunt end of an old, rusty hatchet. Even if Norman *hadn't* killed Mr. Slowik, even if Norman was still back in that other timezone, he was still following her, just like Peterson was following poor scared Alma St. George. He was following her inside her head.

The elevator settled and the doors opened. Rosie stepped out into the lobby, and the man standing by the building directory turned toward her, his face looking both hopeful and tentative. It was an expression that made him look younger than ever . . . a teenager, almost.

"Hi, Rosie," Bill said.

9

She felt a sudden and amazingly strong urge to run, to do it before he could see the way he had staggered her, and then his eyes fixed on hers, caught them, and running away was no longer an option. She had forgotten about the fascinating green undertints in those eyes, like sunrays caught in shallow water. Instead of running for the lobby doors, she walked slowly toward him, feeling simultaneously afraid and happy. Yet what she felt most of all was an overwhelming sense of relief.

"I told you to stay away from me." She could hear the tremble in her voice.

He reached for her hand. She felt sure she should not let him have it, but she couldn't stop it from happening . . . nor her captured hand from turning in his grip so it could close on his long fingers.

"I know you did," he said simply, "but Rosie, I can't."

That frightened her, and she dropped his hand. She studied his face uncertainly. Nothing like this had ever happened to her, *nothing,* and she had no idea of how to react or behave.

He opened his arms, and perhaps it was simply a gesture meant to underline and emphasize his helplessness, but it was all the gesture her tired, hopeful heart needed; it brushed aside the prissy ditherings of her mind and took charge. Rosie found herself stepping like a sleepwalker into the opening his arms made, and when they closed around her, she pressed her face against his shoulder and closed her eyes. And as his hands touched her hair, which she had left unplaited and loose upon her shoulders this morning, she had a strange and marvellous feeling: it was as if she had just woken up. As if she *had* been asleep, not just now, as she entered the circle of his arms, not just this morning since the alarm had blared her out of her motorcycle dream, but for years and years, like Snow White after the apple. But now she was awake again, wide awake, and looking around with eyes that were just beginning to see.

"I'm glad you came," she said.

10

They walked slowly east along Lake Drive, facing into a strong, warm wind. When he put his arm around her, she gave him a small smile. They were three miles west of the lake at this point, but Rosie felt she could walk all the way there if he would just keep his arm around her like that. All the way to the lake, and maybe all the way across it as well, stepping calmly from one wave-top to the next.

"What are you smiling at?" he asked her.

"Oh, nothing," she said. "Just feel like smiling, I guess."

"You're really glad I came?"

"Yes. I didn't sleep much last night. I kept thinking I'd made a mistake. I guess I *did* make a mistake, but . . . Bill?"

"I'm here."

"I did it because I feel more for you than I thought I'd ever feel for any man again in my whole life, and it's all happened so *fast* . . . I must be crazy to be telling you this."

He squeezed her briefly closer. "You're not crazy."

"I called you and told you to stay away because something's happening—*may* be happening—and I didn't want you to be hurt. Not for anything. And I still don't."

"It's Norman, isn't it? As in Bates. He's come looking for you after all."

"My *heart* says he has," Rosie said, speaking very carefully, "and my *nerves* say he has, but I'm not sure I trust my heart—it's been scared for so long—and my nerves . . . my nerves are just shot."

She glanced at her watch, then at the hotdog stand on the corner just ahead. There were benches on a small grassy strip nearby, and secretaries eating their lunches.

"Would you buy a lady a foot-long with sauerkraut?" she asked. Suddenly a case of afternoon burps seemed like the least important thing in the world. "I haven't had one of those since I was a kid."

"I think it could be arranged."

"We can sit on one of those benches and I'll tell you about Norman, as in Bates. Then you can decide if you want to be around me or not. If you decide you don't want to be, I'll understand—"

"Rosie, I won't—"

"Don't say that. Not until I've told you about him. And you'd better eat before I start, or you're apt to lose your appetite."

11

Five minutes later he came over to the bench where she was sitting. He was carefully balancing a tray on which there were two foot-long dogs and two paper cups of lemonade. She took a dog and a cup, set her drink on the bench beside her, then looked at him gravely. "You probably ought to stop buying me meals. I'm starting to feel like the waif on the UNICEF posters."

"I *like* buying you meals," he said. "You're too thin, Rosie."

That's not what Norman says, she thought, but it was hardly the right remark, under the circumstances. She wasn't sure what was, and found herself thinking of the half-witty repartee the characters spouted on TV shows like *Melrose Place.* She could certainly use a little of that bright chatter now. *Silly me, I forgot to bring my screenwriter with me,* she thought. Instead of talking, she looked down at her krautdog and began poking the bun, her forehead creased and her mouth intent, as if this were some arcane pre-ingestion ritual which had been handed down in her family, mother to daughter, over the generations.

"So tell me about Norman, Rosie."

"All right. Just let me think how to start."

She took a bite of her dog, relishing the sting of the sauerkraut against her tongue, then sipped her lemonade. It occurred to her that Bill mightn't want to know her anymore when she had finished, that he would feel nothing but horror and disgust for a woman who could live with a creature like Norman for all those years, but it was too late to start worrying about things like that. She opened her mouth and began to speak. Her voice sounded steady enough, and that had a calming effect on her.

She began by telling him about a fifteen-year-old girl who'd felt extraordinarily pretty with a pink ribbon tied in her hair, and how this girl had gone to a varsity basketball game one night only because her Future Homemakers meeting had been cancelled at the last minute and she had two hours to kill before her father came and picked her up. Or maybe, she said, she'd just wanted people to see how pretty she looked, wearing that ribbon, and the school library was empty. A boy in a letter-jacket had sat down beside her in the bleachers, a big boy with broad shoulders, a senior who would have been out there, running up and down the court with the rest of them, if he hadn't been kicked off the team in December for fighting. She went on, listening to her mouth spill out things she had been positive she would take untold with her to her grave. Not about the tennis racket, that one she *would* take untold to her grave, but about how Norman had bitten her on their honeymoon and how she had tried to persuade herself it was a lovebite, and about the Norman-assisted miscarriage, and about the crucial differences between face-hitting and back-hitting. "So I have to pee a lot," she said, smiling nervously down at her own hands, "but that's getting better." She told him about the times, early in their marriage, when he had burned her toes or the tips of her fingers with his cigarette lighter; hilariously enough, that particular torment had ceased when Norman quit smoking. She told him about the night Norman had come home from work, sat silently in front of the TV during the news, holding his dinner on his lap but not eating it; how he had put his plate aside when Dan Rather had finished and how he had begun poking her with the tip of a pencil that had been lying on the table at one end of the couch. He poked hard enough to hurt and leave little black dots like moles on her skin, but not quite hard enough to draw blood. She told Bill there were other times when Norman had hurt her worse, but that he had never scared her more. Mostly it was his silence. When she talked to him, tried to find out what was wrong, he wouldn't reply. He only kept walking after her as she retreated (she hadn't wanted to run; that would very likely have been like dropping a sulphur match into a barrel of gunpowder), not answering her questions and ignoring her outstretched, splay-fingered hands. He kept poking her arms and her shoulders and her upper chest—she had been wearing one of those shell tops with a mildly scooped neck—with the pencil and making a little plosive noise under his breath every time the pencil's blunt point dug into her skin: *Poo! Poo! Poo!* At last she had been huddled in the corner with her knees up against her breasts and her hands laced over the back of her head and he had been kneeling in front of her, his face serious, almost studious, and he kept poking her with the pencil and making that noise. She told Bill that by then she was sure he was going to kill her, that she was going to be the only woman in the history of the world to be stabbed to death with a Mongol No. 2 pencil . . . and what she remembered telling herself over and over again was that she mustn't scream because the neighbors would hear and she didn't want to be found this way. Not still alive, at least. It was too shameful. Then, just as she was nearing the point where she knew she was going to begin screaming in spite of herself, Norman had gone into the bathroom and shut the door. He was in there a long time and she had thought about running then—just running out the door and into the anywhere—but it had been night, and he had been in the house. If he had come out and found her gone, she said, he would have chased her and caught her and killed her, she knew it. "He would have snapped my neck like the wishbone in a chicken," she told Bill without looking up. She had promised herself that she *would* leave, though; she would do it the very next time he hurt her. But after that night he hadn't laid a hand on her for a long time. Five months, maybe. And when he *did* go after her again, at first it hadn't been so bad and she had told herself that if she could stand up to being poked over and over again with a pencil, she could put up with a few punches. She had gone on thinking that until 1985, when things had suddenly escalated. She told him how scary Norman had been that year, because of the trouble with Wendy Yarrow.

"That was the year you had your miscarriage, wasn't it?" Bill asked.

"Yes," she told her hands. "He broke one of my ribs, too. Or maybe it was a couple. I don't really remember anymore, isn't that *awful?*"

He didn't reply, so she hurried on, telling him that the worst parts (other than the miscarriage, of course) were the long, scary silences when he would simply look at her, breathing so loudly through his nose that he sounded like an animal getting ready to charge. Things had gotten a little better, she said, after her miscarriage. She told him about how she had started to slip a few cogs at the end, how time sometimes got away from her when she was in her rocker and how sometimes, when she was setting the table for supper and listening for the sound of Norman's car pulling into the driveway, she'd realize she'd taken eight or even nine showers in the course of the day. Usually with the bathroom lights off. "I liked to shower in the dark," she said, still not daring to look up from her hands. "It was like a wet closet."

She finished by telling him about Anna's call, which Anna had made in a hurry for one important reason. She had learned a detail which hadn't been in the newspaper story, a detail the police were holding back to help them weed out any false confessions or bad tips they might receive. Peter Slowik had been bitten over three dozen times, and at least one part of his anatomy was missing. The police believed that the killer had taken it with him . . . one way or another. Anna knew from Therapy Circle that Rosie McClendon, whose first significant contact in this city had been with her ex-husband, had been married to a biter. There might be no connection, Anna had been quick to add. But . . . on the other hand . . .

"A biter," Bill said quietly. It sounded almost as if he were talking to himself. "Is that what they call men like him? Is that the term?"

"I guess it is," Rosie said. And then, maybe because she was afraid he wouldn't believe her (would think she had been "fibulating," in Normanspeak), she slid her shoulder briefly out of the pink Tape Engine tee-shirt she was wearing and showed him the old white ring of scar there, like the remnant of a shark-bite. That had been the first one, her honeymoon present. Then she turned up her left forearm, showing him another one. This time it wasn't a bite it made her think of; for some reason it made her think of smooth white faces almost hidden in lush green undergrowth.

"This one bled quite a bit, then got infected," she told him. She spoke in the tone of someone relaying routine information—that Gramma had called earlier, perhaps, or that the mailman had left a package. "I didn't go to the doctor, though. Norman brought home a big bottle of antibiotic tablets. I took them and got better. He knows all sorts of people he can get things from. He calls people like that 'daddy's little helpers.' That's sort of funny when you think of it, isn't it?"

She was still talking mostly to her hands, which were clasped in her lap, but she finally dared a quick look up at him, to gauge his reaction to the things she had been saying. What she saw stunned her.

"What?" he asked hoarsely. "What, Rosie?"

"You're crying," she said, and now her own voice wavered.

Bill looked surprised. "No, I'm not. At least, I don't *think* I am."

She reached out with one finger, drew a gentle semicircle below his eye with it, and then held the tip up for him to see. He examined it closely, biting his lower lip.

"You didn't eat much, either." Half of his dog was still on his plate, with mustardy sauerkraut spilling out of the bun. Bill pitched the paper plate into the trash barrel beside the bench, then looked back at her, absently wiping at the wetness on his cheeks.

Rosie felt a bleak certainty steal over her. Now he would ask why she had stayed with Norman, and while she wouldn't get up off the park bench and leave (any more than she had ever left the house on Westmoreland Street until April), it would put the first barrier between them, because it was a question she couldn't answer. She didn't *know* why she had stayed with him, any more than she knew why, in the end, it had taken just a single drop of blood to transform her entire life. She only knew that the shower had been the best place in the house, dark and wet and full of steam, and that sometimes half an hour in Pooh's Chair felt like five minutes, and that why wasn't a question that had any meaning when you were living in hell. Hell was motiveless. The women in Therapy Circle had understood that; no one had asked her why she stayed. They knew. From their own experiences they knew. She had an idea that some of them might even know about the tennis racket . . . or things even worse than the tennis racket.

But when Bill finally asked a question, it was so different from the one she had expected that for a moment she could only flounder.

"What are the chances he might have killed the woman who was making all the trouble for him back in '85? That Wendy Yarrow?"

She was shocked, but it wasn't the kind of shock one feels when asked an unthinkable question; she was shocked in the manner of one who sees a known face in some fabulously unlikely locale. The question he had spoken aloud was one which had circled, unarticulated and thus not quite formed, at the back of her mind for years.

"Rosie? I asked you what you thought the chances were—"

"I think they might have been . . . well, pretty good, actually."

"It was convenient for him when she died like that, wasn't it? Saved him from watching the whole thing get hung out in civil court."

"Yes."

"If she had been bitten, do you think the newspapers would have printed it?"

"I don't know. Maybe not." She looked at her watch and got quickly to her feet. "Oh, boy, I have to go, and right now. Rhoda wanted to start in again at twelve-fifteen and it's ten past already."

They started back side by side. She found herself wishing he would put his arm around her again, and just as part of her mind was telling her not to be greedy and another part (Practical-Sensible) was telling her not to ask for trouble, he did just that.

I think I'm falling in love with him.

It was the lack of amazement in that thought which prompted the next one: *No, Rosie, I think that's actually yesterday's headline. I think it's already happened.*

"What did Anna say about the police?" he asked her. "Does she want you to go someplace and make a report?"

She stiffened within the circle of his arm, her throat drying out as adrenaline tipped into her system. All it took was that single word. The p-word.

Cops are brothers. Norman had told her this over and over. *Law enforcement is a family and cops are brothers.* Rosie didn't know how true it was, how far they would go to stick up for each other—or *cover* up for each other—but she knew that the cops Norman brought home from time to time seemed eerily like Norman himself, and she knew he had never said a word against any of them, even his first partner on detectives, a crafty, grafty old pig named Gordon Satterwaite, whom Norman had loathed. And of course there was Harley Bissington, whose hobby —at least when in attendance at Casa Daniels—had been undressing Rosie with his eyes. Harley had gotten some kind of skin-cancer and taken early retirement three years ago, but he had been Norman's partner back in 1985, when the Richie Bender/Wendy Yarrow thing had gone down. And if it had gone down the way Rosie suspected it had, then Harley had stuck up for Norman. Stuck up for him big-time. And not just because he'd been in on it himself, either. He'd done it because law enforcement was a family and cops were brothers. Cops saw the world in a different way from the nine-to-fivers ("the Kmart shoppers," in Normanspeak); cops saw it with its skin off and its nerves sizzling. It made all of them different, it made some of them a *lot* different . . . and then there was Norman.

"I'm not going *anywhere near* the police," Rosie said, speaking rapidly. "Anna said I don't have to and nobody can make me. The police are *his* friends. His *brothers.* They stick up for each other, they—"

"Take it easy," he said, sounding a little alarmed. "It's okay, just take it easy."

"I *can't* take it easy! I mean, you don't *know.* That's really why I called you and said I couldn't see you, because you don't know how it is . . . how *he* is . . . and how it works between him and all the rest of them. If I went to the police *here,* they'd check with the police *there.* And if one of them . . . someone who works with him, who's been on stakeouts with him at three in the morning, who's trusted his life to him . . ." It was Harley she was thinking of, Harley who couldn't stop looking at her breasts and always had to check on where the hem of her skirt finished up when she sat down.

"Rosie, you don't have to—"

"Yes I *do!*" she said with a fierceness that was entirely unlike her. "If a cop like that knew how to get in touch with Norman, he *would.* He'd say I'd been talking about him. If I gave them my address—and they make you do that when you file a complaint—he'd give him that, too."

"I'm sure that no cop would—"

"Have you ever had them in your house, playing poker or watching *Debbie Does Dallas?*"

"Well . . . no. No, but . . ."

"I have. I've heard what they talk about, and I know how they look at the rest of the world. They see it that way, as the rest of the world. Even the best of them do. There's them . . . and there's the Kmart shoppers. That's all."

He opened his mouth to say something, he wasn't sure what, then closed it again. The idea that Norman might find out the address of her room on Trenton Street as the result of some cops' jungle telegraph had a sort of persuasiveness to it, but this was not the main reason he kept quiet. The look on her face—the look of a woman who has made a hateful and unwilling regression back to an unhappier time—suggested that he could say nothing which would convince her, anyway. She was scared of the cops, that was all, and he was old enough to know that not all bogies can be slain by mere logic.

"Besides, Anna said I didn't have to. Anna said if it *was* Norman, *they'd* be seeing him first, not me."

Bill thought it over and decided it made sense. "What will she do about it?"

"She's already started. She faxed a women's group back home—where

I came from, anyway—and told them what might be happening here. She asked them if they could send her any information about Norman, and they faxed back a whole bunch of stuff just an hour later, including a picture."

Bill raised his eyebrows. "Fast work, especially after business hours."

"My husband is now a hero back home," she said dully. "Probably hasn't had to pay for a drink in a month. He was in charge of the team that broke up a big drug-ring. His picture was on the front page of the paper two or three days running."

Bill whistled. Maybe she wasn't so paranoid, after all.

"The woman who took Anna's request went a step further," Rosie continued. "She called the Police Department and asked if she could speak to him. She spun a big story about how her group wanted to give him a Women's Commendation Award."

He considered this, then burst out laughing. Rosie smiled wanly.

"The duty sergeant checked his computer and said that Lieutenant Daniels was on vacation. Somewhere out west, he thought."

"But he *could* be vacationing here," Bill said thoughtfully.

"Yes. And if someone gets hurt, it'll be all my f—"

He put his hands on her shoulders and swung her around. Her eyes flew wide, and he saw the beginning of a cringe. It was a look that hurt his heart in a new, strange way. He suddenly remembered a story he had heard at the Zion American Center, where he had gone to religious-study classes and USY until he was nine. Something about how, back in the days of the prophets, people had sometimes been stoned to death. At the time he had thought it the most fabulously cruel form of punishment ever invented, much worse than the firing squad or the electric chair, a form of execution which could never be justified. Now, seeing what Norman Daniels had done to this lovely woman with her fragile, vulnerable face, he wondered.

"Don't say fault," he told her. "You didn't make Norman."

She blinked, as if this were a thought which had never occurred to her before.

"How in God's name could he have found this guy Slowik in the first place?"

"By being me," she said.

Bill looked at her. She nodded.

"It sounds crazy, but it's not. He can really do that. I've *seen* him do it. It's probably how he busted that drug-ring back home."

"Hunch? Intuition?"

"More. It's almost like telepathy. He calls it trolling."

Bill shook his head. "We're talking about a seriously strange guy, aren't we?"

That surprised her into a little laugh. "Oh boy, you don't have any idea! Anyway, the women at D and S have all seen his picture, and they'll be taking special precautions, especially at the picnic on Saturday. Some of them will be carrying Mace . . . the ones who might actually remember to use it in a jackpot situation, Anna says. And that was all sounding good to me, but then she said 'Don't worry, Rosie, we've been through scares like this before' and that turned it around again. Because when a man gets killed—a nice man like the one that rescued me in that horrible bus station—it's *not* just a scare."

Her voice was rising, picking up speed again. He took her hand and stroked it. "I know, Rosie," he said in what he hoped was a soothing voice. "I know it's not."

"She thinks she knows what she's doing—Anna, I mean—that she's been through this before just because she's called the cops on some drunk man who threw a brick through one of the windows or hung around and spit on his wife when she came out to pick up the morning paper. But she's never been through *anything* like Norman, and she doesn't know it, and that's what scares *me*." She paused, working to get control of herself, then smiled up at him. "Anyway, she says I don't have to be involved at all, at least not at this point."

"I'm glad."

The Corn Building was just ahead now. "You didn't say anything about my hair." She looked up again, a quick, shy glance this time. "Does that mean you didn't notice it or you don't like it?"

He glanced at it and grinned. "I *did* notice and I *do* like it, but I had this other thing on my mind—being afraid I might never see you again, I mean."

"I'm sorry you were so upset." She was, but she was also *glad* he had been upset. Had she ever felt even remotely like this when she and Norman had been courting? She couldn't remember. She had a clear memory of him feeling her up under a blanket at a stock-car race one night, but for the moment, at least, everything else was lost in a haze.

"You got the idea from the woman in the painting, didn't you? The one you bought the day I met you."

"Maybe," she said cautiously. Did he think that was strange, and was that maybe the real reason he hadn't said anything about her hair?

But he surprised her again, perhaps this time even more than when he had asked about Wendy Yarrow.

"When most women change their hair color, what they look like is women who've changed their hair color," he said. "Most times men pretend they don't know that, but they do. But you . . . it's like the way your hair looked when you came into the shop was a dye-job and this is the way it really is. Probably that sounds like the most outrageous con you've ever heard, but it's the truth . . . and blondes usually look the least realistic. You ought to braid it like the woman in the picture, too, though. It'd make you look like a Viking princess. Sexy as hell."

That word hit a big red button inside her, kicking off sensations that were both powerfully attractive and terribly alarming. *I don't like sex,* she thought. *I have never liked sex, but—*

Rhoda and Curt were walking toward them from the other direction. The four of them met in front of the Corn Building's elderly revolving doors. Rhoda's eyes scanned Bill up and down with bright curiosity.

"Bill, these are the people I work with," Rosie said. Instead of subsiding, the heat continued to rise in her cheeks. "Rhoda Simons and Curtis Hamilton. Rhoda, Curt, this is—" For one brief, abysmally black second she found herself completely unable to remember the name of this man who already meant so much to her. Then, thankfully, it came. "Bill Steiner," she finished.

"Goodtameetcha," Curt said, and shook Bill's hand. He glanced toward the building, clearly ready to slide his head back between the earphones.

"Any friend of Rosie's, as the saying goes," Rhoda said, and held out her own hand. The slim bracelets on her wrist jangled mutedly.

"My pleasure," Bill said, and turned back to Rosie. "Are we still on for Saturday?"

She thought furiously, then nodded.

"I'll pick you up at eight-thirty. Remember to dress warm."

"I will." She could feel the blush spreading all the way down her body now, turning her nipples hard and even making her fingers tingle. The way he was looking at her hit that hot-button again, but this time it was more attractive than scary. She was suddenly struck by an urge—comical but amazingly strong, nevertheless—to put her arms around him . . . and her legs . . . and then simply climb him like a tree.

"Well, I'll see you, then," Bill said. He bent forward and pecked the corner of her mouth. "Rhoda, Curtis, it was nice to meet you."

He turned and walked off, whistling.

"I'll say this for you, Rosie, your taste is excellent," Rhoda said. "Those *eyes!*"

"We're just friends," Rosie said awkwardly. "I met him . . ." She trailed off. Suddenly explaining how she had met him seemed complicated, not to mention embarrassing. She shrugged, laughed nervously. "Well, you know."

"Yes, I do," Rhoda said, watching Bill's progress up the street. Then she turned back to Rosie and laughed delightedly. "I *do* know. Within this old wreck of femininity there beats the heart of a true romantic. One who hopes you and Mr. Steiner will be very good friends. Meantime, are you ready to go back at it?"

"Yes," Rosie said.

"Are we going to see an improvement over this morning, now that you've got your . . . other business more or less in order?"

"I'm sure there will be a big improvement," Rosie said, and there was.

VI

THE
TEMPLE
OF
THE BULL

1

Before going to bed that Thursday night, Rosie plugged in her new phone again and used it to call Anna. She asked if Anna had heard anything new, or if anyone had seen Norman in the city. Anna gave a firm no to both questions, told her all was quiet, and then offered the old one about no news being good news. Rosie had her doubts about that, but kept them to herself. Instead, she offered Anna hesitant condolences on the loss of her ex-husband, wondering if Miss Manners had rules for handling such situations.

"Thanks, Rosie," Anna said. "Peter was a strange and difficult man. He loved people, but he wasn't very loveable himself."

"He seemed very nice to me."

"I'm sure. To strangers he was the Good Samaritan. To his family and the people who tried to be his friends—I've belonged to both groups, so I know—he was more like the Levite who passed by on the other side. Once, during Thanksgiving dinner, he picked up the turkey and threw it at his brother Hal. I can't remember for sure what the argument was about, but it was probably either the PLO or César Chávez. It was usually one or the other."

Anna sighed.

"There's going to be a remembrance circle for him Saturday afternoon—we all sit around in folding chairs, like drunks at an AA meeting, and take turns talking about him. At least I *think* that's what we do."

"It sounds nice."

"Do you think so?" Anna asked. Rosie could imagine her arching her eyebrows in that unconsciously arrogant way of hers, and looking more like Maude than ever. "*I* think it sounds rather silly, but perhaps you're right. Anyway, I'll leave the picnic long enough to do that, but I'll come back with only a few regrets. The battered women of this city have lost a friend, there's no doubt about that much."

"If it was Norman who did it—"

195

"I knew *that* was coming," Anna said. "I've been working with women who've been bent, folded, stapled, and mutilated for a lot of years, and I know the masochistic grandiosity they develop. It's as much a part of the battered-woman syndrome as the disassociation and the depression. Do you remember when the space shuttle *Challenger* exploded?"

"Yes . . ." Rosie was mystified, but she remembered, all right.

"Later that day, I had a woman come to me in tears. There were red marks all over her cheeks and arms; she'd been slapping and pinching herself. She said it was her fault those men and that nice woman teacher had died. When I asked why, she explained she'd written not one but *two* letters supporting the manned space program, one to the Chicago *Tribune* and one to the U.S. Representative from her district.

"After awhile, battered women start accepting the blame, that's all. And not just for some things, either—for *everything.*"

Rosie thought of Bill, walking her back to the Corn Building with his arm around her waist. *Don't say fault,* he'd told her. *You didn't make Norman.*

"I didn't understand that part of the syndrome for a long time," Anna said, "but now I think I do. *Someone* has to be to blame, or all the pain and depression and isolation make no sense. You'd go crazy. Better to be guilty than crazy. But it's time for you to get past that choice, Rosie."

"I don't understand."

"Yes, you do," Anna said calmly, and from there they had passed on to other subjects.

2

Twenty minutes after saying goodbye to Anna, Rosie lay in bed with her eyes open and her fingers laced together under her pillow, looking up into the darkness as faces floated through her mind like untethered balloons. Rob Lefferts, looking like Mr. Pennybags on the yellow Community Chest cards; she saw him offering her the one that said Get Out of Jail Free. Rhoda Simons with a pencil stuck in her hair, telling Rosie it was nylon stockings, not nylon strokings. Gert Kinshaw, a human version of the planet Jupiter, wearing sweatpants and a man's V-necked undershirt, both size XXXL. Cynthia Someone (Rosie still couldn't quite remember her last name), the cheerful punk-rocker with the tu-tone hair, saying she had once sat for hours in front of a picture where the river had actually seemed to be moving.

And Bill, of course. She saw his hazel eyes with the green undertints, saw the way his dark hair grew back from his temples, saw even the tiny circle of scar on his right earlobe, which he'd once had pierced (perhaps back in college, as the result of a drunken dare) and then allowed to grow back over. She felt the touch of his hand on her waist, warm palm, strong fingers; felt the occasional brush of her hip against his, and wondered if he had been excited, touching her. She was now willing to admit that the touch had certainly excited *her*. He was so different from Norman that it was like meeting a visitor from another star-system.

She closed her eyes. Drifted deeper.

Another face came floating out of the darkness. Norman's face. Norman was smiling, but his gray eyes were as cold as chips of ice. *I'm trolling for you, sweetie,* Norman said. *Lying in my own bed, not all that far away, and trolling for you. Pretty soon I'll be talking to you. Right up close, I'll be talking to you. It should be a fairly short conversation. And when it's over—*

He raised his hand. There was a pencil in it, a Mongol No. 2. It had been sharpened to a razor point.

This time I won't bother with your arms or shoulders. This time I'm going straight for your eyes. Or maybe your tongue. How do you think that would be, sweetie? Having a pencil driven straight through your quacking, lying t—

Her eyes flew open and Norman's face disappeared. She closed them again and summoned Bill's face. For a moment she was sure it wouldn't come, that Norman's face would return instead, but it didn't.

We're going out on Saturday, she thought. *We're going to spend the day together. If he wants to kiss me, I'll let him. If he wants to hold me and touch me, I'll let him. It's nuts, how much I want to be with him.*

She began to drift again, and now she supposed she must be dreaming about the picnic she and Bill were going on the day after tomorrow. Someone else was picnicking nearby, someone with a baby. She could hear it crying, very faintly. Then, louder, came a rumble of thunder.

Like in my picture, she thought. *I'll tell him about my picture while we eat. I forgot to tell him today, because there were so many other things to talk about, but . . .*

The thunder rolled again, closer and sharper. This time the sound filled her with dismay. Rain would spoil their picnic, rain would wash out the Daughters and Sisters picnic at Ettinger's Pier, rain might even cause the concert to be cancelled.

Don't worry, Rosie, the thunder's only in the picture, and this is all a dream.

But if it was a dream, how come she could still feel the pillow lying on her wrists and forearms? How come she could still feel her fingers laced together and the light blanket lying on top of her? How come she could still hear city traffic outside her window?

Crickets sang and hummed: *reep-reep-reep-reep-reep.*

The baby cried.

The insides of her eyelids suddenly flashed purple, as if with lightning, and the thunder rolled again, closer than ever.

Rosie gasped and sat up straight in bed, her heart thumping hard in her chest. There was no lightning. No thunder. She thought she could still hear crickets, yes, but that might just have been her ears playing tricks on her. She looked across the room toward the window and made out the shadowy rectangle leaning against the wall below it. The picture of Rose Madder. Tomorrow she would slip it into a grocery sack and take it to work with her. Rhoda or Curt would probably know a place nearby where she could get it re-framed.

Still, faintly, she could hear crickets.

From the park, she thought, lying back down.

Even with the window closed? Practical-Sensible asked. She sounded dubious, but not really anxious. *Are you sure, Rosie?*

Sure she was. It was almost summer, after all, lots more crickets for your buck, shoppers, and what difference did it make, anyhow? All right, maybe there *was* something odd about the picture. More likely the oddities were in her own mind, where the final kinks were still being worked out, but say it really *was* the picture. So what? She sensed no actual *badness* about it.

But can you say it doesn't feel dangerous, *Rosie?* Now there *was* a touch of anxiety in Practical-Sensible's voice. *Never mind evil, or badness, or whatever you want to call it. Can you say it doesn't feel* dangerous?

No, she *couldn't* say that, but on the other hand, there was danger everywhere. Just look at what had happened to Anna Stevenson's ex-husband.

Except she didn't *want* to look at what had happened to Peter Slowik; she didn't want to go back down what was sometimes called Guilty Street in Therapy Circle. She wanted to think about Saturday, and what it might feel like to be kissed by Bill Steiner. Would he put his hands on her shoulders, or around her waist? What, exactly, would his mouth feel like on hers? Would he . . .

Rosie's head slipped over to the side. Thunder rumbled. The crickets hummed, louder than ever, and now one of them began to hop across the floor toward the bed, but Rosie didn't notice. This time the string tethering her mind to her body had broken, and she floated away into darkness.

3

A flash of light woke her, not purple this time but a brilliant white. It was followed by thunder—not a rumble but a roar.

Rosie sat up in bed, gasping, clutching the top blanket to her neck. There was another flash, and in it she saw her table, the kitchen counter, the little sofa that was really not much more than a loveseat, the door to the tiny bathroom standing open, the daisy-printed shower curtain run back on its rings. The light was so bright and her eyes so unprepared that she continued to see these things even after the room had fallen dark again, only with the colors reversed. She realized she could still hear the baby crying, but the crickets had stopped. And a wind was blowing. That she could feel as well as hear. It lifted her hair from her temples, and she heard the rattle-slither-flump of pages. She had left the Xeroxed sides of the next "Richard Racine" novel on the table, and the wind had sent them cascading all over the floor.

This is no dream, she thought, and swung her feet out of bed. As she did, she looked toward the window and her breath stuck solid in her throat. Either the window was gone, or the wall had become *all* window.

In any case, the view was no longer of Tremont Street and Bryant Park; it was of a woman in a rose madder chiton standing on top of an overgrown hill, looking down at the ruins of a temple. But now the hem of her short gown was rippling against the woman's long, smooth thighs; now Rosie could see the fine blonde hairs which had escaped her plait wavering like plankton in the wind, and the purple-black thunderheads rushing across the sky. Now she could see the shaggy pony's head move as it cropped grass.

And if it was a window, it was wide open. As she watched, the pony poked its muzzle into her room, sniffed at the floorboards, found them uninteresting, pulled back, and began to crop on its own side once more.

More lightning, another roll of thunder. The wind gusted again, and Rosie heard the spilled pages stirring and swirling around in the kitchen alcove. The hem of her nightgown fluttered against her legs as she got up and walked slowly toward the picture which now covered the whole wall from floor to ceiling and side to side. The wind blew back her hair, and she could smell sweet impending rain.

It won't be long now, either, she thought. *I'm going to get drenched. We all are, I guess.*

ROSE, WHAT ARE YOU THINKING? Practical-Sensible screamed. *WHAT IN GOD'S NAME ARE Y—*

Rosie squashed the voice—at that moment it seemed she had heard enough of it to last her a lifetime—and stopped before the wall that was no longer a wall. Just ahead, no more than five feet away, was the blonde woman in the chiton. She hadn't turned, but Rosie could now see the little tilts and adjustments of her upraised hand as she looked down the hill, and the rise and fall of her barely glimpsed left breast as she breathed.

Rosie took a deep breath and stepped into the picture.

4

It was at least ten degrees cooler on the other side, and the high grass tickled her ankles and shins. For a moment, she thought she heard a baby crying again, very faintly, but then the sound was gone. She looked back over her shoulder, expecting to see her room, but it was gone, too. A gnarled old olive tree spread its roots and branches at the place where she had stepped through into this world. Beneath it she saw an artist's easel with a stool in front of it. Standing open on the stool was a painter's box full of brushes and colors.

The canvas propped on the easel was exactly the size of the picture Rosie had bought in the Liberty City Loan & Pawn. It showed her room on Trenton Street, as seen from the wall where she had hung Rose Madder. There was a woman, clearly Rosie herself, standing in the middle of the room, facing the door which gave on the second-floor hallway. Her posture and position were not quite the same as the posture and position of the woman looking down on the ruined temple—her hand was not upraised, for instance—but it was close enough to frighten Rosie badly. There was something else frightening about the picture, as well: the woman had on dark blue tapered slacks and a pink sleeveless top. This was the outfit Rosie had already planned to wear when she went motor-cycling with Bill. *I'll have to wear something different,* she thought wildly, as if by changing her clothes in the future she could change what she was seeing now.

Something nuzzled her upper arm, and Rosie gave a small scream. She turned and saw the pony looking at her with apologetic brown eyes. Overhead, thunder rumbled.

A woman was standing beside the trim pony-cart to which the shaggy little beast was harnessed. She was wearing a many-layered red robe. It was ankle-length but gauzy, almost transparent; Rosie could see the warm tints of her *café-au-lait* skin through its artful layers. Lightning flared across the sky, and for a moment Rosie again saw what she had first seen in the painting not long after Bill had brought her back from Pop's Kitchen: the shadow of the cart lying on the grass, and the shadow of the woman growing out of it.

"Don't you worry, now," the woman in the red robe said. "Radamanthus the *least* of your worries. He don't bite nothing but grass and clover. He's just gettin a little smell on you, that's all."

Rosie felt a sudden, overwhelming sense of relief as she realized that this was the woman Norman had always referred to (in tones of aggrieved bitterness) as "that slutty high-yellow gal." It was Wendy Yarrow, but Wendy Yarrow was dead, and so this was a dream, Q.E.D. No matter how realistic it felt or how realistic the details might be (wiping a tiny bit of moisture off her upper arm, for instance, left there by the pony's enquiring muzzle), it was a dream.

Of course it is, she told herself. *No one actually steps through pictures, Rosie.*

That had little or no power over her. The idea that the woman attending the cart was the long-dead Wendy Yarrow did, however.

The wind gusted, and once again the sound of the crying baby came to her. Now Rosie saw something else: sitting on the pony-cart's seat was a large basket made of green woven rushes. Fluffs of silk ribbon decorated the handle, and there were silk bows on the corners. The hem of a pink blanket, clearly hand-woven, hung over the end.

"Rosie."

The voice was low and sweetly husky. Nevertheless, it sent a scutter of gooseflesh up Rosie's back. There was something wrong with it, and she had an idea that wrongness might be something only another woman could hear—a man heard a voice like that, immediately thought about sex, and forgot everything else. But there *was* something wrong with it. *Badly* wrong.

"Rosie," it said again, and suddenly she knew: it was as if the voice were striving to be human. Striving to remember *how* to be human.

"Girl, don't you look straight at her," the woman in the red robe said. She sounded anxious. "That's not for the likes of you."

"No, I don't want to," Rosie said. "I want to go home."

"I don't blame you, but it's too late for that," the woman said, and stroked the pony's neck. Her dark eyes were grave and her mouth was tight. "Don't touch her, either. She don't mean you no harm, but she ain't got good control of herself no more." She tapped her temple with one finger.

Rosie turned reluctantly toward the woman in the chiton, and took a single step forward. She was fascinated by the texture of the woman's back, her bare shoulder, and the lower part of her neck. The skin was finer than watered silk. But farther up on her neck . . .

Rosie didn't know what those gray shadows lurking just below her hairline could be, and didn't think she *wanted* to know. Bites were her first wild thought, but they weren't bites. Rosie knew bites. Was it leprosy? Something worse? Something contagious?

"Rosie," the sweet, husky voice said for the third time, and there was something in it that made Rosie feel like screaming, the way that seeing Norman smile had sometimes made her feel like screaming.

This woman is mad. Whatever else is wrong with her—the patches on her skin—is secondary to that. She is mad.

Lightning flashed. Thunder rumbled. And, on the fitfully gusting wind, from the direction of the ruined temple at the foot of the hill, came the distant wail of an infant.

"Who are you?" she asked. "Who are you, and why am I here?"

For an answer, the woman held out her right arm and turned it over, revealing an old white ring of scar on the underside. "This one bled quite a bit, then got infected," she said in her sweetly husky voice.

Rosie held out her own arm. It was the left instead of the right, but the mark itself was exactly the same. A small but terrible packet of knowledge came to her then: if she were to put on the short rose madder chiton, she would wear it so that her right shoulder was bare instead of her left, and if she were to own the gold armlet, she would clasp it above her left elbow instead of her right.

The woman on the hill was her mirror image.

The woman on the hill was—

"You're *me,* aren't you?" Rosie asked. And then, as the woman with the plaited hair shifted slightly, she added in a shrill, shaking voice: "Don't turn around, I don't want to see!"

"Don't jump so fast," Rose Madder said in a strange, patient voice. "*You're* really Rosie, *you're* Rosie Real. Don't forget that when you forget everything else. And don't forget one other thing: *I repay.* What you do for me I will do for you. And that's why we were brought together. That is our balance. That is our *ka.*"

Lightning ripped the sky; thunder cracked; wind hissed through the olive tree. The tiny blonde hairs which had escaped from Rose Madder's

202

plait wavered wildly. Even in this chancey light they looked like filaments of gold.

"Go down now," Rose Madder said. "Go down and bring me my baby."

5

The child's cry drifted up to them like something which had labored here from another continent, and Rosie looked down at the ruined temple, whose perspective still seemed strangely and unpleasantly skewed, with new fear. Also, her breasts had begun to throb, as they had often throbbed in the months following her miscarriage.

Rosie opened her mouth, not sure of the words that would come out, only knowing they would be some sort of protest, but a hand gripped her shoulder before she could speak. She turned. It was the woman in red. She shook her head warningly, tapped her temple again, and pointed down the hill at the ruins.

Rosie's right wrist was seized by another hand, one as cold as a gravestone. She turned back and realized at the last moment that the woman in the chiton had turned around and was now facing her. Quickly, with confused thoughts of Medusa filling her mind, Rosie cast her eyes down so as not to see the face of the other. She saw the back of the hand gripping her wrist instead. It was covered with a dark gray blotch that made her think of some hovering ocean predator (a manta ray, of course). The fingernails looked dark and dead. As Rosie watched, she saw a small white worm wriggle out from beneath one of them.

"Go now," Rose Madder said. "Do for me what I cannot do for myself. And remember: *I repay.*"

"All right," Rosie said. A terrible, perverse desire to look up into the other woman's face had seized her. To see what was there. Perhaps to see her own face swimming beneath the dead gray shadows of some ailment that made you crazy even as it ate you alive. "All right, I'll go, I'll try, just don't make me look at you."

The hand let go of her wrist . . . but slowly, as if it would clamp tight again the instant its owner sensed any weakening on Rosie's part. Then the hand turned and one dead gray finger pointed down the hill, as the Ghost of Christmas Yet to Come had pointed out one particular grave marker to Ebenezer Scrooge.

"Go on, then," Rose Madder said.

Rosie started slowly down the hill, eyes still lowered, watching her bare feet slip through the high, rough grass. It wasn't until a particularly vicious crack of thunder tore through the air and she looked up, startled, that she realized the woman in the red robe had come with her.

"Are you going to help me?" Rosie asked.

"I c'n only go that far." The woman in red pointed toward the fallen pillar. "I got what she got, only so far it hasn't done much more than brush me."

She held out an arm, and Rosie saw an amorphous pink blotch squirming on her flesh—*in* her flesh—between the wrist and the fore-arm. There was a similar one in the cup of her palm. This one was almost pretty. It reminded Rosie of the clover she had found between the floor-boards in her room. Her room, the place she had counted on to be her refuge, seemed very distant to her now. Perhaps *that* was the dream, that whole life, and this was the only reality.

"Those are the only two I got, at least for now," she said, "but they're enough to keep me out of there. That bull would smell me and come running. It's me it'd come to, but both of us'd get killed."

"What bull?" Rosie asked, mystified and afraid. They had almost reached the fallen pillar.

"Erinyes. He guards the temple."

"What temple?"

"Don't waste time with man's questions, woman."

"What are you talking about? What are man's questions?"

"Ones you already know the answers to. Come on over here."

"Wendy Yarrow" was standing by the moss-encrusted end segment of the fallen pillar and looking impatiently at Rosie. The temple loomed close by. Looking at it hurt Rosie's eyes in the same way that looking at a movie screen where the picture had gone out of focus hurt them. She saw subtle bulges where she was sure there were none; she saw folds of shadow which disappeared when she blinked her eyes.

"Erinyes is one-eyed, and that one eye is blind, but there ain't nothing wrong with his sense of smell. Is it your time, girl?"

"My . . . time?"

"Time of the *month!*"

Rosie shook her head.

"Good, because we'd'a been done before we was begun if you was. I ain't, neither, ain't had no womanblood since the sickness started to show. Too bad, because that blood would be best. Still—"

The most monstrous crack of thunder yet split the air open just above their heads, and now icy droplets of rain began to fall.

"We got to hurry!" the woman in red told her. "Tear off two pieces of your nightgown—a strip for a bandage and a swatch big enough to wrap a stone in with enough left over to tie it up. Don't argue, and don't go askin no more questions, neither. Just do it."

Rosie bent down, took hold of the hem of her cotton nightgown, and tore a long, wide strip up the side, leaving her left leg bare almost all the way to the hip. *When I walk, I'm going to look like a waitress in a Chinese restaurant,* she thought. She tore a narrower strip from the side of this, and when she looked up, she was alarmed to see that "Wendy" was holding a long and wicked-looking double-sided dagger. Rose couldn't think where it might have come from, unless the woman had had it strapped to her thigh, like the heroine in one of those sweet-savage Paul Sheldon novels, stories where there was a reason, no matter how farfetched, for everything that happened.

That's probably just where she had it, too, Rosie thought. She knew that she herself would want a knife if she was traveling in the company of the woman in the rose madder chiton. She thought again about how the woman who *was* traveling in her company had tapped the side of her head with one finger and told Rosie not to touch her. *She don't mean you no harm,* "Wendy Yarrow" had said, *but she ain't got good control of herself no more.*

Rosie opened her mouth to ask the woman standing by the fallen pillar what she intended doing with that knife . . . and then closed her lips again. If a man's questions were ones you already knew the answers to, then that was a man's question.

"Wendy" seemed to feel her eyes and looked up at her. "It's the big piece you'll want first," she said. "Be ready with it."

Before Rosie could answer, "Wendy" had pierced her own skin with the tip of the dagger. She hissed a few words Rosie didn't understand —maybe a prayer—and then drew a fine line across her forearm, one that matched her dress. It fattened and began to run as the skin and underlying tissue drew back, allowing the wound to gape.

"Oooh, that hurt *bad!*" the woman moaned, then held out the hand with the dagger in it. "Give it to me. The big piece, the big piece!"

Rosie put it in her hand, confused and frightened but not nauseated; the sight of blood did not do that to her. "Wendy Yarrow" folded the strip of cotton cloth into a pad, which she placed over the wound, held, then turned over. Her purpose did not appear to be compression; she only wanted to soak the cloth with her blood. When she handed it back to Rosie, the cotton which had been cornflower blue when Rosie lay down in her Trenton Street bed was a much darker color . . . but a familiar one. Blue and scarlet had combined to make rose madder.

"Now find a rock and tie that piece of cloth around it," she said to Rosie. "When you got that done, take off that thing you're wearing and wrap it around both."

Rosie stared at her with wide eyes, far more shocked by this order than she had been by the sight of the blood pouring off the woman's arm. "I can't do that!" she said. "I don't have anything on underneath!"

"Wendy" grinned humorlessly. "I won't tell if you won't," she said. "Meantime, gimme that other 'un before I bleed to death."

Rosie handed her the narrower strip of cloth, this one still blue, and the brown-skinned woman began to wrap it swiftly around her wounded arm. Lightning exploded on their left like some monstrous firework. Rosie heard a tree go over with a long, rending crash. This sound was followed by a cannonade of thunder. Now she could smell a coppery odor on the air, like pennies that had been flash-fried. Then, as if the lightning had ripped open the sky's bag of waters, the rain arrived. It fell in cold torrents driven almost horizontal by the wind. Rosie saw it hit the pad of cloth in her hand, making it steam, and saw the first runnels of pink, bloody water coming out of it and trickling down her fingers. It looked like strawberry Kool-Aid.

Without any further thought about what she was doing or why, Rosie reached over her shoulder, grasped the back of her nightgown, bowed forward, and stripped it off over her head. She was immediately standing in the world's coldest shower, gasping for breath as the rain needled her cheeks and shoulders and unprotected back. Her skin tightened and then broke out in hundreds of tiny hard goosepimples; they covered her from neck to heels.

"Ai!" she cried in a desperate, breathless little voice. "Oh, ai! So cold!"

She dropped her nightgown, still mostly dry, over the hand holding the bloody rag and spied a rock the size of a cinnamon bun lying between two of the fallen pillar's segments. She picked it up, dropped to her knees, and then spread her nightgown over her head and shoulders, much as a man caught in an unexpected shower might use his newspaper as a makeshift tent. Under this temporary protection she wrapped the bloodsoaked rag around the rock. She was left with two long, sticky ears, and these she tied together, wincing with disgust as "Wendy's" rain-thinned blood ran out of them and pattered to the ground. With the rock tied in the rag, she wrapped her nightgown (no longer even close to dry) around the whole thing, as instructed. Most of the blood was going to wash out anyway, she knew. This wasn't a shower, or even a downpour. This was a flood.

"Go on!" the brown-skinned woman in the red dress told her. "Go on in the temple! Walk right through it, and don't stop for nothing! Don't pick nothing up, and don't believe in anything you see or hear. It's a ghos place, no doubt about that, but even in the Temple of the Bull there ain't no ghos can hurt a livin woman."

Rosie was shivering wildly, water in her eyes doubling her vision, water dripping from the tip of her nose, drops of water hanging from the lobes of her ears like exotic jewelry. "Wendy" stood facing her, hair plastered to her brow and cheeks, dark eyes blazing. Now she had to shout in order to make herself heard over the relentlessly rising wind.

"Pass through the door on the other side of the altar and you gonna find yourself in a garden where all the plants n flowers are dead! Acrost the garden you gonna see a grove of trees, all of *them* dead, too, all cept one! In between the garden and the grove there runs a stream! You dassn't drink from it, no matter how much you might want to— *dassn't*—or even touch it! Use the steppin-stones to get acrost! Wet so much as a single finger in that water, you gonna forget everythin you ever knew, even your own name!"

Electricity raced through the clouds in a glare of light, turning the thunderheads into strangulated goblin faces. Rosie had never been so cold in her life, or so aware of her heart's strange exhilaration as it tried to force a flush of heat to her rain-chilled skin. And the thought came to her again: this was no more a dream than the water cascading down from the sky was a sprinkle.

"Go in the grove! Into the dead trees! The one tree still livin is a pom'granate tree! Gather the seeds that you find in the fruit around the base of that tree, but don't taste the fruit or even put the hand that touches the seeds into your mouth! Go down the stairs by the tree and into the halls beneath! Find the baby and bring her out, but 'ware the bull! 'Ware the bull Erinyes! Now go! Hurry!"

She was afraid of the Temple of the Bull, with its curiously twisted perspectives, so it was something of a relief for Rosie to discover that her desperate desire to get out of the storm had now superseded every-thing. She wanted to get away from the wind and rain and lightning, but she also wanted to be under cover in case the rain decided to turn to hail. She found the idea of being naked in a hailstorm, even if it *was* a dream, extremely unpleasant.

She went a few steps, then turned back to look at the other woman.

"Wendy" looked as naked as Rosie did herself, her gauzy red gown now plastered to her body like paint.

"Who's Erinyes?" Rosie shouted. *"What is he?"* She ventured a glance at the temple over her shoulder, almost as if she expected the god to come at the sound of her voice. No god appeared; there was only the temple, shimmering in the downpour.

The brown-skinned woman rolled her eyes. *"Why you act so stupid, girl?"* she yelled back. *"Go on, now! Go on while you still can!"* And she pointed wordlessly at the temple, much as her mistress had done.

6

Rosie, naked and white, holding the soaked ball of her nightgown against her stomach to protect it as much as she could, started toward the temple. Five paces took her to the fallen stone head lying in the grass. She peered down at it, expecting to see Norman. Of course it would be Norman, and she might as well be prepared for it. That was the way things worked in dreams.

Except it wasn't. The receding hairline, fleshy cheeks, and luxurious David Crosby moustache belonged to the man who had been leaning in the doorway of The Wee Nip tavern on the day Rosie had gotten lost looking for Daughters and Sisters.

I'm lost again, she thought. *Oh boy, am I.*

She walked past the fallen stone head with its empty eyes that seemed to be weeping and the long wet strand of weed that lay across its cheek and brow like a green scar and it seemed to be whispering from behind her as she approached the strangely configured temple: *Hey baby wanna get it on nice tits whaddaya say wanna get it on wanna do some low ridin wanna do the dog whaddaya say?*

She walked up the steps, which were slippery and treacherous with overgrown vines and creepers, and seemed to sense that head rolling on its stone cranium, squelching muddy water up from the soaked earth, wanting to watch the flex of her bare bottom as she climbed toward the darkness.

Don't think about it, don't think about it, don't think.

She resisted the urge to run—both from the rain and from that imagined stare—and went on picking her way, avoiding the places where the stone had been cracked open by the elements, leaving jagged gaps where one might twist or even break an ankle. Nor was that the worst possibility; who knew what sorts of poisonous things might be coiled up in those dark places, waiting to sting or bite?

Water dripped from her shoulderblades and ran straight down the course of her spine and she was colder than ever, but she nevertheless stopped on the top step, looking at the carving above the temple's wide, dark doorway. She hadn't been able to see it in her picture; it had been lost in the darkness under the roof's overhang.

It showed a hard-faced boy leaning against what could have been a telephone pole. His hair fell over his forehead and the collar of his jacket was turned up. A cigarette hung from his lower lip and his slouched, hipshot posture proclaimed him as Mr. Totally Cool, Late Seventies Edition. And what else did that posture say? *Hey baby* was what it said. *Hey baby hey baby, want to get down? Want to do some low riding? Want to do the dog with me?*

It was Norman.

"No," she whispered. It was almost a moan. "Oh, no."

Oh *yes*. It was Norman, all right, Norman when he had still been the Ghost of Beatings Yet to Come, Norman leaning against the phone pole on the corner of State Street and Highway 49 in downtown Aubreyville (downtown Aubreyville, now *there* was a joke), Norman watching the cars go by while the sound of the Bee Gees singing "You Should Be Dancing" came drifting out of Finnegan's Pub, where the door had been chocked open and the Seeburg turned up loud.

The wind dropped momentarily and Rosie could hear the baby crying again. It didn't sound hurt, exactly; rather as if it might be very hungry. The faint howls got her eyes off that wretched carving and got her bare feet moving, but just before she passed into the temple doorway, she looked up again . . . she couldn't help herself. The boy-Norman was gone, if he had ever been there at all. Now she saw carved words directly above her. SUCK MY AIDS-INFECTED COCK, they said.

Nothing stays steady in dreams, she thought. *They're like water.*

She looked back over her shoulder and saw "Wendy," still standing by the fallen pillar, looking bedraggled in the collapsed cobwebs of her dress. Rosie raised the hand that wasn't holding the wadded nightgown in a tentative wave. "Wendy" raised her own hand in return, then just stood watching, seemingly oblivious of the pelting rain.

Rosie stepped through the wide, cool doorway and into the temple. She stood at the back, tense, ready to dart out again at once if she saw . . . well . . . if she saw she didn't know what. "Wendy" had told her not to sweat the ghosts, but Rosie thought the woman in the red dress could afford to be sanguine; she was back there, after all.

She guessed it was warmer inside than out, but it didn't *feel* warmer —there was the deep chill of damp stone about the place, the chill of crypts and mausoleums, and for a moment she wasn't sure she could make herself walk up the shadowy aisle, scattered with long-dead drifts and swirls of autumn leaves, which lay ahead of her. It was just too cold . . . and cold in too many ways. She stood shivering and gasping for breath in short little pulls of air, with her arms crossed tightly over her breasts and little ribbons of steam rising from her skin. She touched her left nipple with the tip of her finger and was not much surprised to find it was like touching a chip of rock.

It was the thought of going back to the woman on the hill that got her moving—the thought of having to face Rose Madder empty-handed. She stepped into the aisle, moving slowly and carefully, listening to the distant howl of the infant. It sounded miles away, carried to her by some thin, magical communication.

Go down and bring me my baby.

Caroline. The name she had planned to give her own baby, the one Norman had beaten out of her, came easily and naturally to her mind. The fugitive throb in her breasts began again. She touched them, and winced. They were tender.

Her eyes were adjusting to the gloom now, and it occurred to her that the Temple of the Bull had a strangely Christian look to it—that it looked, in fact, quite a bit like the First Methodist Church of Aubrey-ville, where she had gone twice a week until she had married Norman. First Methodist was where that marriage had taken place, and it was from there that her father, mother, and kid brother had been buried after the road accident which had taken their lives. There were rows of old wooden pews, the ones at the back overturned and half-buried in drifts of cinnamon-smelling leaves. Closer down toward the front they were still upright, and ranked in neat rows. Lying on them at regular intervals were fat black books that might have been the *Methodist Book of Hymns and Praise* Rosie had grown up with.

The next thing she became aware of—this as she walked down the center aisle like some strange naked bride—was the smell of the place. Under the good smell of the leaves which had blown in through the open door over the years there lurked a less pleasant odor. It was a little like mold, a little like mildew, a little like late-stage decay, and really not like any of those things. Old sweat, perhaps? Yes, perhaps. And perhaps other fluids, as well. Semen came to her mind. So did blood.

After her awareness of the smell came the almost undeniable sensation of being watched by malevolent eyes. She sensed them studying her nakedness carefully, brooding over it, perhaps, marking each undraped curve and line, memorizing the movement of her muscles beneath her wet, sleek skin.

Talk to you up close, the temple seemed to sigh to her beneath the hollow drumming of the rain and the crackle of the old leaves beneath her bare feet. *Talk to you right up close . . . but we won't have to talk long to say the things we need to say. Will we, Rosie?*

She stopped near the front of the temple and picked up one of the black books from where it lay in the second pew. When she opened it, a gasp of putrefaction so strong it almost choked her wafted up. The picture at the top of the page was a stark line drawing which had never appeared in the Methodist hymnals of her youth; it showed a woman on her knees, performing fellatio on a man whose feet were not feet at all, but hooves. His face was suggested rather than actually rendered, but Rosie saw a hideous similarity just the same . . . or thought she did. He looked like Norman's old partner Harley Bissington, who had always checked her hem so assiduously whenever she sat down.

Below the drawing, the yellowed page was crammed with Cyrillic lettering, unreadable but familiar. It took her only a moment of thought to understand why; they were the same letters which had filled the newspaper Peter Slowik had been reading when she had approached the Travelers Aid booth and asked him for help.

Then, with shocking suddenness, the drawing began to move, its lines seeming to crawl toward her white, rain-wrinkled fingers, leaving little snail-trails of sludge behind. It was alive, somehow. She slammed the book shut and her throat clenched at the wet squelching noise that came from inside it. She dropped it, and either the bang it made when it hit the pew or her own revolted cry woke a flutter of bats in the shadowy area she supposed was the choir loft. Several of them turned aimless figure-eights overhead, black wings dragging loathsomely plump brown bodies through the dank air, and then they retreated back into their holes. Ahead was the altar, and she was relieved to see a narrow door standing open to its left and letting in an oblong of clean white light.

Yerrr reeely Roww-zey, the tongueless voice of the temple whispered, bleakly amused. *And yerrr Rowww-zey Reeel . . . come over here and I'll give yewww . . . a grrreat big feeeeel . . .*

She refused to look around; she kept her eyes fixed on the door and the daylight beyond it. The rain had abated, the hollow rushing sound from overhead now down to a steady low mutter.

It's for men only, Rowww-zey, the temple whispered, and then added what Norman always said when he didn't want to answer one of her questions, but wasn't really mad at her, either: *It's a guy thing.*

She looked into the altar area as she passed it, then quickly looked away. It was empty—there was no pulpit, no symbols, no arcane books—but she saw another hovering manta-shadow, this one lying on the bare stones. Its rusty color suggested to her that it was blood, and the size of the shadow suggested that a lot of it had been spilled here over the years. A lot.

It's like the Roach Motel, Rowww-zie, the room whispered, and the leaves on the stone floor stirred, making a sound like laughter slipping between gumless teeth. *They check in, but they don't check owwwwwt.*

She walked steadily toward the door, trying to ignore that voice, keeping her eyes fixed straight ahead. She half-expected it to slam shut in her face when she got close to it, but it didn't. No capering bogey with Norman's face leaped through it, either. She stepped out onto a small stone stoop, stepped into the cool smell of rain-freshened grass, and into air which had begun to warm again even though the rain had not completely stopped. Water dripped and rustled everywhere. Thunder boomed (but it was going-away thunder now, she felt sure). And the baby, of which she had not been aware for several minutes, resumed its distant wailing.

The garden was divided into two parts—flowers on the left, veggies on the right—but it was all dead. Cataclysmically dead, and the lush greenery which surrounded it and the Temple of the Bull like encircling arms made that dead acre look so much the worse by contrast—like a corpse with its eyes open and its tongue lolling. Huge sunflowers with yellowy, fibrous stalks, brown centers, and curling, faded petals towered over everything else, like diseased turnkeys in a prison where all the inmates have died. The flowerbeds were full of blown petals that made her think, in an instant of nightmarish recall, of what she had seen when she had gone back to the cemetery where her family was buried a month after their interment. She had walked to the back of the little graveyard after putting fresh flowers on their graves, wanting to collect herself, and had been horrified to find drifts of rotting flowers piled in the declivity between the stone wall and the woods behind the cemetery. The stink of their dying perfume had made her think of what was happening to her mother and father and brother under the ground. How they were changing.

Rosie looked hastily away from the flowers, but at first what she saw in the moribund vegetable patch was no better: one of the rows appeared to be full of blood. She wiped water out of her eyes, looked again, and sighed with relief. Not blood but tomatoes. A twenty-foot row of fallen, rotting tomatoes.

Rosie.

Not the temple this time. This was Norman's voice, it was *right behind her,* and she suddenly realized she could smell Norman's cologne. *All my men wear English Leather or they wear nothing at all,* she thought, and felt ice creep up her spine.

He was behind her.

Right behind her.

Reaching for her.

No. I don't believe that. I don't believe it even if I do.

That was a completely stupid thought, of course, probably stupid enough to rate at least a small entry in the *Guinness Book of Records,* but it steadied her somehow. Moving slowly—knowing if she tried to go even a little faster she was apt to lose it completely—Rosie went down the three stone steps (much humbler even than those at the front of the building) and into the remains of what she mentally named Bull Gardens. The rain was still falling, but gently, and the wind had dropped to a sigh. Rosie walked down an aisle formed by two ranks of brown and leaning cornstalks (there was no way she was going to walk through those rotting tomatoes in her bare feet, feeling them burst beneath her soles), listening to the stony roar of a nearby stream. The sound grew steadily louder as she walked, and when she stepped out of the corn she saw the stream flowing past less than fifteen feet away. It was perhaps ten feet across and ordinarily shallow, judging from its mild banks, but now it was swollen with runoff from the downpour. Only the tops of the four large white stones which crossed it showed, like the bleached shells of turtles.

The water of the stream was a tarry, lightless black. She walked slowly toward it, barely aware that she was squeezing her hair with her free hand, wringing the water out of it. As she drew close, she smelled a peculiar mineral odor coming up from the stream, heavily metallic yet oddly attractive. She was suddenly thirsty, very thirsty, her throat as parched as a hearthstone.

You dassn't drink from it, no matter how much you want to. Dassn't.

Yes, that was what she'd said; she'd told Rosie that if she wet so much as a finger in that water, she would forget everything she had ever known, even her own name. But was that such a bad deal? When you thought things over, was that really such a bad deal, especially when one of the things she could forget was Norman, and the possibility that he wasn't done with her yet, that he had killed a man because of her?

She swallowed and heard a dust-dry click in her throat. Again, acting with almost no awareness of what she was doing, Rosie ran a hand up her side, over the swell of her breast, and across her neck, collecting moisture and then licking it out of her palm. This did not slake her thirst but only fully awakened it. The water gleamed a slick black as it flowed around the stepping-stones, and now that queerly attractive mineral smell seemed to fill her whole head. She knew how the water would taste—flat and airless, like some cold syrup—and how it would fill her throat and belly with strange salts and exotic bromides. With the taste of memoryless earth. Then there would be no more thoughts of the day when Mrs. Pratt (white as snow she had been, except for her lips, which were the color of blueberries) had come to the door and told her that her family, *her whole family,* had been killed in a highway wreck, no more thoughts of Norman with the pencil or Norman with the tennis racket. No more images of the man in the doorway of The Wee Nip or the fat lady who had called the women at Daughters and Sisters welfare lesbians. No more dreams of sitting in the corner while the pain from her kidneys made her sick, reminding herself over and over to throw up in her apron if she had to throw up. Forgetting those things would be good. Some things deserved forgetting, and others—things like what he had done to her with the tennis racket—*needed* forgetting . . . except most people never got the chance, not even in a dream.

Rosie was trembling all over now, her eyes welded to the water flowing past like transparent silks filled with smooth black ink; her throat burned like a brushfire and her eyes pulsed in their sockets and she could see herself going down flat on her belly, sticking her whole head into that blackness and drinking like a horse.

You'd forget Bill, too, Practical-Sensible whispered, almost apologeti-cally. *You'd forget the green undertint in his eyes, and the little scar on his earlobe. These days some things are worth remembering, Rosie. You know that, don't you?*

With no further hesitation (she didn't believe even the thought of Bill would have been able to save her if she'd waited much longer), Rosie stepped onto the first stone with her hands held out to either side for balance. Red-tinted water dripped steadily from the damp ball of her nightgown, and she could feel the rock at the center of the bundle, like the pit in a peach. She stood with her left foot on the stone and her right on the bank, summoned up her courage, and put the foot behind her on the stone ahead of her. All right so far. She lifted her left foot and strode to the third stone. This time her balance shifted a little and she tottered to the right, waving her left arm to keep her balance while the babble of the strange water filled her ears. It was probably not as close as it seemed, and a moment later she was standing on the stones in the middle of the stream with her heartbeat thudding emphatically in her ears.

Afraid she might freeze if she hesitated too long, Rosie stepped onto the last stone and then up to the dead grass of the far bank. She had taken only three steps toward the grove of bare trees ahead when she realized that her thirst had passed like a bad dream.

It was as if giants had been buried alive here at some time in the past and had died trying to pull themselves out; the trees were their fleshless hands, reaching fruitlessly at the sky and silently speaking of murder. The dead branches were interlaced, creating strange, geometric patterns against the sky. A path led into them. Guarding it was a stone boy with a huge erect phallus. His hands were held straight up over his head, as if he were signalling that the extra point was good. As Rosie passed, his pupilless stone eyes rolled toward her. She was sure of it.

Hey baby! the stone boy spat inside her head. *Want to get down? Want to do the dog with me?*

She backed away from it, raising her own hands in a warding-off gesture, but the stone boy was just a stone boy again . . . if, that was, he had been anything else, even for a moment. Water dripped from his comically oversized penis. *No problems maintaining an erection there,* Rosie thought, looking at the stone boy's pupilless eyes and somehow too-knowing smile (had it been smiling before? Rosie tried to remember and found she couldn't). *How Norman would envy you that.*

She hurried past the statue and along the path leading into the dead grove, restraining an urge to look over her shoulder and make sure the statue wasn't following her, wanting to put that stone hardon to work. She didn't dare look. She was afraid her overstrained mind might see it even if it wasn't there.

The rain had backed off to a hesitant drizzle, and Rosie suddenly realized she could no longer hear the baby. Perhaps it had gone to sleep. Perhaps the bull Erinyes had gotten tired of listening to it and gobbled it like a canapé. In either case, how was she supposed to find it, if it didn't cry?

One thing at a time, Rosie, Practical-Sensible whispered.

"Easy for *you* to say," Rosie whispered.

She went on, listening to the rainwater drip from the dead trees and realizing—reluctantly—that she could see faces in the bark. It wasn't like lying on your back and looking at clouds, where your imagination did ninety per cent of the work; these were real faces. *Screaming* faces. To Rosie they looked like women's faces, for the most part. Women who had been talked to right up close.

After she had walked a little way she rounded a bend and found the path blocked by a fallen tree which had apparently been struck by lightning at the height of the storm. One side was splintered and black. Several of the branches on that side still smoldered sullenly, like the ashes of a carelessly doused campfire. Rosie was afraid to climb over it; gouges and splinters and jags of wood stuck up all over the burst trunk.

She began edging around it on the right, where the roots had torn out of the ground. She had gotten most of the way back to the path when one of the tree's roots suddenly jerked, quivered, then slid around her upper thigh like a dusty brown snake.

Hey, baby! Want to do the dog? Want to do the dog, you bitch?

The voice came drifting out of the crumbling dry cave of earth where the tree had so recently stood. The root slid higher on her thigh.

Want to put all four on the floor, Rosie? That sound good? I'll be your back-door man, gobble you like a toasted-cheese sandwich. Or would you rather suck my AIDS-infected—

"Let me go," Rosie said quietly, and pressed the crumpled wad of her nightgown against the root that was holding her. It loosened and fell away immediately. She hurried the rest of the way around the tree and resumed the path. The root had squeezed hard enough to leave a red ring on her thigh, but the mark faded quickly. She supposed she should have been terrified by what had just happened, that perhaps something *meant* for her to be terrified. If so, it hadn't worked. She decided that this was a pretty cutrate chamber of horrors, all in all, for someone who had lived with Norman Daniels for fourteen years.

7

Another five minutes brought her to the end of the path. It opened into a perfectly circular clearing, and within it was the only living thing in all this desolation. It was the most beautiful tree Rosie had ever seen in her life, and for several moments she actually forgot to breathe. She had been a faithful attendee of Methodist Little Folks Sunday School back in Aubreyville, and now she remembered the story of Adam and Eve in the Garden of Eden and thought that if there really *had* been a

Tree of Good and Evil standing at the center of that place, it must have looked just like this.

It was densely dressed in long, narrow leaves of polished green, and its branches hung heavy with a perfect bounty of reddish-purple fruit. The falls surrounded the tree in a rose madder drift which exactly matched the color of the short gown worn by the woman Rosie hadn't dared to look at. Many of these falls were still fresh and plump; they had probably been struck from the tree in the storm which had just passed. Even those well advanced in rot looked almost unbearably sweet; Rosie's mouth cramped pleasurably at the thought of picking up one of those fruits and biting deeply into it. She thought the taste would be both tart and sweet, something like a stalk of rhubarb picked early in the morning, or raspberries taken from the bush the day before they came to perfect ripeness. As she looked at the tree, one of the fruits (to Rosie it looked no more like a pomegranate than it looked like a bureau drawer) dropped from an overloaded branch, struck the ground, and split open in rose madder folds of flesh. She could see the seeds amid its trickling juices.

Rosie took a step toward the tree and stopped. She kept swinging back and forth between two poles: her mind's belief that all this had to be a dream, and her body's equally emphatic assertion that it couldn't be, that no one on earth had ever had a dream this real. Now, like a troubled compass needle caught in a landscape where there are too many mineral deposits, she swung doubtfully back toward the dream thesis. Standing to the left of the tree was something that looked like a subway entrance. Broad white steps led down into darkness. Above them was an alabaster plinth upon which a single word had been carved: MAZE.

Really, this is too much, Rosie thought, but she walked toward the tree just the same. If this *was* a dream, it couldn't hurt to follow instructions; doing so might even hasten the moment when she finally woke up in her own bed, groping for the alarm-clock, wanting to silence its self-righteous yell before it could split her head open. How she would welcome its cry this time! She was chilly, her feet were dirty, she had been groped by a root and ogled by a stone boy who, in a properly made world, would have been too young to know what the hell he was looking at. Most of all she felt that if she didn't get back to her room soon, she was apt to come down with a really wonderful cold, maybe even bronchitis. That would take care of her date on Saturday, and keep her out of the recording studio all next week as well.

Not seeing the absurdity of believing one could become ill as the result of an excursion made in a dream, Rosie knelt down just beyond the fallen fruit. She surveyed it carefully, wondering again how it would taste (like nothing you found in the produce aisle of the A&P, that was for sure), then unfolded a corner of her nightgown. She tore off another chunk, wanting to provide herself with a square of cloth and succeeding better than she had expected to do. She laid it down, then began to pick seeds up off the ground, placing each one on the cloth she intended using to carry them.

A good plan, too, she thought. *Now if I only knew* why *I was carrying them.*

The tips of her fingers went numb right away, as if they had been shot full of Novocain. At the same time, the most wonderful aroma filled her nose. Sweet but not flowery, it made Rosie think of the pies, cakes, and cookies that had come from her gramma's stove. It made her think of something else, as well, something which was light-years from Gramma Weeks's kitchen with its faded linoleum and Currier & Ives prints: of how she had felt when Bill's hip brushed against hers as they were walking back to the Corn Building.

She laid two dozen seeds on the square of cloth, hesitated, shrugged, and added two dozen more. Would that be enough? How could she know, when she didn't know what they were for to begin with? In the meantime, she'd better be moving. She could hear the baby again, but the cries were now little more than echoey whimpers—the sounds babies made when they were getting ready to give up and go to sleep.

She folded the damp cloth over and then tucked the edges in, making a little envelope that reminded her of the seed-packets her dad had gotten from the Burpee Company late each winter, back in the days when she had still been a regular attendee at Little Folks Sunday School. She had now grown comfortable enough with her nakedness to be exasperated by it rather than ashamed: she wanted a pocket. Well, if wishes were pigs, bacon would always be on sa—

The part of her that was practical and sensible realized what she was about to do with her rose madder–stained fingers less than a second before they would have been in her mouth. She snatched them away with her heart pounding and that sweet/tart smell filling her head. *Don't taste the fruit,* "Wendy" had told her. *Don't taste the fruit or even put the hand that touches the seeds into your mouth!*

This place was full of traps.

She got up, looking at her stained and tingling fingers as if she had never seen them before. She backed away from the tree standing in its circle of fallen fruit and spilled seeds.

It's not the Tree of Good and Evil, Rosie thought. *It's not the Tree of Life, either. I think this is the Tree of Death.*

A little gust of wind puffed past her, rustling through the pomegranate tree's long, polished leaves, and they seemed to rattle out her name in a hundred small, sarcastic whispers: *Rosie-Rosie-Rosie!*

She knelt again, wishing for live grass, but there was none. She put down her nightgown with the rock inside it, placed the little packet of seeds on top of it, then snatched up big handfuls of wet, dead grass. She scrubbed the hand which had touched the seeds as well as she could. The rose madder stain faded but didn't disappear completely, and it remained bright beneath her nails. It was like looking at a birthmark which nothing will completely bleach out. Meantime, the baby's cries were becoming ever more occasional.

"Okay," Rosie muttered to herself, getting up. "Just keep your damned fingers out of your mouth. You'll be all right if you do that!"

She walked to the stairs which led beneath the white stone and stood at the head of them for a moment, dreading the darkness and trying to nerve herself up to face it. The alabaster stone with MAZE carved into its surface no longer looked like a plinth to her; it looked like a marker standing at the end of a narrow, open grave.

The baby was down there, though, whimpering as babies do when no one comes to comfort them and they finally set about doing the job as well as they can themselves. It was that lonely, self-comforting sound which finally set her feet in motion. No baby should have to cry itself to sleep in such a lonely place.

Rosie counted steps as she went down. At seven she passed beneath the overhang and the stone. At fourteen she looked over her shoulder at the white rectangle of light she was leaving behind, and when she faced forward again, that shape hung before her eyes in the screening darkness like a bright ghost. She went down and down, bare feet slapping on stone. There would be no talking herself out of the terror which now filled her heart, no talking herself through it, either. She would be doing well just to live with it.

Fifty steps. Seventy-five. A hundred. She stopped at a hundred and twenty-five, realizing she could see again.

That's nuts, she thought. *Imagination, Rosie, that's all.*

It wasn't, though. She raised a hand slowly toward her face. It and the little packet of seeds it held glowed a dull, witchy green. She raised her other hand, the one holding the rock in the remains of her nightgown, beside it. She could see, all right. She turned her head first one way, then the other. The walls of the stairwell were glowing with a faint green light. Black shapes rose and twisted lazily in it, as if the walls were actually the glass faces of aquaria in which dead things twisted and floated.

Stop it, Rosie! Stop thinking that way!

Except she couldn't. Dream or no dream, panic and blind retreat were now very close.

Don't look, then!

Good idea. *Great* idea. Rosie dropped her eyes to the dim X-ray ghosts of her own feet and resumed her descent, now whispering her count under her breath. The green light continued to brighten as she went down, and by the time she reached two hundred and twenty, the last step, it was as if she were standing on a stage lit with low-level green gels. She looked up, trying to steel herself for what she might see. The air down here was moving, damp but fresh enough . . . yet it brought her a smell she didn't much like. It was a zoo smell, as if something wild were penned up down here. Something was, of course: the bull Erinyes.

Ahead were three free-standing stone walls facing her edge-on and running away into the gloom. Each was about twelve feet high, much too tall for her to see over. They glowed with that sullen green light, and Rosie nervously examined the four narrow passages they made. Which one? Somewhere far ahead of her, the baby continued to whimper . . . but the sound was fading relentlessly. It was like listening to a radio which is being slowly but steadily turned down.

"Cry!" Rosie shouted, then cringed from the returning echoes of her own voice: *"Iy! . . . iy! . . . iy!"*

Nothing. The four passages—the four entrances to the maze—gawped silently at her, like narrow vertical mouths wearing identical expressions of prissy shock. Not far inside the second from the right, she saw a dark pile of something.

You know damned well what that is, she thought. *After fourteen years of listening to Norman and Harley and all their friends, you'd have to be pretty stupid not to know bullshit when you see it.*

This thought and the memories that went with it—memories of those men sitting around in the rec room, talking about the job and drinking beer and talking about the job and smoking cigarettes and talking about the job and telling jokes about niggers and spicks and taco-benders and then talking about the job a little more—made her angry. Instead of denying the emotion, Rosie went against a lifetime of self-training and welcomed it. It felt *good* to be angry, to be anything other than terrified. As a kid she'd had a really piercing playground yell, the sort of high, drilling cry that could shatter window-glass and almost rupture eyeballs. She had been scolded and shamed out of using it around the age of ten, on the grounds that it was unladylike as well as brain-destroying. Now Rosie decided to see if she still had it in her repertoire. She drew the damp underground air into her lungs, all the way to the bottom, closed her eyes, and remembered playing Capture the Flag behind Elm Street School or Red Rover and Texas Rangers in Billy Calhoun's jungly, overgrown back yard. For a moment she thought she could almost smell the comforting aroma of her favorite flannel shirt, the one she wore until it practically fell apart on her back, and then she peeled back her lips and let loose with the old ululating, yodeling cry.

She was delighted, almost ecstatic, when it came out sounding just as it had in the old days, but there was something even better: it made her *feel* the way it had in the old days, like a combination of Wonder Woman, Supergirl, and Annie Oakley. And it still affected others as it had back then, it seemed; the baby had begun to cry again even before she had finished sending her schoolyard warwhoop into the stony dark. It was, in fact, screaming at the top of its lungs.

Quick now, Rosie, you have to be. If she's really tired, she won't be able to manage that volume for very long.

Rosie took a couple of steps forward, eyeing each of the four entrances to the maze, then walked past each of them, listening. The wail of the baby might have sounded a bit louder coming out of the third passage-way. That could have been no more than imagination, but at least it was a place to begin. She started down it, bare feet slapping on the stone floor, then halted with her head cocked and her teeth working at her lower lip. Her old warcry had stirred up more than the baby, it seemed. Somewhere in here—how close or far away was impossible to tell be-cause of the echo—hooves were running on rock. They moved at a lazy lope, seeming to grow closer, then fading a little, then growing closer again, then (somehow this was more frightening than the sound itself) stopping altogether. She heard a low, wet snort. It was followed by an even lower grunting sound. Then there was only the baby, its bellows already beginning to subside again.

Rosie found herself able to imagine the bull all too well, a vast animal with a bristly hide and thick black shoulders humping grimly above its dropped head. It would have a gold ring in its nose, of course, like the Minotaur in her childhood book of myths, and the green light sweating out of the walls would reflect off that ring in tiny stitches of liquid light. Erinyes was standing quietly now in one of the passages ahead, its horns tipped forward. Listening for her. Waiting for her.

She walked down the faintly glowing corridor, trailing one hand along the wall, listening for the baby and the bull. She kept an eye out for more droppings, too, but saw none. Not yet, anyway. After perhaps three minutes, the passage she was following emptied into a T-junction. The sound of the baby seemed slightly louder to the left (*or do I just have a dominant ear to match my dominant hand?* she wondered), so she turned in that direction. She had taken only two steps when she stopped short. All at once she knew what the seeds were for: she was Gretel underground, with no brother to share her fear. She went back to the T-junction, knelt, and unfolded one side of her packet. She placed a seed on the floor with the sharp end pointing back in the direction from which she had come. At least, she reflected, there were no birds down here to gobble up her backtrail.

Rosie got to her feet and began walking again. Five paces brought her to a new passage. She peered down it and saw that it divided into three branches just a short way up. She chose the center branch, marking it with a pomegranate seed. Thirty paces and two turns later, this passage dead-ended in a stone wall upon which seven black words had been slashed: WANT TO DO THE DOG WITH ME?

Rosie returned to the three-way junction, stooped to pick up her seed, and laid it at the head of a new path.

8

She had no idea how long it took her to find her way to the center of the maze in this fashion, because time quickly lost all meaning for her. She knew it couldn't have taken terribly long, because the baby's cries continued . . . although by the time Rosie began to get really close, they had become intermittent. Twice she heard the bull's hooves go thudding dully along the stone floor, once at a distance, once so close that she stopped short, hands clasped between her breasts, as she waited for it to appear at the head of the passageway she was in.

If she had to backtrail, she always picked up the last seed so she should suffer no confusion on her way back out. She had started with almost fifty; when she finally came around a corner and observed a much brighter green glow straight ahead, she was down to three.

She walked to the end of the passageway and stood at its mouth, looking into a square stone-floored room. She glanced up briefly, looking for a roof, and saw only a cavernous blackness that made her dizzy. She looked down again, registered several more large pats of dung scattered across the floor, and then turned her attention to the center of the room. Lying there on a pad of blankets was a plump, fair-haired baby. Her eyes were swollen with crying and her cheeks were wet with tears, but she had fallen quiet again, at least for the time being. Her feet were in the air and she appeared to be trying to examine her toes. Every now and then she gave out a watery, sobbing little gasp. These sounds moved Rosie's heart in a way the baby's all-out wails had not been able to do; it was as if the infant knew somehow that she had been abandoned.

Bring me my baby.

Whose *baby? Who is she, really? And who brought her here?*

She decided she didn't care about the answer to those questions, at least not now. It was enough that she was lying here, perfectly sweet and all alone, trying to comfort herself with her own toes in the chilly green light at the center of the maze.

And that light can't be good for her, Rosie thought distractedly, hurrying toward the center of the room. *It must be some kind of radiation.*

The baby turned her head, saw Rosie, and raised her arms toward her. The gesture won Rosie's heart completely. She wrapped the top blanket in the pile over the child's chest and belly, then picked her up. The infant looked to be about three months old. She put her arms around Rosie's neck and then dropped her head—*clunk!*—down on Rosie's shoulder. She began to sob again, but very weakly.

"That's all right," Rosie said, patting the tiny, blanket-wrapped back gently. She could smell the infant's skin, warm and sweeter than any perfume. She put her nose against the fine hair which floated around the perfectly made skull. "That's all right, Caroline, everything's fine, we're going to get out of this nasty old—"

She heard thudding hooves approaching from behind her and shut her mouth, praying that the bull hadn't heard her alien voice, praying that the hooves would turn and begin to fade as Erinyes chose some path that would lead it away from her again. This time that didn't happen. The hoofbeats grew closer—sharper, too, as the bull closed in. Then they stopped, but she could hear something big breathing hard, like a heavy-set man who has just climbed a flight of stairs.

Slowly, feeling old and stiff, Rosie turned toward the sound with the baby in her arms. She turned to Erinyes, and Erinyes was there.

That bull would smell me and come running. That was what the woman in the red dress had told her . . . and something else. *It's me it'd come to, but both of us'd get killed.* Had Erinyes smelled her? Smelled her even though the moon was not full for her? Rosie didn't think so. She thought it was the bull's job to guard the baby—perhaps to guard *what-*

ever might be at the center of the maze—and that it had been drawn by the sound of the baby's cries, just as Rosie had been. Perhaps that mattered, perhaps it didn't. In any case, the bull was here, and it was the ugliest brute Rosie had ever seen in her life.

It stood at the mouth of the passageway it had just run, somehow as unsettled in its shape as the temple she had passed through—it was as though she were looking at it through currents of clear, rapidly moving water. Yet the bull itself was, for the moment at least, completely still. Its head was lowered. One huge front hoof, cloven so deeply it almost looked like a gigantic bird's talon, pawed restlessly at the stone floor. Its shoulders overtopped Rosie's five-feet-six by at least four inches and she guessed its weight at two tons, minimum. The top of its dropped head was flat as a hammer and shiny as silk. Its horns were stubby, no more than a foot in length, but sharp and thick. Rosie had no trouble imagining how easily they would punch into her naked belly . . . or into her back, if she tried to run. She couldn't imagine how such a death would *feel,* however; not even after all her years with Norman could she imagine that.

The bull raised its head slightly and she saw it did indeed have only one eye, a filmy blue thing, huge and freakish, above the center of its snout. As it lowered its head and began to thud its cloven hoof restlessly against the floor again, she understood something else, as well: it was getting ready to charge.

The baby let out an earsplitting howl, almost directly into Rosie's ear, making her jump.

"Hush," she said, bouncing it up and down in her arms. "Hush-a-baby, no fear, no fear."

But there *was* fear, plenty of it. The bull standing over there in its narrow slot of doorway was going to unzip her guts for her and decorate these peculiar glowing walls with them. She supposed they would look black against the green, like the shapes which occasionally seemed to twist deep in the stone. There was nothing in this center chamber to hide behind, not so much as a single pillar, and if she ran for the passage she'd come out of, the blind bull would hear her feet on the stone and cut her off before she had gotten halfway—it would gore her, toss her against the wall, gore her again, and then trample her to death. The baby as well, if she managed to keep hold of it.

One-eyed blind, but there ain't nothing wrong with his sense of smell.

Rosie stood watching it with wide eyes, mesmerized by the tapping front hoof. When that tapping finally stopped—

She looked down at the damp, crumpled ball of nightgown in her hand. The ball of nightgown with the rag-wrapped stone in the center. *Nothing wrong with his sense of smell.*

She dropped to one knee, keeping her eyes trained on the bull and holding the baby against her shoulder with her right hand. She used the left to open out her nightgown. The piece she had wrapped around the rock had been a dark red, rich with "Wendy Yarrow's" blood, but the downpour had washed much of it away, and the fabric was now a fading pink. Only the ears of cloth, where she had tied it over the rock, were brighter—were, in fact, rose madder.

Rosie cupped the stone in her left hand, feeling the heft of it. Just as the bull's haunches flexed, she underhanded the stone, bowling it along the floor to the bull's left. Its head swung heavily in that direction, its nostrils flared, and it charged toward what it both heard and smelled.

Rosie was on her feet again in a flash. She left the crumpled remnant of her nightgown lying beside the baby's pad of blankets. The little packet containing the last three pomegranate seeds was still in her hand, but Rosie wasn't aware of them. She was aware only of sprinting across the room toward the passageway she wanted, while behind her Erinyes charged the rock, kicked it aslant with one flying hoof, chased it down again, butted it with the flat hammer of its head, sent it flying into one of the other passages, and then chased after it, grunting thickly in its throat. She was sprinting, yes, but in slow motion, and now all this seemed like a dream again, because this was the way one *always* ran in dreams, especially the bad ones where the fiend was always just two steps behind. In nightmares, escape became an underwater ballet.

She burst into the narrow corridor just as she heard the hoofbeats wheel around and begin to approach again. They came fast, bearing down on her, and as they closed in, Rosie screamed and clutched the yowling, frightened baby to her breasts and ran for her life. It did no good. The bull was faster. It overtook her . . . and then passed by on the far side of the wall to her right. Erinyes had discovered the ruse of the stone in time to double back and catch her, but it had chosen the wrong passageway by one.

Rosie hurried on, gasping, dry-mouthed, feeling the rapid rhythm of her heartbeat in her temples, her throat, her eyeballs. She hadn't the slightest idea of where she was, or in which direction she was traveling; now everything depended on the seeds. If she had forgotten so much as a single one, she might wander in here for hours, until the bull finally found her and ran her down.

She reached a five-way junction, looked down, and saw no seed. She *did* see a gleaming, aromatic spatter of bullpiss, however, and it gave rise to a horribly plausible idea. Suppose there *had* been a seed? She couldn't remember dropping one here, true enough, so in itself the lack of one meant nothing. But she couldn't remember *not* dropping one, either. Suppose she had, and suppose the bull had picked it up on its hoof as it raced through the intersection with its head down and its short, sharp horns sorting through the air, spraying piss as it went?

You can't think of that, Rosie—plausible or not, you can't think of it. You'll freeze, and eventually the bull will kill both of you.

She dashed across the intersection, holding the baby's neck with one hand, not wanting her head to go whipping back and forth. The passage ran straight on for twenty yards, made a right-angle, then ran another twenty yards to a T-junction. She hurried down to it, telling herself not to lose her head if she found no seed there. In that case, she would simply retrace her steps to the five-way and try another choice, easy as pie, simple as could be, zero perspiration . . . if she kept her head, that was. And even as she was preparing herself with these thoughts, an alien, frightened voice at the back of her mind was moaning, *Lost, this is what you get for leaving your husband, this is how it all turns out, lost in the maze, playing hide-and-seek with a bull in the dark, doing errands for madwomen . . . this is what happens to bad wives, to wives who get above their place in the scheme of things. Lost in the dark . . .*

She saw the seed, its sharp end pointing clearly into the righthand arm of the junction, and sobbed with relief. She kissed the baby's cheek and saw she had fallen asleep again.

9

Rosie turned right and began walking with Caroline—it was as good a name as any, surely—cradled in her arms. She never quite lost that nightmarish floating feeling, nor her fear that she would eventually come to an intersection she had forgotten to mark with a seed, but at every choosing-point the seed was there. Erinyes was there, too, however, and the thudding of his hooves on stone, sometimes far-off and muffled, sometimes close and terrifyingly sharp, reminded her of the time she and her parents had gone to New York City when she had been only five or six. The two things she remembered best about that trip were the Rockettes high-kicking their way across the stage at Radio City Music Hall, their legs moving in perfect unison, and the intimidating bustle and confusion of Grand Central Station, with its echoes and huge lighted signs and its tidal flows of people. The people in Grand Central had fascinated her much as the Rockettes had (and for many of the same reasons, although this idea would not come to her until later), but the sound of the trains had scared her badly, because you couldn't tell where they were coming from or where they were going. The disembodied squeals and rumbles swelled and faded, swelled and faded, sometimes distant, sometimes seeming to shake the very floor under one's feet. Listening to the bull Erinyes charge blindly through the maze brought that memory back with amazing clarity. Rosie understood that she, who had never wagered a single dollar on the state lottery or played a single card of church Bingo for a turkey or a set of glassware, was now running in a game of chance where the prize was her life and the forfeit would be her death . . . and the baby's death, too. She thought of the man in Portside, the one with the handsome, unreliable face and the game of three-card monte set up on top of his suitcase. Now *she* was the ace of spades. The cold fact was that the bull didn't necessarily need its ears or its sense of smell to find them; it might stumble upon them by dumb luck.

But that didn't happen. Rosie came around a final corner and saw the stairs ahead. Gasping, crying, and laughing all at the same time, she hurried out of the passageway and ran for them. She climbed half a dozen, then turned and looked back. From here she could see the maze twisting and sprawling its way into the dimness, a right-and-left-angled confusion of turns, junctions, and blind alleys. Somewhere far off to the right she could hear Erinyes galloping. Galloping *away.* They were safe from it, and Rosie's shoulders sagged in relief.

The voice of "Wendy" filled her head: *Ne'mine that—you get on back here with the child. You done good, but you ain't done yet.*

No, she certainly was not. She had over two hundred stairs to climb, this time with a child in her arms, and she was exhausted already.

One at a time, dear, Practical-Sensible said. *That's how you have to do it. One step at a time.*

Yes, yes. Ms. P & S, Queen of the Twelve-Step Philosophy.

Rose started up (one step at a time), looking over her shoulder from time to time and thinking half formed

(can bulls climb stairs?)

dreadful thoughts as the maze fell behind her. The baby grew heavier and heavier in her arms, as if some weird mathematical law had come into force here: the closer to the surface, the heavier the kid. She could see a starpoint of daylight above her, and she fixed her eyes on it. For awhile it seemed to mock her, growing no closer at all as her breath came faster and the blood pounded in her temples. For the first time in almost two weeks her kidneys really began to hurt again, throbbing in dull counterpoint to her laboring heart. She ignored all of these things —as well as she could, anyway—and kept her eyes fixed on the star-point. At last it began to swell and to take on the shape of the opening at the top of the stairs.

Five steps from the top, a paralyzing cramp sank into the big muscles of her right thigh, knotting the flesh from the back of her knee almost all the way up to her right buttock. When she reached down to massage her leg, it was at first like trying to knead stone. Groaning softly, her mouth pulled down in a trembling moue of pain, she worked on the muscles (this was something else she had done for herself many times during the years of her marriage) until they finally began to loosen. She flexed the leg at the knee, waiting to see if the cramp would seize her again. When it didn't, she cautiously climbed the last few stairs, favoring the leg as she went. At the top, she stood looking around with the dazed eyes of a miner who has, contrary to all his expectations, survived a terrible cave-in.

The clouds had rolled away during her time underground, and the day was now filled with hazy summer light. The air was heavy and humid, but Rosie thought she had still never drawn a sweeter breath in her entire life. She turned her face, wet with sweat and tears, gratefully up to the faded blue denim she could see between the unravelling clouds. Somewhere in the distance thunder continued to rumble balefully, like a beaten bully making empty threats. That made her think of Erinyes, running in the darkness below, still looking for the woman who had invaded its domain and stolen its prize. *Cherchez la femme,* Rosie thought with a trace of a smile. *You can* cherchez *all you want, big fella; this* femme*—not to mention her* petite fille*—is gone.*

10

Rosie walked slowly away from the stairs. At the head of the path leading back into the grove of dead trees, she sat down with the baby in her lap. All she wanted was to regain her breath, but the hazy sun was warm on her back, and when she raised her head again, some small change in the lie of her shadow made her think she might have dozed a little.

As she got to her feet, wincing at the pain that shot through the muscles of her right thigh, she heard the harsh, squabbling cry of many birds—they sounded like a big family having a rancorous argument at

Sunday dinner. The child in her arms made a soft snorting sound as Rosie shifted her to a more comfortable position, blew a little spit-bubble between her pursed lips, then fell silent again. Rosie was both amused by and deeply envious of her placid, sleeping confidence.

She started down the path, then stopped and looked back at the single living tree with its shiny green leaves, its bounty of deadly reddish-purple fruit, and the Classical Fables subway entrance standing nearby. She looked at these things for a long moment, filling her eyes and mind with them.

They're real, she thought. *How can things I see so clearly be anything but real? And I dozed off, I know I did. How can you go to sleep in a dream? How can you go to sleep when you're sleeping already?*

Forget it, Practical-Sensible said. *That's the best thing, at least for the time being.*

Yes, probably it was.

Rosie started off again, and when she reached the fallen tree blocking the path, she was amused and rather exasperated to see that her arduous detour around the snarl of roots could have been avoided: there was an easy path around the top of the tree.

At least there is now, she thought as she went around it. *Are you sure there was before, Rosie?*

The rocky babble of the black stream rose in her ears, and when she reached it, she saw that the level had already begun to drop and the stepping-stones no longer looked so perilously small; now they looked almost the size of floor-tiles, and the scent of the water had lost its ominously attractive quality. Now it just smelled like very hard water, the kind that would leave an orange ring around the tub and toilet-bowl.

The squabble of the birds—*You did, No I didn't, Yes you did*—started up again, and she observed twenty or thirty of the largest birds she had ever seen in her life lined up along the peak of the temple's roof. They were much too big to be crows, and after a moment she decided they were this world's version of buzzards or vultures. But where had they come from? And why were they here?

Without realizing she was doing it until the infant squirmed and protested in her sleep, Rosie hugged the baby tighter to her breast as she gazed at the birds. They all took off at the same instant, their wings flapping like sheets on a clothesline. It was as if they had seen her looking at them and didn't like it. Most of them flew off to roost in the dead trees behind her, but several remained in the hazy sky overhead, circling like bad omens in a western movie.

Where did they come from? What do they want?

More questions to which Rosie had no answers. She pushed them away and crossed the stream on the stones. As she approached the temple, she saw a neglected but faintly visible path leading around its stone flank. Rosie took it without a single moment of interior debate, although she was naked and both sides of the path were lined with thorn-bushes. She walked carefully, turning sideways to keep her hip from being scratched, holding

(Caroline)

the baby up and out of thorns' way. Rosie took one or two swipes in spite of her care, but only one—across her badly used right thigh—was deep enough to draw blood.

As she came around the corner of the temple and glanced up at the front, it seemed to her that the building had changed somehow, and that the change was so fundamental that she wasn't quite able to grasp it. She forgot the idea for a moment in her relief at seeing "Wendy" still standing beside the fallen pillar, but after she'd taken half a dozen steps toward the woman in the red dress, Rosie stopped and looked back, opening her eyes to the building, opening her *mind* to it.

This time she saw the change at once, and a little grunt of surprise escaped her. The Temple of the Bull now looked stiff and unreal . . . two-dimensional. It made Rosie think of a line of poetry she'd read back in high school, something about a painted ship upon a painted ocean. The odd, unsettling sense that the temple was out of perspective (or inhabiting some strange, non-Euclidean universe where all the laws of geometry were different) had departed, and the building's aura of menace had departed with it. Now its lines looked straight in all the places where one expected such a building to look straight; there were no sudden turns or jags in the architecture to trouble the eye. The building looked, in fact, like a painting rendered by an artist whose mediocre talent and run-of-the-mill romanticism have combined to create a piece of bad art—the sort of picture which always seems to end up gathering dust in a basement corner or on an attic shelf, along with old issues of the *National Geographic* and stacks of jigsaw puzzles with a piece or two missing.

Or in the seldom-browsed third aisle of a pawnshop, perhaps.

"Woman! You, woman!"

She swung back toward "Wendy" and saw her beckoning impatiently.

"Hurry up n get that baby over here! This ain't no tourist 'traction!"

Rosie ignored her. She had risked her life for this child, and she didn't intend to be hurried. She folded back the blanket and looked at a body which was as naked and female as her own. That was where the resemblance ended, however. There were no scars on the child, no marks that looked like the fading teeth of old traps. There was not, as far as Rosie could see, so much as a single mole on that small and lovely body. She traced a finger slowly up the baby's entire length, from ball of ankle to ball of hip to ball of shoulder. Perfect.

Yes, perfect. And now that you have *risked your life for her, Rosie, now that you've saved her from the dark and the bull and God knows what else that might have been down there, do you intend to turn her over to these two women? Both have some sort of disease working on them, and the one up on the hill has a mental problem, as well. A* serious *mental problem. Do you intend to give this kid to them?*

"She be all right," the brown-skinned woman said. Rosie wheeled in the direction of the voice. "Wendy Yarrow" was now standing at her shoulder, and looking at Rosie with perfect understanding.

"Yes," she said, nodding as if Rosie had spoken her doubts aloud. "I know what you're thinkin and I tell you it's all right. She mad, no doubt in the world 'bout *that,* but her madness don't extend to the child. She knows that although she bore it, this child ain't hers to keep, no more than it's yours to keep."

Rosie glanced toward the hill, where she could just see the woman in the chiton, standing by the pony and waiting for the outcome.

"What's her name?" she asked. "The baby's mother? Is it—"

"Ne'mine," the brown woman in the red dress replied, cutting in quickly, as if to keep Rosie from speaking some word better left unsaid. "Her name don't matter. Her state o' mind does. She a mighty impatient lady these days, along with all her other woes. We best be goin up with no more jabber."

Rosie said, "I'd made up my mind to call my baby Caroline. Norman said I could. He didn't really care one way or the other." She began to cry.

"Seems like a nice enough name to me. A *fine* name. Don't you cry, now. Don't you carry on." She slipped an arm around Rosie's shoulders and they began walking up the hill. The grass whispered gently against Rosie's bare legs and tickled her knees. "Will you listen to a piece o' my advice, woman?"

Rosie looked at her curiously.

"I know advice is hard to take in matters o' sorrow, but think about my qualifications to give it: I was born in slavery, raised in chains, and ransomed to freedom by a woman who's not quite a goddess. *Her.*" She pointed to the woman who stood silently watching and waiting for them.

"She's drunk the waters of youth, and she made me drink, too. Now we go on together, and I don't know 'bout her, but sometimes when I look in the mirror I wish for wrinkles. I've buried my children, and their children, and their children's children into the fifth generation. I've seen wars come n go like waves on a beach that roll in n rub out the footprints and wash away the castles in the sand. I've seen bodies on fire and heads by the hundreds poked onto poles along the streets of the City of Lud, I've seen wise leaders assassinated and fools put up in their places, and still I live."

She sighed deeply.

"Still I live, and if there's anything that qualifies me to give advice, it's that. Will you hear it? Answer quick. It's not advice I'd have *her* overhear, and we're drawin close."

"Yes, tell me," Rosie said.

"It's best to be ruthless with the past. It ain't the blows we're dealt that matter, but the ones we survive. Now remember, for your sanity's sake if not your life's, *don't look at her!*"

The woman in red spoke these last words in an emphatic little mutter. Less than a minute later, Rosie was once more standing in front of the blonde woman. She fixed her eyes firmly on the hem of Rose Madder's chiton, and she didn't realize she was clutching the baby too tightly again until "Caroline" wriggled in her arms and waved an indignant arm. The child had awakened and was looking up at Rosie with bright interest. Her eyes were the same hazy blue as the summer sky overhead.

"You've done well, so you have," that low and sweetly husky voice told her. "I thank you. Now give her to me."

Rose Madder held out her hands. They swarmed with shadows. And now Rosie saw something she liked even less: a thick, gray-green sludge was growing between the woman's fingers like moss. Or scales. Without thinking about what she was doing, Rosie held the baby against her. This time she wriggled more strongly, and voiced a short cry.

A brown hand reached out and squeezed Rosie's shoulder. "It's all right, I tell you. She'd never hurt it, and I'll have most the care of it until our journey's done. That won't be long, and then she'll turn the child over to . . . well, that part don't matter. For a little while longer, the baby's hers. Give it over, now."

Feeling it was the hardest thing she'd ever had to do in a life full of hard things, Rosie held out the baby. There was a soft little grunt of satisfaction as the shadowy hands took her. The baby gazed up into the face which Rosie was forbidden to look at . . . and laughed.

"Yes, yes," the sweet, husky voice crooned, and there was something in it like Norman's smile, something that made Rosie feel like screaming. "Yes, sweet one, it was dark, wasn't it? Dark and nasty and bad, oh yes, Mamma knows."

The mottled hands lifted the baby against the rose madder gown. The child looked up, smiled, then laid her head on her mother's breast and closed her eyes again.

"Rosie," the woman in the chiton said. Her voice was musing, thoughtful, insane. The voice of a despot who will soon seize personal control of imaginary armies.

"Yes," Rosie nearly whispered.

"*Really* Rosie. Rosie Real."

"Y-Yes. I guess."

"Do you remember what I told you before you went down?"

"Yes," Rosie said. "I remember very well." She wished she didn't.

"What was it?" Rose Madder asked greedily. "What did I tell you, Rosie Real?"

" 'I repay.' "

"Yes. I repay. Was it bad for you, down in the dark? Was it bad for you, Rosie Real?"

She thought this over carefully. "Bad, but not the worst. I think the worst was the stream. I wanted to drink."

"There are many things in your life that you would forget?"

"Yes. I guess there are."

"Your husband?"

She nodded.

The woman with the sleeping baby against her breast spoke with a queer, flat assurance that chilled Rosie's heart. "You shall be divorced of him."

Rosie opened her mouth, found herself quite incapable of speech, and closed it again.

"Men are beasts," Rose Madder said conversationally. "Some can be gentled and then trained. Some cannot. When we come upon one who cannot be gentled and trained—a rogue—should we feel that we have been cursed or cheated? Should we sit by the side of the road—or in a rocking chair by the bed, for that matter—bewailing our fate? Should we rage against *ka*? No, for *ka* is the wheel that moves the world, and the man or woman who rages against it will be crushed under its rim. But rogue beasts must be dealt with. And we must go about that task with hopeful hearts, for the next beast may always be different."

Bill isn't a beast, Rosie thought, and knew she would never dare say that aloud to this woman. It was too easy to imagine this woman seizing her and tearing her throat out with her teeth.

"In any case, beasts will fight," Rose Madder said. "That is their way, to lower their heads and rush at each other so they may try their horns. Do you understand?"

Rosie suddenly thought she *did* understand what the woman was saying, and it terrified her. She raised her fingers to her mouth and touched her lips. They felt dry, feverish. "There isn't going to be any fight," she said. "There isn't going to be any fight, because they don't know about each other. They—"

"Beasts will fight," Rose Madder repeated, and then held something out to Rosie. It took her a moment to realize what it was: the gold armlet she'd been wearing above her right elbow.

"I . . . I can't . . ."

"Take it," the woman in the chiton said with sudden harsh impatience. "Take it, take it! And don't whine anymore! For the sake of every god that ever was, *stop your stupid sheep's whining!*"

Rosie reached out with a trembling hand and took the armlet. Although it had been against the blonde woman's flesh, it felt cold. *If she asks me to put it on, I don't know what I'll do,* Rosie thought, but Rose Madder did not ask her to put it on. Instead she reached out with her mottled hand and pointed toward the olive tree. The easel was gone, and the picture—like the one in her room—had grown to an enormous size. It had changed, as well. It still showed the room on Tremont Street, but now there was no woman facing the door. The room was in darkness. Just a fluff of blonde hair and a single bare shoulder showed above the blanket on the bed.

That's me, Rosie thought in wonder. *That's me sleeping and having this dream.*

"Go on," Rose Madder said, and touched the back of her head. Rosie took a step toward the picture, mostly to get away from even the lightest touch of that cold and awful hand. As she did, she realized she could hear—very faintly—the sound of traffic. Crickets jumped around her feet and ankles in the high grass. "Go on, little Rosie Real. Thank you for saving my baby."

"*Our* baby," Rosie said, and was instantly horrified. A person who corrected this woman had to be insane herself.

But the woman in the reddish-purple chiton sounded amused rather than angry when she replied. "Yes, yes, if you like—*our* baby. Go on, now. Remember what you have to remember, and forget what you need to forget. Protect yourself while you are outside the circle of my regard."

You bet, Rosie thought. *And I won't be coming around, looking for favors, you can count on it. That would be like hiring Idi Amin to cater a garden-party, or Adolf Hitler to—*

The thought broke off as she saw the woman in the painting shift in her bed and pull the blanket up over her exposed shoulder.

Not a painting, not anymore.

A window.

"Go on," the woman in the red dress said softly. "You done fine. Get gone before she change her mind 'bout how she feel."

Rosie stepped toward the picture, and from behind her Rose Madder spoke again, her voice neither sweet nor husky now but loud and harsh and murderous: *"And remember: I repay!"*

Rosie's eyes winced shut at this unexpected shout, and she lunged forward, suddenly sure that the woman in the chiton had forgotten the service Rosie had done her and had decided to kill her after all. She tripped over something (the bottom edge of the painting, perhaps?) and then there was a sense of falling. She had time to feel her stomach turn over like a circus tumbler, and then there was only darkness, rushing past her eyes and ears. In it she seemed to hear some ominous sound, distant but drawing closer. Perhaps it was the sound of trains in the deep tunnels beneath Grand Central Station, perhaps it was the rumble of thunder, or perhaps it was the bull Erinyes, running the blind depths of his maze with his head down and his short, sharp horns sorting the air.

Then, for a little while, at least, Rosie knew nothing at all.

11

She floated silently and thoughtlessly, like an undreaming embryo in its placental sac, until seven o'clock in the morning. Then the Big Ben beside the bed tore her out of sleep with its ruthless howl. Rosie sat bolt-upright, flailing at the air with hands like claws and crying out something she didn't understand, words from a dream that was already forgotten: *"Don't make me look at you! Don't make me look at you! Don't make me! Don't make me!"*

Then she saw the cream-colored walls, and the sofa that was really just a loveseat with delusions of grandeur, and the light flooding in through the window, and used these things to lock in the reality she needed. Whoever she might have been or wherever she might have gone in her dreams, she was now Rosie McClendon, a single woman who recorded audio books for a living. She had stayed for a long time with a bad man, but had left him and met a good one. She lived in a room at 897 Trenton Street, second floor, end of the hall, good view of Bryant Park. Oh, and one other thing. She was a single woman who never intended to eat another foot-long hotdog in her life, especially one smothered in sauerkraut. They did not agree with her, it seemed. She couldn't remember what she had dreamed

(remember what you have to remember and forget what you need to forget)

but she knew how it had started: with her walking into that damned painting like Alice going through the looking-glass.

Rosie sat where she was for a moment, wrapping herself in her Rosie Real world as firmly as she could, then reached out for the relentless alarm-clock. Instead of gripping it, she knocked it onto the floor. It lay there, bawling its excited, senseless cry.

"Hire the handicapped, it's fun to watch em," she croaked.

She leaned over and groped for the clock, fascinated all over again by the blonde hair she saw from the corner of her eye, locks so fabulously unlike those of that obedient little creepmouse Rose Daniels. She got hold of the clock, felt with her thumb for the stud that shut off the alarm, and then paused as something else registered. The breast pressing against her right forearm was naked.

She silenced the alarm, then sat up with the clock still in her left hand. She pushed down the sheet and light blanket. Her bottom half was as bare as her top half.

"Where's my nightie?" she asked the empty room. She thought she had never heard herself sounding so exceptionally stupid . . . but of course, she wasn't used to going to bed with her nightgown on and waking up naked. Even fourteen years of marriage to Norman had not prepared her for anything quite that peculiar. She put the clock back on the nighttable, swung her legs out of bed—

"Ow!" she cried, both startled and frightened by the pain and stiffness in her hips and thighs. Even her butt hurt. *"Ow, ow, OW!"*

She sat on the edge of the bed and gingerly flexed her right leg, then her left. They moved, but they *hurt,* especially the right one. It was as if she'd spent most of yesterday doing the granddaddy of all workouts, rowing machine, treadmill, StairMaster, although the only exercise she had taken was her walk with Bill, and that had been no more than a leisurely stroll.

The sound was like the trains in Grand Central Station, she thought.

What sound?

For a moment she thought she almost had it—had *something,* anyway—and then it was gone again. She got slowly and cautiously to her feet, stood beside the bed for a moment, then walked toward the bathroom. *Limped* toward the bathroom. Her right leg felt as if she had actually strained it somehow, and her kidneys ached. What in God's name—?

She remembered reading somewhere that people sometimes "ran" in their sleep. Perhaps *that* was what she had been doing; perhaps the jumble of dreams she couldn't quite remember had been so horrible that she'd actually made an effort to run away from them. She stopped in the bathroom doorway and looked back at her bed. The ground-sheet was rumpled, but not twisted or tangled or pulled loose, as she would have expected if she had been *really* active in her sleep.

Rosie saw one thing she didn't like much, however, something that flashed her back to the bad old days with terrible and unexpected suddenness: blood. They were the prints of thin lines rather than drops, however, and they were too far down to have come from a punched nose or a split lip . . . unless, of course, her sleeping movements had been so vigorous she'd actually turned around in her bed. Her next thought was that she'd had a visit from the cardinal (this was how her mother had insisted Rosie speak of her menstrual periods, if she had to speak of them at all), but it was entirely the wrong time of the month for that.

Is it your time, girl? Is the moon full for you?

"What?" she asked the empty room. "What about the moon?"

Again, something wavered, almost held, and then floated away before she could grasp it. She looked down at herself, and one mystery was solved, at least. She had a scratch on her upper right thigh, quite a nasty one, from the look. That was undoubtedly where the blood on the sheet had come from.

Did I scratch myself in my sleep? Is that what—

This time the thought which came into her mind held a little longer, perhaps because it wasn't a thought at all, but an image. She saw a naked woman—herself—edging carefully sideways along a path which was overgrown with thorn-bushes. As she turned on the shower and held one hand under the spray to test the temperature, she found herself wondering if you could bleed spontaneously in a dream, if the dream was vivid enough. Sort of like those people who bled from their hands and feet on Good Friday.

Stigmata? Are you saying that on top of everything else, you're suffering stigmata?

I'm not saying anything because I don't know *anything,* she answered herself, and how true that was. She supposed she could believe—just about barely—that a scratch might appear spontaneously on a sleeping person's skin, matching a scratch that was occurring at that same moment in the person's dream. It was a stretch, but not entirely out of the question. What *was* out of the question was the idea that a sleeping person could make the nightgown disappear right off her body simply by dreaming she was naked.

(Take off that thing you're wearing.

(I can't do that! I don't have anything on underneath!

(I won't tell if you won't . . .)

Phantom voices. One she recognized as her own, but the other?

It didn't matter; surely it didn't. She had taken her nightgown off in her sleep, that was all, or perhaps in a brief waking interlude which she now remembered no better than her weird dreams about running around in the dark or using white stepping-stones to cross streams of black water. She had taken it off, and when she got around to looking, she would no doubt find it wadded up under the bed.

"Right. Unless I ate it, or someth—"

She pulled back the hand which had been testing the water and looked at it curiously. There were fading reddish-purple stains on the tips of her fingers, and a slightly brighter residue of the same stuff under her nails. She raised the hand slowly to her face, and a voice deep down in her mind—not the voice of Practical-Sensible this time, at least she didn't think so—responded with unmistakable alarm. *Dassn't put the hand that touches the seeds into your mouth! Dassn't, dassn't!*

"What seeds?" Rosie asked, frightened. She smelled her fingers and caught just a ghost of an aroma, a smell that reminded her of baking and sweet cooked sugar. "*What* seeds? What happened last night? Is it—" She made herself stop there. She knew what she had been about to say, but didn't want to hear the question actually articulated, hanging in the air like unfinished business: *Is it* still *happening?*

She got into the shower, adjusted the water until it was as hot as she could take it, and then grabbed the soap. She washed her hands with particular care, scrubbed them until she could not see so much as a trace of that rose madder stain, even under her nails. Then she washed her hair, beginning to vocalize as she did so. Curt had suggested nursery rhymes in different keys and vocal registers, and that was what she did, keeping her voice low so as not to disturb the people above or below her. When she got out five minutes later and dried off, her body was starting to feel a little more like real flesh and a little less like something constructed out of barbed wire and broken glass. Her voice had almost returned to normal, as well.

She started to put on jeans and a tee-shirt, remembered that Rob Lefferts was taking her to lunch, and put on a new skirt instead. Then she sat down in front of the mirror to plait her hair. It was slow going, because her back, shoulders, and upper arms were also stiff. Hot water had improved the situation but not entirely cured it.

Yes, it was a good-sized baby for its age, she thought, so absorbed in getting the plait just right that what she was thinking did not even really register. But as she was finishing, she looked into the mirror which reflected the room behind her and saw something which widened her eyes. The morning's other, more minor discordancies slipped from her mind in an instant.

"Oh my God," Rosie said in a strengthless little voice. She got up and walked across the room on legs which felt as nerveless as stilts.

In most regards the picture was just the same. The blonde woman still stood on top of her hill with her plaited hair hanging down between her shoulderblades and her left arm raised, but now the hand shading her eyes made sense, because the thunderheads which had overhung the scene were gone. The sky above the woman in the short gown was the faded blue denim of a humid day in July. A few dark birds which hadn't been there before circled in that sky, but Rosie hardly noticed them.

The sky's blue because the storm is over, she thought. *It ended while I was . . . well . . . while I was somewhere else.*

All she could remember for sure about that somewhere else was that it had been dark and scary. That was enough; she didn't *want* to remember any more, and she thought maybe she didn't want to have her picture re-framed, after all. She knew she had changed her mind about showing it to Bill tomorrow, or even mentioning it. It would be bad if he saw the change from overcast and thunderheads to hazy sunshine, yes, but it would be even worse if he saw no change at all. That would mean she was losing her mind.

I'm not sure I want the damned thing anymore at all, she thought. *It's scary. Do you want to hear something really hilarious? I think it might be haunted.*

She picked the unframed canvas up, holding the edges with her palms, denying her conscious mind access to the thought

(careful Rosie don't fall in)

that caused her to handle it that way. There was a tiny closet to the right of the door leading out into the hall, with nothing in it yet but the lowtop sneakers she'd been wearing when she left Norman and a new sweater made out of some cheap synthetic stuff. She had to put the picture down in order to open the door (she could have tucked it under her arm long enough to free one hand, of course, but somehow didn't like to do that), and when she picked it up again she paused, looking fixedly at it. The sun was out, definitely new, and there were big black birds circling in the sky above the temple, *probably* new, but wasn't there something else, as well? Some other change? She thought so, and she thought she wasn't seeing it because it wasn't an addition but a deletion. Something was gone. Something—

I don't want to know, Rosie told herself brusquely. *I don't even want to think about it, so there.*

Yes, so there. But she was sorry to feel the way she did, because she'd begun by thinking of the picture as her personal good-luck charm, a kind of rabbit's foot. And of one thing there was absolutely no doubt: it was thinking of Rose Madder, standing there so fearlessly on top of her hill, that had pulled her through on her first day in the recording studio, when she'd suffered the panic attack. So she didn't want to be having these unpleasant feelings about the picture, and most assuredly didn't want to be afraid of it . . . but she was. After all, the weather in oil-paintings usually didn't clear up overnight, and the amount of stuff you could see in them usually didn't grow and contract, as if some un-seen projectionist were switching back and forth between lenses. She didn't know what she was going to do with the picture in the long run, but she knew where it was going to spend today and the coming week-end: in the closet, keeping her old sneaks company.

She put it in there, propped it against the wall (resisting an urge to turn it around so it would also face the wall), and then closed the door. With that done, she slipped into her only good blouse, took her purse, and left the room. As she walked down the long, dingy corridor leading to the stairs, two words whispered up from the very bottom of her mind: *I repay.* She stopped at the head of the stairs, shivering so violently she almost dropped her purse, and for a moment her right leg ached almost all the way up to her buttock, as if she had been struck with a savage cramp. Then it passed, and she went quickly down to the first floor. *I won't think about it,* she told herself as she walked down the street to the bus stop. *I don't have to if I don't want to, and I most definitely don't want to. I'll think about Bill instead. Bill, and his motorcycle.*

12

Thinking about Bill got her to work and into the dark-toned world of *Kill All My Tomorrows* without a hitch, and at lunch there was even less time to think of the woman in the painting. Mr. Lefferts took her to a tiny Italian place called Della Femmina, the nicest restaurant Rosie had ever been in, and while she was eating her melon, he offered her what he called "a more solid business arrangement." He proposed signing her to a contract which would pay her eight hundred dollars a week for twenty weeks or twelve books, whichever came first. It wasn't the thousand a week Rhoda had urged her to hold out for, but Robbie also promised to put her together with an agent who would set her up with as many radio spots as she wanted.

"You can make twenty-two thousand dollars by the end of the year, Rose. More, if you want it . . . but why knock yourself out?"

She asked him if she could have the weekend to think about it. Mr. Lefferts told her she certainly could. Before he left her in the lobby of the Corn Building (Rhoda and Curt were sitting together on a bench by the elevator, gossiping like a couple of thieves), he held his hand out to her. She returned the gesture, expecting her hand to be shaken. Instead he took it in both of his, bowed, and kissed it. The gesture—no one had ever kissed her hand before, although she had seen it done in lots of movies—sent a shiver up her back.

It was only as she sat in the recording booth, watching Curt thread up a fresh reel in the other room, that her thoughts returned to the picture which was now safely

(you hope Rosie you hope)

stashed away in her closet. Suddenly she knew what the other change had been, what had been subtracted from the picture: the armlet. The woman in the rose madder chiton had been wearing it above her right elbow. This morning her arm had been bare all the way to her shapely shoulder.

13

When she got back to her room that night, Rosie dropped to her knees and peered beneath her unmade bed. The gold armlet lay all the way in the back, standing on edge in the dark and gleaming softly. To Rosie it looked like the wedding ring of a giantess. Something else lay beside it: a small folded square of blue cloth. She'd found a piece of her missing nightgown after all, it seemed. There were reddish-purple spatters on it. These looked like blood, but Rosie knew they weren't; they were the spill of fruits better not tasted. She had scrubbed similar stains off her fingers this morning in the shower.

The armlet was extremely heavy—a pound at least, perhaps even two. If it was made of the stuff it looked like it was made of, how much might it be worth? Twelve thousand dollars? Fifteen? Not bad, considering it had somehow come out of a painting she'd gotten by trading away a nearly worthless engagement ring. Still, she didn't like to touch it, and she put it on the nighttable beside the lamp.

She held the little packet of blue cotton in her hand for a moment, sitting there like a teenager with her back propped against the bed and her feet crossed, and then she unfolded one side. She saw three seeds, three little seeds, and as Rosie looked at them with hopeless and unreasoning horror, those merciless words recurred, clanging in her head like iron bells:

I repay.

VII

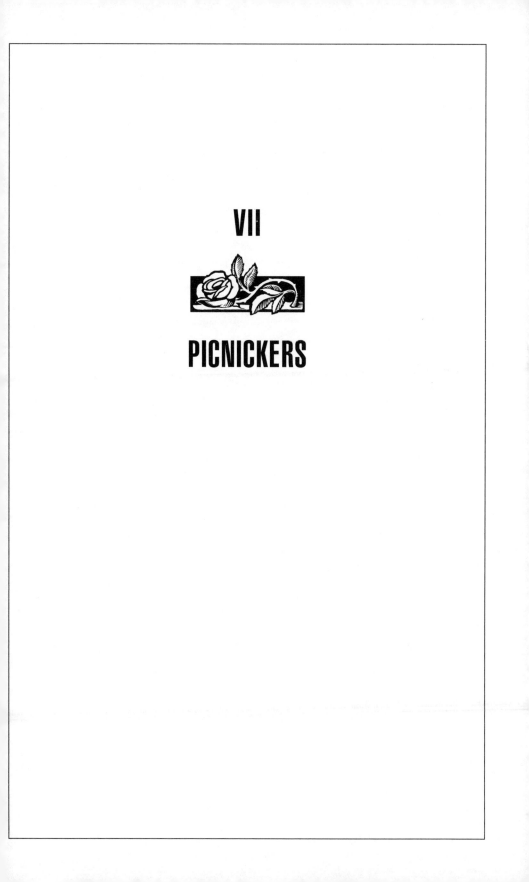

PICNICKERS

1

Norman had been trolling for her.

He lay awake late in his hotel room on Thursday night and across midnight's dark knife-edge into Friday morning. He turned off all the lights except for the fluorescent bar over the bathroom sink; it threw a diffuse glow across the room that he liked. It made him think of the way streetlights looked when you saw them through a heavy mist. He lay almost exactly as Rosie had lain before falling asleep on that same Thursday night, only with just one hand under his pillow instead of both. He needed the other to smoke with, and to convey the bottle of Glenlivet standing on the floor to his lips.

Where are you, Rosie? *he asked the wife who was no longer there.* Where are you and where did you ever find the nerve to cut and run, a scared little creepmouse like you?

It was this second question he cared about the most—how she had dared. The first one didn't matter all that much, not in any practical sense, because he knew where she was going to be on Saturday. A lion doesn't have to bother himself about where the zebra feeds; all he has to do is wait by the waterhole where it drinks. So far, so good, but still . . . how had *she ever dared leave him in the first place? Even if there was no life for him beyond their final conversation, he wanted to know that. Had it been planned? An accident? An aberration born of a single impulse? Had anyone helped her (besides, that was, the late Peter Slowik and the Cavalcade of Cunts on Durham Avenue)? What had she been doing since she'd hit the bricks of this charming little city by the lake? Waitressing? Shaking farts out of sheets in some fleabag like this? He didn't think so. She was too lazy to do menial work, you only had to look at the way she kept house to see that, and she had no skills to do anything else. If you wore tits, that left just one other choice. She was out there someplace right now, selling it on some streetcorner. Of course she was; what else? God knew she was a lousy lay, screwing her had been about as exciting as fucking mud, but pussy was something men would pay for even if it didn't do anything but lie there and drool a little after the rodeo was over. So yes, sure, she was probably out there selling it.*

He'd ask her about it, though. He would ask her everything. And when he had all the answers he needed, all the answers he ever wanted from the likes of her, he would wrap his belt around her neck so she couldn't scream, and then he would bite . . . and bite . . . and bite. His mouth and jaws still ached from what he had done to Thumper the Amazing Urban Jewboy, but he wouldn't let that stop him, or even slow him down. He had three Percodans at the bottom of his traveling bag, and he would take them before he went to work on his lost lamb, his sweet little rambling Rose. As for afterward, after it was over, after the Percs wore off . . .

But he couldn't see that, and he didn't want to see that. He had an idea that there was going to be no after, only darkness. And that was all right. In fact, a long dose of darkness might be just what the doctor ordered.

He lay in bed and drank the best Scotch in the world and burned one cigarette after another, watching the smoke drift up to the ceiling in silky reefs that turned blue when they passed through the soft white radiance from the bathroom, and he trolled for her. He trolled for her, and his hook slipped through nothing but water. There was nothing there and it was driving him crazy. It was as if she had been abducted by aliens, or something. At one point, quite drunk by then, he had dropped a live cigarette into his hand and clenched his fist around it, imagining it was her hand instead of his, that he was holding his hands over hers, clamping hers tight on the heat. And as the pain bit in and wisps of smoke curled out around his knuckles, he whispered, "Where are you, Rose? Where are you hiding, you thief?"

Not long after that he drifted off. He woke up around ten on Friday morning, unrested and hungover and vaguely frightened. He had dreamed peculiar dreams all night long. In them he was still awake and still lying in his bed here on the ninth floor of the Whitestone, and the light from the bathroom was still cutting softly through the darkness of his room, and the cigarette smoke was still rising through it in shifting blue membranes. Only in his dreams, he could see pictures like movies in the smoke. He could see Rose in the smoke.

There you are, he thought as he watched her walk through a dead garden in a pelting rainstorm. *Rose was naked for some reason, and he felt an unexpected bite of lust. He hadn't felt anything at the sight of her nakedness but weary revulsion for eight years or more, but now she looked different. Pretty good, in fact.*

It isn't that she's lost weight, *he thought in the dream,* although it looks like she has . . . a little, anyway. Mostly it's something about the way she's moving what she's got. What is it?

Then it came to him. She had the look of a woman who's fucking someone and hasn't had anywhere near enough just yet. If it had even crossed his mind to doubt this assessment—to say What, Rosie? *You got to be kidding, cousin—one look at her hair would have been enough to settle the question once and for all. She'd dyed it slut-blonde, as if she thought she was Sharon Stone, or maybe Madonna.*

He watched the smoke-Rose leave the weird dead garden and approach a stream so dark it looked more like ink than water. She crossed it on a path of stepping-stones, holding her arms out for balance, and he saw that she had some sort of wet, crumpled rag in one hand. It looked like a nightgown to Norman and he thought: Why don't you put it on, you brazen bitch? Or are you expecting your boyfriend to come by and give your ticket a punch? I'd like to see that. I really would. Tell you one thing—if I so much as catch you holding hands with a guy when I finally track you down, the cops are going to find his goddam trouser-rat sticking out of his asshole like a birthday candle.

No one came by, though—not in the dream, anyway. The Rose over his bed, the smoke-Rose, walked down a path through a grove of trees that looked as dead as . . . well, as dead as Peter Slowik. At last she came into a clearing where there was one tree which still looked alive. She knelt down, picked up a bunch of seeds, and wrapped them in what looked like another piece of her nightgown. With that done she got up, went to a set of stairs near the tree (in dreams you never knew what fucked-up thing was going to happen next), and disappeared down them. He was waiting around for her to come back up when he began to feel a presence behind him, something as cold and chill as a draft from an open meat-locker. He'd handled some fairly scary people during his years as a cop—the PCP addicts he and Harley Bissington had had to deal with from time to time were probably the scariest—and you developed a sense of their presence after awhile. Norman was feeling that now. Someone was coming up behind him, and he never doubted for a moment that it was someone dangerous.

"I repay," *a woman's voice whispered. It was a sweet voice, and soft, but it was terrifying, just the same. There was no sanity in it.*

"Good for you, bitch," *Norman said in his dream.* "You try to repay me and I'll change your whole fucking outlook."

She screamed, a sound that seemed to go directly to the center of his head without even passing through his ears, and he sensed her lunging toward him with her hands out. He drew in a deep breath and blew the cigarette smoke apart. The woman disappeared. Norman felt her go. For a little while after that there was only darkness, with him floating peacefully in the middle of it, untouched by the fears and desires which haunted him when he was awake.

He woke up at ten past ten on Friday morning and shifted his eyes from the clock by the bed to the hotel room ceiling, almost expecting to see phantom figures moving through decaying stacks of cigarette smoke. There were no figures, of course, phantom or otherwise. No smoke, for that matter—just the lingering smell of Pall Malls, in hoc signo vinces. *There was only Detective Norman Daniels, lying here in a sweaty bed that smelled of tobacco and used booze. His mouth tasted as if he had spent the previous evening sucking the end of a freshly polished cordovan shoe, and his left hand hurt like a mad bastard. He opened it and saw a shiny blister in the center of his palm. He looked at it for a long time, while pigeons fluttered and cooed at each other on the shit-encrusted ledge that ran past his window. At last the memory of blistering himself with the cigarette came back, and he nodded. He'd done it because he couldn't see Rose no matter how hard he tried . . . and then, as if in compensation, he'd had crazy dreams about her all night long.*

He placed two fingers on the sides of the blister and squeezed, slowly increasing the pressure until it popped. He wiped his hand on the sheet, relishing the waves of stinging pain. He lay looking at his hand—watching it throb, almost—for a minute or so. Then he reached under his bed for his traveling bag. There was a Sucrets tin at the bottom, and in it were a dozen or so assorted pills. A few were speedy, but most were downers. As a general rule, Norman found he could get up with no pharmacological help at all; it was getting back down again that sometimes presented a problem.

He took a Percodan with a small swallow of Scotch, then lay back, looking up at the ceiling and once again smoking one cigarette after another, stubbing them out in the overflowing ashtray when they were done.

This time it wasn't Rose he was thinking of, at least not directly; this time it was the picnic he was considering, the one being thrown by her new friends. He had been to Ettinger's Pier, and what he saw there wasn't encouraging. It was large—a combination beach, picnic area, and amusement park—and he didn't see any way he could stake it out with any confidence of seeing her arrive or leave. If he'd had six men (even four, if they knew what they were doing), he would have felt differently, but he was on his own. There were three ways in, assuming she didn't come by boat, and he could hardly watch all three of them at the same time. That meant working the crowd, and working the crowd would be a bitchkitty. He wished he could believe that Rose would be the only one there to-morrow who would recognize him, but if wishes were pigs, bacon would always be on sale. He had to assume they would be looking for him, and he would also have to assume they had received pictures of him from one of their sister groups back home. He didn't know about the x, but he was coming to believe that the first two letters in fax stood for Fucked Again.

That was one part of the problem. The other part was his own belief, backstopped by more than one bitter experience, that disguises were a recipe for disaster in situations like this. The only quicker, surer route to failure in the field was probably wearing the ever-popular wire, where you could lose six months' worth of surveillance and setup if a kid happened to be running a radio-controlled boat or racecar in the area where you were planning to bring the hammer down on some shitbag.

All right, *he thought.* Don't bitch about it. Remember what old Whitey Slater used to say—the situation is what the situation is. How you're going to work around it is the only question. And don't even think of putting it off. Their goddam party is just twenty-four hours away, and if you miss her there, you could hunt for her until Christmas and not find her. In case you hadn't noticed, this is a big city.

He got up, walked into the bathroom, and showered with his blistered hand stuck out through the shower curtain. He dressed in faded jeans and a nondescript green shirt, putting on his CHISOX *cap and tucking the cheap sunglasses into his shirt pocket, at least for the time being. He took the elevator down to the lobby and went to the newsstand to get a paper and a box of Band-Aids. While he was waiting for the dope behind the counter to figure out his change, he looked over the guy's shoulder and through a glass panel at the back of the newsstand alcove. He could see the service elevators through this panel, and as he watched, one of them opened. Three chattering, laughing chambermaids stepped out. They were carrying their purses, and Norman guessed they were on their way to lunch. He had seen the one in the middle—slim, pretty, fluffy blonde hair—someplace else. After a moment it came to him. He had been on his way to check out Daughters and Sisters. The blonde had walked beside him for a little while. Red slacks. Cute little ass.*

"Here you are, sir," *the counterman said. Norman stuffed his change into his pocket without looking at it. Nor did he look at the trio of maids as he shouldered past them, not even at the one with the cute tush. He had cross-referenced her automatically, that was all—it was a cop reflex, a knee that jerked on its own. His conscious mind was fixed on one thing and one thing only: the best way to spot Rose tomorrow without being spotted himself.*

He was heading up the corridor toward the doors when he heard two words which he at first thought must have come out of his own head: Ettinger's Pier.

His stride faltered, his heart kicked into overdrive, and the blister in the palm of his hand began to throb fiercely. It was a single missed step, that was all—that one little hesitation, and then he went on heading toward the revolving doors with his head down. Someone looking at him might have thought he'd felt a brief muscle-twinge in his knee or calf, no more than that, and that was good. He didn't dare *falter, that was the hell of it. If the woman who'd spoken was one of the cunts from their clubhouse over on Durham Avenue, she might recognize him if he drew attention to himself . . . might have* already *recognized him, if the speaker of those two magic words was the little honey he'd crossed the street beside the other day. He knew it was unlikely—as a cop he'd had first-hand experience of how amazingly, numbingly unobservant most civilians were—but from time to time it did happen. Killers and kidnappers and bank-thieves who had eluded capture long enough to make the FBI's Ten Most Wanted List suddenly found themselves back in the slam, dropped by a 7-Eleven clerk who read* True Detective *or a meter maid who watched all the reality-crime shows on TV. He didn't dare stop, but—*

—but he had *to stop.*

Norman knelt abruptly to the left of the swinging door with his back to the women. He dropped his head and pretended to tie his shoe.

"—sorry to miss the concert, but if I want that car, I can't pass up the—"

Out the door they went, but what Norman had heard convinced him: it was *the picnic the woman was talking about, the picnic and the concert that was going to round off the day, some group called the Indian Girls, probably lezzies. So there was a chance that this woman knew Rosie. Not a good chance—lots of people who weren't tight with Daughters and Sisters would be at Ettinger's Pier tomorrow—but a chance, just the same. And Norman was a man who believed emphatically in the fickle finger of fate. The hell of it was, he did not yet know which of the three had been talking.*

Let it be Blondie, *he prayed as he got quickly to his feet and went out through the swinging door.* Let it be Blondie with the big eyes and the cute ass. Let it be her, what do you say?

It was dangerous to follow, of course—you could never tell when one of them might glance idly around and win the super bonus round of Place the Face—but at this point he could do nothing else. He sauntered along behind them, his head casually turned to one side, as if the junkola in the shop windows he was passing was of vital interest to him.

"How are you making out on pillowcases today?" the tub of guts walking on the inside asked the other two.

"For once, they're all there," the older woman walking on the outside said. "How about you, Pam?"

"I haven't counted yet, it's too depressing," Blondie replied, and they all laughed—those high, giggly sounds that always made Norman feel as if his fillings were cracking in his mouth. He stopped at once, looking in a window at a bunch of sporting goods, letting the maids pull ahead. It was her, all right—no question about it. Blondie was the one who had said the magic words Ettinger's Pier. *Maybe it changed everything, maybe it changed nothing. Right now he was too excited to figure it out. It was certainly an amazing stroke of luck, though—the kind of miraculous, coincidental break you always hoped for when you were working a longshot case, the break that happened more often than anyone would ever believe.*

For now he would file this in the back of his mind and proceed with Plan A. He wouldn't even ask about Blondie back at the hotel, at least not yet. He knew her name was Pam, and that was plenty to start with.

Norman walked to the bus stop, waited fifteen minutes for the airport shuttle, and then hopped on board. It was a long ride; the terminal was on the edge of the city. When he finally disembarked in front of Terminal A, he slipped on his dark glasses, crossed the street, and made his way to the longterm parking area. The first car he tried jumping had been there so long the battery was dead. The second one, a nondescript Ford Tempo, started all right. He told the man in the collection booth that he'd been in Dallas for three weeks and had lost his ticket. He was always losing them, he said. He lost laundry tickets, too, and he was always having to show his driver's license at Photomat when he stopped in to pick up his snapshots. The man in the collection booth nodded and nodded, the way you do at a boring story you've already heard about ten thousand times. When Norman humbly offered him an extra ten dollars in lieu of the ticket, the man in the collection booth perked up a little. The money disappeared.

Norman Daniels drove out of longterm parking at almost exactly the same moment that Robbie Lefferts was offering his fugitive wife what he termed "a more solid business arrangement."

Two miles down the road, Norman parked behind a beat-to-shit Le Sabre and swapped license plates. Another two miles on, he stopped at a Robo-Wash. He had a bet with himself that the Tempo would turn out

*to be dark blue, but he lost. It was green. He didn't think it mattered—
the man in the collection booth had only taken his eyes off his little black-
and-white TV when the tenspot had appeared under his nose—but it was
best to play safe. It increased the comfort level.*

*Norman turned on the radio and found an oldies station. Shirley Ellis
was on, and he sang along as Shirley instructed, "If the first two letters
are ever the same / Drop them both and say the name / Like Barry-Barry,
drop the B, oh-Arry / That's the only rule that is contrary." Norman realized he knew every word of that stupid old song. What kind of world
was it where you couldn't remember the fucking quadratic equation or
the various forms of the French verb* avoir *two years after you got out of
high school, but when you were getting on for forty years old you could
still remember* Nick-Nick-bo-bick, banana-fanna-fo-fick, fee-fi-mo-mick,
Nick? *What kind of world was that?*

One that's slipping behind me now, *Norman thought serenely, and yes,
that seemed to be the truth. It was like in those science fiction movies
where the spacemen saw Earth dwindling in the viewscreens, first a ball,
then a coin, then a tiny glowing dot, then all gone. That was what the
inside of his head was like now—a spacecraft headed out on a five-year
mission to explore new worlds and go where no man had gone before. The
Starship* Norman, *approaching warp-speed.*

*Shirley Ellis finished up and something by the Beatles came on. Norman
twisted the radio's volume knob off so hard he broke it. He didn't want
to listen to any of that hippy-dippy "Hey Jude" crap today.*

*He was still a couple of miles from where the real city began when he
saw a place called The Base Camp.* ARMY SURPLUS LIKE YOU NEVER FIND!
*the sign out front read, and for some reason that made him burst out
laughing. He thought it was in some ways the single most peculiar motto
he'd seen in his whole life; it seemed to mean* something, *but it was
impossible to say just what. Anyway, the sign didn't matter. The store
probably had one of the things he was looking for, and that did.*

There was a big banner reading ALWAYS BE SAFE, NEVER BE SORRY *over
the middle aisle. Norman inspected three different kinds of "stun-gas,"
pepper-gas pellets, a rack of Ninja throwing-stars (the perfect weapon for
home defense if you should happen to be attacked by a blind quadriplegic),
gas guns that fired rubber bullets, slingshots, brass knuckles both plain and
studded, blackjacks and bolas, whips and whistles.*

*Halfway down this aisle was a glass case containing what Norman con-
sidered to be the only really useful item in The Base Camp. For sixty-
three-fifty he purchased a taser which produced a large (although probably
not the 90,000 volts promised on the label) wallop of juice between its*

two steel poles when the triggers were pushed. Norman considered this weapon every bit as dangerous as a small-caliber pistol, and the best part was that one did not have to sign one's name anywhere in order to purchase one.

"You wah niy-vole baddery widdat?" the clerk asked. He was a bullet-headed young man with a harelip. He wore a teeshirt which said BETTER TO HAVE A GUN AND NOT NEED ONE THAN NEED ONE AND NOT HAVE ONE. To Norman he looked like the sort of fellow whose parents might have been blood relatives. "Dass waddit runs on—a niy-vole."

Norman realized what the young man with the harelip was trying to say and nodded. "Give me two," he said. "Let's live a little."

The young man laughed as if this was the funniest line he'd ever heard, even funnier than Army Surplus Like You Never Find!, and then he bent down, got two nine-volt batteries from under the counter, and slapped them down beside Norman's Omega taser.

"Dull-feetcha!" the young man cried, and laughed some more. Norman figured this one out, too, after a moment, and laughed right along with Young Mister Harelip and later he thought that was the exact moment when he hit warp-speed and all the stars turned into lines. All ahead, Mr. Sulu—this time we're going way past the Klingon Empire.

He drove the stolen Tempo back into the city and in a part of town where the smiling models on the cigarette billboards started being black rather than white, he found a barber shop by the charming name of Cut Me Some Slack. He went in and found a young black man with a cool moustache sitting in an old-fashioned barber chair. There were Walkman earphones on his head and a copy of Jet in his lap.

"Whatchoo want?" the black barber asked. He spoke perhaps more brusquely than he would have to a black man, but not discourteously, either. You weren't discourteous to a man like this without a damned good reason, especially when you were alone in your shop. He was six-two at least, with broad shoulders and big, thick legs. Also, he smelled like a cop.

Above the mirror were photographs of Michael Jordan, Charles Barkley, and Jalen Rose. Jordan was wearing a Birmingham Barons baseball uniform. Above his picture was a slip of paper with THE ONCE & FUTURE BULL typed on it. Norman pointed. "Do me like that," he said.

The black barber looked at Norman carefully, first making sure he wasn't drunk or stoned, then trying to make sure he wasn't joking. The second was harder than the first. "Whatchoo saying, brother? Are you saying you want a cleanhead?"

"That's exactly what I'm saying." Norman ran a hand through his hair, *which was a thick black just starting to show flecks of gray at the temples. It was neither exceptionally short nor exceptionally long. He had worn it at this same length for almost twenty years. He looked at himself in the mirror, trying to imagine what he was going to look like, as bald as Michael Jordan, only white. He couldn't do it. With luck, Rose and her new friends wouldn't be able to, either.*

"You sure?"

Suddenly Norman felt almost sick with the desire to knock this man down and drop both knees onto his chest and lean over and bite his entire upper lip, cool moustache and all, right off his face. He supposed he knew why, too. He looked like that memorable little cocksucker, Ramon Sanders. The one who had tried to cash in on the ATM card his lying bitch of a wife had stolen.

Oh, barber, *Norman thought.* Oh barber, you're so close to being nothing but taillights. Ask one more question, say one more wrong word in my face, and that's all you'll be. And I can't say anything to you; I couldn't warn you even if I wanted to, because right now my own voice is all the firing-pin I'd need. So here we are, and here we go.

The barber gave him another long, careful look. Norman stood where he was and let him do it. Now he felt composed. What happened would be what happened. It was all in this jiggedy-jig's hands.

"All right, I guess you are," the barber said at last. His voice was mild and disarming. Norman relaxed his right hand, which had been shoved deep into his pocket and gripping the handle of the taser. The barber put his magazine on the counter beside his bottles of tonic and cologne (there was a little brass sign there that said SAMUEL LOWE), *then got up and shook out a plastic apron. "You wanna be like Mike, let's do it."*

Twenty minutes later, Norman was staring at himself thoughtfully in the mirror. Samuel Lowe stood beside his chair, watching him look. Lowe seemed apprehensive, but he also seemed interested. He looked like a man seeing something familiar from an entirely new perspective. Two new customers had come in. They were also looking at Norman look at himself, and they wore identical expressions of appraisal.

"The man be handsome," one of the newcomers said. He spoke in a tone of faint surprise, and mostly to himself.

Norman couldn't get entirely straight in his mind the fact that the man in the mirror was still him. He winked and the mirror-man winked, he smiled and the mirror-man smiled, he turned and the mirror-man turned, but it didn't help. Before, he'd had the brow of a cop; now he had the brow of a mathematics professor, a brow that went into the stratosphere. He couldn't get over the smooth, somehow sensuous curves of his bald

*skull. And its whiteness. He hadn't thought he had anything like a tan,
but compared to his pallid skull, the rest of his skin was as brown as a
lifeguard's. His head looked strangely fragile, and too weirdly perfect to
belong to the likes of him. To belong to any human being, especially a
male. It looked like a piece of Delft china.*

"You ain't got a bad head 'tall, man," Lowe said. *He spoke tentatively,
but Norman had no sense he was trying to flatter him, and that was good,
because Norman was in no mood to have someone blow smoke up his ass.*
"Look good. Look younger. Don't he, Dale?"

"Ain't bad," *the other newcomer agreed.* "Nossir, not half."

"How much did you say?" *Norman asked Samuel Lowe. He tried to
turn away from the mirror and was distressed and a little frightened to
find that his eyes tried to follow the top of his head, to see how it looked
in the back. That sense of disassociation was stronger within him than
ever. He* wasn't *the man in the mirror, the man with the scholar's bald
head rising above heavy black eyebrows; how could he be? This was some
stranger, that was all, some fantastic Lex Luthor up to no good in Me-
tropolis, and the things he did from here on out didn't matter. From here
on out, nothing mattered. Except catching Rose, of course. And talking
to her.*

Up close.

*Lowe was giving him that cautious look again, breaking it off to dart
glances at the other two patrons, and Norman suddenly realized he was
checking to see if they'd help him, if the big white man—the big* bald
white man—suddenly went berserk.

"I'm sorry," *he said, trying to make his voice soft and conciliatory.* "You
were talking, weren't you? What did you say?"

"I said thirty sounds about right to me. How's it sound to you?"

*Norman took a folded-over packet of bills out of his left front pocket,
slid two twenties out from under the tarnished old moneyclip, and held
them out.*

"Thirty sounds too low," *he said.* "Take forty, along with my apologies.
You did a great job. I've just had a bitch of a week, that's all." *You don't
know the half of it, buddy,* he thought.

Samuel Lowe relaxed visibly and took the money. "No prob, bro," *he
said.* "And I wasn't kiddin—you ain't got a bad-lookin head at all. You
ain't Michael, but ain't nobody Michael."

" 'Cept Michael," *the newcomer named Dale said. The three black
men laughed heartily and nodded at one another. Although he could
have killed all three of them without turning a hair, Norman nodded
and laughed along with them. The newcomers in the barber shop had*

changed things. It was time to be careful again. Still laughing, he went out.

A trio of teenagers, also black, were leaning against a fence near the Tempo, but they hadn't bothered doing anything to the car, possibly because it was too much of a dog to bother with. They eyed Norman's pallid white head with interest, then glanced at each other and rolled their eyes. They were fourteen or so, boys without much trouble in them. The one in the middle started to say "You lookin at me?*" like Robert De Niro in* Taxi Driver. *Norman seemed to sense this and stared at him—just at* him, *it seemed, ignoring the other two completely. The one in the middle decided that maybe his De Niro imitation needed a little more work and quit it.*

Norman got into his freshly washed stolen car and drove away. Six blocks in toward the center of the city, he went into a used-clothing store called Play It Again, Sam. There were several browsers in the store, and they all looked at him, but that was okay. Norman didn't mind being looked at, especially if it was his freshly shaven skull they were paying attention to. If they were looking at the top of his head, they wouldn't have the slightest fucking idea what his face looked like five minutes after he left.

He found a motorcycle jacket that gleamed with studs and zippers and small silver chains and creaked in every fold when he took it off its hanger. The clerk opened his mouth to ask two hundred and forty dollars for the jacket, looked at the haunted eyes peering out from beneath the awesome white desert of that freshly shaven skull, and told Norman the jacket was one-eighty, plus tax. He would have gone lower had Norman dickered, but Norman didn't. He was tired now, his head was throbbing, and he wanted to go back to the hotel and go to sleep. He wanted to sleep right through until tomorrow. He needed all the rest he could get, because tomorrow was going to be a busy day.

He made two more stops on the way back. The first was at a store which sold ostomy supplies. Here Norman bought a motorless second-hand wheelchair which would fit, folded up, into the trunk of the Tempo. Then he went to the Women's Cultural Center and Museum. Here he paid six dollars to get in but looked at no exhibits and did not so much as peer into the auditorium, where a panel discussion on natural childbirth was being held. He made a quick trip to the gift shop, then left.

Back at the Whitestone, he went upstairs without asking anyone about Blondie with the cute little ass. He would not have trusted himself to ask for a glass of club soda in his current condition. His newly shaven head was pounding like a steel-forge, his eyes were beating in their sockets, his teeth hurt and his jaws throbbed. Worst of all, his mind now seemed to be bobbing along above him like a float in the Macy's Thanksgiving Day Parade; it felt as if it were tethered to the rest of him by a single fragile thread and might break away at any moment. He had to lie down. To sleep. Maybe then his mind would go back inside his head, where it belonged. As for Blondie, his best course would be to treat her as an ace in the hole, something to be used only if absolutely necessary. Break Glass in Case of Emergency.

Norman went back to bed at four o'clock on Friday afternoon. The throbbing behind his temples was no longer anything resembling a hangover; it was now one of the headaches he called his "specials." He got them frequently when he was working hard, and since Rose had left and his big drug-case had heated up, two a week weren't unusual. As he lay in bed looking up at the ceiling, his eyes ran and his nose leaked and he could see funny bright zigzag patterns pulsing around the edges of things. The pain had reached the point where it felt like there was some horrible fetus in the middle of his head, trying to be born; the point where there was nothing to do but hunker down and wait for it to be over, and the way you did that was by getting through the moments one at a time, going from one to the next the way a person might use stepping-stones to cross a stream. That tugged some hazy memory far back in his mind, but it couldn't get past the relentless throbbing, and Norman let it go. He rubbed his hand back and forth across the top of his head. The smoothness up there felt like nothing that could be a part of him; it was like touching the hood of a freshly waxed car.

"Who am I?" he asked the empty room. "Who am I? Why am I here? What am I doing? Who am I?"

Before he could stab at an answer to any of these questions he fell asleep. The pain followed him for quite a distance into its dreamless depths, like a bad idea that won't let go, but finally Norman left it behind. His head sagged to one side on his pillow, and a wetness which was not precisely tears ran out of his left eye and left nostril and trickled down his cheek. He began to snore thickly.

When he woke up twelve hours later, at four o'clock on Saturday morning, his headache was gone. He felt fresh and energized, as he almost always did after one of his specials. He sat up, put his feet on the floor, and looked out the window at darkness. The pigeons were out there on the ledge, cooing to each other even in their sleep. He knew, completely and surely and without any doubt, that this day was going to see the end of it. Probably the end of him, *as well, but that was a minor matter. Just knowing there would be no more headaches, not ever, made that seem like a fair trade.*

Across the room, his new motorcycle jacket hung over a chair like a black and headless ghost.

Wake up early, Rose, *he thought almost tenderly.* Wake up early, honeybunch, and get a good look at the sunrise, why don't you? You ought to get the best look you can, because it's the last one you're ever going to see.

2

Rosie woke at a few minutes past four on Saturday morning and fumbled for the lamp by the bed, terrified, sure that Norman was in the room with her, sure she could smell his cologne, all my men wear English Leather or they wear nothing at all.

She almost knocked the lamp onto the floor in her panicky efforts to make a light, but when it was finally on (with the base hanging halfway over oblivion) her fear subsided quickly. It was just her room, small and neat and sane, and the only thing she could smell was the faint, bedwarm fragrance of her own skin. No one was here but her . . . and Rose Madder, of course. But Rose Madder was safely put away in the closet, where she undoubtedly still stood with one hand raised to shade her eyes, looking down at the ruins of the temple.

I was dreaming about him, she thought as she sat up. *I was having another nightmare about Norman, that's why I woke up so scared.*

She pushed the lamp back on the table. It clinked against the armlet. Rose picked it up and looked at it. Strange, how hard it was to remember

(what you have to remember)

how she'd come by this trinket. Had she bought it in Bill's shop, because it looked like the one the woman in her picture was wearing? She didn't know, and that was troubling. How could you forget

(what you need to forget)

a thing like that?

Rosie lifted the circlet, which felt as heavy as gold but was probably just gilded potmetal, and looked across the room through it, like a woman looking through a telescope.

As she did, a fragment of her dream came back, and she realized it hadn't been about Norman at all. It had been about Bill. They had been on his motorcycle, but instead of taking her to a picnic place by the lake, he had driven her down a path that wound deeper and deeper into a sinister forest of dead trees. After awhile they came into a clearing, and in the clearing was a single live tree, laden with fruit the color of Rose Madder's chiton.

Oh, what a great first course! Bill had cried cheerily, hopping off his motorcycle and hurrying toward the tree. *I've heard about these—eat one and you can see out of the back of your head, eat two and you live forever!*

That was where the dream had crossed the line from the merely unsettling into real nightmare country. She knew somehow that the fruit of that tree wasn't magic but horribly poisonous and she ran to him, wanting to stop him before he could bite into one of the tempting fruits. But Bill wouldn't be convinced. He merely put an arm around her, gave her a little hug, and said, *Don't be silly, Rosie—I know pomegranates, and these aren't them.*

That was when she'd awakened, shivering madly in the dark and thinking not about Bill but about Norman . . . as if Norman were lying in bed someplace near and thinking about *her.* This idea made Rosie cross her arms over her breasts and hug herself. It was all too possible that he was doing just that. She put the armlet back down on the table, hurried into the bathroom, and turned on the shower.

Her troubling dream of Bill and the poisoned fruit, her questions about where or how she might have come by the armlet, and her confused feelings about the picture she'd bought, then unframed, then hidden away in the closet like a secret . . . all these things faded behind a larger and more immediate concern: her date. It was today, and every time she thought of that she felt something like a hot wire in her chest. She was both afraid and happy, but more than anything else she was curious. Her date. *Their* date.

If he even comes, a voice inside whispered ominously. *It could have all been a joke, you know. Or you might have scared him off.*

Rosie started to step into the water, and realized just in the nick of time that she was still wearing her panties.

"He'll come," she murmured as she bent and slipped them off. "He'll come, all right. I know he will."

As she ducked under the spray and reached for the shampoo, a voice far back in her mind —a very different voice, this time—whispered, *Beasts will fight.*

"What?" Rosie froze with the plastic bottle in one hand. She was frightened and didn't quite know why. "What did you say?"

Nothing. She couldn't even remember exactly what it was that she'd thought, only that it was something else about that damned picture, which had gotten into her head like the chorus of a song you can't forget. As she began to lather her hair, Rosie decided abruptly to get rid of it. The thought of doing that made her feel better, like the thought of quitting some bad habit—smoking, drinking at lunch—and by the time she stepped out of the shower, she was humming.

<h1 style="text-align:center">3</h1>

Bill didn't torture her with doubt by being late. Rosie had pulled one of the kitchen chairs over by the window so she could watch for him (at quarter past seven she had done this, three full hours after she'd stepped out of the shower), and at twenty-five past eight a motorcycle with a cooler strapped to the carrier-rack pulled into one of the spaces in front of the building. The driver's head was covered by a big blue helmet and the angle was wrong for her to see his face, but she knew it was him. Already the line of his shoulders was unmistakable to her. He gunned the engine once, then killed it and used a booted heel to drop the Harley's kickstand. He swung one leg off, and for a moment the line of his thigh was clearly visible against his faded jeans. Rosie felt a tremor of timid but unmistakable lust go through her and thought: *That's what I'll be thinking about tonight while I'm waiting to go to sleep; that's what I'm going to see. And if I'm very, very lucky, it's what I'll dream about.*

She thought of waiting for him up here, of letting him come to her the way a girl who is comfortable in the home of her parents might wait for the boy who is going to take her to the Homecoming Dance, waiting even after he has come, watching in her strapless party dress from behind the curtain of her bedroom window, smiling a small secret smile as he gets out of his father's newly washed and waxed car and comes to the door, self-consciously adjusting his bowtie or tugging on his cummerbund.

She thought of it, then opened the closet door, reached in, and snatched out her sweater. She hurried down the hall, slipping into it as she went. It crossed her mind as she came to the head of the stairs and saw him already halfway up, his head raised to look at her, that she had reached the perfect age: too old to be coy for the sake of coyness, but still too young not to believe that some hopes—the ones that really matter—may turn out against all odds to be justified.

"Hi," she said, looking down from her place. "You're on time."

"Sure," he said, looking up from his. He seemed faintly surprised. "I'm *always* on time. It's the way I was raised. I think it might have been

260

bred in my genes, too." He held one gloved hand up to her, like a cavalier in a movie. He smiled. "Are you ready?"

This was a question she didn't yet know how to answer, so she just met him where he was and took his hand and let him lead her down and out into the sunlight washing over the first Saturday of June. He stood her on the curb beside the leaning bike, looked her critically up and down, then shook his head. "Nope, nope, the sweater doesn't make it," he said. "Luckily, my Boy Scout training has never deserted me."

There were saddlebags on either side of the Harley's carrier-rack. He unbuckled one of them and pulled out a leather jacket similar to his own: zipper pockets high and low on either side, but otherwise black and plain. No studs, epaulets, lightning bolts, or geegaws. It was smaller than the one Bill wore. She looked at it hanging flat in his hands like a pelt, troubled by the obvious question.

He saw the look, understood it at once, and shook his head. "It's my dad's jacket. He taught me to ride on an old Indian hammerhead he took in trade for a dining-room table and a bedroom set. The year he turned twenty-one, he rode that bike all over America, he says. It was the kind you had to kick-start, and if you forgot to put the gearshift in neutral, it was apt to go tearing right out from under you."

"What happened? Did he crash it?" She smiled a little. "Did *you* crash it?"

"Neither one. It died of old age. Since then they've all been Harleys in the Steiner family. This is a Heritage softail, thirteen-forty-five cc." He touched the nacelle gently. "Dad hasn't ridden for five years or so now."

"Did he get tired of it?"

Bill shook his head. "No, he got glaucoma."

She slipped into the jacket. She guessed that Bill's father must be at least three inches shorter and maybe forty pounds lighter than his son, but the jacket still hung comically on her, almost to her knees. It was warm, though, and she zipped it up to her chin with a kind of sensuous pleasure.

"You look good," he said. "Kind of funny, like a kid playing dress-up, but good. Really."

She thought she could now say what she hadn't been able to when she and Bill had been sitting on the bench and eating hotdogs, and it suddenly seemed very important that she should say it.

"Bill?"

He looked at her with that little smile, but his eyes were serious. "Yeah?"

"Don't hurt me."

He considered this, the little smile staying on, his eyes still grave, and then he shook his head. "No. I won't."

"Do you promise?"

"Yeah. I promise. Come on, climb aboard. Have you ever ridden an iron pony before?"

She shook her head.

"Well, those little pegs are for your feet." He bent over the back of the bike, rummaged, and came up with a helmet. She observed its red-purple color with absolutely no surprise. "Have a brain-bucket."

She slipped it on over her head, bent forward, looked solemnly at herself in one of the Harley's side-mirrors, then burst out laughing. "I look like a football player!"

"Prettiest one on the team, too." He took her by the shoulders and turned her around. "It buckles under your chin. Here, let me." For a moment his face was kissing distance from hers, and she felt light-headed knowing that if he wanted to kiss her, right here on the sunny sidewalk with people going about their leisurely Saturday-morning errands, she would let him.

Then he stepped back.

"That strap too tight?"

She shook her head.

"Sure?"

She nodded.

"Say something, then."

"Iss sap's ot ooo ite," she said, and burst out laughing at his expression. Then he was laughing with her.

"Are you ready?" he asked her again. He was still smiling, but his eyes had returned to their former look of serious consideration, as if he knew that they had embarked on some grave enterprise, where any word or movement might have far-reaching consequences.

She made a fist, rapped the top of her helmet, and grinned nervously. "I guess I am. Who gets on first, you or me?"

"Me." He swung his leg over the saddle of the Harley. "Now you."

She swung her leg over carefully, and put her hands on his shoulders. Her heart was beating very fast.

"No," he said. "Around my waist, okay? I have to keep my arms and hands free to run the controls."

She slipped her hands in between his arms and sides and clasped them in front of his flat stomach. All at once she felt as if she were dreaming again. Had all of this come out of one small drop of blood on a sheet?

An impulse decision to walk out of her front door and just keep going? Was that even possible?

Dear God, please let this not be a dream, she thought.

"Feet up on the pegs, check?"

She put them there, and was fearfully enchanted when Bill rocked the bike upright and booted back the kickstand. Now, with only his feet holding them steady, it felt to her like the moment when a small boat's last mooring is slipped and it floats beside the dock, nodding more freely on the waves than previously. She leaned a little closer to his back, closed her eyes, and inhaled deeply. The smell of sunwarmed leather was pretty much as she had imagined it would be, and that was good. It was all good. Scary and good.

"I hope you like this," Bill said. "I really do."

He pushed a button on the right handlebar and the Harley went off like a gun beneath them. Rosie jumped and slipped closer to him, her grip tightening and becoming a little less self-conscious.

"Everything okay?" he called.

She nodded, realized he couldn't see that, and shouted back that yes, everything was fine.

A moment later the curb to their left was rolling backward. He snatched a quick glance over her shoulder for traffic, then swung across Trenton Street to the right side. It wasn't like a turn in a car; the motorcycle *banked,* like a small airplane lining itself up with the runway. Bill twisted the throttle and the Harley scooted forward, blowing a rattle of wind into her helmet and making her laugh.

"I thought you'd like it!" Bill called back over his shoulder as they stopped at the traffic light on the corner. When he put his foot down it was as if they were tethered to solid land once more, but by the thinnest of lines. When the light turned green the engine roared under her again, with more authority this time, and they swung onto Deering Avenue, running beside Bryant Park, rolling through the shadows of old oaks that were printed on the pavement like inkblots. She looked up over his right shoulder and saw the sun leading them through the trees, flashing in her eyes like a heliograph, and when he leaned the bike onto Calumet Avenue, she leaned with him.

I thought you'd like it, he'd said as they started off, but she only liked it while they were crossing the north side of the city, hopscotching through increasingly suburban neighborhoods where the hip-to-hip frame houses made her think of *All in the Family* and there seemed to be a Wee Nip on every corner. By the time they were on the Skyway out of the city she was not just liking it but loving it, and when he left the Skyway for Route 27, two-lane blacktop which traced the edge of the lake all the way up into the next state, she felt she would have been happy to go on forever. If he'd asked her what she thought about going all the way to Canada, maybe catch a Blue Jays game in Toronto, she would simply have laid her helmeted head against the leather between his shoulderblades so he could feel her nod.

Highway 27 was the best. Later in the summer it would be heavy with traffic even at this hour of the morning, but today it was almost empty, a black ribbon with a yellow stitch running down the middle. On their right, the lake winked a fabulous blue through the running trees; on their left they passed dairy farms, tourist cabins, and souvenir shops just opening for the summer.

She felt no need to talk, was not sure she *could* have talked, even if called upon to do so. He gradually twisted the Harley's throttle until the red speedometer needle stood straight up from its pin like a clock hand indicating noon, and the wind rattled harder in her helmet. To Rosie it was like the dreams of flying she'd had as a young girl, dreams in which she had gone racing with fearless exuberance over fields and rock walls and rooftops and chimneys with her hair rippling like a flag behind her. She had awakened from those dreams shaking, sweat-drenched, both terrified and delighted, and she felt that way now. When she looked to her left, she saw her shadow flowing along beside her as it had in those dreams, but now there was another shadow with it, and that made it better. If she had ever in her whole life felt as happy as she did at that moment, she didn't know when it had been. The whole world seemed perfect around her, and she perfect within it.

There were delicate fluctuations of temperature, cold as they flew through wide swales of shadow or descended into dips, warm when they passed into the sun again. At sixty miles an hour the smells came in capsules, so concentrated it was as if they were being fired out of ramjets: cows, manure, hay, earth, cut grass, fresh tar as they blipped by a drive-way repaving project, oily blue exhaust as they came up behind a laboring farm truck. A mongrel dog lay in the back of the truck with its muzzle on its paws, looking at them without interest. When Bill swung out to pass on a straight stretch, the farmer behind the wheel raised a hand to Rosie. She could see the crow's feet around his eyes, the red-dened, chapped skin on the side of his nose, the glint of his wedding ring in the sunshine. Carefully, like a tightrope walker doing a stunt without a net, she slid one hand out from under Bill's arm and waved back. The farmer smiled at her, then slipped behind them.

Ten or fifteen miles out of the city, Bill pointed ahead at a gleaming metal shape in the sky. A moment later she could hear the steady beat of the helicopter's rotors, and a moment after that she could see two men seated in the Perspex bubble. As the chopper flashed over them in a clattery rush, she could see the passenger leaning over to shout something in the pilot's ear.

I can see everything, she thought, and then wondered why that should seem so amazing. She really wasn't seeing anything she couldn't see from a car, after all. *Except I am,* she thought. *I am because I'm not looking at it through a window and that makes it stop being just scenery. It's the* world, *not scenery, and I'm in it. I'm flying across the world, just like in the dreams I used to have, but now I'm not doing it alone.*

The motor throbbed steadily between her legs. It wasn't a sexy feeling, exactly, but it made her very aware of what was down there and what it was for. When she wasn't looking at the passing countryside, she found herself looking with fascination at the small dark hairs on the nape of Bill's neck, and wondering how it would feel to touch them with her fingers, to smooth them down like feathers.

An hour after leaving the Skyway they were in deep country. Bill walked the Harley deliberately down through the gears to second, and when they came to a sign reading SHORELAND PICNIC AREA CAMPING BY PERMIT ONLY, he dropped to first and turned onto a gravel lane.

"Hang on," he said. She could hear him clearly now that the wind was no longer blowing a hurricane through her helmet. "Bumps."

There *were* bumps, but the Harley rode them easily, turning them into mere swells. Five minutes later they pulled into a small dirt parking area. Beyond it were picnic tables and stone barbecue pits spotted on a wide, shady expanse of green grass which dropped gradually down to a rocky shingle which could not quite be termed a beach. Small waves came in, running up the shingle in polite, orderly procession. Beyond them, the lake opened out all the way to the horizon, where any line marking the point where the sky and the water met was lost in a blue haze. Shoreland was entirely deserted except for them, and when Bill switched the Harley off, the silence took her breath away. Over the water, gulls turned and turned, crying toward the shore in their high-pitched, frantic voices. Somewhere far to the west there was the sound of a motor, so dim it was impossible to tell if it was a truck or a tractor. That was all.

He scraped a flat rock toward the side of the bike with the toe of his boot, then dropped the kickstand so the foot would rest on the rock. He got off and turned toward her, smiling. When he saw her face, the smile turned to an expression of concern.

"Rosie? Are you all right?"

She looked at him, surprised. "Yes, why?"

"You've got the funniest look—"

I'll bet, she thought. *I'll just bet.*

"I'm fine," she said. "I feel a little bit like all of this is a dream, that's all. I keep wondering how I got here." She laughed nervously.

"But you're not going to faint, or anything?"

Rosie laughed more naturally this time. "No, I'm fine, really."

"And you liked it?"

"Loved it." She was fumbling at the place where the strap wove through the helmet's locking rings, but without much success.

"Those're hard the first time. Let me help you."

He leaned close to slip the strap free, kissing distance again, only this time he didn't draw away. He used the palms of his hands to lift the helmet off her head and then kissed her mouth, letting the helmet dangle by its straps from the first two fingers of his left hand while he put his right against the small of her back, and for Rosie the kiss made everything all right, the feel of his mouth and the pressure of his palm was like coming home. She felt herself starting to cry a little, but that was all right. These tears didn't hurt.

He pulled back from her a little, his hand still on the small of her back, the helmet still bumping softly against her knee in little pendulum strokes, and looked into her face. "All right?"

Yes, she tried to say, but her voice had deserted her. She nodded instead.

"Great," he said, and then, gravely, like a man doing a job, he kissed her cool wet cheeks high up and in toward her nose—first under her right eye and then under her left. His kisses were as soft as fluttering eyelashes. She had never felt anything like them, and she suddenly put her arms around his neck and hugged him fiercely, with her face against the shoulder of his jacket and her eyes, still trickling tears, shut tight. He held her, the hand which had been pressed against her back now stroking the plait of her hair.

After awhile she pulled back from him and rubbed her arm across her eyes and tried to smile. "I don't always cry," she said. "You probably don't believe that, but it's true."

"I believe it," he said, and took off his own helmet. "Come on, give me a hand with this cooler."

She helped him unsnap the elastic cords which held it, and they carried it down to one of the picnic tables. Then she stood looking down at the water. "This must be the most beautiful place in the world," she said. "I can't believe there's nobody here but us."

"Well, Highway 27's a little off the regular tourist-track. I first came here with my folks, when I was just a little kid. My dad said he found it almost by accident, rambling on his bike. Even in August there aren't many people here, when the rest of the lakeside picnic areas are jammed."

She gave him a quick glance. "Have you brought other women here?"

"Nope," he said. "Would you like to take a walk? We could work up an appetite for lunch, and there's something I could show you."

"What?"

"It might be better to just show you," he said.

"All right."

He led her down by the water, where they sat side by side on a big rock and took off their footgear. She was amused by the fluffy white athletic socks he had on under the motorcycle boots; they were the kind she associated with junior high school.

"Leave them or take them?" she asked, holding up her sneakers.

He thought about it. "You take yours, I'll leave mine. Damn boots are almost impossible to put back on even when your feet are dry. If they're wet, you can forget it." He stripped off the white socks and laid them neatly across the blocky toes of the boots. Something in the way he did it and the prim way they looked made her smile.

"What?"

She shook her head. "Nothing. Come on, show me your surprise."

They walked north along the shore, Rosie with her sneakers in her left hand, Bill leading the way. The first touch of the water was so cold it made her gasp, but after a minute or two it felt good. She could see her feet down there like pale shimmering fish, slightly separated from the rest of her body at the ankles by refraction. The bottom felt pebbly but not actually painful. *You could be cutting them to pieces and not know,* she thought. *You're numb, sweetheart.* But she wasn't cutting them. She felt he would not *let* her cut them. The idea was ridiculous but powerful.

About forty yards along the shore they came to an overgrown path winding up the embankment, grainy white sand amid low, tough juniper bushes, and she felt a small shiver of *déjà vu,* as if she had seen this path in a barely remembered dream.

He pointed to the top of the rise and spoke in a low voice. "We're going up there. Be as quiet as you can."

He waited for her to slip into her sneakers and then led the way. He stopped and waited for her at the top, and when she joined him and started to speak, he first put a finger on her lips and then pointed with it.

They were at the edge of a small brushy clearing, a kind of overlook fifty feet or so above the lake. In the center was a fallen tree. Beneath the tangle of the soil-encrusted roots lay a trim red fox, giving suck to three kits. Nearby a fourth was busily chasing his own tail in a patch of sunlight. Rosie stared at them, entranced.

He leaned close to her, his whisper tickling her ear and making her feel shivery. "I came down day before yesterday to see if the picnic area was still here, and still nice. I hadn't been here in five years, so I couldn't be sure. I was walking around and found these guys. *Vulpes fulva*—the red fox. The little ones are maybe six weeks old."

"How do you know so much about them?"

Bill shrugged. "I like animals, that's all," he said. "I read about them, and try to see them in the wild when I can."

"Do you hunt?"

"God, no. I don't even take pictures. I just look."

The vixen had seen them now. Without moving she grew even more still within her skin, her eyes bright and watchful.

Don't you look straight at her, Rosie thought suddenly. She had no idea of what this thought meant; she only knew it wasn't her voice she was hearing in her head. *Don't you look straight at her, that's not for the likes of you.*

"They're beautiful," Rosie breathed. She reached out for his hand and enfolded it in both of hers.

"Yes, they are," he said.

The vixen turned her head to the fourth kit, who had given up on his tail and was now pouncing at his own shadow. She uttered a single high-pitched bark. The kit turned, looked impudently at the newcomers standing at the head of the path, then trotted to his mother and lay down beside her. She licked the side of his head, grooming him quickly and competently, but her eyes never left Rosie and Bill.

"Does she have a mate?" Rosie whispered.

"Yeah, I saw him before. A good-sized dog."

"Is that what they're called?"

"Uh-huh, dogs."

"Where is he?"

"Somewhere around. Hunting. The little ones probably see a lot of gulls with broken wings dragged home for dinner."

Rosie's eyes drifted to the roots of the tree beneath which the foxes had made their den, and she felt *déjà vu* touch her again. A brief image of a root moving, as if to clutch, came to her, shimmered, then slipped away.

"Are we scaring her?" Rosie asked.

"Maybe a little. If we tried to get closer, she'd fight."

"Yes," Rosie said. "And if we messed with them, she'd repay."

He looked at her oddly. "Well, I guess she'd try, yeah."

"I'm glad you brought me to see them."

His smile lit his whole face. "Good."

"Let's go back. I don't want to scare her. And I'm hungry."

"All right. I am, too."

He raised one hand and waved solemnly. The vixen watched with her bright, still eyes . . . and then wrinkled back her snout in a soundless growl, showing a row of neat white teeth.

"Yeah," he said, "you're a good mama. Take care of them."

He turned away. Rosie started to follow, then looked back once, into those bright, still eyes. The vixen's snout was still rolled back, exposing her teeth as she suckled her kits in the silent sunshine. Her fur was orange rather than red, but something about that shade—its violent contrast to the lazy green around it—made Rosie shiver again. A gull swooped overhead, printing its shadow across the brushy clearing, but the vixen's eyes never left Rosie's face. She felt them on her, watchful and deeply concentrated in their stillness, even when she turned to follow Bill.

4

"**W**ill they be all right?" she asked when they reached the waterside again. She held his shoulder, balancing, as she removed first her left sneaker and then her right.

"You mean will the kits be hunted down?"

Rosie nodded.

"Not if they stay out of gardens and henhouses, and Mom and Pop'll be wise enough to keep them away from farms—if they keep normal, that is. The vixen's four years old at least, the dog maybe seven. I wish you'd seen him. He's got a brush the color of leaves in October."

They were halfway back to the picnic area, ankle deep in the water. She could see his boots up ahead on the rock where he'd left them with the prim white socks lying across the square toes.

"What do you mean, 'if they keep normal'?"

"Rabies," he said. "More often than not it's rabies that leads them to gardens and henhouses in the first place. Gets them noticed. Gets them killed. The vixens get it more often than the dogs, and they teach the kits dangerous behavior. It knocks the dogs down quick, but a vixen can carry rabies a long time, and they keep getting worse."

"Do they?" she asked. "What a shame."

He stopped, looked at her pale, thoughtful face, then gathered her into his arms and hugged her. "It doesn't have to happen," he said. "They've got along fine so far."

"But it could happen. It *could.*"

He considered this, and nodded. "Sure, yeah," he said at last. "Anything could. Come on, let's eat. What do you say?"

"I say that sounds like a good idea."

But she thought she wouldn't eat much, that she'd been haunted out of her appetite by the vixen's bright regard. When he began laying out the food, however, she was instantly ravenous. Breakfast had been orange juice and a single slice of dry toast; she'd been as excited (and fearful) as a bride on the morning of her wedding. Now, at the sight of bread and meat, she forgot all about the foxes' earth north of the beach.

He kept taking food out of the cooler—cold beef sandwiches, tuna sandwiches, chicken salad, potato salad, coleslaw, two cans of Coke, a Thermos of what he said was iced tea, two pieces of pie, a large slab of cake—until it made her think of clowns piling out of the little car at the circus, and she laughed. It probably wasn't polite, but she had enough confidence in him now not to feel she had to be merely polite. That was good, because she wasn't sure she could have helped herself, anyway.

He looked up, holding a salt shaker in his left hand and a pepper shaker in his right. She saw he had carefully put Scotch tape over the holes in case they fell over, and that made her laugh harder than ever. She sat down on the bench running down one side of the picnic table and put her hands over her face and tried to get a grip. She'd almost made it when she peeked through her fingers and saw that amazing stack of sandwiches—half a dozen for two people, each cut on the diagonal and neatly sealed in a Baggie. That set her off again.

"What?" he asked, smiling himself. "What, Rosie?"

"Were you expecting friends to drop by?" she asked, still giggling. "A Little League team, maybe? Or a Boy Scout troop?"

His smile widened, but his eyes continued to hold that serious look. It was a complicated expression, one that said he understood both what was funny here and what was not, and in it she finally saw that he really *was* her own age, or close enough not to matter. "I wanted to make sure you'd have something that you liked, that's all."

Her giggles were tapering off, but she continued to smile at him. What struck her most was not his sweetness, which made him seem younger, but his openness, which now made him seem somehow older.

"Bill, I can eat just about anything," she said.

"I'm sure you can," he said, sitting down beside her, "but that's not what this is about. I don't care so much about what you can stand or what you can manage as I do about what you like and want to have. Those are the kinds of things I want to give to you, because I'm crazy about you."

She looked at him solemnly, the laughter gone, and when he took her hand, she covered it with her other one. She was trying to get what he'd just said straight in her mind and finding it hard going—it was like trying to get a bulky, balky piece of furniture through a narrow doorway, turning it this way and that, trying to find an angle where everything would finally work.

"Why?" she asked. "Why me?"

He shook his head. "I don't know. Fact is, Rosie, I don't know very much about women. I had a girlfriend when I was a junior in high school, and we probably would have slept together eventually, but she moved away before it could happen. I had a girlfriend when I was a freshman in college, and I *did* sleep with her. Then, five years ago, I got engaged to a wonderful girl I met in the city zoo, of all places. Her name was Bronwyn O'Hara. Sounds like something out of Margaret Mitchell, doesn't it?"

"It's a lovely name."

"She was a lovely girl. She died of a brain aneurysm."

"Oh, Bill, I'm so sorry."

"Since then, I've dated a couple of girls, and I'm not exaggerating—I've dated a couple of girls, period, end of story. My parents fight over me. My father says I'm dying on the vine, my mother says 'Leave the boy alone, stop scolding.' Only she says it *scoldink.*"

Rosie smiled.

"Then you walked into the shop and found that picture. You knew you had to have it from the word go, didn't you?"

"Yes."

"That's how I felt about you. I just wanted you to know that. Nothing that's happening here is happening out of kindness, or charity, or duty. None of what's happening here is happening because poor Rosie has had such a hard, hard life." He hesitated and then said, "It's happening because I'm in love with you."

"You can't know that. Not yet."

"I know what I know," he said, and she found the gentle insistence in his tone a little frightening. "Now that's enough soap opera. Let's eat."

They did. When they were done and Rosie's stomach felt stretched drumhead-tight against the waistband of her pants, they repacked the cooler and Bill strapped it onto the Harley's carrier again. No one had come; Shoreland was still all theirs. They went back down to the waterside and sat on the big rock again. Rosie was starting to feel very strongly about this rock; it was, she thought, the kind of rock you could come to visit once or twice a year, just to say thanks . . . if things turned out well, that was. And she thought they were, at least so far. She could not, in fact, think of a day that had been better.

Bill put his arms around her, then placed the fingers of his left hand on her right cheek, turning her face toward him. He began kissing her. Five minutes later she *did* feel close to fainting, half in a dream and half out, excited in a way she had never conceived of, excited in a way that made sense of all the books and stories and movies she hadn't really understood before but had taken on faith, the way a blind person will take on faith a sighted person's statement that a sunset is beautiful. Her cheeks were burning, her breasts felt flushed and tender from his gentle touch through her blouse, and she found herself wishing that she hadn't worn a bra. The thought made her cheeks flush brighter than ever. Her heart was racing, but that was good. It was all good. Over the line and into wonderful, in fact. She put her hand on him down there, felt how hard he was. It was like touching stone, except stone would not have throbbed beneath her palm like her own heart.

He left her hand where it was for a minute, then raised it gently and kissed the palm. "No more now," he said.

"Why not?" She looked at him candidly, without artifice. Norman was the only man she had known sexually in her entire life, and he was not the sort of man who got hot simply because you touched him there through his pants. Sometimes—increasingly, in the last few years—he didn't get hot at all.

"Because I won't be able to stop without suffering a most severe case of blue balls."

She looked at him with such frowning, earnest puzzlement that he burst out laughing.

"Never mind, Rosie. It's just that I want everything to be right the first time we make love—no mosquitoes biting our butts, no rolling in the poison oak, no kids from U.C. showing up at a vital moment. Besides, I promised to have you back by four so you could sell tee-shirts, and I don't want you to have to race the clock."

She looked down at her watch and was startled to see it was ten past two. If they had been sitting on the rock and making out for only five or ten minutes, how was that possible? She came to the reluctant but rather marvellous conclusion that it wasn't. They had been here for half an hour at least, maybe closer to forty-five minutes.

"Come on," he said, sliding off the rock. He grimaced as the soles of his feet splashed into the cold water, and she caught just a glimpse of the bulge in his pants before he turned away. *I did that,* she thought, and was astonished at the feelings which came with the thought: pleasure, amusement, even a slight smugness.

She slipped off the rock next to him and was holding his hand in hers before she realized she had taken it. "Okay; what now?"

"How about a little walk before we start back? Cool off."

"All right, but let's stay away from the foxes. I don't want to disturb them again."

Her, she thought, *I don't want to disturb* her *again.*

"All right. We'll walk south."

He started to turn away. She squeezed his hand to make him turn back again and when he did, Rosie stepped into his arms and slipped her own arms around his neck. The hardness below his waist wasn't gone entirely, not yet, and she was glad. She'd had no idea until today that there was something in that hardness a woman could really like— she'd honestly thought it a fiction of those magazines whose main job it was to sell clothes and makeup and hair-care products. Now she knew a little more, perhaps. She pressed herself firmly against that hard place and looked into his eyes.

"Do you mind if I say something my mother taught me to say when I went to my first birthday party? I was four or five, I think."

"Go ahead," he said, smiling.

"Thank you for a lovely time, Bill. Thank you for the most lovely day I've had since I grew up. Thank you for asking me."

Bill kissed her. "It's been nice for me too, Rosie. It's been years since I felt this happy. Come on, let's walk."

They went south along the shore this time, walking hand in hand. He led her up another path and into a long, narrow hayfield that looked as if it hadn't been touched in years. The afternoon light lay across it in dusty beams, and butterflies skittered through the timothy grass, weaving aimless courses. Bees droned, and off to their left, a woodpecker tack-hammered a tree relentlessly. He showed her flowers, naming most of them. She thought he got a couple wrong but didn't tell him. Rosie pointed out a cluster of fungi around the base of an oak at the edge of the field, and told him they were toadstools, but not too dangerous because they were bitter. It was the ones that didn't taste bitter that could get you in trouble, or get you killed.

By the time they got back to the picnic area, the college kids Bill had spoken of had arrived—a van and a four-wheel-drive Scout full of them. They were amiable but noisy as they went about carrying coolers filled with beer into the shade and then setting up their volleyball net. A boy of about nineteen was carrying his girlfriend, clad in khaki shorts and a bikini top, around on his shoulders. When he broke into a trot, she began to scream happily and beat the top of his crewcut head with the palms of her hands. As she watched them, Rosie found herself wondering if the girl's screams carried to the vixen in her clearing, and supposed they did. She could almost see her lying there with her brush curled over her sleeping, milk-stuffed kits, listening to the human screams from down the beach, her ears cocked, her eyes bright and crafty and all too capable of madness.

It knocks the dogs down quick, but a vixen can carry it a long time, Rosie thought, and then recalled the toadstools she'd spotted on the edge of the overgrown meadow, growing in the shadows where it was damp. Spider toadstools, her grandmother had called them when she pointed them out to Rosie one summer, and while that was a name that must have been special to Gramma Weeks—certainly it was not one Rosie had ever seen since in any book of plants—she had never forgotten the somehow nasty look of them, the pale and waxy flesh swarming with dark spots that *did* look a little like spiders, she supposed, if your imagination was good . . . and hers had been.

A vixen can carry rabies a long time, she thought again. *It knocks the dogs down quick, but . . .*

"Rosie? Are you cold?"

She looked at him, not understanding.

"You were shivering."

"No, I'm not cold." She looked at the kids, who did not see her and Bill because they were past the age of twenty-five, and then back to him. "But maybe it's time to go back."

He nodded. "I think you're right."

5

The traffic was heavier on the return trip, and heavier still once they left the Skyway. It slowed them down but never quite stopped them. Bill darted the big Harley through holes when they appeared, making Rosie feel a little as if she were riding on the back of a trained dragonfly, but he took no unreasonable chances and she never doubted him, even when he took them up the dotted line between lanes, passing big semis on either side, lined up like patient mastodons as they waited for their turn to go through the Skyway tollbooths. By the time they began passing signs which read WATERFRONT and AQUARIUM and ETTINGER'S PIER & AMUSEMENT PARK, Rosie was glad they had left when they had. She was going to be on time for her shift in the tee-shirt booth, and that was good. She was going to introduce Bill to her friends, and that was even better. She was sure they were going to like him. As they passed beneath a bright pink banner reading *SWING INTO SUMMER WITH DAUGHTERS AND SISTERS!*, Rosie felt a burst of happiness which she would remember later on that long, long day with sickened horror.

She could see the roller coaster now, all curves and complicated strut-work silhouetted against the sky, could hear the screams drifting off it like vapor. She hugged Bill tighter for a moment, and laughed. Everything was going to be all right, she thought, and when she remembered—for just a moment—the vixen's dark and watchful eye, she pushed the memory away, as one will push away a memory of death at a wedding.

6

While Bill Steiner was negotiating his motorcycle carefully up the lane leading to Shoreland, Norman Daniels was negotiating his stolen car into a huge parking lot on Press Street. This lot was about five blocks from Ettinger's Pier, and served half a dozen lakeside attractions—the amusement park, the aquarium, the Old Towne Trolley, the shops and restaurants. There was parking closer in to all these points of interest and refreshment, but Norman didn't want to get closer in. He might feel it necessary to leave this area at some speed, and he didn't want to find himself mired in traffic if that turned out to be the case.

The front half of the Press Street lot was nearly deserted at quarter to ten on Saturday morning, not good for a man who wanted to keep a low profile, but there were plenty of vehicles in the day- and week-rate section, most the property of ferry customers who were off somewhere up north, on day trips or weekend fishing expeditions. Norman eased the Ford Tempo into a space between a Winnebago with Utah plates and a gigantic RoadKing RV from Massachusetts. The Tempo was all but invisible between these big guys, and that suited Norman fine.

He got out, then took his new leather jacket off the seat and put it on. From one of its pockets he took a pair of sunglasses—not the same ones he'd worn the other day—and slipped these on, as well. Then he walked to the rear of the car, took a look around to make sure he was unobserved, and opened the trunk. He took out the wheelchair and unfolded it.

He had pasted the bumper stickers he'd bought in the gift shop of the Women's Cultural Center all over it. They might have lots of smart people giving lectures and attending symposia upstairs in the meeting rooms and the auditorium, but downstairs in the gift shop they sold exactly the sort of shrill, nonsensical shit Norman had been hoping for. He had no use for keychains with the female sign on them, or the poster of a woman being crucified (JESUSINA DIED FOR YOUR SINS) on Golgotha, but the bumper stickers were perfect. A WOMAN NEEDS A MAN LIKE A FISH NEEDS A BI-CYCLE, said one. Another, obviously written by someone who'd never seen a bimbo with her eyebrows and half her hair singed off by a malfunctioning crackpipe, read WOMEN ARE NOT FUNNY! There were stickers that said I'M PRO-CHOICE AND I VOTE, SEX IS POLITICAL, and R-E-S-P-E-C-T, FIND OUT WHAT IT MEANS TO ME. Norman wondered if any of these braless wonders knew that song had been written by a man. He bought them all, though. His favorite was the one he had carefully pasted in the center of the wheelchair's imitation leather backrest, next to the little customized holster for his Walkman: I AM A MAN WHO RESPECTS WOMEN, it said.

And that's true enough, *he thought, taking another quick check of the parking lot to make sure there was no one observing the cripple as he climbed spryly into his wheelchair.* As long as they behave themselves, I respect them fine.

He saw no one at all, let alone anyone watching him specifically. He pivoted the wheelchair and looked at his reflection in the side of the freshly washed Tempo. Well? *he asked himself.* What do you think? Will it work?

He thought it would. Since disguise was out of the question, he had tried to go beyond disguise—to create a real person, the way a good actor can create a real person on stage. He had even come up with a name for this new guy: Hump Peterson. Hump was an army vet who'd come back home and ridden with an outlaw biker gang for ten years or so, one of the ones where the women have only two or three very limited uses. Then the accident had happened. Too many beers, wet pavement, a bridge abutment. He'd been paralyzed from the waist down, but had been nursed back to health by a saintly young woman named . . .

"Marilyn," Norman said, thinking of Marilyn Chambers, who for years had been his favorite porn star. His second favorite was Amber Lynn, but Marilyn Lynn sounded fake as hell. The next name to occur to him was McCoo, but that was no good, either; Marilyn McCoo was the bitch who had sung with the Fifth Dimension, back in the seventies, when life hadn't been as weird as it was these days.

There was a sign in a vacant lot across the street—ANOTHER QUALITY DELANEY CONSTRUCTION PROJECT WILL GO UP IN THIS SPACE NEXT YEAR! *it said—and Marilyn Delaney was as good a name as any. He would probably not be asked to tell his life's story by any of the women from Daughters and Sisters, but to paraphrase the sentiment on the shirt the clerk in* The Base Camp *had been wearing, it was better to have a story and not need one than to need one and not have one.*

And they would believe in Hump Peterson. They would have seen more than a few guys just like him, guys who'd had some sort of life-changing experience and were trying to atone for their past behavior. And the Humps of the world, of course, atoned the way they had done everything else in their lives, by going right to the firewall. Hump Peterson was trying to turn himself into a kind of honorary woman, that was all. Norman had seen similar scagbags turn themselves into passionate anti-drug advocates, Jesus freaks, and Perotistas. At the bottom they were really just the same one-note assholes they'd always been, singing the same old tune in a different key. That wasn't the important thing, though. The important thing was that they were always around, hanging on the fringes of whatever scene it was they wanted to be in. They were like tumbleweeds in the desert or icicles in Alaska. So yes—he thought Hump would be accepted as Hump, even if they were on the lookout for Inspector Daniels. Even the most cynical of them would be apt to dismiss him as no more than a horny crip using the old "sensitive, caring man" routine to get himself laid on a Saturday night. With just a smidge of luck, Hump Peterson would be both as visible and as little noticed as the guy on stilts who plays Uncle Sam in the Fourth of July parade.

Beyond this, his plan was simplicity itself. He would find the main concentration of women from the group home, and he would watch them as Hump from the sidelines—their games and conversational groups, their picnic. When someone brought him a hamburger or a corndog or a slice *of pie, as some helpful cunt undoubtedly would (you couldn't propagandize their deep need to bring food to the menfolks out of them—that was instinct, by God), he'd take it with thanks, and he'd eat every bite. He would speak when spoken to, and if he should chance to win a stuffed animal playing ringtoss or Pitch Til U Win, he'd give it to some little kid . . . always being careful not to pat the rugmuffin on the head; even that could get you busted for molestation these days.*

But mostly he'd just watch. Watch for his rambling Rose. He could do that with no problem at all, once he had been accepted as a valid part of the scene; he was a champ at the art of surveillance. After he spotted her, he could take care of his business right here on the Pier, if he wanted to; just wait until she had to use the potty, follow her, and snap her neck like a chickenbone. It would be over in seconds, and that, of course, was just the problem. He didn't want *it to be over in seconds. He wanted to be able to take his time. Have a nice, leisurely chat with her. Get a complete rundown on her activities since she'd walked out on him with his ATM card in her pocket. The full report, so to speak, from chowder to cashews. He could ask her how it had felt to punch in his pin-number, for instance, and find out if she'd gotten off when she'd bent down to scoop the cash out of the slot—the cash he'd worked for, the cash he'd earned by staying up until all hours and busting scumholes who'd do anything to anybody if there weren't guys like him around to stop them. He wanted to ask her how she'd ever thought she could get away with it. How she'd thought she could get away from* him.

And after she'd told him everything he wanted to hear, he would *talk to* her.

Except maybe talk *wasn't exactly the right word for what he had in mind.*

Step one was to spot her. Step two was to keep an eye on her from a discreet distance. Step three was to follow her when she'd finally had enough and left the party . . . probably after the concert, but maybe earlier if he was lucky. He could ditch the wheelchair once he was clear of the amusement park. There would be fingerprints on it (a pair of studded biker gauntlets would have taken care of that problem and also added to the Hump Peterson image, but he'd only had so much time, not to mention one of his horrible headaches, his specials), but that was all right. He had an idea that fingerprints were going to be the least of his problems from here on out.

He wanted her at her place, and Norman thought he was probably going to get what he wanted. When she got on the bus (and it would be *the bus; she had no car and wouldn't want to waste money on a cab), he would get on right behind her. If she happened to spot him at some point along the line between Ettinger's Pier and the crib where she was turning her tricks, he'd kill her on the spot, and devil take the consequences. If things went well, though, he'd follow her right in through her door, and on the other side of that door she was going to suffer as no woman on the face of the earth had ever suffered before.*

Norman wheeled his way to the booth marked ALL-DAY PASSES, *saw that adult admission was twelve bucks, handed the money to the guy in the booth, and started into the park. The way was clear; it was early and Ettinger's wasn't really bustling yet. Of course, that had its downside, too. He'd have to be very careful not to attract the wrong sort of attention. But he could do that. He—*

"Buddy! Hey, buddy! Come back here!"

Norman stopped at once, his hands frozen on the wheels of his chair, blank eyes staring at the Haunted Ship and the giant robot in old-time ship's captain's clothes that stood out in front. "Ahoy for terror, *matey!" the robot ship's captain called over and over again in his mechanical drone of a voice. No, he didn't want to attract the wrong sort of attention . . . and here he was, doing precisely that.*

"Hey baldy! You in the wheelchair!"

People turning to look at him. One was a fat black bitch in a red jumper who looked about half as bright as The Base Camp clerk with the harelip. She also looked vaguely familiar, but Norman dismissed that as plain paranoia—he didn't know anyone in this city. She turned and walked on, clutching a purse the size of a briefcase, but plenty of other people were still looking. Norman's crotch suddenly felt humid with sweat.

"Hey, man, come back here! You gave me too much!"

For a moment the sense of this didn't come through to him—it was like something spoken in a foreign language. Then he understood, and an enormous sense of relief—mingled with feelings of disgust at his own stupidity—washed over him. Of course he had given the guy in the booth too much. He had forgotten he was not an Adult Male but a Handicapped Person.

He pivoted and wheeled back to the booth. The guy leaning out of it was fat, and he looked as disgusted with Norman as Norman felt with himself. He was holding out a five-dollar bill. "Seven bucks handicap, can'tcha read?" he asked Norman, first pointing at the sign on the booth with the bill and then shoving it in Norman's face.

Norman entertained a brief vision of jamming the fivespot into the fat fuck's left eye, then took it and stuffed it into one of his jacket's many pockets. "Sorry," he said humbly.

"Yeah, yeah," the man in the booth said, and turned away.

Norman began wheeling himself into the park again, his heart pounding. He had carefully constructed a character . . . made simple but adequate plans to accomplish his aims . . . and then, at the outset, had done some-thing not just stupid but incredibly *stupid. What was happening to him?*

He didn't know, but from this point on he was going to have to work around it.

"I can do that," he muttered to himself. "Goddam right I can."

"Ahoy for terror, *matey!" the robot sailor droned down at him as Nor-man rolled past. In one hand he waved a corncob pipe the size of a toilet bowl. "Ahoy for* terror, *matey! Ahoy for* terror, *matey!"*

"Whatever you say, Cap'n," Norman muttered under his breath, and kept rolling. He came to a three-way intersection with arrows pointing to the Pier, the midway, and the picnic area. Beside the one pointing to the picnic area was a small sign which read GUESTS AND FRIENDS OF DAUGH-TERS AND SISTERS EAT AT NOON, EAT AT SIX, CONCERT AT EIGHT   ENJOY! REJOICE!

You bet, *Norman thought, and began to roll his bestickered wheelchair down one of the concrete flower-bordered paths which led into the picnic area. It was actually a park, and a good one. There was playground equip-ment for children who had tired of the rides or found them too stressful. There were jolly topiary animals like the ones at Disney World, horseshoe pits, a softball diamond, and lots of picnic tables. An open-sided canvas tent had been set up and Norman could see men in cooks' whites inside, preparing to barbecue. Beyond the tent was a row of booths which had clearly been put up just for today's events—at one you could buy chances on a couple of hand-made quilts, at another you could buy tee-shirts (many bearing the same sentiments which decorated "Hump's" wheelchair), at another you could get any sort of pamphlet you wanted . . . as long as you wanted to find out how to leave your husband and find joy with your lesbian soul-sisters.*

If I had a gun, he thought, *something heavy and fast like a Mac-10, I could make the world a much better place in just twenty seconds.* Much *better.*

Most of the people here were women, but there were enough men that Norman did not feel particularly conspicuous. He rolled past the booths, being pleasant, nodding when nodded to, smiling when smiled at. He bought a chance on the snowflake quilt, putting his name down as Richard Peterson. It might not be such a good idea to call himself Hump—not here. He picked up a pamphlet called Women Have Estate Rights, Too *and told the lesbo queen minding the booth he was going to send it to his sister Jeannie in Topeka. The lesbo queen smiled and told him to have a nice day. Norman smiled and said right back atcha. He looked at everything in general and for one person in particular: Rose. He didn't see her yet, but that was okay; the day was young. He felt almost positive that she'd be here for the sitdown meal at noon, and once he'd gotten a confirmed sighting of her, all would be well, all would be well, and all manner of things would be well. Okay, he had screwed up a little at the All-Day booth, but so what? That was behind him now and he wouldn't screw up again. Absolutely not.*

"Cool wheelchair, my friend," a young woman in leopardskin shorts said cheerfully. She was leading a little boy by the hand. The little boy had a cherry Sno-Kone in his free hand and appeared to be trying to coat his entire face with it. To Norman he looked like a world-class booger. "Cool sentiments, too."

She held out a hand for Norman to slap, and Norman wondered—just for a moment—how fast that stupid little I-brake-for-cripples smirk would disappear from her face if he bit off a couple of her fingers instead of giving her the low five she was expecting. It was her left hand she was holding out and Norman wasn't surprised to see there was no wedding ring on it, although the rugrat with the cherry shit all over his face looked just like her.

You slut, *he thought.* I look at you and I see everything that's wrong with this fucked-up world. What did you do? Get one of your dyke friends to knock you up with a turkey-baster?

He smiled and slapped her outstretched hand lightly. "You the best, girl," he said.

"Do you have a friend here?" the woman asked.

"Well, you," he said promptly.

She laughed, pleased. "Thanks. But you know what I mean."

"Nope, just diggin the scene," he said. "If I'm in the way, or if it's a private gig, I can always head out."

"No, no!" she said, looking horrified at the idea . . . as Norman had known she would. "Stay. Hang out. Enjoy. Could I bring you something to eat? It would be my pleasure. Cotton candy? A hotdog, maybe?"

"No, thanks," Norman said. "I was in a motorcycle accident awhile back—that's how I lucked into the wonderful wheelchair." The bitch was nodding sympathetically; he could have her bawling in about three minutes, if he felt like it. "I don't seem to have much appetite since then." He grinned tremulously at her. "But I enjoy life, by God!"

She laughed. "Good for you! Have a great day."

He nodded. "Goes back double. You have a good day too, son."

"Sure," the kid said noncommittally, and looked at Norman with hostile eyes from above his cherry-lathered cheeks. Norman had a moment of real panic, a sense that the boy was looking into him and seeing the Norman who was hiding behind Hump Peterson's studhorse cleanhead and many-zippered jacket. He told himself it was simple garden-variety paranoia he was feeling, no more and no less—he was, after all, an imposter in the court of his enemies and it was perfectly normal to feel paranoid under such circumstances—but he went on his way quickly just the same.

He thought he would start to feel better again once he was away from the kid with the hostile eyes, but he didn't. His brief burst of optimism had been replaced by an antsy feeling. The noon meal was close now, people would be sitting down in fifteen minutes or so, and there was still no sign of her. Some of the women were off doing the rides, and it was possible that Rose was among them, but he didn't think it was very likely. Rose wasn't a Crack the Whip kind of gal.

No, you're right, she never was . . . but maybe she's changed, *a voice inside whispered. It started to say something else, but Norman muzzled it savagely before it could get a single word out. He didn't want to hear that crap, even though he knew that* something *in Rose must have changed, or she'd still be at home, ironing his shirts every Wednesday, and none of this would be happening. The idea of Rose's changing enough to walk out of the house with his goddam ATM card took hold again in his mind, took hold in a gnawing, beavery way he could hardly stand. Thinking about it made him feel panicky, as if there were a weight on his chest.*

Stay in control, *he told himself.* That's what you've got to do. Think of it as being on stakeout, as a job you've done a thousand times before. If you can think of it just that way, everything will be fine. Tell you what you do, Normie: forget it's *Rose* you're looking for. Forget it's Rose until you actually see her.

He tried. It helped that things were going pretty much as he had expected; Hump Peterson had been accepted as a valid part of the scene. Two dykes wearing tee-shirts cut off to display their overbuilt arms included him briefly in their Frisbee game, and an older woman with white hair on top and really ugly varicose veins down below brought him a Yogurt Pop because, she said, he looked really hot and uncomfortable, stuck in that chair. "Hump" thanked her gratefully and said yes, he was *a little hot.* But you're not, sweetie, *he thought as the woman with the graying hair started away.* No wonder you're with these lesbo queens—you couldn't get a man if your life depended on it. The Yogurt Pop was good, though—cool—and he ate it down greedily.

The trick was never to stay in one place for too long. He moved from the picnic area to the horseshoe pit, where two inept men were playing doubles against two equally inept women. To Norman it looked as if the game might go on until the sun went down. He rolled past the cook-tent, where the first hamburgers were coming off the grill and potato salad was being dished into serving bowls. Finally he headed for the midway and the rides, wheeling along with his head down, sneaking little peeks at the women who were now heading for the picnic tables, some pushing strollers, some carrying trumpery prizes under their arms. Rose was not among them.

She did not seem to be anywhere.

7

Norman was too busy looking for Rose to see that the black woman who had noticed him earlier was noticing him again. This was an extremely large woman, one who actually did bear a slight resemblance to William "Refrigerator" Perry.

Gert was in the playground, pushing a little boy on a swing. Now she stopped and shook her head, as if to clear it. She was still looking at the cripple in the motorcycle jacket, although now she could only see him from behind. There was a bumper sticker on the back-support of his wheelchair. I AM A MAN WHO RESPECTS WOMEN, it said.

You're also a man who looks familiar, Gert thought. *Or is it just that you look like some movie actor?*

"Come on, Gert!" Melanie Huggins's little boy commanded. "Push! I wanna go high! I wanna loop the loop!"

Gert pushed higher, although little Stanley wasn't going to get anywhere near looping the loop—not in *this* litigious age, thank you very much. Still, his laughter was a kick; it made her grin herself. She pushed him a little higher, dismissing the man in the wheelchair from her mind. From the *front* of her mind.

"I wanna loop the loop, Gert! Please! Come on, *pleeeese!*"

Well, Gert thought, *maybe once wouldn't hurt.*

"Hold on tight, hero," she said. "Here we go."

8

Norman *kept rolling even after he knew he'd gone by the last incoming picknickers. He felt it wise to make himself scarce while the women from Daughters and Sisters and their friends were eating. Also, his sense of* *panic had continued to grow, and he was afraid someone might notice something wrong with him if he stuck around. Rose should be here, and he should have seen her by now, but he hadn't. He didn't think she was here, and that made no sense. She was a mouse, for Christ's sake, a mouse, and if she wasn't here with her fellow Mouska-Cunts, where was she? Where did she have to go, if not here?*

He wheeled beneath an arch reading WELCOME TO THE MIDWAY *and traveled along the broad paved way, not paying much attention to where he was going. The best thing about riding in a wheelchair, he was discovering, was people watched out for* you.

The park was filling up, and he supposed that was good, but nothing else was good. His head was throbbing again, and the hurrying crowds made him feel strange, like an alien inside his own skin. Why were so many of them laughing, *for instance? What in God's name did they have to laugh about? Didn't they understand what the world was like? Didn't they see that everything—everything!—was on the verge of going down the tubes? He realized with dismay that they all looked like lovergirls and fagboys to him now, all of them, as if the world had degenerated into a cesspool of one-sex lovers, women who were thieves, men who were liars, none of them with any respect for the glue that held society together.*

His headache was getting worse, and the bright little zigzags had started to show around the edges of things again. The noises of this place had grown maddeningly loud, as if some cruel gnome inside his head had taken over the controls and was gradually turning the volume all the way up to max decibels. The rumble of the cars mounting the first slope of the rollercoaster track sounded like an avalanche, and the screams of the riders as the cars fell into the first drop tore at his ears like shrapnel. The calliope farting out its steamy tunes, the electronic chatter from the video arcade, the buglike whine of go-karts speeding around the Rally Racer track . . . these sounds converged inside his confused and frightened mind like hungry monsters. Worst of all, pervading everything and digging into the meat of his brain like the blade of a dull auger, was the chant of the mechanical sailor in front of the Haunted Ship. He felt that if he had to listen to it bellow "Ahoy for terror, matey!" just one more time, his mind would snap like a dry stick of kindling. Either that or he would simply bolt out of this dumb fucking chair and go screaming through—

Stop, Normie.

He wheeled into a small empty space between the booth selling fried dough and the one selling pizza by the slice, and there he did *stop, facing away from the milling crowds. When that particular voice came, Norman always listened. It was the voice which had told him nine years ago that the only way to shut Wendy Yarrow up was to kill her, and it was also the voice which had finally persuaded him to take Rose to the hospital the time she'd broken a rib.*

Normie, you've gone crazy, *that calm, lucid voice said now.* By the standards of the courtrooms where you've testified thousands of times, you're as nutty as a Payday candybar. You know that, don't you?

Faintly, blowing to him on the breeze off the lake: "Ahoy for terror, *matey!"*

Normie?

"Yeah," he whispered. He began to massage his aching temples with the tips of his fingers. "Yeah, I guess I do know that."

All right; a person can work with his handicaps . . . if he's willing to acknowledge them. You have to find out where she is, and that means taking a risk. But you took a risk just coming here, right?

"Yeah," he said. "Yeah, Daddy, I did."

Okay, the bullshit stops here. Listen up, Normie.

Norman listened up.

9

Gert pushed Stan Huggins on the swings for a little while longer, his cries for her to "loop him around the loop some more" becoming steadily more tiresome. She had no intention of doing that again; the first time he'd damned near fallen out, and for one second Gert had been sure she was going to drop dead of a heart attack.

Also, her mind had returned to the guy. The bald guy.

Did she know him from somewhere? Did she?

Could it have been Rosie's husband?

Oh, that's insane. Paranoia deluxe.

Probably, yeah. Almost certainly. But the idea nibbled. The size looked about right . . . although when you were looking at a guy in a wheelchair it was hard to tell, wasn't it? A man like Rosie's husband would know that, of course.

Quit it. You're jumping at shadows.

Stan tired of the swings and asked Gert if she'd climb on the jungle gym with him. She smiled and shook her head.

"Why *not?*" he asked, pouting.

"Because your old pal Gert hasn't had a jungle gym body since she ditched the diapers and rubber pants," she said. She saw Randi Franklin over by the slide and suddenly made a decision. If she didn't chase this a little, it would drive her nuts. She asked Randi if she'd keep an eye on Stan for awhile. The young woman said sure and Gert called her an angel, which Randi definitely was not . . . but a little positive reinforcement never hurt anyone.

"Where you goin, Gert?" Stan asked, clearly disappointed.

"Got to run an errand, big boy. Chase on over there and slide awhile with Andrea and Paul."

"Slidin's for babies," Stan said morosely, but he went.

10

Gert walked up the path which led from the picnic area to the main drag, and when she got there she made her way to the entrance booths. There were long lines at both the All-Day and the Half-Day, and she was nearly positive the man she wanted to talk to would not be helpful—she had already seen him in operation.

The back door of the All-Day booth was open. Gert stood where she was a moment longer, gathering her resolve, and then marched toward it. She had no official capacity at Daughters and Sisters, never had, but she loved Anna, who had helped her out of a relationship with a man who had sent her to the emergency room nine times when Gert had been between the ages of sixteen and nineteen. Now she was thirty-seven, and had been Anna's informal second-in-command for almost fifteen years. Teaching battered newcomers what Anna had taught her —that they didn't have to keep going back to abusive husbands and boyfriends and fathers and step-parents—was only one of her functions. She taught self-defense skills (not because they saved lives but because they salvaged dignity); she helped Anna plan fundraisers like this one; she worked with Anna's frail and elderly accountant to keep the place on something which resembled a paying basis. And when there was security work to be done, she tried her best to do it. It was in this capacity that she moved forward now, unsnapping the clasp of her handbag as she did so. It was Gert's traveling office.

"Beg pardon, sir," she said, leaning in the open back door. "Could I speak to you a second?"

"Customer Service booth is to the left of the Haunted Ship," he said without turning around. "If you have a problem, go there."

"You don't understand," Gert said. She took a deep breath and worked to speak evenly. "This is a problem only you can help me with."

"That's twenty-four dollars," the ticket-agent said to the young couple on the other side of the window, "and six is your change. Enjoy your day." To Gert, still without turning his head: "I'm busy here, lady, in case you didn't notice. So if you want to complain about how the games are rigged, or something of that nature, you just toddle on down to Customer Service and—"

That was it; Gert had no intention of listening to this guy tell her to toddle *anywhere,* especially not in that insufferable the-world-is-full-of-fools voice. Maybe the world *was* full of fools, but she wasn't one of them, and she knew something this self-important idiot didn't: Peter Slowik had been bitten over eighty times, and it wasn't impossible that the man who had done it was here right now, looking around for his wife. She stepped into the booth—it was a squeeze, but she made it—and seized the agent by the shoulders of his blue uniform shirt. She turned him around. The name-tag on the breast pocket of his shirt said CHRIS. Chris stared into the dark moon of Gert Kinshaw's face, astonished to be touched by a customer. He opened his mouth, but Gert spoke before he got a chance.

"Shut up and listen. I think there's a chance that you sold a day-pass to a very dangerous man this morning. A murderer. So don't bother telling me how tough your day's been, Chris, because I don't . . . fucking . . . care."

Chris looked at her, bug-eyed with surprise. Before he could recover either his voice or his attitude, Gert had taken a slightly blurred fax photograph from her oversized purse and shoved it under his eyes. *Detective Norman Daniels, who led the drug-busting undercover task force,* read the caption beneath.

"You want Security," Chris said. His tone was both injured and apprehensive. Behind him, the man now at the head of the line—he was wearing an idiotic Mr. Magoo hat and a tee-shirt reading WORLD'S GREATEST GRANDPA—abruptly raised a videocam and began to shoot, possibly anticipating a confrontation that would land his footage on one of the network reality shows.

If I'd known how much fun this was going to be, I never would have hesitated at all, Gert thought.

"No, I don't want them, not yet, anyway; I want you. Please. Just take one good look and tell me—"

"Lady, if you knew how many people I see in a single d—"

"Think about a guy in a wheelchair. Early. Before the rush, okay? Big guy. Bald. You leaned out of the booth and yelled after him. He came back. He must have forgotten his change, or something."

A light had gone on in Chris's eyes. "No, that wasn't it," he said. "He thought he was giving me the right money. I know he did, because it was a ten and two ones. He either forgot the handicapped price of an all-day pass, or he never noticed it."

Yeah, Gert thought. *Just the kind of thing a man who's only* pretending *to be a cripple might forget, if his mind was on other things.*

Mr. Magoo, apparently deciding there wasn't going to be a punchup after all, lowered his videocam. "Would you sell me a ticket for me and my grandson, please?" he asked through the speaker-hole.

"Hold your water," Chris said. He was an all-around charmer if Gert had ever met one, but this was not the time to offer him helpful hints on how he could upgrade his performance. This was a time for diplomacy. When he turned back to her, looking weary and put-upon, she held out the picture again and spoke in a soft tell-me-o-wise-one voice.

"Was this the man in the wheelchair? Imagine him without hair."

"Aw, lady, come on! He was wearing sunglasses, too."

"Try. He's dangerous. If there's even a chance he's here, I *will* have to talk to your Security people."

Boink, a mistake. She knew it almost at once, but that was still a couple of seconds too late. The flicker in his eyes was brief but still hard to misunderstand. If she wanted to go to Security about some problem that didn't concern him, that was fine. If it *did* concern him, even tangentially, it *wasn't* fine. He'd had trouble with Security before, maybe, or maybe he'd just been reprimanded about being a short-tempered asshole. In either case, he had decided this whole business was an aggravation he didn't need.

"It isn't the guy," he said. He'd taken the photo for a closer look. Now he attempted to hand it back. Gert raised her hands with her palms against her chest, above the formidable swell of her bosom, refusing to take it, at least for the time being.

"Please," she said. "If he's here, he's looking for a friend of mine, and not because he wants to take her on the Ferris Wheel."

"Hey!" someone shouted from the growing All-Day line. "Let's go, let's go!"

There were cries of agreement, and Monsieur World's Greatest Grandpa raised his videocam again. This time he seemed interested only in capturing Gert's new friend, Mr. Congeniality, on tape. Gert saw Chris look at him, saw the color mounting into his cheeks, saw the abortive move to cover the side of his face with his hand, like a crook coming out of the county courthouse after his arraignment. Any chance she might have had of finding something out here had now passed.

"It's *not* the *guy!*" Chris snapped. "Completely different! Now get your fat ass out of here, or I'll have you tossed out of the park."

"Look who's talking," Gert sniffed. "I could set a twelve-course meal on what you're carrying behind you and never drop a single fork down the crack in the middle."

"Get out! Right now!"

Gert stalked back toward the picnic area, her cheeks flaming. She felt like a fool. How could she have blown that so badly? She tried to tell herself it was the place—too loud, too confusing, too many people running around like lunatics, trying to have fun—but it wasn't the place. She was scared, that was why it had happened. The idea that Rosie's husband might have killed Peter Slowik was bad, but the idea that he might be *right here today,* masquerading as a paralyzed iron horseman, was a thousand times worse. She had run into craziness before, but craziness combined with this degree of craft and obsessive determination . . .

Where was Rosie, anyhow? Not here, that was all Gert knew for sure. *Not here* yet, she amended to herself.

"I blew it," she muttered aloud, and then remembered what she told almost all the women who came to D & S: *If you know it, own it.*

All right, she'd own it. That meant Pier Security was out, at least for the time being—convincing them might be impossible, and even if she succeeded, it might take too long. She had seen the bald biker in the wheelchair hanging around the picnic, though, talking to several people, most of them women. Lana Kline had even brought him something to eat. Ice cream, it had looked like.

Gert hurried back to the picnic area, needing to pee now but ignoring it. She looked for Lana or for any of the women who'd been talking to the bald guy, but it was like looking for a cop—there was never one around when you needed one.

And now she *really* had to go; it was killing her. Why had she drunk so goddam much iced tea?

11

Norman *rolled slowly back down the amusement park midway and toward the picnic area. The women were still eating, but not for much longer—he could see the first dessert trays being passed. He'd have to move fast if he wanted to act while most of them were still in one place.*

He wasn't worried, though; the worry had passed. He knew just where to go in order to find one woman alone, one woman he could talk to up close. Women can't stay away from bathrooms, Normie, *his father had once told him.* They're like dogs that can't pass a single damn lilac bush without stopping to squat and piddle.

Norman wheeled his chair briskly past the sign reading TO COMFORT STATIONS.

Just one, *he thought.* Just one walking by herself, one who can tell me where Rose has gone if she's not here. If it's San Francisco, I'll follow her there. If it's Tokyo, I'll follow her there. And if it's hell, I'll follow her there. Why not? That's where we're going to end up, anyway, and probably keeping house together.

He passed through a little grove of ornamental firs and went freewheeling down a mild slope toward a windowless brick building with a door at either end—men on the right, women on the left. Norman rolled his chair past the door marked WOMEN *and parked on the far side of the building. This was a very satisfactory location, in Norman's view—a narrow strip of bare earth, a line of plastic garbage cans, and a high stake privacy fence. He got out of the wheelchair and peered around the corner of the building, sliding his head out farther and farther until he could see the path. He felt all right again, calm and settled. His head still ached, but the pain had receded to a dull throb.*

A pair of women came out of the toy grove—no good. That was the worst thing about his current stakeout position, of course, the way women so often went to the john in pairs. What did they do in there, for Chrissake? Finger each other?

These two went in. Norman could hear them through the nearest vent, laughing and talking about someone named Fred. Fred did this, Fred did that, Fred did the other thing. Apparently Fred was quite the boy. Every time the one doing most of the talking paused for breath the other one would giggle, a sound so jagged it made Norman feel as if someone were rolling his brain in broken glass the way a baker would roll a doughnut in sugar. He stood where he was, though, so he could watch the path, and he stood perfectly still, except for his hands, which opened and closed, opened and closed.

At last they came out, still talking about Fred and still giggling, walking so close together that their hips brushed and their shoulders touched, and Norman found himself hard-put to keep from rushing after them and seizing their slutwhore heads, one head for the palm of each hand, so he could bring them together and shatter them like a couple of pumpkins stuffed full of high explosive.

"Don't," he whispered to himself. Sweat ran down his face in large, clear droplets and stood out all over his freshly shaven skull. "Oh don't, not now, for Christ's sake don't lose it now." He was shivering, and his headache had come back full force, pounding like a fist. The bright zigzags boogied and hustled around the edges of his vision, and his nose had begun to leak from the right nostril.

The next woman who came into view was alone, and Norman recognized her—white hair on top, ugly varicose veins on the bottom. The woman who'd given him the Yogurt Pop.

I got a pop for you, he thought, tensing as she started down the concrete path. I got a pop for you, and if you don't give me the answers I'm looking for, and right away, you're apt to find yourself eating every goddam inch of it.

Then someone else came out of the little grove of trees. Norman had seen her, too—the fat, nosy bitch in the red jumper, the one who had looked him over when the guy in the booth called him back. Once again he felt that maddening sense of recognition, like a name that dances impudently on your tongue, darting back every time you try to catch it. Did he know her? If only his head wasn't aching—

She still had her oversized purse, the one which looked more like a briefcase, and she was pawing around in it. What you looking for, Fat Girl? Norman thought. Couple of Twinkies? A few Mallow Cremes? Maybe a—

And suddenly, just like that, he had it. He'd read about her in the library, in a newspaper article about Daughters and Sisters. There had been a picture of her crouched down in some asshole karate posture, looking more like a doublewide trailer than Bruce Lee. She was the bitch who told the reporter men weren't their enemies . . . "but if they hit, we hit back." Gert. He didn't remember the last one, but her first name had been Gert.

Get out of here, Gert, Norman thought at the big black woman in the red jumper. His hands were tightly clenched, the nails digging into his palms.

But she didn't. "Lana!" she called instead. "Hey, Lana!"

The white-haired woman turned, then walked back to Fat Girl, who looked like The Fridge in a dress. He watched the white-haired woman named Lana lead old Dirty Gertie back into the trees. Gertie was holding something out to her as they went. It looked like a piece of paper.

Norman armed sweat out of his eyes and waited for Lana to finish her confab with Gert and come down to the toilet. On the other side of the grove, in the picnic area, desserts were now being finished up, and when they were gone, the trickle of women coming down here to use the bath-

291

room would become a flood. If his luck didn't change, and change soon, this could turn into a real mess.

"Come on, come on," Norman muttered under his breath, and as if in answer, someone came out of the trees and started down the path. It was neither Gert nor Lana the Yogurt Pop lady, but it was someone else Norman recognized, just the same—one of the whores he'd seen in the garden on the day he'd reconned Daughters and Sisters. It was the one with the tu-tone rock-star hair. The bold bitch had even waved at him.

Scared the hell out of me, too, *he thought,* but turnabout's fair play, isn't it? Come on, now. Just come on down here to Papa.

Norman felt himself getting hard, and his headache was entirely gone. He stood as still as a statue, with one eye peeking around the corner of the building, praying that Gert would not pick this particular moment to come back, praying that the girl with the half-green, half-orange hair wouldn't change her mind. No one came out of the trees and the girl with the fucked-up hair kept approaching. Ms. Punky-Grungy Scumbucket of 1994, come into my parlor said the spider to the fly, closer and closer, and now she was reaching out for the doorhandle but the door never opened because Norman's hand closed on Cynthia's thin wrist before she could touch the handle.

She looked at him, startled, her eyes opening wide.

"Come around here," he said, dragging her after him. "Come on around here so I can talk to you. So I can talk to you up close."

12

Gert Kinshaw was hurrying for the bathroom, almost running, when—wonder of wonders—she saw the very woman she'd been looking for just ahead. She immediately opened her capacious purse and began hunting for the photograph.

"Lana!" she called. "Hey, Lana!"

Lana came back up the path. "I'm looking for Cathy Sparks," she said. "Have you seen her?"

"Sure, she's throwing horseshoes," Gert said, cocking a thumb back toward the picnic area. "Saw her not two minutes ago."

"Great!" Lana started in that direction at once. Gert cast one yearning glance at the comfort station, then fell in beside her. She guessed her bladder would hold a little longer. "I thought maybe she'd had one of her panic attacks and just fired on out of here," Lana was saying. "You know how she gets."

"Uh-huh." Gert handed Lana the fax photo just before they reentered the trees. Lana studied it curiously. It was her first look at Norman, because she wasn't a D & S resident. She was a psychiatric social worker who lived in Crescent Heights with her pleasant, non-abusive husband and her three pleasant, non-dysfunctional kids.

"Who's this?" Lana asked.

Before Gert could answer, Cynthia Smith walked by. As always, even under these circumstances, her weird hair made Gert grin.

"Hi, Gert, love your shirt!" Cynthia said smartly. This was not a compliment but just something the girl said, a little Cynthia-ism.

"Thanks. I like your shorts. But I bet if you really tried, you could find a pair that let even more of your cheeks hang out."

"Hey, tell me about it," Cynthia said, and went on her way with her small but undeniably cute fanny ticking back and forth like the pendulum of a clock. Lana looked at her with amusement, then turned her attention back to the photo. As she studied it she absently stroked her long white hair, which she had tied into a ponytail.

"Do you know him?" Gert asked.

Lana shook her head, but Gert thought she was expressing doubt rather than saying no.

"Imagine him without the hair."

Lana did better than that; she covered the photo from the hairline up. Then she studied it more closely than ever, her lips moving, as if she were reading it rather than looking at it. When she looked up at Gert again, her face was both puzzled and concerned.

"I gave a Yogurt Pop to a guy this morning," she began hesitantly. "He was wearing sunglasses, but—"

"He was in a wheelchair," Gert said, and although she knew this was where the work really began, she felt a great weight slip off her shoulders, just the same. It was better to know than not to know. Better to be sure.

"Yes. Is he dangerous? He is, isn't he? I'm here with a couple of women who've been through a great deal of trauma in the last few years. They're pretty delicate. Is there going to be trouble, Gert? I'm asking for them, not me."

Gert thought it over carefully before saying, "I think everything's going to be all right. I think the scary part's almost over."

13

Norman tore off Cynthia's sleeveless blouse, baring her teacup-sized breasts. He clamped one hand over her mouth, simultaneously pinning her to the wall and muzzling her. He rubbed his crotch against hers. He felt her trying to pull back, but of course there was no way she could do that and that excited him more, how he had her trapped here. But it was only his body that was excited. His mind was floating about three feet over his head, watching serenely as Norman leaned forward and clamped his teeth on Miss Punky-Grungy's shoulder. He battened on her like a vampire and began drinking her blood when it burst through the skin. It was hot and salty, and when he ejaculated in his pants, he was hardly aware of it, any more than he was aware of her screaming against his hard palm.

14

"Go on back and hang with your patients until I give you the all-clear," Gert told Lana. "And do me a favor—don't mention this to *anyone,* not yet. Your friends aren't the only women here today who are psychologically delicate."

"I know."

Gert squeezed her arm. "It'll be fine. I promise."

"Okay, you know best."

"Yeah, right, dream on. But I *do* know he shouldn't be hard to find, if he's still cruising around in that wheelchair. If you see him, keep away from him. Do you understand? *Keep away from him!"*

Lana looked at her with deep dismay. "What are you going to do?"

"Take a leak before I die of uremic poisoning. Then go to the Security office and tell them that a man in a wheelchair tried to snatch my purse. We'll go from there, but step one is getting him the hell away from our picnic." Rosie wasn't here, she might have a date, or some other appointment, and Gert had never been so grateful for anything in her life. She was his trigger; with Rosie not around, they had a chance of neutralizing him before he did any damage.

"Do you want me to wait for you while you go to the toilet?" Lana asked nervously.

"I'll be fine."

Lana frowned at the path leading back through the grove. "Maybe I'll wait anyway," she said.

Gert smiled. "Okay. This won't take long, believe me."

She had almost reached the comfort station when a sound impinged on her thoughts: someone panting, and hard. No—*two* someones. A smile curved the corners of Gert's large mouth. Someone was enjoying a little afternoon delight behind the toilets, from the sound. Just having a nice little—

"*Talk* to me, you bitch!"

The voice, so low it sounded almost like the growl of a dog, froze the smile on Gert's lips.

"Tell me where she is, and do it *right now!*"

15

Gert ran around the side of the squat brick building so fast she barely avoided hitting the abandoned wheelchair and going ass over teakettle. The bald man in the motorcycle jacket—Norman Daniels—was standing with his back to her, holding Cynthia so tightly by her thin upper arms that his thumbs had nearly disappeared into her scant flesh. His face was jammed down against hers, but Gert could see the peculiar cant to Cynthia's nose. She'd seen that before, once in her own mirror. The girl's nose had been broken.

"Tell me where she is or you'll never have to bother with lipstick again, because I'll bite your fucking kisser right off your fa—"

Gert stopped thinking then, stopped hearing. She went on autopilot. Two steps took her to where Daniels was. As she took them, she laced the fingers of both hands together to make a cudgel. She raised this over her right shoulder, getting as much height as she could; she wanted all the velocity she could muster. Just before she brought her hands down, Cynthia's terrified eyes shifted to her, and Rosie's husband saw it happen. He was quick, Gert had to give him that. He was terribly quick. Her locked hands caught him and caught him hard, but not on the nape of the neck, where she had wanted to hit him. He had already started to wheel around, and her hands caught him on the side of his face and the angle of his jaw instead. Her chance for a quick no-fuss, no-muss knockout had passed. As he turned to face her, Gert's first thought was that he had been eating strawberries. He grinned at her with teeth that were still dripping blood. The grin horrified Gert, and filled her with the certainty that she had only managed to make sure two women were going to die back here instead of one. This wasn't a man at all. This was Grendel in a motorcycle jacket.

"Why, it's Dirty Gertie!" Norman exclaimed. "You wanna *rassle,* Gertie? Is that what you want? To *rassle?* Gonna whip me into submission with those 52-Ds of yours, is that what you're gonna do?" He laughed, patting the flat of one hand against his chest to communicate how tickled he was by the idea. The zippers on his jacket jingled.

Gert snatched a glance at Cynthia, who was looking down at herself as if wondering where her shirt had gone.

"Cynthia, run!"

Cynthia gave her a dazed look, took two hesitant steps backward, then simply leaned against the comfort station, as if just the thought of escape had tired her out. Gert could already see bruises rising on her cheeks and forehead, like fresh dough.

"Gert-Gert-bo-Bert," Norman crooned, starting toward her. "Banana-fanna-fo-Fert, fee-fi-mo-Mert . . . *Gert!*" He laughed like a child at this, then armed some of Cynthia's blood off his mouth. Gert could see beads of sweat clinging to his naked skull. They looked like sequins. "Oooh, Gertie," Norman crooned, and now his upper body began to sway from side to side, like the body of a cobra emerging from a snake-charmer's basket. "Oooh, *Gertie.* I'm gonna roll you like a doughnut. I'm gonna turn you inside out like a pair of gloves. I'm—"

"Then why don't you come on and do it?" she barked at him. "This ain't the high-school prom, you chickenshit asshole! If you want me, come and get me!"

Daniels stopped weaving and gaped at her, seemingly unable to believe that this tub of guts had shouted at him. Had *taunted* him. Behind him, Cynthia retreated another two or three tired stumble-steps, the seat of her shorts whispering against the brick of the comfort station, then leaned against the wall again.

Gert cocked her arms and held them out in front of her. The palms of her hands faced each other, about twenty inches apart. Her fingers were splayed. She dropped her head between her shoulders, hulking like a mother bear. Norman observed this defensive posture, and his expression of surprise dissolved into amusement.

"What you gonna do, Gert?" he asked her. "You think you're gonna run some Bruce Lee moves on me? Hey, I got news for you, he's *dead,* Gertie. Just like you're gonna be in about fifteen seconds—just a fat old nigger bitch lying dead on the ground." He laughed.

Gert suddenly thought of Lana Kline, glancing nervously around and saying that maybe she would wait for Gert to use the bathroom.

"Lana!" she screamed at the top of her voice. *"He's here! If you're still there, run and get help!"*

Rosie's husband looked startled again for a moment, then relaxed. His smile resurfaced. He snatched a quick glance over his shoulder to make sure Cynthia was still there, then looked back at Gert. His upper body resumed its back-and-forth swaying.

"Where's my wife?" he asked. "Tell me that and maybe I'll only break one of your arms. Hell, I might even let you go. She stole my bank card. I want it back, that's all."

Can't rush him, Gert thought. *He has to come to me—there's no other way I have even a chance of handling him. But just how am I supposed to make him do that?*

Her thoughts turned to Peter Slowik—the parts that had been missing, and the places where the concentration of bite-marks had been the heaviest—and thought she might know.

"You give the term *eat me* a whole new meaning, don't you, fagboy? Just sucking his cock wasn't enough for you, was it? So what do you say? Are you coming for me, or do women scare you too much?"

The smile did not just slip from his face this time; when she called him a fagboy it fell off so suddenly that Gert almost heard it shatter like an icicle on the steel toes of his boots. The weaving stopped.

"I'LL KILL YOU, YOU BITCH!" Norman screamed, and charged.

Gert turned sideways, just as she had when Cynthia charged her on the day Rosie had brought her new picture down to the basement rec room at D & S. She kept her hands lowered longer than she did when she was teaching throw-holds to the girls, knowing that not even his blind rage was enough to guarantee her success—this was a powerful man, and if she didn't suck him all the way in, she'd be chewed up like a rat in a threshing machine. Norman reached for her, his lips already peeling back from his teeth, getting ready to bite. Gert tucked even further, her fanny slapping against the brick wall, and thought, *Help me, God.* Then she seized both of Norman's thick, hairy wrists.

Don't spoil it by thinking about it, she told herself, and turned back toward him, socking one big hip into his side and then snap-pivoting to her left. Her legs spread, then bunched, and her corduroy jumper never had a chance; it split up the back almost all the way to her waist with a sound like a pineknot exploding in a fireplace.

The move worked like a charm. Her hip had become a ball-bearing and Norman went flying helplessly across it, his expression of rage turning to a faceful of shock. He crashed headfirst into the wheelchair. It overturned and landed on top of him.

"Wheee," Cynthia said in a husky little croak from where she was leaning against the wall.

Lana Kline's brown eyes peered cautiously around the side of the building. "What is it? What are you shouting ab—" She saw the bleeding man trying to crawl out from beneath the overturned wheelchair, saw the bright malevolence in his eyes, and stopped talking.

"Run and get help," Gert snapped at her. "Security. Right now. Scream your head off."

Norman shoved the wheelchair away. His forehead was only dripping blood, but his nose was gushing like a fountain. "I'm going to kill you for that," he whispered.

Gert had no intention of giving him a chance to try. As Lana turned and fled, howling at the top of her lungs, Gert landed on Norman Daniels in a flying drop that Hulk Hogan would have envied. There was a lot of her to drop—two hundred and eighty pounds at last count—and Norman's efforts to get to his feet ceased at once. His arms collapsed like the legs of a card-table that has been asked to hold a truck engine, his already wounded nose slammed into the hard-packed dirt between the brick wall and the fence, and his balls were driven into one of the wheelchair footrests with paralyzing force. He tried to scream—his face certainly looked like the face of a man who is screaming—and produced only a harsh wheezing sound.

Now she was sitting on top of him, the jumper's split skirt hiked almost all the way to her hips, and as she sat there, wondering what to do next, she found herself remembering the first two or three times in Therapy Circle when Rosie had finally mustered enough courage to speak. The first thing she told them was that she had terrible backaches, backaches that even lying down in a hot bath could sometimes not ease. And when she had told them why, many of the women had nodded in recognition and understanding. Gert had been one of the nodders. Now she reached down and pulled the split skirt higher, revealing a pair of vast blue cotton underpants.

"Rosie says you're a kidney man, Norman. She says that's because you're one of those shy guys who don't like to leave marks. Also, you like the way she looks when you hit her there, don't you? That sick look. All the color goes out of her face, doesn't it? Even her lips. I know, because I had a boyfriend who was that way. When you see that sick look on her face, it fixes something inside you, doesn't it? At least temporarily."

". . . bitch . . ." he whispered.

"Yeah, you're a kidney man, sure, I can tell a lot from faces, it's a

talent I have." She was using her knees to wriggle her way up his body.
She had made it almost to his shoulders. "Some guys are leg men, some
guys are ass men, some guys are tit men, and then there are *some* guys,
weirded-out assholes like you, Norman, who are kidney men. Well, you
probably know the old saying—'To each her own, said the old maid as
she kissed the cow.'"

". . . off me . . ." he whispered.

"Rosie's not here, Norm," she said, ignoring him and wriggling a little
higher, "but she left you a little message from her kidneys, by way of
my kidneys. I hope you're ready, because here it comes."

She knee-walked one final step, positioned herself over his upturned
face, and let go. Ah, sweet relief.

At first Norman didn't appear to realize what was happening. Then
understanding came. He screamed and tried to buck her off. Gert felt
herself rising and used her buttocks to thump herself back down on top
of him. She was surprised he was able to make as much of an effort as
he had, after the pounding he had taken.

"No, you don't, me foine bucko," she said, and went on voiding her
bladder. He was in no danger of drowning, but she had never seen such
revulsion and anger on a human face. And over what? A little hot water.
And if anyone in the history of the world had ever needed pissing on,
it was this sick fu—

Norman gave a vast, inarticulate cry, reached up with both hands,
grabbed her forearms, and sank his nails into them. Gert screamed
(mostly in surprise, although it *did* hurt like hell) and shifted her weight
backward. He timed her move perfectly and flung himself up again as
she made it, harder than before this time, and succeeded in tipping her
over. She went sprawling against the brick wall to her left. Norman
stumble-staggered to his feet, his face and bald head running with moisture, his motorcycle jacket dripping with it, the plain white tee-shirt
beneath the jacket plastered to his body.

"You pissed on me, you cunt," he wheezed, and lunged for her.

Cynthia stuck her foot out. Norman tripped over it and went sprawling
face-first into the wheelchair again. He scrambled away from it on his hands
and knees, then turned. He tried to get up, almost made it, then fell back,
panting, looking at Gert with his bright gray eyes. Crazy eyes. Gert started
toward him, meaning to put him down and keep him down. She would
break his back like a snake if that was what it took, and this was the time to
do it, before he found enough strength to get on his feet again.

He reached into one of the motorcycle jacket's many pockets, and for
one stomach-freezing moment she was sure he had a gun, that he was

going to shoot her two or three times in the gut. *At least I'll die with an empty bladder,* she thought, and stopped where she was.

It wasn't a gun, but it was bad enough: he had a taser. Gert knew a crazy homeless woman downtown who had one and used it to kill rats with, the ones so big they thought they were Cocker Spaniels who just didn't happen to have pedigree papers.

"You want some of this?" Norman asked, still on his knees. He waved the taser back and forth in front of him. "You want a little, Gertie? You might as well come and get it, because you're gonna get some of it whether you want it or . . ."

He trailed off, looking doubtfully toward the corner of the building. Cries of female excitement and dismay drifted from that direction. They were still distant, but they were getting closer.

Gert used his moment of distraction to take a step backward, grab the handles of the fallen wheelchair, and jerk it upright. She stepped behind it, the chair's push handles completely lost in her big brown fists. She darted it at him in quick little pushes.

"Yeah, come on," she said. "Come on, kidney-man. Come on, chickenshit. Come on, fagboy. You want to zap me? Got your phaser set to stun, do you? Come on, then. I think we got time for one more tango before the men in the white coats show up to take you away to Sunnydale Acres, or wherever they store weird fucks like y—"

He got to his feet, glancing again toward the sound of the approaching voices, and Gert thought, *What the fuck, I only have one life, let me live it as a blonde* and shoved the wheelchair at him as hard as she could. It struck him dead-center and he went over again with a yell. Gert lunged after him, hearing Cynthia's teary, wavering scream just one instant too late:

"Look out Gert he's still got it!"

There was a small but vicious crackling sound—*ziiittttt!*—and a bolt of chrome-plated agony shot up from Gert's ankle, where he had applied the taser, all the way to her hip. The fact that her skin was wet with urine probably made Norman's weapon even more effective. All the muscles in her left leg clenched eye-wateringly tight, then let go completely. Gert spilled to the ground. As she went, she grabbed onto the wrist of the hand with the taser in it and twisted it as hard as she could. Norman howled with pain and kicked out both booted feet. One missed completely, but the heel of the other caught her high up in the diaphragm, just below her breasts. The pain was so sudden and so strong that Gert forgot all about her leg, at least temporarily, but she held onto the taser, twisting his wrist until his fingers opened and the nasty gadget fell to the ground.

He scrambled back from her, blood bubbling from his mouth and snorting out of his nose in fine droplets. His eyes were wide and disbelieving; the idea that a woman had administered this beating hadn't sunk in, perhaps *couldn't* sink in. He staggered up, glanced in the direction of the approaching voices—they were very close now—and then fled along the board fence, back toward the amusement park. Gert didn't think he would get far before attracting the interest of Park Security; he looked like an extra from a *Friday the 13th* movie.

"Gert . . ."

Cynthia was crying and attempting to crawl to where Gert lay on her side, watching Norman disappear from view. Gert turned her attention to the girl and saw she'd taken a much worse beating than Gert had thought at first. A bruise like a thundercloud was puffing up over her right eye, and her nose would probably never be the same.

Gert struggled to her knees and crawled toward Cynthia. They met and held each other that way, arms locked around necks to keep them from tumbling over. Speaking with enormous effort through her puffy lips, Cynthia said: "I would have thrown him myself . . . like you taught us . . . only he took me by surprise."

"That's all right," Gert said, and kissed her gently on the temple. "How bad are you hurt?"

"Don't know . . . not coughing up blood . . . step in the right direction." She was trying to smile. It was clearly painful, but she was trying, anyway. "Pissed on him."

"Yes. I did."

"Bitchin-good," Cynthia whispered, and then began to cry again. Gert took her in her arms, and that was how the first group of women, closely followed by a pair of Pier Security guards, found them: on their knees between the back of the bathroom and the abandoned, overturned wheelchair, each with her head against the shoulder of the other, clinging together like shipwrecked sailors.

16

Rosie's first blurred impression of the East Side Receiving Hospital Emergency Room was that everyone from Daughters and Sisters was there. As she crossed the room toward Gert (barely registering the men clustered around her), she saw at least three were missing: Anna, who might still be at the memorial service for her ex-husband; Pam, who was working; and Cynthia. It was this last which most sparked her dread.

"Gert!" she cried, pushing through the men with barely a glance at them. "Gert, where's Cynthia? Is she—"

"Upstairs." Gert tried to give Rosie a reassuring smile, but it wasn't much of a success. Her eyes were swollen and red with tears. "They admitted her and she's probably going to be here awhile, but she'll be okay, Rosie. He beat her up pretty bad, but she'll be okay. Do you know you're wearing a motorcycle helmet? It's sort of . . . cute."

Bill's hands were on the buckle under her chin again, but Rosie was hardly even aware of the helmet's being removed. She was looking at Gert . . . Consuelo . . . Robin. Looking for eyes that said she was infected, that she had brought a plague into their previously clean house. Looking for the hate.

"I'm sorry," she said hoarsely. "I'm so sorry for everything."

"Why?" Robin asked, sounding honestly surprised. "*You* didn't beat Cynthia up."

Rosie looked at her uncertainly, then back to Gert. Gert's eyes had shifted, and when Rosie followed them, she felt a surge of dread. For the first time she consciously registered the fact that there were cops here as well as women from D & S. Two in plainclothes, three in uniform. *Cops.*

She reached out with a hand that felt numb and grasped Bill's fingers.

"You have to talk to this woman," Gert was telling one of the cops. "Her husband was the one who did this. Rosie, this is Lieutenant Hale."

They were all turning to look at her now, to look at the cop's wife who'd had the deadly impudence to steal her husband's bank card and then try to flee from his life.

Norman's brothers, looking at her.

"Ma'am?" the plainclothes cop named Hale said, and for a moment he sounded so much like Harley Bissington she thought she might scream.

"Steady, Rosie," Bill murmured. "I'm here and I'm staying here."

"Ma'am, what can you tell us about this?" At least he didn't sound like Harley anymore. That had only been a trick of her mind.

Rosie looked out the window toward a freeway entrance ramp. She looked east—the direction from which night would come rising out of the lake not so many hours from now. She bit her lip, then looked back at the cop. She placed her other hand over Bill's and spoke in a husky voice she hardly recognized as her own.

"His name is Norman Daniels," she told Lieutenant Hale.

You sound like the woman in the painting, she thought. *You sound like Rose Madder.*

"He's my husband, he's a police detective, and he's crazy."

VIII

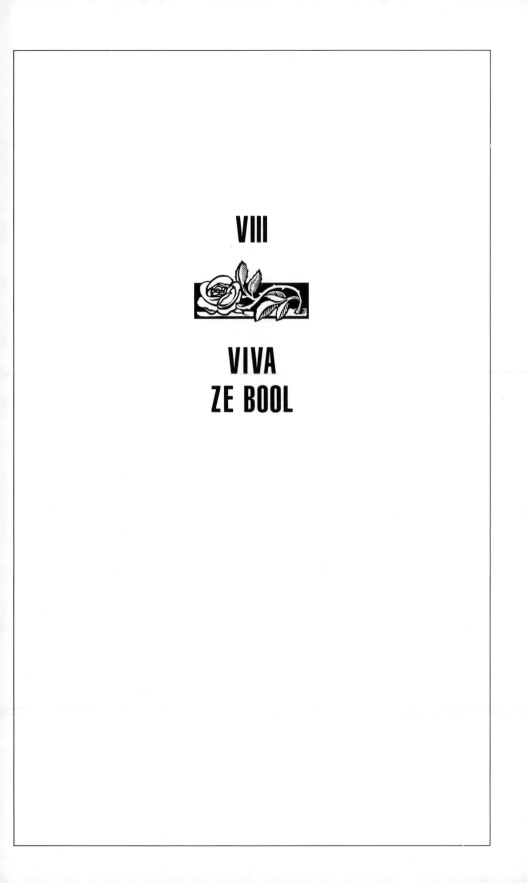

VIVA
ZE BOOL

1

He *had felt as if he were floating above his own head, somehow, but when Dirty Gertie pissed on him, all that changed.* Now, *instead of feeling like a helium-filled balloon, his head felt like a flat rock which some strong hand had sent skipping across the surface of a lake. He was no longer* floating; *now he seemed to be* leaping.

He still couldn't believe what the fat black bitch had done to him. He knew *it,* yes, *but knowing and believing were sometimes worlds apart, and this was one of those times. It was as if a dark transmutation had occurred, changing him into some new creature, a thing that went skittering helplessly along the surface of perception, allowing him only brief periods of thought and strange, disconnected snatches of experience.*

He remembered staggering to his feet that last time behind the shithouse, face bleeding from half a dozen cuts and scrapes, his nose stuffed halfway shut, aching all over from repeated confrontations with his own wheelchair, his ribs and guts throbbing from having about three hundred pounds of Dirty Gertie perched on top of him . . . but he could have lived with any of that—that and more. It was the wetness from her and the smell of her, not just urine but a woman's *urine, that made his mind feel as if it were buckling each time it turned back that way. Thinking of what she had done made him want to scream, and it made the world—which he badly needed to stay in touch with, if he didn't want to end up behind bars, probably laced into a straitjacket and stuffed full of Thorazine—begin to fuzz out.*

As he staggered along the fence he thought, Get her, get her, you have to turn around and get her, get her and kill her for what she did, it's the only way you'll ever be able to sleep again, it's the only way you'll ever be able to *think* again.

Some part of him knew better, though, and instead of getting her, he ran.

Probably Dirty Gertie thought it was the sound of approaching people that drove him off, but it wasn't. He ran because his ribs hurt so badly that he could only draw half-breaths, at least for the time being, and his stomach ached, and his testicles were throbbing with that deep, desperate pain only men know about.

Nor was the pain the only reason he ran—it was what the pain meant. He was afraid that if he took after her again, Dirty Gertie might do better than just fight him to a draw. So he fled, lurching along beside the board fence as fast as he could, and Dirty Gertie's voice chased him like a mocking ghost: She left you a little message . . . her kidneys by way of *my* kidneys . . . a little message, Normie . . . here it comes . . .

Then one of those skips happened, a short one, the stone of his mind striking the flat surface of reality and flying up and off it again, and when he came back into himself, some little length of time—maybe as short as fifteen seconds, maybe as long as forty-five—had passed. He was running down the midway toward the amusements area, running as thoughtlessly as a cow in a stampede, actually running away *from the park exits instead of toward them, running toward the Pier, running toward the lake, where it would be child's play to first bottle him up and then bring him down.*

Meanwhile, his mind shrieked in the voice of his father, the world-class crotchgrabber (and, on at least one memorable hunting trip, world-class cockgobbler, as well). It was a woman! Ray Daniels was screaming. How could you let your clock get cleaned by some cunt, Normie?

He shoved that voice out of his mind. The old man had shouted enough at him while he was alive; Norman was damned if he was going to listen to that same old bullshit now that the old man was dead. He could take care of Gertie, he could take care of Rose, he could take care of all of them, but he had to get away from here in order to do it . . . and before every Security cop in the place was looking for the bald guy with the bloody face. Already far too many people were gawking, and why not? He stank of piss and looked as if he'd been clawed by a catamount.

He turned into an alley running between the video arcade and the South Seas Adventure ride, no plan in mind, wanting only to get away from the geeks on the midway, and that was when he won the lottery.

The side door of the arcade opened and someone Norman assumed was a kid came out. It was impossible to tell for sure. He was short like a kid and dressed like a kid—jeans, Reeboks, Michael McDermott tee-shirt (I LOVE A GIRL CALLED RAIN, it said, whatever the fuck that meant)—but his entire head was covered by a rubber mask. It was Ferdinand the Bull. Ferdinand had a big, sappy smile on his face. His horns were decorated with garlands of flowers. Norman never hesitated, simply reached out and snatched the mask off the kid's head. He got a pretty good handful of hair, too, but what the fuck.

"Hey!" the kid screamed. With the mask off, he looked about eleven years old. Still, he sounded more outraged than fearful. "Gimme that back, that's mine, I won it! What do you think you're—"

Norman reached out again, took the kid's face in his hand, and shoved him backward, hard. The side of the South Seas Adventure ride was canvas, and the kid went billowing through it with his expensive sneakers flying up in the air.

"Tell anybody, I'll come back and kill you," Norman said into the still-billowing canvas. Then he walked rapidly toward the midway, pulling the bullmask down over his head. It stank of rubber and its previous owner's sweaty hair, but neither smell bothered Norman. The thought that the mask would soon also stink of Gertie's piss did.

Then his mind took another of those skips, and he disappeared into the ozone for awhile. When he came back this time, he was trotting into the parking lot at the end of Press Street with one hand pushing against his ribcage on the right side, where every breath was now agony. The inside of the mask smelled exactly as he had feared it would and he pulled it off, gasping gratefully at cool air which didn't stink of piss and pussy. He looked down at the mask and shivered—something about that vapid, smiling face creeped him out. A bull with a ring through his nose and garlands of posies on his horns. A bull wearing the smile of a creature that has been robbed of something and is too stupid to even know what it is. His first impulse was to throw the goddam thing away, but he restrained himself. There was the parking-lot attendant to think about, and while he would undoubtedly remember a man driving off in a Ferdinand the Bull mask, he might not immediately associate that man with the man the police were shortly going to be asking about. If it bought him a little more time, the mask was worth holding onto.

He got behind the wheel of the Tempo, tossed the mask onto the seat, then bent and crossed the ignition wires. When he bent over that way, the smell of piss coming off his shirt was so tart and clear that it made his eyes water. *Rosie says you're a kidney man,* he heard Dirty Gertie, the jiggedy-jig from hell, say inside his head. He was terribly afraid she'd always *be* inside his head now—it was as if she had somehow raped him, and left him with the fertilized seed of some malformed and freakish child.

You're one of those shy guys who don't like to leave marks.

No, he thought. *No, stop it, don't think about it.*

She left you a little message from her kidneys, by way of *my* kidneys

. . . and then it had flooded his face, stinking and as hot as a childhood fever.

"No!" This time he screamed it aloud, and brought his fist down on the padded dashboard. "No, she can't! *She* can't! SHE CAN'T DO THAT TO ME!" He pistoned his fist forward, slamming it into the rear-view mirror and knocking it off its post. It struck the windshield and rebounded onto the floor. He lashed out at the windshield itself, hurting his hand, his Police Academy ring leaving a nest of cracks that looked like an oversized asterisk. He was getting ready to start hammering on the steering wheel when he finally got hold of himself. He looked up and saw the parking-lot ticket tucked under the sun-visor. He focused on that, working to get himself under control.

When he felt he had some, Norman reached into his pocket, took out his cash, and slipped a five from the moneyclip. Then, steeling himself against the smell (except there was really no way you could defend yourself against it), he pulled the Ferdinand mask back down over his head and drove slowly over to the booth. He leaned out of the window and stared at the parking attendant through the eyeholes. He saw the attendant grab for the side of the booth's door with an unsteady hand as he bent forward to take the offered bill, and Norman realized an utterly splendid thing: the guy was drunk.

"Viva ze bool," the parking-lot attendant said, and laughed.

"Right," the bull leaning out of the Ford Tempo said. "El toro grande."

"That'll be two-fifty—"

"Keep the change," Norman said, and pulled out.

He drove half a block and then pulled over, realizing that if he didn't get the goddam mask off his head right away he was going to make things exponentially worse by puking into it. He scrabbled at it, pulling with the panicky fingers of a man who realizes he has a leech stuck on his face, and then everything was gone for a little while, it was another of those skips, with his mind lifting off from the surface of reality like a guided missile.

When he came back to himself this time he was sitting barechested behind the steering wheel at a red light. On the far corner of the street, a bank clock flashed the time: 2:07 p.m. He looked around and saw his shirt lying on the floor, along with the rear-view mirror and the stolen mask. Dirty Ferdie, looking deflated and oddly out of perspective, stared up at him from blank eyes through which Norman could see the passenger-side floormat. The bull's happy, sappy smile had wrinkled into a somehow knowing grin. But that was all right. At least the goddam thing was off his head. He turned on the radio, not easy with the knob busted off, but perfectly possible, oh yes. It was still tuned to the oldies station, and here

were Tommy James and the Shondells singing "Hanky Panky." Norman
immediately began to sing along.

In the next lane, a man who looked like an accountant was sitting
behind the wheel of a Camry, looking at Norman with cautious curiosity.
At first Norman couldn't understand what the man was so interested in,
and then he remembered that there was blood on his face—most of it
crusting now, by the feel. And his shirt was off, of course. He'd have to
do something about that, and soon. Meanwhile . . .

He leaned over, picked up the mask, slipped one hand into it, and
gripped the rubber lips with the tips of his fingers. Then he held it up in
the window, moving the mouth with the song, making Ferdinand sing
along with Tommy James and the Shondells. He rolled his wrist back and
forth, so Ferdinand also appeared to be sort of bopping to the beat. The
man who looked like an accountant faced forward again quickly. Sat still
for a moment. Then leaned over and banged down the doorlock on the
passenger side.

Norman grinned.

He tossed the mask back on the floor, wiping the hand that had been
inside it on his bare chest. He knew how weird he must look, how nuts,
but he was damned if he was going to put that pissy shirt back on again.
The motorcycle jacket was lying on the seat beside him, and at least that
was dry on the inside. Norman put it on and zipped it up to the chin. The
light turned green as he was doing it, and the Camry beside him exploded
through the intersection like something fired from a gun. Norman also
rolled, but more leisurely, singing along with the radio: "I saw her walkin
on down the line . . . You know I saw her for the very first time . . . A
pretty little girl, standin all alone . . . Hey, pretty baby, can I take you
home?" It made him think of high school. Life had been good back then.
No sweet little Rose around to fuck everything up, cause all this trouble.
Not until his senior year, at least.

Where are you, Rose? he thought. Why weren't you at the bitch-
picnic? Where the fuck are you?

"She's at her own picnic," ze bool whispered, and there was something
both alien and knowing in that voice—as if it spoke not in speculation
but with the simple inarguable knowledge of an oracle.

Norman pulled over to the curb, unmindful of the NO PARKING LOAD-
ING ZONE sign, and snatched the mask up off the floor again. Slid it over
his hand again. Only this time he turned it toward himself. He could see
his fingers in the empty eyesockets, but the eyesockets seemed to be looking
at him, anyway.

"What do you mean, her own picnic?" he asked hoarsely.

His fingers moved, moving the bull's mouth. He couldn't feel them, but he could see them. He supposed the voice he heard was his own voice, but it didn't sound *like his voice, and it didn't seem to be coming from his throat; it seemed to be coming out from between those grinning rubber lips.*

"She likes the way he kisses her," Ferdinand said. "Wouldn't you know it? She likes the way he uses his hands, too. She wants him to do the hanky panky with her before they have to come back." The bull seemed to sigh, and its rubber head rocked from side to side on Norman's wrist in a strangely cosmopolitan gesture of resignation. "But that's what all the women like, isn't it? The hanky panky. The dirty boogie. All night long."

"Who?" Norman shouted at the mask. Veins stood out at his temples, pulsing. "Who's kissing her? Who's feeling her up? And where are they? You tell me that!"

But the mask was silent. If, that was, it had ever spoken at all.

What are you going to do, Normie? *That voice he knew.* Dad's voice. *A pain in the ass, but not scary. That* other *voice* had *been scary. Even if it had come out of his own throat, it had been scary.*

"Find her," he whispered. "I'm going to find her, and then I'm going to teach her how to do the hanky panky. My version *of it."*

Yes, but how? How *are you going to find her?*

The first thought that came to him was their clubhouse on Durham Avenue. There'd be a record of where Rose was living there, he was sure of it. But it was a bad idea, just the same. The place was a modified fortress. You'd need a keycard of some sort—one that probably looked quite a lot like his stolen bank card—to get in, and maybe a set of numbers to keep the alarm system from going off, as well.

And what about the people there? Well, he could shoot the place up, if it came to that; kill some of them and scare the rest off. His service revolver was back at the hotel in the room safe—one of the advantages of traveling by bus—but guns were usually an asshole's solution. Suppose the address was in a computer? It probably was, everyone used those pups these days. He'd very likely still be fucking around, trying to get one of the women to give him the password and file name, when the police showed up and killed his ass.

Then something came to him—another voice. This one drifted up from his memory like a shape glimpsed in cigarette smoke: . . . sorry to miss the concert, but if I want that car, I can't pass up the . . .

Whose voice was that, and what couldn't its owner afford to pass up?

After a moment, the answer to the first question came to him. It was Blondie's voice. Blondie with the big eyes and cute little ass. Blondie, whose real name was Pam something. Pam worked at the Whitestone, Pam might well know his rambling Rose, and Pam couldn't afford to pass something up. What might that something be? When you really thought about it, when you put on that old deerstalker hat and put that brilliant detective's mind to work, the answer wasn't all that difficult, was it? When you wanted that car, the only thing you couldn't afford to pass up was a few extra hours at work. And since the concert she was passing up was this evening, the chances were good that she was at the hotel right now. Even if she wasn't, she would be soon. And if she knew, she would tell. The punk-rock bitch hadn't, but that was only because he hadn't had time enough to discuss the matter with her. This time, though, he'd have all the time he needed.

He would make sure of it.

2

Lieutenant Hale's partner, John Gustafson, drove Rosie and Gert Kinshaw to the District 3 police station in Lakeshore. Bill rode behind them on his Harley. Rosie kept turning in her seat to make sure he was still there. Gert noticed but did not comment.

Hale introduced Gustafson as "my better half," but Hale was what Norman called the alpha-dog; Rosie knew that from the moment she saw the two men together. It was in the way Gustafson looked at him, even in the way he watched Hale get into the shotgun seat of the unmarked Caprice. Rosie had seen these things for herself a thousand times before, in her own home.

They passed a bank clock—the same one Norman had passed not so long before—and Rosie bent her head to read the time. 4:09 p.m. The day had stretched out like warm taffy.

She looked back over her shoulder, terrified that Bill might be gone, sure in some secret part of her mind and heart that he would be. He wasn't, though. He shot her a grin, lifted one hand, and waved at her briefly. She raised her own hand in return.

"Seems like a nice guy," Gert said.

"Yes," Rosie agreed, but she didn't want to talk about Bill, not with the two cops in the front seat undoubtedly listening to every word they said. "You should have stayed at the hospital. Let them take a look at you, make sure he didn't hurt you with that taser thing."

"Shit, it was *good* for me," Gert said, grinning. She was wearing a huge blue-and-white-striped hospital bathrobe over her split jumper.

"First time I've felt absolutely and completely awake since I lost my virginity at Baptist Youth Camp, back in 1974."

Rosie tried for a matching grin and could manage only a wan smile. "I guess that's it for Swing into Summer, huh?" she said.

Gert looked puzzled. "What do you mean?"

Rosie looked down at her hands and was not quite surprised to see they were rolled into fists. "*Norman's* what I mean. The skunk at the picnic. One big fucking skunk." She heard that word, that *fucking,* come out of her mouth and could hardly believe she'd said it, especially in the back of a police car with a couple of detectives in the front seat. She was even more surprised when her fisted left hand shot out sideways and struck the door panel, just above the window crank.

Gustafson jumped a little behind the wheel. Hale looked back, face expressionless, then faced forward again. He might have murmured something to his partner. Rosie didn't know for sure, didn't care.

Gert took her hand, which was throbbing, and tried to soothe the fist away, working on it like a masseuse working on a cramped muscle. "It's all right, Rosie." She spoke quietly, her voice rumbling like a big truck in neutral.

"No, it's not!" Rosie cried. "No, it's *not,* don't you say it is!" Tears were pricking her eyes now, but she didn't care about that, either. For the first time in her adult life she was weeping with rage rather than with shame or fear. "Why won't he go away? Why won't he leave me *alone*? He hurts Cynthia, he spoils the picnic . . . fucking Norman!" She tried to strike the door again, but Gert held her fist prisoner. *"Fucking skunk Norman!"*

Gert was nodding. "Yeah. Fuckin' skunk Norman."

"He's like a . . . a birthmark! The more you rub and try to get rid of it, the darker it gets! Fucking Norman! Fucking, stinking, crazy Norman! I hate him! *I hate him!"*

She fell silent, panting for breath. Her face was throbbing, her cheeks wet with tears . . . and yet she didn't feel exactly bad.

Bill! Where's Bill?

She turned, *certain* he would be gone this time, but he was there. He waved. She waved back, then faced forward again, feeling a little calmer.

"You be mad, Rosie. You've got a goddam right to be mad. But—"

"Oh, I'm mad, all right."

"—but he didn't spoil the day, you know."

Rosie blinked. "What? But how could they just go on? After . . ."

"How could *you* just go on, after all the times he beat you?"

Rosie only shook her head, not comprehending.

"Some of it's endurance," Gert said. "Some, I guess, is plain old stubbornness. But what it is mostly, Rosie, is showing the world your gameface. Showing that we can't be intimidated. You think this is the first time something like this has happened? Huh-uh. Norman's the worst, but he's not the first. And what you do when a skunk shows up at the picnic and sprays around is you wait for the breeze to blow the worst of it away and then you go on. That's what they're doing at Ettinger's Pier now, and not just because we signed a play-or-pay contract with the Indigo Girls, either. We go on because we have to convince ourselves that we can't be beaten out of our lives . . . our *right* to our lives. Oh, some of them will have left—Lana Kline and her patients are history, I imagine—but the rest will rally 'round. Consuelo and Robin were heading back to Ettinger's as soon as we left the hospital."

"Good for you guys," Lieutenant Hale said from the front seat.

"How could you let him get away?" Rosie asked him accusingly. "Jesus, do you even know how he did it?"

"Well, strictly speaking, *we* didn't let him get away," Hale said mildly. "It was Pier Security's baby; by the time the first metro cops got there, your husband was long gone."

"We think he stole some kid's mask," Gustafson said. "One of those whole-head jobs. Put it on, then just boogied. He was lucky, I'll tell you that much."

"He's *always* been lucky," Rose said bitterly. They were turning into the police station parking lot now, Bill still behind them. To Gert she said, "You can let go of my hand now."

Gert did and Rosie immediately hit the door again. The hurt was worse this time, but some newly aware part of her relished that hurt.

"Why won't he let me *alone?*" she asked again, speaking to no one. And yet she was answered by a sweetly husky voice which spoke from deep in her mind.

You shall be divorced of him, that voice said. *You shall be divorced of him, Rosie Real.*

She looked down at her arms and saw that they had broken out all over in gooseflesh.

3

His *mind lifted off again, up up and away, as that foxy bitch Marilyn McCoo had once sung, and when he came back he was easing the Tempo into another parking space. He didn't know where he was for sure, but he thought it was probably the underground parking garage half a block down from the Whitestone, where he'd stowed the Tempo before. He caught sight of the gas gauge as he leaned over to disconnect the ignition wires and saw something interesting: the needle was all the way over to F. He'd stopped for gas at some point during his last blank spot. Why had he done that?*

Because gas wasn't really what I wanted, *he answered himself.*

He leaned forward again, meaning to look at himself in the rear-view mirror, then remembered it was on the floor. He picked it up and looked at himself closely. His face was bruised, swelling in several places; it was pretty goddam obvious that he'd been in a fight, but the blood was all gone. He had scrubbed it away in some gas-station restroom while a self-serve pump filled the Tempo's tank on slow automatic feed. So he was fit to be seen on the street—as long as he didn't press his luck—and that was good.

As he disconnected the ignition wires he wondered briefly what time it was. No way to tell; he wasn't wearing a watch, the shitbox Tempo didn't have a clock, and he was underground. Did it matter? Did it—

"Nope," a familiar voice said softly. "Doesn't matter. The time is out of joint."

He looked down and saw the bullmask staring up at him from its place in the passenger-side footwell: empty eyes, disquieting wrinkled smile, absurd flower-decked horns. All at once he wanted it. It was stupid, he hated the garlands on the horns and hated the stupid happy-to-be-castrated smile even more . . . but it was good luck, maybe. It didn't really talk, of course, all of that was just in his mind, but without the mask he certainly never would have gotten away from Ettinger's Pier. That was for damned sure.

Okay, okay, *he thought,* viva ze bool, *and he leaned over to get the mask.*

Then, with seemingly no pause at all, he was leaning forward and clamping his arms around Blondie's waist, squeezing her tight-tight-tight so she couldn't get enough breath to scream. She had just come out of a door marked HOUSEKEEPING, *pushing her cart in front of her, and he thought he'd probably been waiting out here for her quite awhile, but that didn't matter now because they were going right back into* HOUSEKEEPING, *just Pam and her new friend Norman, viva ze bool.*

She was kicking at him and some of the blows landed on his shins, but she was wearing sneakers and he hardly felt the hits. He let go of her waist with one hand, pulled the door closed behind him, and shot the bolt across. A quick look around, just to make sure the place was empty except for the two of them. Late Saturday afternoon, middle of the weekend, it should have been . . . and was. The room long and narrow, with a short row of lockers standing at the far end. There was a wonderful smell—a fragrance of clean, ironed linen that made Norman think of laundry day at their house when he was a kid.

There were big stacks of neatly folded sheets on pallets, Dandux laundry baskets full of fluffy bathtowels, pillowcases piled on shelves. Deep stacks of coverlets lined one wall. Norman shoved Pam into these, watching with no interest at all as the skirt of her uniform flipped up high on her thighs. His sex-drive had gone on vacation, perhaps even into permanent retirement, and maybe that was just as well. The plumbing between his legs had gotten him into a lot of trouble over the years. It was a hell of a note, the sort of thing that might lead you to think that God had more in common with Andrew Dice Clay than you maybe wanted to believe. For twelve years you didn't notice it, and for the next fifty—or even sixty— it dragged you around behind it like some raving baldheaded Tasmanian devil.

"Don't scream," he said. "Don't scream, Pammy. I'll kill you if you do." It was an empty threat—for now, at least—but she wouldn't know that.

Pam had drawn in a deep breath; now she let it out in a soundless rush. Norman relaxed slightly.

"Please don't hurt me," she said, and boy, was that *original, he'd certainly never heard* that *one before, nope, nope.*

"I don't *want to hurt you," he said warmly. "I certainly don't." Something was flopping in his back pocket. He felt for it and touched rubber. The mask. He wasn't exactly surprised. "All you have to do is tell me what I want to know, Pam. Then you go on your happy way and I go on mine."*

"How do you know my name?"

He gave her that evocative interrogation-room shrug, the one that said he knew lots *of things, that was his job.*

She sat in the pile of tumbled dark maroon coverlets just like the one on his bed up on the ninth floor, smoothing her skirt down over her knees.

Her eyes were a really extraordinary shade of blue. A tear gathered on the lower lid of the left one, trembled, then slipped down her cheek, leaving a trail of mascara-soot.

"Are you going to rape me?" she asked. She was looking at him with those extraordinary baby blues of hers, great eyes—who needs to pussywhip a man when you've got eyes like those, right, Pammy?—but he didn't see the look in them he wanted to see. That was a look you saw in the interrogation room when a guy you'd been whipsawing with questions all day and half the night was finally getting ready to break: a humble look, a pleading look, a look that said I'll tell you anything, anything at all, just let off me a little. He didn't see that look in Pammy's eyes.

Yet.

"Pam—"

"Please don't rape me, please don't, but if you do, if you have to, please wear a condom, I'm so scared of AIDS."

He gawped at her, then burst out laughing. It hurt his stomach to laugh, it hurt his diaphragm even worse, and most of all it hurt his face, but for awhile there was just no way he could stop. He told himself he had to stop, that some hotel employee, maybe even the house dick, might happen by and hear laughter coming from in here and wonder what it meant, but not even that helped; in the end, the throe had to pass on its own.

Blondie watched him with amazement at first, then smiled tentatively herself. Hopefully.

Norman at last managed to get himself under control, although his eyes were streaming with tears by that time. "I'm not going to rape you, Pam," he said at last—when he was capable of saying anything without laughing it into insincerity.

"How do you know my name?" she asked again. Her voice was a little stronger this time.

He hauled the mask out, stuck his hand inside it, and manipulated it as he had for the asshole accountant in the Camry. "Pam-Pam-bo-Bam, banana-fanna-fo-Fam, fee-fi-mo-Mam," he made it sing. He bopped it back and forth, like Shari Lewis with fucking Lamb Chop, only this was a bull, not a lamb, a stupid fucking fagbull with flowers on its horns. Not a reason in the world why he should like the fucking thing, but the fact was, he sort of did.

"I sort of like you, too," Ferd the fagbull said, looking up at Norman with its empty eyes. Then it turned back to Pam, and with Norman to move its lips, it said: "You got a problem with that?"

"N-N-No," she said, and the look he wanted still wasn't in her eyes,

not yet, but they were making progress, she was terrified of him—of them—that much was for sure.

Norman squatted down, hands dangling between his thighs, Ferdinand's rubber horns now pointing at the floor. He looked at her sincerely. "Bet you'd like to see me out of this room and out of your life, wouldn't you, Pammy?"

She nodded so vigorously her hair bounced up and down on her shoulders.

"Yeah, I thought so, and that's fine by me. You tell me one thing and I'll be gone like a cool breeze. It's easy, too." He leaned forward toward her, Ferd's horns dragging on the floor. "All I want to know is where Rose is. Rose Daniels. Where does she live?"

"Oh my God." What color there still was in Pammy's face—two spots of red high up on her cheekbones—now disappeared, and her eyes widened until it seemed they must tumble from their sockets. "Oh my God, you're him. You're Norman."

That startled and angered him—he was supposed to know her name, that was how it worked, but she wasn't supposed to know his—and everything else followed upon that. She was up and off the coverlets while he was still reacting to his name in her mouth, and she almost got away completely. He sprang after her, reaching out with his right hand, the one that still had the bullmask on it. Faintly he could hear himself saying that she wasn't going anywhere, that he wanted to talk to her and intended to do it right up close.

He grabbed her around the throat. She gave a strangled cry that wanted to be a scream and lunged forward with surprising, sinewy strength. Still he could have held her, if not for the mask. It slipped on his sweaty hand and she tore away, fell away toward the door, arms out to either side, flailing, and at first Norman didn't understand what happened next.

There was a noise, a meaty sound that was almost a pop like a champagne cork, and then Pam began to flail wildly, her hands beating at the door, her head back at a strange stiff angle, like someone staring intently at the flag during a patriotic ceremony.

"Huh?" Norman said, and Ferd rose up in front of his eyes, askew on his hand. Ferdinand looked drunk.

"Ooops," said the bull.

Norman yanked the mask off his hand and stuffed it in his pocket, now aware of a pattering sound, like rain. He looked down and saw that Pam's left sneaker was no longer white. Now it was red. Blood was pooling around it; it ran down the door in long drips. Her hands were still fluttering. To Norman they looked like small birds.

She looked almost nailed to the door, and as Norman stepped forward, he saw that, in a way, she was. There was a coathook on the back of the damned thing. She'd torn free of his hand, plunged forward, and impaled herself. The coathook was buried in her left eye.

"Oh Pam, shit, you fool," Norman said. He felt both furious and dismayed. He kept seeing the bull's stupid grin, kept hearing it say Ooops, *like some wiseass character in a Warner Bros. cartoon.*

He yanked Pam off the coathook. There was an unspeakable gristly sound as she came. Her one good eye—bluer than ever, it seemed to Norman—stared at him in wordless horror.

Then she opened her mouth and shrieked.

Norman never thought about it; his hands acted on their own, grabbing her face by the cheeks, planting his big palms beneath the delicate angles of her jaw, and then twisting. There was a single sharp crack—the sound of someone stamping on a cedar shingle—and she went limp in his arms. She was gone, and whatever she had known about Rose was gone with her.

"Oh you dopey gal," Norman breathed. "Put your eye out on the fucking coathook, how stupid is that?"

He shook her in his arms. Her head flopped bonelessly from side to side. She now wore a wet red bib on the front of her white uniform. He carried Pam back over to the coverlets and dropped her there. She sprawled with her legs apart.

"Brazen bitch," Norman said. "You can't even quit when you're dead, can you?" He crossed her legs. One of her arms dropped off her lap and thumped onto the coverlets. He saw a kinky purple bracelet around her wrist—it looked almost like a short length of telephone cord. On it was a key.

Norman looked at this, then toward the lockers at the far end of the room.

You can't go there, Normie, *his father said.* I know what you're thinking, but you're nuts if you go anywhere near their place on Durham Avenue.

Norman smiled. You're nuts if you go there. *That was sort of funny, when you thought about it. Besides, where else was there to go? What else was there to try? He didn't have much time. His bridges were burning merrily behind him, all of them.*

"The time is out of joint," Norman Daniels murmured, and stripped the key-bracelet off Pam's wrist. He went down to the lockers, holding the bracelet between his teeth long enough to stick the bullmask back on

his hand. Then he held Ferd up and let him scan the Dymotapes on the lockers.

"This one," Ferd said, and tapped the locker marked PAM HAVERFORD *with his rubber face.*

The key fit the lock. Inside was a pair of jeans, a tee-shirt, a sports bra, a shower-bag, and Pam's purse. Norman took the purse over to one of the Dandux baskets and spilled out the contents on the towels. He cruised Ferdinand over the stuff like some bizarre spy satellite.

"There you go, big boy," Ferd murmured.

Norman plucked a thin slice of gray plastic from the rubble of cosmetics, tissues, and papers. It would open the front door of their clubhouse, no doubt about that. He picked it up, started to turn away—

"Wait," ze bool said. It went to Norman's ear and whispered, flower-decked horns bobbing.

Norman listened, then nodded. He stripped the mask off his sweaty hand again, stuffed it back into his pocket, and bent over Pam's purse-litter. He sifted carefully this time, much as he would have if he had been investigating what was called "an event scene" in the current jargon . . . only then he would have used the tip of a pen or pencil instead of the tips of his fingers.

Fingerprints certainly aren't a problem here, *he thought, and laughed.* Not anymore.

He pushed her billfold aside and picked up a small red book with TEL-EPHONE ADDRESS *on the front. He looked under* D, *found an entry for Daughters and Sisters, but it wasn't what he was looking for. He turned to the front page of the book, where a great many numbers had been written over and around Pam's doodles—eyes and cartoon bowties, mostly. The numbers all looked like phone numbers, though.*

He turned to the back page, the other likely spot. More phone numbers, more eyes, more bowties . . . and in the middle, neatly boxed and marked with asterisks, this:

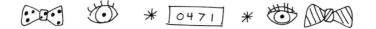

"Oh boy," he said. "Hold your cards, folks, but I think we have a Bingo. We do, don't we, Pammy?"

Norman tore the back page out of Pam's book, stuffed it in his front pocket, and tiptoed back to the door. He listened. No one out there. He let out a breath and touched the corner of the paper he'd just stuck in his

*pocket. His mind lifted off in another one of those skips as he did so, and
for a little while there was nothing at all.*

4

Hale and Gustafson led Rosie and Gert to a corner of the squadroom
that was almost like a conversation-pit; the furniture was old but fairly
comfortable, and there were no desks for the detectives to sit behind.
They dropped instead onto a faded green sofa parked between the soft-
drink machine and the table with the Bunn-O-Matic on it. Instead of a
grim picture of drug addicts or AIDS victims, there was a travel-agency
poster of the Swiss Alps over the coffee-maker. The detectives were calm
and sympathetic, the interview was low-key and respectful, but neither
their attitude nor the informal surroundings helped Rosie much. She was
still angry, more furious than she had ever been in her life, but she was
also terrified. It was being in this place.

Several times as the Q-and-A went on, she came close to losing control
of her emotions, and each time this happened she would look across the
room to where Bill was sitting patiently outside the waist-high railing
with its sign reading POLICE BUSINESS ONLY BEYOND THIS POINT,
PLEASE.

She knew she should get up, go over to him, and tell him not to wait
any longer—to just take himself on home and call her tomorrow. She
couldn't bring herself to do it. She needed him to be there the way she'd
needed him to be behind her on the Harley when the detectives had
been driving them here, needed him as an overimaginative child needs
a nightlight when she wakes up in the middle of the night.

The thing was, she kept having crazy ideas. She *knew* they were crazy,
but knowing didn't help. For awhile they would go away, she would
simply answer their questions and not have the crazy ideas, and then she
would catch herself thinking that they had Norman down in the basement, that they were *hiding* him down there, sure they were, because
law enforcement was a family, cops were brothers, and cops' wives
weren't allowed to run away and have lives of their own no matter what.
Norman was safely tucked away in some tiny sub-basement room where
no one could hear you even if you screamed at the top of your lungs, a
room with sweaty concrete walls and a single bare bulb hanging down
from a cord, and when this meaningless charade was over, they would
take her to him. They would take her to Norman.

Crazy. But she only fully *knew* it was crazy when she looked up and saw Bill on the other side of the low railing, watching her and waiting for her to be done so he could take her home on the back of his iron pony.

They went over it and over it, sometimes Gustafson asking the questions, sometimes Hale, and while Rosie had no sense that the two men were playing good-cop/bad-cop, she wished they would finish with their interminable questions and their interminable forms and let them go. Maybe when she got out of here, those paralyzing swoops between rage and terror would abate a little.

"Tell me again how you happened to have Mr. Daniels's picture in your purse, Ms. Kinshaw," Gustafson said. He had a half-completed report in front of him and a Bic in one hand. He was frowning horribly; to Rosie he looked like a kid taking a final he hasn't studied for.

"I've told you that twice already," Gert said.

"This'll be the last time," Hale said quietly.

Gert looked at him. "Scout's Honor?"

Hale grinned—a very winning grin—and nodded. "Scout's Honor."

So she told them again how she and Anna had tentatively connected Norman Daniels to the murder of Peter Slowik, and how they had gotten Norman's picture by fax. From there she went to how she had noticed the man in the wheelchair when the ticket-agent shouted at him. Rosie was familiar with the story now, but Gert's bravery still amazed her. When Gert got to the confrontation with Norman behind the comfort station, relating it in the matter-of-fact tones of a woman reciting a shopping list, Rosie took her big hand and squeezed it hard.

When she finished this time, Gert looked at Hale and raised her eyebrows. "Okay?"

"Yes," Hale said. "Very okay. Cynthia Smith owes you her life. If you were a cop, I'd put you in for a citation."

Gert snorted. "I'd never pass the physical. Too fat."

"Just the same," Hale said, not smiling, meeting her eyes.

"Well, I appreciate the compliment, but what I really want to hear from you is that you're going to catch the guy."

"We'll catch him," Gustafson said. He sounded absolutely sure of himself and Rosie thought, *You don't know my Norman, Officer.*

"Are you done with us?" Gert asked.

"With you, yes," Hale said. "I have a few more questions for Ms. McClendon . . . can you deal with that? If not, they could wait." He paused. "But they really *shouldn't* wait. I think we both know that, don't we?"

Rosie closed her eyes briefly, then opened them. She looked toward Bill, who was still sitting outside the railing, and then back at Hale.

"Ask what you have to," she said. "Just finish as soon as you can. I want to go home."

5

This time when he came back into his own head he was getting out of the Tempo on a quiet street he recognized almost at once as Durham Avenue. He was parked a block and a half down from the Pussy Palace. It wasn't dark yet, but getting there; the shadows under the trees were thick and velvety, somehow luscious.

He looked down at himself and saw that he must have gone to his room before leaving the hotel. His skin smelled of soap and he was wearing different clothes. They were good clothes for this errand, too: chinos, a white roundneck tee-shirt, and a blue work-shirt with the tails hanging out. He looked like the sort of guy who might turn out on a weekend to check a faulty gas connection or . . .

"Or to check the burglar alarm," Norman said under his breath, and grinned. "Pretty brazen, Señor Daniels. Pretty goddam bra—"

Panic struck like a thunderclap then, and he slapped at the lefthand rear pocket of the chinos he was now wearing. He felt nothing but the lump of his wallet. He slapped at the righthand rear and let out a harsh sigh of relief as the limp rubber of the mask flopped against his hand. He had forgotten his service revolver, apparently—left it back in the room safe—but he'd remembered the mask, and right now the mask seemed a lot more important than the gun. Probably crazy, but there it was.

He started up the sidewalk toward 251. If there were only a few cunts there, he'd try to take them all hostage. If there were a lot, he'd hold onto as many as he could—maybe half a dozen—and send the rest scampering for the hills. Then he'd simply start shooting them, one by one, until somebody coughed up Rose's address. If none of them knew it, he'd shoot them all and start checking files . . . but he didn't think it would come to that.

What will you do if the cops are there, Normie? his father asked nervously. Cops out front, cops inside, cops protecting the place from you?

He didn't know. And didn't much care.

He passed 245, 247, 249. There was a hedge between that last one and the sidewalk, and as Norman reached the end of it he stopped suddenly, *looking at 251 Durham Avenue with narrow, suspicious eyes. He had been prepared to see a lot of activity or a little activity, but he had not been prepared for what he was seeing, which was no activity at all.*

Daughters and Sisters stood at the end of its narrow, deep lawn with the second- and third-story shades pulled against the heat of the day. It was as silent as a relic. The windows to the left of the porch were unshaded but dark. There were no shapes moving in there. No one on the porch. No cars in the driveway.

I can't just stand here, *he thought, and got moving again. He walked past the place, looking into the vegetable garden where he'd seen the two whores before—one of them the whore he'd grabbed at the comfort station. The garden was also empty this evening. And from what he could see of the back yard, that was empty, too.*

It's a trap, Normie, *his father said.* You know that, don't you?

Norman walked as far as a Cape Cod with 257 on the door, then turned and began to saunter casually back down the sidewalk. He knew it looked like a trap, the father-voice was right about that, but somehow it didn't feel like *a trap.*

Ferdinand the Bull rose up before his eyes like a cheesy rubber ghost— Norman had pulled the mask out of his back pocket and put it on his hand without even realizing it. He knew this was a bad idea; anyone looking out a window would be sure to wonder why the big man with the swollen face was talking to the rubber mask . . . and making the mask answer back by wiggling its lips. Yet none of that seemed to matter, either. Life had gotten very . . . well, basic. Norman sort of liked that.

"Nah, it's not a trap," *Ferdinand said.*

"Are you sure?" *he asked. He was almost in front of 251 again.*

"Yeah," *Ferdinand said, nodding his garlanded horns.* "They just went on with their picnic, that's all. Right now they're probably all sitting around toasting marshmallows while some dyke in a granny dress sings 'Blowin' in the Wind.' You didn't amount to any more than a temporary wrinkle in their day."

He stopped in front of the walk leading up to Daughters and Sisters, looking down at the mask, thunderstruck.

"Hey—sorry, guy," *ze bool said apologetically,* "but I don't make the news, you know, I only report it."

Norman was stunned to discover there was something almost as bad as coming home to find out your wife had absconded for parts unknown with your bank card in her purse: there was being ignored.

Being ignored by a bunch of women.

"Well, then, teach them not to do that," *Ferd said.* "Teach them a *lesson. Go on, Norm. Teach them who you are. Teach them so they'll never forget it."*

"So they'll never forget it," Norman muttered, and the mask nodded enthusiastically on his hand.

He stuffed it into his back pocket again and pinched Pam's keycard and the slip of paper he'd taken from her address book out of his left front one as he went up the walk. He climbed the porch steps, glancing up once—casually, he hoped—at the TV camera mounted over the door. He held the keycard against his leg. Eyes might be watching, after all. He would do well to remember that, lucky or not, Ferdinand was only a rubber mask with Norman Daniels's hand for a brain.

The keycard slot was just where he had expected it would be. There was a talkbox beside it, complete with a little sign instructing visitors to press and speak.

Norman pressed the button, leaned forward, and said: "Midland Gas, checking for a leak in the neighborhood, ten-four?"

He let go of the button. Waited. Glanced up at the camera. Black-and-white, probably wouldn't show how swollen his face was . . . he hoped. He smiled to show he was harmless as his heart pumped away in his chest like a small, vicious engine.

No answer. Nothing.

He pushed the button again. "Anybody home, gals?"

He gave them time, counting slowly to twenty. His father whispered that it was a trap, exactly the sort of trap he himself would have set in this situation, lure the scumbucket in, make him believe the place was empty, then land on him like a load of bricks. And yes, it was the kind of trap he himself would have set . . . but there was no one here. He was almost sure of it. The place felt as empty as a discarded beercan.

Norman put the keycard into the slot. There was a single loud click. He pulled the card out, turned the doorknob, and stepped into the front hall of Daughters and Sisters. From his left came a low, steady sound: meep-meep-meep-meep. *It was a keypad burglar alarm. The words* FRONT DOOR *were flashing on and off in its message window.*

Norman looked at the slip of paper he'd brought with him, took a second to pray the number on it was what he thought it was, and punched 0471. For one heartstopping moment the alarm continued to meep, *and then it stopped. Norman let out his breath and closed the door. He reset the alarm without even thinking about it, just cop instinct at work.*

He looked around, noted the stairs going up to the second floor, then walked down the main hall. He poked his head into the first room on the right. It looked like a schoolroom, with chairs set up in a circle and a

blackboard at one end. Written on the blackboard were the words DIG-
NITY, RESPONSIBILITY, *and* FAITH.

"Words of wisdom, Norm," *Ferdinand said. He was back on Norman's
hand again. He'd gotten there like magic.* "Words of wisdom."

"If you say so; looks like the same old shit to me." *He looked around,
then raised his voice. It seemed almost sacrilegious to shout into this somehow dusty silence, but a man had to do what a man had to do.*

"Hello? Anybody here? Midland Gas!"

"Hello?" *Ferd shouted from the end of his arm, looking brightly around
with his empty eyes. He spoke in the comic-German voice Norman's father
had sometimes used when he was drunk.* "Hello, vas you dere, Cholly?"

"Shut up, you idiot," *Norman muttered.*

"Yessir, Cap'n," *ze bool replied, and fell silent at once.*

*Norman turned slowly around and then went on down the hall. There
were other rooms along the way—a parlor, a dining room, what looked
like a little library—but they were all empty. The kitchen at the end of
the hall was empty, too, and now he had a new problem: where did he go
to find what he was looking for?*

*He drew in a breath and closed his eyes, trying to think (and trying to
stave off the headache, which was trying to come back). He wanted a
cigarette but didn't dare light one; for all he knew, they might have the
smoke detectors turned up enough to shriek at the first whiff of tobacco.*

*He drew in another deep breath, drew it all the way down to the floor of
his lungs, and now recognized the smell in here for what it was—not the smell
of dust but the smell of women, women who had been long entrenched with
their own kind, women who had knitted themselves into a communal shroud
of self-righteousness in an effort to block out the real world. It was a smell of
blood and douche and sachet and hair spray and roll-on deodorant and per-
fumes with fuck-me names like My Sin and White Shoulders and Obsession.
It was the vegetable smell of what they liked to eat and the fruity smell of the
teas they liked to drink; that smell was not dust but something like yeast,
a fermentation, and it produced a smell cleaning could never remove: the
smell of women without men. All at once that smell was filling his nose,
filling his throat, filling his heart, gagging him, making him feel faint,
almost suffocating him.*

"Get hold of yourself, Cholly," *Ferdinand said sharply.* "All you smell
is last night's spaghetti sauce! I mean, Cheezus-pleezus!"

*Norman blew out a breath, took in another one, opened his eyes. Spa-
ghetti sauce, yes. A red smell, like blood. But spaghetti sauce was really
all it was.*

"Sorry, got a little flaky there for a minute," *he said.*

"Yup, but who wouldn't?" Ferd said, and now his empty eyes seemed to express both sympathy and understanding. "This is where Circe turns men into pigs, after all." The mask swivelled on Norman's wrist, scanning with its blank eyes. "Yas, dis be de place."

"What are you talking about?"

"Nothing. Never mind."

"I don't know where to go," Norman said, also looking around. "I've got to hurry, but Christ, the place is so big! There must be twenty rooms, at least."

The bull pointed its horns at a door across the kitchen. "Try that one."

"Hell, that's probably just the pantry."

"I don't think so, Norm. I don't think they'd put a sign that says PRIVATE on the pantry, do you?"

It was a point. Norman crossed the room, stuffing the bullmask back into his pocket as he did (and noticing the spaghetti colander which had been left to drip-dry in the rack beside the sink), then rapped on the door. Nothing. He tried the knob. It turned easily. He opened the door, felt inside on the right, and flipped a switch.

The overhead fixture illuminated a dinosaur of a desk heaped high with clutter. Balanced atop one pile was a gold plaque which read ANNA STEVENSON and BLESS THIS MESS. On the wall was a framed picture of two women Norman recognized. One was the late great Susan Day. The other was the white-haired bitch from the newspaper photo, the one who looked like Maude. They had their arms around each other and were smiling into each other's eyes like true lesbos.

The side of the room was lined with filing cabinets. Norman walked over to them, dropped to one knee, started to reach for the cabinet labelled D-E, then stopped. She wasn't using Daniels anymore. He couldn't remember if that was something Ferdinand had told him or something he'd either found out or intuited for himself, but he knew it was true. She had gone back to her maiden name.

"You'll be Rose Daniels until the day you die," he said, and reached for the M cabinet instead. He tugged. Nothing. It was locked.

A problem, but not a big one. He'd get something in the kitchen to pry it open with. He turned, meaning to go back out, then stopped, his eye caught by a wicker basket standing on the corner of the desk. There was a card hanging from the basket's handle. GO THEN, LITTLE LETTER was written on it in Old English script. There was a small stack of what looked like outgoing mail in the basket, and below a billpayer envelope addressed to Lakeland Cable TV, he saw this poking out:

endon
renton Street

—endon?

McClendon?

He snatched the letter up, overturning the basket and dumping most of the outgoing mail on the floor, his eyes wide and greedy.

Yes, McClendon, by God—Rosie McClendon! And right below it, firmly and legibly printed, the address he'd gone through hell to get: 897 Trenton Street.

There was a long, chrome-plated letter-opener lying half under a stack of leftover Swing into Summer fliers. Norman grabbed it, slit the letter open, and shoved the opener into his back pocket without even thinking about it. He pulled out the mask again at the same time and slid it onto his hand. The single sheet of paper bore an embossed letterhead which read ANNA STEVENSON in big letters and Daughters and Sisters in slightly smaller ones.

Norman gave this small ego-signal a quick glance, then began to cruise the mask over the paper, letting Ferdinand read it for him. Anna Stevenson's handwritten script was large and elegant—arrogant, some might have termed it. Norman's sweaty fingers shook and tried to clench inside Ferdinand's head, sending the rubber mask through a series of convulsive winces and leers as it moved.

Dear Rosie,

I just wanted to send you a note in your new "digs" (I know how important those first few letters can be!), telling you how glad I am that you came to us at Daughters and Sisters, and how glad I am we could help you. I also want to say how pleased I am with your new job—I have an idea you won't be living on Trenton Street for long!

Every woman who comes to Daughters and Sisters renews the lives of all the others—those there with her during her first period of healing and all those who come after she's left, for each one leaves a bit of her experience, strength, and hope behind. *My hope is to see you here often, Rosie,* not just because your recovery is a long way from complete and because you have many feelings (chiefly anger, I should surmise) which you haven't yet dealt with, but because you have an obligation to pass on what you've learned here. I probably don't need to tell you these things, but—

A click, not much of a sound but loud in the silence. This was followed by another sound: meep-meep-meep-meep.

The burglar alarm.

Norman had company.

6

Anna never noticed the green Tempo parked by the curb a block and a half down from Daughters and Sisters. She was deep in a private fantasy, one she had never told anyone, not even her therapist, the necessary fantasy she saved for horrible days like today. In it she was on the cover of *Time* magazine. It wasn't a photo but a vibrant oil painting which showed her in a dark blue shift (blue was her best color, and a shift would obscure the depressing way she had been thickening around the middle these last two or three years). She was looking over her left shoulder, giving the artist her good side to work with, and her hair spilled over her right shoulder in a snowdrift. A *sexy* snowdrift.

The caption beneath the picture read simply: AMERICAN WOMAN.

She turned into the driveway, reluctantly putting the fantasy away (she had just reached the point where the writer was saying, "Although she has reclaimed the lives of over fifteen hundred battered women, Anna Stevenson remains surprisingly, even touchingly, modest . . ."). She turned off the engine of her Infiniti and just sat there for a moment, delicately rubbing at the skin beneath her eyes.

Peter Slowik, whom she had usually referred to at the time of their divorce as either Peter the Great or Rasputin the Mad Marxist, had been a promiscuous babbler when alive, and his friends had seemed determined to remember him in that same spirit. The talk had gone on and on, each "remembrance bouquet" (she thought that she could cheerfully machine-gun the politically correct buttholes who spent their days thinking such smarmy phrases up) seemingly longer than the last, and by four o'clock, when they'd finally gotten up to eat the food and drink the wine—domestic and dreadful, just what Peter would have picked if he'd been the one doing the shopping—she was sure the shape of the folding chair on which she'd been sitting must have been tattooed into her ass. The idea of leaving early—perhaps slipping out after one finger-sandwich and a token sip of wine—had never crossed her mind, however. People would be watching, evaluating her behavior. She was Anna Stevenson, after all, an important woman in the political structure of this town, and there were certain people she had to speak to after the formal ceremonies were over. People she wanted other people to *see* her talking to, because that was how the carousel turned.

And, just to add to the fun, her pager had gone off three times in a space of forty-five minutes. *Weeks* went by when it sat mutely in her purse, but this afternoon, during a meeting where there were long periods of silence broken by people who seemed incapable of speaking above a tearful mutter, the gadget had gone crazy. After the third time she got tired of the swivelling heads and turned the Christing thing off. She hoped nobody had gone into labor at the picnic, that nobody's kid had taken a thrown horseshoe in the head, and most of all she hoped Rosie's husband hadn't shown up. She doubted that he had, though; he would know better. In any case, anyone who'd called her pager would have called D & S first, and she'd make the answering machine in her study stop number one. She could listen to the messages while she peed. In most cases, that would be fitting.

She got out of the car, locked it (even in a good neighborhood like this you couldn't be too careful), and went up the porch steps. She used her keycard and silenced the *meep-meep-meep* of the security system without even thinking of it; sweet shreds of her daydream

(*only woman of her time to be loved and respected by* all *factions of the increasingly divergent women's movement*)

still swirled in her head.

"Hello, the house!" she called, walking down the hall.

Silence replied, which was what she'd expected . . . and, let's face it, hoped for. With any luck, she might have two or even three hours of blessed silence before the commencement of that night's giggling, hissing showers, slamming doors, and cackling sitcoms.

She walked into the kitchen, wondering if maybe a long leisurely bath, Calgon and all, wouldn't smooth off the worst of the day. Then she stopped, frowning across at her study door. It was standing ajar.

"Goddammit," she muttered. "God *damn* it!"

If there was one thing she disliked above all others—except maybe for touchy-huggy-feely people—it was having her privacy invaded. She had no lock on her study door because she did not believe she should be reduced to that. This was *her* place, after all; the girls and women who came here came through her generosity and at her sufferance. She shouldn't need a lock on that door. Her desire that they should stay out unless invited in ought to have been enough.

Mostly it was, but every now and then some woman would decide she *really needed* some piece of her documentation, that she *really needed* to use Anna's photocopier (which warmed up faster than the one downstairs in the rec room), that she *really needed* a stamp, and so this disrespectful person would come in, she'd track through a place that wasn't hers, maybe look at things that weren't hers to look at, junk up the air with the smell of some cheap drugstore perfume . . .

Anna paused with one hand on the study doorknob, looking into the dark room which had been a pantry when she was a little girl. Her nostrils flared slightly and the frown on her face deepened. There was a smell, all right, but it wasn't quite perfume. It was something that reminded her of the Mad Marxist. It was . . .

All my men wear English Leather or they wear nothing at all.

Jesus! Jesus Christ!

Her arms crawled with gooseflesh. She was a woman who prided herself on her practicality, but suddenly it was all too easy to imagine Peter Slowik's ghost waiting for her inside her study, a shade as insubstantial as the stink of that ludicrous cologne he'd worn . . .

Her eyes fixed on a light in the darkness: the answering machine. The little red lamp was stuttering madly, as if everyone in the city had called today.

Something *had* happened. All at once she knew it. It explained the pager, too . . . and like a dummy she'd turned it off so people would stop staring at her. Something had happened, probably at Ettinger's Pier. Someone hurt. Or, God forbid—

She stepped into the office, feeling for the light-switch beside the door, then stopped, puzzled by what her fingers had found. The switch was already up, which meant the overhead light should be on, but it wasn't.

Anna flipped the switch up and down twice, started to do it a third time, and then a hand dropped on her right shoulder.

She screamed at that settling touch, the sound coming out of her throat as full and frantic as any scream ever voiced by a horror-movie heroine, and as another hand clamped on her upper left arm and turned her around on her heels, as she saw the shape silhouetted against the flooding light from the kitchen, she screamed again.

The thing which had been standing behind the door and waiting for her wasn't human. Horns sprouted from the top of its head, horns which appeared to be swollen with strange, tumorous growths. It was—

"Viva ze bool," a hollow voice said, and she realized it *was* a man, a man wearing a mask, but that didn't make her feel any better because she had a very good idea of who the man was.

She tore out of his grip and backed toward the desk. She could still smell English Leather, but she could smell other things now, as well. Hot rubber. Sweat. And urine. Was it hers? Had she wet herself? She didn't know. She was numb from the waist down.

"Don't touch me," she said in a trembling voice utterly unlike her usual calm and authoritative tone. She reached behind her and felt for the button that summoned the police. It was there someplace, but buried under drifts of paper. "Don't you dare touch me, I'm warning you."

"Anna-Anna-bo-Banna, banana-fanna-fo-Fanna," the creature in the horned mask said in a tone of deep meditation, and then swept the door shut behind it. Now they were in total darkness.

"Stay away," she said, moving along the desk, sliding along the desk. If she could get into the bathroom, lock the door—

"Fee-fi-mo-Manna . . ."

From her left. And close. She lunged to the right, but not soon enough. Strong arms enfolded her. She tried to scream again, but the arms tightened, and her breath came out in a silent rush.

If I were Misery Chastain, I'd— she thought, and then Norman's teeth were on her throat, he was nuzzling her like a horny kid parked on Lovers' Lane, and then his teeth were *in* her throat, and something was spraying warm all down the front of her, and she thought no more.

7

By the time the final questions were asked and the final statement was signed, it was long past dark. Rosie's head spun, and she felt a little unreal to herself, as she had after those occasional all-day tests they threw at you in high school.

Gustafson went off to file his paperwork, bearing it before him as if it were the Holy Grail, and Rosie got to her feet. She began moving toward Bill, who was also getting up. Gert had gone in search of the ladies' room.

"Ms. McClendon?" Hale asked from her elbow.

Rosie's weariness was supplanted by a sudden, horrid premonition. It was just the two of them; Bill was too far away to overhear anything Hale might say to her, and when he began to speak, he would do so in a low, confidential voice. He would tell her that she would stop all this foolishness about her husband right now, while there was still time, if she knew what was good for her. That she would keep her mouth shut around cops from here on out, unless one of them either (a) asked her a question, or (b) unzipped his fly. He would remind her that this was a family thing, that—

"I *am* going to bust him," Hale said mildly. "I don't know if I can completely convince you of that no matter what I say, but I need you to hear me say it, anyway. I *am* going to bust him. It's a promise."

She looked at him with her mouth open.

"I'm going to do it because he's a murderer, and crazy, and dangerous. I'm also going to do it because I don't like the way you look around the squadroom and jump every time a door slams somewhere. Or the way you cringe a little every time I move one of my hands."

"I don't . . ."

"You *do*. You can't help it and you do. That's all right, though, because I understand *why* you do. If I was a woman and I'd been through what you've been through . . ." He trailed off, looking at her quizzically. "Has it ever occurred to you how magic-goddam-lucky you are just to be alive?"

"Yes," Rosie said. Her legs were trembling. Bill was standing at the gate, looking at her, clearly concerned. She forced a smile for him and raised a single finger—one more minute.

"You bet you are," Hale said. He glanced around the squadroom, and Rosie followed his eyes. At one desk, a cop was writing up a weeping teenager in a high-school letter-jacket. At another, this one by the chickenwired floor-to-ceiling windows, a uniformed cop and a detective with his jacket off so you could see the .38 Police Special clipped to his belt were examining a stack of photos, their heads close together. At a row of VDT screens all the way across the room, Gustafson was discussing his reports with a young bluesuit who looked no older than sixteen to Rosie.

"You know a lot about cops," Hale said, "but most of what you know is wrong."

She didn't know how to answer that, but it was okay; he didn't seem to require an answer.

"You want to know what my *biggest* motivation for busting him is, Ms. McClendon? Numero uno on the old hit parade?"

She nodded.

"I'm going to bust him *because* he's a cop. A hero cop, for God's sake. But the *next* time his puss is on the front page of the old hometown paper, he's either going to be the *late* Norman Daniels or he's going to be in legirons and an orange tracksuit."

"Thank you for saying that," Rosie said. "It means a lot."

He led her over to Bill, who opened the gate and put his arms around her. She hugged him tight, her eyes shut.

Hale asked, "Ms. McClendon?"

She opened her eyes, saw Gert come back into the room, and waved. Then she looked at Hale shyly but not fearfully. "You can call me Rosie, if you want."

He smiled briefly at that. "Would you like to hear something that'll maybe make you feel a little better about your first less-than-enthusiastic reaction to this place?"

"I . . . I guess so."

"Let *me* guess," Bill said. "You're having problems with the cops back in Rosie's hometown."

Hale smiled sourly. "Indeed we are. They're being shy about faxing us what they know about Daniels's blood-medicals, even his prints. We're already dealing with police lawyers. Cop-shysters!"

"They're protecting him," Rosie said. "I knew they would."

"So far, yes. It's an instinct, like the one that tells you to drop everything and go after the killer when a cop gets gunned down. They'll stop trying to throw sand in the gears when they finally get it through their heads that this is real."

"Do you really believe that?" Gert asked.

He thought this over, then nodded. "Yes. I do."

"What about police protection for Rosie until this is over?" Bill asked.

Hale nodded again. "There's already a black-and-white outside your place on Trenton Street, Rosie."

She looked from Gert to Bill to Hale, dismayed and frightened all over again. The situation kept sandbagging her. She'd start to feel she was getting a handle on it, and then it would whop her flat all over again, from some new direction.

"Why? *Why?* He doesn't know where I live, he *can't* know where I live! That's why he came to the picnic, because he thought I'd be there. Cynthia didn't tell him, did she?"

"She says not." Hale accented the second word, but so lightly Rosie didn't catch it. Gert and Bill did, and they exchanged a look.

"Well, there! And Gert didn't tell him, either! Did you, Gert?"

"No, ma'am," Gert said.

"Well, I like to play safe—leave it at that. I've got the guys in front of your building, and backup cars—at least two—in the neighborhood. I don't want to scare you all over again, but a nut who knows police procedure is a special nut. Best not to take chances."

"If you think so," Rosie said in a small voice.

"Ms. Kinshaw, I'll send someone around to take you wherever you want to go—"

"Ettinger's," Gert said, and stroked her robe. "I'm going to make a fashion statement at the concert."

Hale grinned, then put his hand out to Bill. "Mr. Steiner, good to meet you."

Bill shook it. "Same here. Thanks for everything."

"It's my job." He glanced from Gert to Rosie. "Good night, girls." He looked back at Gert, fast, and his face broke into a grin that knocked fifteen years off his age in an instant. "Gotcha," he said, and laughed. After a moment's thought, Gert laughed with him.

8

On the steps outside, Bill and Gert and Rosie huddled together a little. The air was damp, and fog was drifting in off the lake. It was still thin, really no more than a nimbus around the streetlights and low-lying smoke over the wet pavement, but Rose guessed that in another hour it would be almost thick enough to cut.

"Want to come back to D and S tonight, Rosie?" Gert asked. "They'll be coming in from the concert in another couple of hours; we could have the popcorn all made."

Rosie, who most definitely did not want to go back to D & S, turned to Bill. "If I go home, will you stay with me?"

"Sure," he said promptly, and took her hand. "It'd be a pleasure. And don't worry about the accommodations—I never saw a couch yet that I couldn't sleep on."

"You haven't seen mine," she said, knowing that her sofa wasn't going to be a problem, because Bill wasn't going to be sleeping there. Her bed was a single, which meant they'd be cramped, but she thought they would still manage quite nicely. Close quarters might even add something.

"Thanks again, Gert," she said.

"No problem." Gert gave her a brief, hard hug, then leaned forward and put a healthy smack on Bill's cheek. A police car came around the corner and stopped, idling. "Take care of her, guy."

"I will."

Gert went to her ride, then stopped to point at Bill's Harley, heeled over on its kickstand in one of the parking spaces stencilled POLICE BUSINESS ONLY. "And don't dump that thing in the goddam fog."

"I'll take it easy, Ma, I promise."

She drew back one big fist, mock-scowling, and Bill stuck out his chin with half-closed eyes and a longsuffering expression that made Rosie laugh hard. She had never expected to be laughing on the steps of a police station, but a lot of things she'd never expected had happened this year.

A *lot.*

9

In spite of all that had happened, Rosie enjoyed the ride back to Trenton Street almost as much as the one out to the country that morning. She clung to Bill as they cut across the city on the surface streets, the big Harley-Davidson slicing smoothly through the thickening fog. The last three blocks were like riding through a dream lined with cotton. The Harley's headlight was a brilliant, cloudy cylinder, boring into the air like the beam of a flashlight cutting across a smoky room. When Bill finally turned onto Trenton Street, the buildings were little more than ghosts and Bryant Park was a vast white blank.

The black-and-white Hale had promised was parked in front of 897. The words *To Serve and Protect* were written on the side. The space in front of the car was empty. Bill swung his motorcycle into it, kicked the gearshift up into neutral with his foot, and killed the engine. "You're shivering," he said as he helped her off.

She nodded and found she had to make a conscious effort to keep her teeth from chattering when she spoke. "It's more the damp than the cold." And yet, even then, she supposed she knew it was really neither; knew on some deep level that things were not as they should be.

"Well, let's get you into something dry and warm." He stowed their helmets, locked the Harley's ignition, and dropped the key into his pocket.

"Sounds like the idea of the century to me."

He took her hand and walked her down the sidewalk to the apartment building steps. As they passed the radio-car, Bill raised his hand to the cop behind the wheel. The cop lifted his own hand out the window in a lazy return salute, and the streetlight gleamed on the ring he wore. His partner appeared to be sleeping.

Rosie opened her purse, got out the key she would need to open the front door at this advanced hour, and turned it in the lock. She had only the faintest idea of what she was doing; her good feelings were gone and her earlier terror had crashed back in on her like some huge dead iron object falling through floor after floor of an old building, an object destined to drop all the way to the basement. Her stomach was suddenly freezing, her head was throbbing, *and she didn't know why.*

She had seen something, *something,* and she was so focused on her effort to think what it might have been that she did not hear the driver's door of the police car open and then chunk softly shut. She did not hear the faintly gritting footsteps on the sidewalk behind them, either.

"Rosie?"

Bill's voice, coming out of darkness. They were in the vestibule now, but she could barely see the picture of the old geezer (she thought maybe it was Calvin Coolidge) hanging on the wall to her right, or the scrawny shape of the coat-tree, with its brass feet and its bristle of brass hooks, standing by the stairs. Why was it so damned *dark* in here?

Because the overhead light-fixture was out, of course; that was simple. She knew a harder question, though: Why had the cop on the passenger side of the black-and-white been sleeping in such an uncomfortable position, with his chin way down on his chest and his cap pulled so low over his eyes that he looked like a thug in a gangster movie from the thirties? Why was he sleeping at all, for that matter, when the subject he was detailed to watch was due at any moment? *Hale would be angry if he knew that,* she thought distractedly. *He'd want to talk to that bluesuit. He'd want to talk to him right up close.*

"Rosie? What's wrong?"

The footsteps behind them were hurrying now.

She rolled mental footage backward like a videotape. Saw Bill raising his hand to the bluesuit behind the wheel of the cruiser, saying hi there, good to see you, without even opening his mouth. She saw the cop raise his own hand in return; saw the gleam of the streetlamp on the ring he wore. She hadn't been close enough to read the words on it, but all at once she knew what they were. She'd seen them printed backward on her own flesh many times, like an FDA stamp on a cut of meat.

Service, Loyalty, Community.

Footsteps hurried eagerly up the steps behind them. The door slammed violently shut. Someone was panting low and fast in the dark, and Rosie could smell English Leather.

10

Norman's mind took another of those big skips while he was standing at the sink in the Daughters and Sisters kitchen with his shirt off, washing fresh blood from his face and chest. The sun had been low on the horizon, glaring orange into his eyes when he raised his head and reached for the towel. He touched it, and then, without a single break that he was aware of, not so much as an eyeblink, he was outside and it was dark. He was wearing the White Sox ballcap again. He was also wearing a London Fog topcoat. God knew where he'd picked it up, but it was very appropriate, since a rapidly thickening fog had settled over the city. He rubbed one hand over the expensive waterproofed fabric of the coat, liking the feel. An elegant item. He tried again to think of how he'd come by it and couldn't. Had he killed someone else? Might have, friends and neighbors, might have; anything was possible when you were on vacation.

He looked up Trenton Street and saw a city police-car—what they called a Charlie-David car back in Norman's bailiwick—parked hubcap-deep in the mist about three-quarters of the way to the next intersection. He reached into the deep left pocket of the coat—a really nice coat, somebody certainly had good taste—and touched something rubbery and crumpled. He smiled happily, like a man shaking hands with an old friend. "Ze bool," he whispered. "El toro grande." He reached into the other pocket, not sure what he was going to find, only sure that there was something in there he would want.

He stabbed the tip of his middle finger into it, winced, and brought it carefully out. It was the chromed letter-opener from his pal Maude's desk.

How she screamed, he thought, and smiled as he turned the letter-opener over in his hands, letting the light from the streetlamps run off its blade like white liquid. Yes, she had screamed . . . but then she had stopped. In the end the gals always stopped screaming, and what a relief that was.

Meantime, he had a formidable problem to solve. There would be two —count em, two—motor-patrolmen in the car parked up there; they'd be armed with guns while he was armed only with a chrome-plated letter-opener. He had to take them out, and as silently as possible. A pretty problem, and one he didn't have the slightest idea of how to solve.

"Norm," a voice whispered. It came from his left pocket.

He reached in and pulled out the mask. Its empty eyeholes gazed up at him with blank rapt attention, and the smile once more looked like a *knowing sneer. In this light, the garlands of flowers decking the horns might have been clots of blood.*

"What?" He spoke in a low, conspiratorial whisper. "What is it?"

"Have a heart attack," ze bool whispered, so that was what he did. He plodded slowly up the sidewalk toward where the cruiser was parked, plodding slower and slower as he got closer and closer. He was careful to keep his eyes down and look at the car only with his peripheral vision. They would have seen him by now, even if they were inept—they'd have to, he was the only thing moving out here—and what he wanted them to see was a man looking at his own feet, a man who was working for every step. A man who was either drunk or in trouble.

His right hand was now inside his coat, massaging the left side of his chest. He could feel the blade of the letter-opener, which he was holding in that hand, making little digs in his shirt. As he drew close to his objective he staggered—just one moderate-to-heavy stagger—and then stopped. He stood perfectly still with his head down for a slow five-count, not allowing his body to sway so much as a quarter-inch to one side or the other. By now their first assumption—that this was Mr. Ginhead making his slow way home after a few hours at the Dew Drop Inn—should be giving way to other possibilities. But he wanted them to come to him. He'd go to them if he absolutely had to, but if he had to do that, they would probably take him down.

He took another three steps, not toward the cruiser now but toward the nearest stoop. He grabbed the cold, fog-beaded iron railing which ran up its side and stood there panting, head still down, hoping he looked like a man who was having a heart attack and not one with a lethal instrument hidden inside his coat.

Just when he was beginning to think he had made a serious error here, the doors of the police car swung open. He heard this rather than saw it, and then he heard an even happier sound: feet hurrying toward him. Cheezit, Rocky, da cops, he thought, and then risked a small look. He had to risk it, had to know where they were in relation to each other. If they weren't close together, he would have to stage a collapse . . . and that held its own ironic danger. In such a case one of them would very likely run back to the cruiser in order to radio for an ambulance.

They were a typical Charlie-David team, one vet and one kid still wet behind the ears. To Norman, the rookie looked weirdly familiar, like someone he might have seen on TV. That didn't matter, though. They were close together, almost shoulder to shoulder, and that did matter. That was very nice. Cozy.

"Sir?" the one on the left—the older one—asked. "Sir, do you have a problem?"

"Hurts like a bastard," Norman wheezed.

"What hurts?" Still the older one. This was a crucial moment, not quite crunch-time, but almost. The older cop could order his partner to radio for EMT backup at any moment and he would be hung, but he couldn't strike just yet; they were just a tiny bit too far away.

At this moment he felt more like his old self than he had since starting on this expedition: cold and clear and totally here, *aware of everything, from the droplets of fog on the iron railing to a dirty-gray pigeon feather lying in the gutter next to a crumpled potato chip bag. He could hear the soft, steady susurrus of the cops' breathing.*

"It's in here," Norman gasped, rubbing under his coat with his right hand. The blade of the letter-opener poked through his shirt and pricked his skin, but he hardly felt it. "It's like having a gallbladder attack, only in my chest."

"Maybe I better call an ambulance," the younger cop said, and suddenly Norman knew who the young cop reminded him of: Jerry Mathers, the kid who'd played Beaver on Leave It to Beaver. *He'd watched all those shows in reruns on Channel 11, some of them five and six times.*

The older cop didn't look a bit like the Beav's brother Wally, though.

"Hang on a sec," the older cop said, and then, incredibly, gave away the store. "Let me take a look. I was a medic in the army."

"Coat . . . buttons . . ." Norman said, keeping an eye on the Beav from the corner of his eye.

The older cop took another step forward. He was now standing right in front of Norman. The Beav also took a step forward. The older cop undid the top button of Norman's newfound London Fog. Then the second one. When he undid the third one, Norman pulled the letter-opener out and plunged it into the man's throat. Blood burst out in a torrent, gushing down his uniform. In the foggy darkness it looked like steak sauce.

The Beav turned out not to be a problem. He stood, paralyzed with horror, as his partner raised his hands and beat weakly at the handle of the thing in his throat. He looked like a man trying to rid himself of some exotic leech. "Bluh!" he choked. "Ahk! Bluh!"

The Beav turned to Norman. In his shock he seemed totally unaware that Norman had had anything to do with what had just befallen his partner, and this didn't surprise Norman at all. It was a reaction he had seen before. In his shock and surprise, the cop looked about ten years old, now not just something like *the Beav, but a dead ringer.*

"Something happened to Al!" the Beav said. *Norman knew something else about this young man who was about to join the city's Roll of Honor: inside his head he thought he was shouting, he really did, when what was actually coming out was only a little bitty whisper. "Something happened to Al!"*

"I know," Norman said, and delivered an uppercut to the kid's chin, a dangerous punch if your opponent is dangerous, but a sixth-grader could have dealt with the Beav as he was now. The blow connected squarely, knocking the young cop back into the iron railing Norman had been clutching not thirty seconds ago. The Beav wasn't as out as Norman had hoped, but his eyes had gone cloudy and vague; there was going to be no trouble here. His hat had tumbled off. The hair beneath was short, but not too short to grab. Norman got a handful and yanked the kid's head sharply down as he brought his knee up. The sound was muffled but terrific; the sound of a man with a mallet whacking a padded bag full of china.

The Beav dropped like a lead bar. Norman looked around for his partner, and here was something incredible: the partner was gone.

Norman wheeled around, eyes glaring, and spotted him. He was walking up the sidewalk very slowly, with his hands held out in front of him like a zombie in a fright-film. Norman turned a complete circle on his heels, looking for witnesses to this comedy. He didn't see any. There was a lot of hooting and hollering drifting over from the park, teenagers running around in there, playing grab-ass in the fog, but that was all right. So far his luck had been fantastic. If it held for another forty-five seconds, a minute at most, he'd be home free.

He ran after the older cop, who had now stopped to have another go at pulling Anna Stevenson's letter-opener out of his throat. He had actually managed to get about twenty-five yards.

"Officer!" Norman said in a low peremptory voice, and touched the cop's elbow.

The cop turned jerkily. His eyes were glassy and bulging from their sockets, the eyes of something that belonged mounted on the wall of a hunting lodge, Norman thought. His uniform was drenched scarlet from neck to knees. Norman didn't have the slightest idea how this man could still be alive, let alone conscious. I guess they must build cops tougher in the midwest, *he thought.*

"Caw!" the cop said urgently. *"Caw! Fuh! Bah-up!"* The voice was bubbly and choked, but still amazingly strong. Norman even knew what the guy was saying. He'd made a bad mistake back there, a rookie's mistake, but Norman thought this was a man he could have been proud to serve with, just the same. The letter-opener handle sticking out of his

throat bobbed up and down when he tried to talk, in a way that reminded Norman of how the bullmask looked when he manipulated the lips from the inside.

"Yes, I'll call for backup." Norman spoke with soft, urgent sincerity. He closed one hand on the cop's wrist. "But for now, let's get you back to the car. Come on. This way, Officer!" He would have used the cop's name, but didn't know what it was; the name-tag on his uniform shirt was covered with blood. He couldn't very well call him Officer Al. He gave the cop's arm another gentle tug, and this time got him moving.

Norman led the staggering, bleeding Charlie-David cop with the letter-opener in his throat back to his own black-and-white, expecting someone to come out of the steadily thickening fog at any moment—a man who'd gone to get a sixpack, a woman who'd been to the movies, a couple of kids on their way home from a date (maybe, God save the King, an amusement-park date at Ettinger's)—and when that happened he'd have to kill them, too. Once you got started killing people it never seemed to stop; the first one spread like ripples on a pond.

But no one came. There were only the disembodied voices floating across from the park. It was a miracle, really, like how Officer Al could still be on his feet even though he was bleeding like a stuck pig and had left a trail of blood behind him so wide and thick it was starting to puddle up in places. The puddles gleamed like engine oil in the fog-faded glow of the streetlamps.

Norman paused to pluck the Beav's fallen hat off the steps, and when they passed the open driver's-side window of the black-and-white, he leaned through quickly to drop it on the seat and pluck the keys from the ignition. There were a formidable number of them on the ring, so many that they couldn't lie flat against one another but stuck out like sunrays in a child's crayon drawing, but Norman had no trouble picking out the one which opened the trunk of the car.

"Come on," he whispered comfortingly. "Come on, just a little further, then we can get backup rolling." He kept expecting the cop to collapse, but he didn't. He had given up on trying to pull the letter-opener out of his throat, though.

"Watch the curb here, Officer, whoops-a-daisy."

The cop stepped off the curb. When his black uniform shoe came down in the gutter, the wound in his throat gaped open around the blade like the gill of a fish and more blood squirted onto the collar of his shirt.

Now I'm a cop-killer, too, Norman thought. He expected the idea to be devastating, but it wasn't. Perhaps because a deeper, wiser part of him knew that he really hadn't killed this fine, tough police officer; someone *else had. Some*thing. *Most likely it had been the bull. The longer Norman thought about it, the more plausible that sounded.*

"Hold it, Officer, here we are."

The cop stopped where he was, at the back of the car. Norman used the key he had picked out to open its trunk. There was a spare tire in there (bald as a baby's ass, too, he saw), a jack, two flak vests—kapok, not Kevlar—a pair of boots, a grease-stained copy of Penthouse, *a toolkit, a police radio with half its guts spilling out. A pretty full trunk, in other words, like the trunk of every other police-car he'd ever seen. But like the trunk of every other police-car he'd ever seen, there was always room for one more thing. He moved the toolkit to one side and the police radio to the other while the Beav's partner stood swaying beside him, now completely silent, his eyes seemingly fixed on some distant point, as if he now saw the place where his new journey would begin. Norman tucked the jack behind the spare tire, then looked from the empty space to the person for whom he had created it.*

"Okay," he said. "Good. But I need to borrow your hat, okay?"

The cop said nothing, simply swayed back and forth on his feet, but Norman's sly bag of a mother had been fond of saying "Silence gives consent," and Norman thought it a good motto, certainly better than his father's favorite, which had been "If they're old enough to pee, they're old enough for me." Norman took off the cop's hat and put it on his own bald head. The baseball cap went into the trunk.

"Bluh," said the cop, holding one smeared hand out to Norman. His eyes didn't bother; they seemed to have floated away completely.

"Yes, I know, blood, that goddam bull," Norman said, and shoved the cop into the trunk. He lay there limply, with one twitching leg still sticking out. Norman bent it at the knee, loaded it in, and slammed the trunk shut. Then he went back to the rookie. The rook was trying to sit up, although his eyes said he was still mostly unconscious. His ears were bleeding. Norman dropped to one knee, settled his hands around the young cop's throat, and began to squeeze. The cop fell backward. Norman sat on him and kept squeezing. When the Beav had ceased all movement, Norman put his ear against the young man's chest. He heard three heartbeats from in there, random and disordered, like fish flopping on a riverbank. Norman sighed and slid his hands around the Beav's throat again, thumbs pressing into his windpipe. Now someone will come, *he thought,* now someone'll come for sure, *but no one did. Someone called, "Yo, muthafucka!" from the white blank of Bryant Park, and there was shrill laughter, the kind only drunks and the mentally retarded can manage, but that was all. Norman bent his ear against the cop's chest again. This guy was stage-*

dressing, and he didn't want his stage-dressing coming to life at a crucial moment.

This time there was nothing ticking but the Beav's watch.

Norman picked him up, carted him around to the passenger side of the Caprice, and loaded him in. He jammed the rookie's hat down as far as he could—black and swollen, the kid's face was now the face of a troll— and slammed the door. Now every part of Norman's body was throbbing, but the worst pain of all had once more settled in his teeth and jaws.

Maude, *he thought.* That's all about Maude.

Suddenly he was very glad he couldn't remember what he had done with Maude . . . or to her. And of course it really hadn't been him at all; it had been ze bool, el toro grande. But dear God, how everything hurt. *It was as if he were being dismantled from the inside out, taken apart a bolt and a screw and a cog at a time.*

The Beav was sliding slowly to the left, his dead eyes bulging out of his face like croaker marbles. "No you don't, whoa, Nellie," Norman said, and pulled him upright again. He reached in farther and buckled the Beav's seatbelt and harness. That did the trick. Norman stood back a little and took a critical look. He didn't think he'd done badly, all in all. The Beav just looked conked out, catching an extra forty or fifty winks.

He leaned in the window again, careful not to disturb the Beav's position, and pawed open the glove compartment. He expected to find a first-aid kit, and he wasn't disappointed. He popped the lid, took out a dusty old bottle of Anacin, and swallowed five or six. He was leaning against the side of the car, chewing them and wincing at the sharp, vinegary taste, when his mind took another of those skips.

When he came back to himself time had passed, but probably not too much; his mouth and throat were still filled with the sour taste of aspirin. He was in the vestibule of her building, snapping the light-switch up and down. Nothing happened when he did it; the little room stayed dark. He'd done something to the lights, then. That was good. He had one of the Charlie-David cops' guns in his other hand. He was holding it by the barrel, and he had an idea he'd used the butt to hammer something. Fuses, maybe? Had he been down cellar? Maybe, but it didn't matter. The lights here didn't work, and that was enough.

This was a rooming-house—a nice one, but still a rooming-house. It was impossible to mistake the smell of cheap food, the kind that always got cooked on a hotplate. It was a smell that seeped into the walls after awhile, and nothing could get rid of it. Two or three weeks from now the characteristic sound of rooming-houses in summer would be added to that smell: the low, intermingled whine of small fans set in many different windows, trying to cool rooms that would be walk-in ovens in August. She had traded her nice little house for this cramped desperation, but there was no time to puzzle over that mystery now. The question right now was how many roomers lived in this building, and how many of them would be in early on a Saturday night. How many, in other words, might be a problem?

None of them will be, *said the voice from the pocket of Norman's new topcoat. It was a comfy voice.* None of them will be, because what happens after doesn't matter, and that simplifies everything. If anyone gets in your way, just kill them.

He turned, went out onto the stoop, and pulled the vestibule door shut behind him. He tried it and found it locked. He supposed he'd picked his way in—the lock certainly didn't look like much of a challenge—but it was mildly disquieting not to know for sure. And the lights. Why had he gone to the trouble of killing them, when she would most likely come in alone? For that matter, how did he know she wasn't in already?

This second was easy—he knew she wasn't in because the bull had told him she wasn't, and he believed it. As to the first question, she might not *be alone. Gertie might be with her, or . . . well, ze bool had said something about a boyfriend. Norman found that frankly impossible to believe, but . . . "She likes the way he kisses her," Ferd had said. Stupid, she'd never dare . . . but it never hurt to be safe.*

He started down the steps, meaning to go back to the cop car, meaning to slide behind the wheel and start waiting for her to show up, and that was when the last flip happened, and it was *a flip this time, a flip and not a skip, he went up like a coin flipped from the thumbnail of a referee in a pregame ritual, who to kick, who to receive, and when he came back down he was slamming the vestibule door behind him, lunging into the darkness, and locking his hands around the neck of Rose's boyfriend. He didn't know how he knew the man* was *her boyfriend and not just some plainclothes cop who had been charged with seeing her home safe, but who cared? He* did *know, and that was enough. His whole head was vibrating with outrage and fury. Had he seen this guy*

(she likes the way he kisses her)

swapping spit with her before going in, maybe with his hands sliding down from her waist to cup her ass? He couldn't remember, didn't want *to remember, didn't* need *to remember.*

"I told you!" the bull said; even in its fury its voice was perfectly lucid. "I told you, didn't I? That's what her friends have taught her! Nice! Very nice!"

"I'm going to kill you, motherfucker," he whispered into the unseen

face of the man who was Rose's boyfriend, and forced him back against the vestibule wall. "And oh boy, if I can, if God lets me, I'm gonna kill you twice."

He clamped his hands around Bill Steiner's throat and began to squeeze.

11

"**N**orman!" Rosie screamed in the darkness. *"Norman, let him go!"*

Bill's hand, which had lightly been touching the back of her arm ever since she had pulled her key out of the door, was suddenly gone. She heard stumbling footfalls—foot-*thuds*—in the darkness. Then there was a heavier bump as someone drove someone else into the vestibule wall.

"I'm going to kill you, motherfucker," came whispering out of the dark. "And oh boy, if I can, if God lets me—"

I'm gonna kill you twice, she finished in her head before he could finish out loud; it was one of Norman's favorite threats, often yelled at the TV screen when an umpire made a call that went against Norman's beloved Yankees, or when someone cut him off in traffic. *If God lets me, I'm gonna kill you twice.* And now she heard a choking, gargly sound, and of course that was Bill. That was Bill in the process of having the life choked out of him by Norman's large and powerful hands.

Instead of the terror Norman had always roused in her, she felt a return of the rage she'd experienced in Hale's car and then at the police station. This time it seemed almost to engulf her. *"Let him alone, Norman!"* she screamed. *"Get your fucking hands off him!"*

"Shut up, you whore!" came out of the darkness, but she could hear surprise as well as anger in Norman's voice. Until now she'd never given him a single command—not in the entire course of their marriage—or spoken to him in such a tone.

And something else—there was a band of dull heat above the place where Bill had been touching her. It was the armlet. The gold armlet the woman in the chiton had given her. And in her mind, Rosie heard her snarl *Stop your stupid sheep's whining!* at her.

"Quit it, I'm warning you!" she screamed at Norman, and then started toward the place from which the choking sounds and the effortful grunts were coming. She went with her hands held out before her like the hands of a blind woman, her lips drawn back from her teeth.

You're not going to choke him, she thought. *You're not, I won't let you. You should have gone away, Norman. You should have gone away and left us alone while you still could.*

Feet, drumming helplessly against the wall just ahead of her, and she could imagine Norman holding Bill up against it, lips drawn back in his biting smile, and suddenly she was a glass woman filled with a pale red liquid, and that liquid was pure and untinctured fury.

"You shit, didn't you hear me? PUT HIM DOWN, I SAID!"

She reached out with her left hand, which now felt as strong as an eagle's talon. The armlet was burning fiercely—she felt she should almost be able to see it, even through her sweater and the jacket Bill had loaned her, glowing like a dull ember. But there was no pain, only a kind of dangerous exhilaration. She grabbed the shoulder of the man who had beaten her for fourteen years and dragged him backward. It was astoundingly easy. She squeezed his arm through the slippery waterproof fabric of his coat, then whipped her own arm out and slung him off into the darkness. She heard the rapid rattle of his stumbling feet, then a thud, then an explosion of breaking glass. Cal Coolidge, or whoever it was in the picture over there, had taken a dive.

She could hear Bill coughing and gagging. She groped for him with splayed fingers, found his shoulders, and settled her hands upon them. He was hunched over, tearing for each breath and immediately coughing it back out. This didn't surprise her. She knew how strong Norman was.

She slipped her right hand down his left arm and grasped him above the elbow. She was afraid to use her left hand, afraid she might hurt him with it. She could feel power humming in it, throbbing through it. Perhaps the most terrifying thing about the sensation was how much she liked it.

"Bill," she whispered. "Come on. Come with me."

She had to get him upstairs. She didn't know exactly why, not yet, but she did not doubt at all that when she needed to know, the knowing would come. But he didn't move. He only leaned on his hands, coughing and making those gagging noises.

"Come on, goddammit!" she whispered in a harsh peremptory voice . . . and she had come so close to saying *you,* as in *Come on, goddam you!* And she knew who she sounded like, oh yes indeed, even in these desperate circumstances, she knew very well.

He got moving, though, and for now that was all that mattered. Rosie led him across the vestibule with the confidence of a seeing-eye dog. He was still coughing and half-retching, but he was able to walk.

"Halt!" Norman shouted from his part of the darkness. He sounded both official and desperate. "Halt, or I'll shoot!"

No you won't, that would spoil all your fun, she thought, but he *did* shoot, the dead cop's .45 slanted up at the ceiling, the sound terrific in the enclosed space of the vestibule, the smell of burnt cordite sharp enough to make the eyes water. There was also a momentary shutterflash of reddish-yellow light, so bright it printed afterimages on her eyes like tattoos, and she supposed that was why he'd done it: to get a look at the landscape, and a look at where she and Bill were in that landscape. At the foot of the stairs, in fact.

Bill made a choked vomiting sound and staggered against her, sending her into the wall of the staircase. As she struggled to keep from going to her knees, she heard a rush of footsteps in the dark as Norman came for them.

12

She lunged up the first two steps, hauling Bill with her. He paddled with his feet, trying to help; perhaps he even did, a little. As Rosie gained the second step, she flung her left hand out behind her and swept the coat-tree across the foot of the stairs like a roadblock. As Norman crashed into it and began cursing, she let go of Bill, who slumped but did not fall. He was still gagging and she sensed him bending over again, trying to get his breath back, trying to get his windpipe to work again.

"Hang in," she murmured. "Just hang in there, Bill."

She went up two stairs, then came back down on the other side of him, so she could use her left arm. If she was going to get him to the top of the stairs, she'd need all the power the gold armlet was putting out. She slipped her arm around his waist, and suddenly it was easy. She started to go up with him, breathing hard and canted over to the right, like a woman counterbalancing a heavy weight, but not gasping or buckling in the knees. She had an idea she could have hauled him up a high ladder like this, if that had been required. Every now and then he'd put a foot down and push, trying to help, but mostly his toes just dragged up the risers and across the carpeted stair-levels. Then, as they reached the tenth step—the halfway point, by her count—he started to help a little more. That was good, because there was a splintering sound from behind and below them as the coat-tree snapped beneath Norman's two hundred and twenty pounds. Now she could hear him coming again, not on his feet—at least it didn't sound that way—but crawling on his hands and knees.

"You don't want to play with me, Rose," he panted. How far behind? She couldn't tell. And while the coat-tree had slowed him down, Norman wasn't dragging a man who was hurt and only three-quarters conscious. "Stop right where you are. Quit trying to run. I only want to talk to y—"

"Stay away!" Sixteen . . . seventeen . . . eighteen. The light was off up here, too, and with no windows it was as dark as a mineshaft. Then she was staggering forward, the foot that had been searching for the nineteenth step finding only more level going. Apparently there were only eighteen stairs in the flight, not twenty. How marvellous. They had made it to the top ahead of him; at least they had managed to do that much. *"Stay away from me, Nor—"*

A thought struck her then, one so terrible that it froze her where she was. She sucked the last syllable of her husband's name back into herself like someone who has been punched in the stomach.

Where were her keys? Had she left them dangling from the lock in the outside door?

She let go of Bill so she could feel in the lefthand pocket of the leather jacket he had loaned her, and as she did, Norman's hand closed softly and persuasively around her calf, like the coil of a snake which squeezes its prey rather than poisoning it with venom. Without thinking, she kicked powerfully backward with her other foot. The sole of her sneaker connected squarely with Norman's already battered nose, and he gave voice to a sick howl of pain. This changed to a yell of surprise as he grabbed for the bannister, missed it, and toppled backward into the darkened stairwell. Rosie heard a double crash as he somersaulted twice, heels over head.

Break your neck! she screamed silently at him as her hand closed on the comforting round shape of the keyring in her jacket pocket—she had stuck it in there after all, thank Christ, thank God, thank all the angels in the Kingdom of Heaven. *Break your neck, let it end right here in the dark, break your stinking neck, die and leave me alone!*

But no. She could already hear him stirring and moving around down there, and then he was cursing her, and then there was the unmistakable marching thud of his knees as he started crawling up the stairs again, calling her all his names—cunt and dyke and whore and bitch—as he came.

"I can walk," Bill said suddenly. His voice was pinched and small, but she was grateful to hear it just the same. "I can walk, Rosie, let's get to your room. The crazy bastard is coming again."

Bill started coughing. Below them—but not much below—Norman laughed. "That's right, Sunny Jim, the crazy bastard is coming again. The crazy bastard is going to poke your eyeballs right out of your fucking head and then make you eat them. I wonder how they'll taste?"

"STAY AWAY, NORMAN!" Rosie shrieked, and began to guide Bill down the pitch-black hall. Her left arm was still wrapped around his midsection; with her right hand she felt the wall, trailing her fingers along it, hunting for her door. Her left hand was a fist against Bill's side with the only three keys she had so far accumulated in this new life—front door key, mailbox key, and room key—clutched in it. *"STAY AWAY, I'M WARN-ING YOU!"*

And from the dark behind her—still on the stairs but now very close to the top of them again—the ultimate absurdity came floating: *"Don't you DARE warn me, you BITCH!"*

The wall notched in to a door that had to be hers. She let go of Bill, picked out the key that opened this one—unlike the one to the front door, her room key had a square head—and then jabbed it at the lock in the dark. She could no longer hear Norman. Was he on the stairs? In the hall? Right behind them, and reaching toward the sounds of Bill's choked breathing? She found the lock, pressed her right index finger over the vertical slot of the keyway as a guide, then brought the key to it. It wouldn't go in. She could feel the tip of it pressing into the slot, but it refused to budge beyond that point. She felt panic starting to rip at her mind with busy little rat-teeth.

"It won't go in!" she panted at Bill. "It's the right key but it won't go in!"

"Turn it over. You're probably trying it upside-down."

"Say, what's going on down there?" This was a new voice, farther down the hall and above them. Probably on the third-floor landing. It was followed by the fruitless *click-click-click* of a light switch. "And why're the lights out?"

"Stay—" Bill shouted, and immediately started coughing again. He made a terrific grinding sound in his throat, trying to clear his voice. *"Stay where you are! Don't come down here! Call the p—"*

"I *am* the police, fuckstick," a soft, strangely muffled voice said from the darkness right beside them. There was a low, thick grunt, a sound that was both eager and satisfied. Bill was jerked away from her just as she finally managed to run her room key into its slot.

"No!" she screamed, flailing in the dark with her left hand. On her upper arm, the circlet was hotter than ever. *"No, leave him alone! LEAVE HIM ALONE!"*

She grasped smooth leather—Bill's jacket—and then it slipped away. The horrible choking sounds, the sounds of someone whose throat is being packed tight with fine sand, began again. Norman laughed. This sound was also muffled. Rosie stepped toward it, arms in front of her, hands splayed and questing. She touched the shoulder of Bill's jacket, reached over it, and touched something gruesome—it felt like dead flesh that was also somehow alive. It was lumpy . . . rubbery . . .

Rubbery.

He's wearing a mask, Rosie thought. *Some kind of mask.*

Then her left hand was seized and pulled into a humid dampness that she had just time to recognize as his mouth before his teeth clamped down on her fingers and she was bitten all the way to the bone.

The pain was terrific, but once again her reaction to it was not fear and the helpless urge to give in, to let Norman have his way as Norman had always had his way, but a rage so great it was like insanity. Instead of trying to pull free of his grinding, baleful teeth, she folded her fingers at the second knuckle, pressing the pads of her fingers against the gum-line inside his front teeth. Then she set the heel of her preternaturally strong left hand against his chin and pulled.

There was a strange creaking sensation under her hand, the sound a board under a man or woman's knee might make just before it snapped. She felt Norman jerk, heard him make a hollow interrogative sound which seemed to consist solely of vowels—*Aaaoouuuu?*—and then his lower face slid forward like a bureau drawer, coming dislocated from the hinges of his jaw. He screamed in agony and Rosie pulled her bleeding hand free, thinking *That's what you get for biting, you bastard, try to do it now.*

She heard him go reeling backward, tracking him by his screams and the sound of his shirt sliding along the wall. *Now he'll use the gun,* she thought as she turned back to Bill. He leaned against the wall, a darker shape in the darkness, coughing desperately again.

"Hey, you guys, come on, a joke's a joke and enough's enough." It was the man from upstairs, sounding petulant and put-out, only now he sounded as if he was *downstairs,* at the far end of this hallway, and Rosie's heart filled with foreknowing even as she twisted the key in the lock and shoved her door open. She didn't sound like herself at all when she screamed, she sounded like the other one.

"Get out of here, you fool! He'll kill you! Don't—"

The gun went off. She was looking to her left and had a nightmarish glimpse of Norman, sitting on the floor with his legs folded under him. There wasn't enough time in that flash for her to recognize what he was wearing on his head, but she did, just the same: it was a bullmask with a vapidly grinning face. Blood—hers—ringed the mouth-hole. She could see Norman's haunted eyes looking out at her, the eyes of a cave-dweller who is about to commence some final, cataclysmic battle.

The complaining tenant screamed as Rosie pulled Bill in through the door and slammed it behind them. Her room was filled with shadows, and the fog had muted the glow from the streetlamp which usually cast a bar of light across the floor, but the place seemed bright after the vestibule, staircase, and upstairs hall.

The first thing Rosie saw was the armlet, glimmering softly in the dark. It was lying on the nighttable beside the base of the lamp.

I did it myself, she thought. Her amazement was so great she felt stupid with it. *I did it all myself, just* thinking *I was wearing it was enough—*

Of course, another voice replied: Practical-Sensible. *Of course it was, because there was never power in the armlet,* never, *the power was always in* her, *the power was always in—*

No, no. She wouldn't go any further down that road, absolutely not. And at that moment her attention was diverted anyway, because Norman hit the door like a freight-train. The cheap wood splintered under his weight; the door groaned on its hinges. Farther away, the upstairs neighbor, a man Rosie had never met, began to wail.

Quick, Rosie, quick! You know what to do, where to go—

"Rosie . . . call . . . have to call . . ." Bill got that far, then began coughing again—too hard to finish. She had no time to listen to such foolishness, anyway. Later his ideas might be good, but now all they were apt to do was get them killed. Now her job was to take care of him, shelter him . . . and that meant getting him to a place where he might be safe. Where they might *both* be safe.

Rose jerked open the closet door, expecting to see that strange other world filling it, the way it had filled her bedroom wall when she had awakened to the sound of thunder. Sunlight would come streaming out, dazzling their dark-adapted eyes . . .

But it was only a closet, small and musty and nothing at all in it—she was wearing the only two items of clothing she had stored in there, a sweater and a pair of sneakers. Oh yes, the picture was there, propped against the wall where she had put it, but it hadn't grown or changed or opened up or whatever it was it did. It was only a picture broken out of its frame, the sort of mediocre painting a person was apt to find in the back of a curio shop or a flea market or a pawnshop. Nothing more than that.

Out in the hall, Norman rammed the door again. The crack was louder this time; a long splinter jumped out of the wood and clattered onto the floor. A few more hits would do it; two or three might be enough. Rooming-house doors were not built to withstand insanity.

"It was more than just some goddam picture!" Rosie cried. "It was left there for me, and it was more than just some goddam picture! It went into some other world! *I know it did, because I've got her bracelet!*"

She turned her head, looked at it, then ran over to the nighttable and snatched it up. It felt heavier than ever. And hot.

"Rosie," Bill said. She could just make him out, holding his hands against his throat. She thought there was blood on his mouth. "Rosie we have to call the—" Then he cried out as bright light washed the room . . . except it wasn't bright enough to be the hazy summer sunlight she had expected. It was moonlight, flooding out of the open closet and washing across the floor. She walked back to Bill with the armlet in her hand and looked in. Where the closet's back wall had been she saw the hilltop, saw tall grasses rippling in a soft and intermittent night breeze, saw the livid lines and columns of the temple gleaming in the dark. And above all was the moon, a bright silver coin riding in a purple-black sky.

She thought of the mother fox they had seen today, a thousand years ago, looking up at such a moon. The vixen looking up as her kits slept beside her in the lee of the fallen trunk, looking raptly up at the moon with her black eyes.

Bill's face was bewildered. The light lay on his skin like silver gilt. "Rosie," he said in a weak and worried voice. His lips continued to move, but he said no more.

She took his arm. "Come on, Bill. We have to go."

"What's happening?" He was pitiful in his hurt and confusion. The expression on his face roused strange and contrasting emotions in her: wild impatience at his slow, oxlike responses, and fierce love—not quite maternal—that felt like a flame in her mind. She would protect him. Yes. Yes. She would protect him unto death, if that was what it took.

"Never mind what's happening," she said. "Only trust me, the way I trusted you to drive the motorcycle. Trust me and come. *We have to go right now!*"

She pulled him forward with her right hand; the armlet dangled from her left like a gold doughnut. He resisted for a moment, and then Norman screamed and hit the door again. With a cry of fear and rage, Rosie renewed her grip on Bill's arm. She yanked him into the closet and then into the moonlit world which now lay beyond its far wall.

13

T hings started to go seriously wrong when the bitch pushed the coat-tree in front of the stairs. Norman got tangled in it somehow, or at least the London Fog he'd liked so much did. One of the brass coathooks somehow ran right through a buttonhole, neatest trick of the week, and another was in his pocket, like an inept pickpocket groping for a wallet. A third speared one blunt brass finger into his much-abused balls. Roaring, cursing her, he tried to lurch forward and upward. The hideous, clinging coat-tree refused to let go of him, and even dragging it along behind him proved to be an impossibility; one of its claw-feet had somehow hooked the newel post, clutching like a grappling-hook and holding like an anchor.

He had to get up there, had to. He didn't want her locking herself and the cocksucker with her into her little bolthole before he could get there. He had no doubt he could break the door down if he had to, he'd broken down a shitload of them in his years as a cop, some of them pretty tough old babies, but time was becoming a factor here. He didn't want to shoot her, that would be too quick and far, far too easy for the likes of his rambling Rose, but if the course he was running didn't smooth out a little, and soon, that might be the only option left to him. What a shame that would be!

"Put me in, coach!" the bull cried from the topcoat pocket. "I'm tanned, I'm fit, I'm rested, I'm ready!"

Yes, that was a goddam good idea. Norman snatched the mask out of his pocket and yanked it over his head, inhaling the smell of piss and rubber. The smells weren't bad at all, when you got them together like that; in fact, they were sort of nice. Sort of comforting.

"Viva ze bool!" he cried, and wriggled out of the topcoat. He lunged forward again, gun in hand. The damned coat-tree snapped under his weight, but not before trying to drive one of its goddam hooks through his left knee. Norman hardly felt it. He was grinning and snapping his teeth savagely together inside the mask, liking the heavy click they made, a sound like colliding billiard balls.

"You don't want to play with me, Rose." He tried for his feet and the kneecap the coat-tree had poked buckled under him. "Stop right where you are. Quit trying to run. I only want to talk to you."

She screamed back at him, words, words, words, they didn't matter. He resumed crawling, going as fast as he could and being as quiet as he could. At last he sensed movement above him. He shot his arm out, seized her *left calf, dug in with his nails. How good it felt!* Got you! *he thought, savagely triumphant.* Got you, by God! Got—

Her foot came out of the dark with the unexpected suddenness of a buckshot-loaded blackjack, striking his nose and smashing it in a new place. The pain was terrible—it felt as if a swarm of African bees had been set loose in his head. She tore away from him, but Norman was hardly aware of this; already he was toppling backward, groping for the bannister and doing nothing but skidding his fingers briefly along its underside. He went tumbling all the way back down to the coat-tree, holding onto the gun with his finger outside the trigger-guard so he wouldn't blow a hole in himself . . . and the way things were going, that seemed all too possible. He lay in a heap for a moment, then shook his head in order to clear it and started back up again.

There was no actual skip in his thoughts this time, no complete break in consciousness, but he didn't have the slightest idea what they might have shouted at him from the top of the stairs or what he might have shouted back. His retraumatized nose was in front of everything, laying down a red screen of pain.

He was aware that someone else was trying to horn in on the party, the fabled innocent bystander, and Rosie's little cocksucker friend was telling him to stay away. The nice thing about that was the way it located the cocksucker friend for him, no problem at all. Norman reached for the cocksucker friend and the cocksucker friend was there. He put his hands around the cocksucker friend's neck and started choking him again. This time he meant to finish the job, only all at once he felt Rosie's hand on the side of his face . . . on the skin of the mask. It was like being caressed after you'd been given a shot of Novocain.

Rosie. Rosie touching him. She was here. For the first time since she'd walked out with his goddam bank card in her purse she was right *here, and Norman lost all interest in loverboy. He seized her hand, stuffed it through the mouth-hole in the mask, and bit down as hard as he could. It was ecstasy. Only—*

Only then something happened. Something bad. Something horrible. *It felt as if she had ripped his lower jaw right out of its sockets. Pain leaped up the sides of his head in polished steel darts, meeting with a bang at the crown. He screamed and reeled back from her, the bitch, oh the dirty bitch, what had happened to change her from the predictable thing she had been into this monster?*

The innocent bystander spoke up then, and Norman was pretty sure he shot him. He'd shot someone, *anyway; people who screamed like that had either been shot or burned. Then, as he turned the gun toward the place where Rose and the cocksucker friend were, he heard a door slam shut. The bitch had beaten him into her room after all.*

For the time being, even that was of secondary importance. His jaw had replaced his nose as the center of pain now, just as his nose had replaced his jammed knee and his outraged balls. What had she done to him? The lower half of his face felt not just torn open but extended, somehow; his teeth seemed to be satellites floating somewhere out beyond the end of his nose.

Don't be an idiot, Normie, *his father whispered.* She's dislocated your jaw, that's all. You know what to do about that, so do it!

"Shut up, you old queer," Norman tried to say, but with his face pulled out of shape, what emerged was Ut uh, ooo ole heer! *He put down the gun, hooked up the sides of the mask with his thumbs (he hadn't pulled it all the way down when he put it on, which made this part of the job easier), and then gently pressed the heels of his hands against the points of his jaw. It was like touching ball-bearings that had jumped out of their sockets.*

Steeling himself against the pain, he slid his hands farther down, tilted them up, and shoved sharply. There was pain, all right, but mostly because only one side of his jaw went back into place at first. That left the lower part of his face askew, like a dresser drawer that's been pushed in crooked.

Squinch your face that way for long, Norman, and it'll freeze that way! *his mother spat inside his head—the old venom he remembered so well.*

Norman shoved up on the right side of his face again. This time he heard a click deep inside his head as the right half of his jaw socked back into place. The whole thing felt weirdly loose, however, as if the tendons had been savagely stretched and might take quite some time to tighten up again. He had the oddest sensation that, if he yawned, his jaw might plummet all the way to his belt-buckle.

The mask, Normie, *his father whispered.* The mask'll help, if you pull it all the way down.

"That's right," the bull said. Its voice was muffled because of the way it was rumpled up on the sides of his face, but Norman had no trouble understanding it.

He pulled it down carefully, all the way this time, getting the hem well under his jawline, and it did *help; it seemed to hold his face in place like an athletic supporter.*

"Yep," ze bool said. "Just think of me as a jawstrap."

Norman breathed deeply as he struggled to his feet, stuffing the cop's .45 into the waistband of his pants as he did. All's cool, he thought.

Nobody in here but the boys; no gals allowed. *It even seemed as if he could see more clearly through the eyeholes of the mask now, as if his vision had been in some way boosted. Undoubtedly just his imagination, but it really did feel that way, and it was a nice feeling to have. A confidence-builder.*

He pressed himself back against the wall, then sprang forward and hit the door she and her cocksucker friend had gone through. It made his jaw waggle painfully even inside the tight webbing of the mask, but he went again, and just as hard, with no hesitation. The door rattled in its frame and a long sliver of wood popped out of the upper panel.

He found himself wishing suddenly that Harley Bissington were here. The two of them could have taken the door in one hit, and he could've let Harley have a go at his wife while he, Norman, took care of her friend. Having a go at Rose had been one of the great unexpressed desires of Harley's life, something Norman did not understand but had read in the man's eyes every time he came over to the house.

He hit the door again.

On the sixth hit—or maybe it was lucky seven, he'd lost count—the lock tore free and Norman catapulted into the room. She was in here, both of them were, had to be, but for the moment he saw neither. Sweat ran into his eyes, momentarily blurring his vision. The room looked empty, but it couldn't be. They hadn't gone out the window; it was closed and locked.

He charged across the room, running through the listless light thrown by the fog-wrapped streetlamp outside, swinging his head from side to side, Ferdinand's horns goring the air. Where was she? The bitch! Where in Christ's name could she have gone?

He spotted an open door on the far side of the room, and the closed lid of a commode. He chased across to it and stood peering into the bathroom. Empty. Unless—

He drew the pistol and fired two shots through the shower curtain, opening a pair of surprised black eyes in the flower-patterned vinyl. Then he rattled it back on its rings. The tub was empty. The bullets had blown a couple of porcelain tiles off the wall; that was the extent of the damage. But maybe that was all right. He hadn't wanted to shoot her, anyway.

No, but where had she gone?

Norman charged back into the room, dropped to his knees (wincing at the pain but not really feeling it), and swept the muzzle of the gun back and forth under the bed. Nothing. He pounded his fist on the floor in frustration.

He started toward the window in spite of what his eyes had told him, because the window was all that was left . . . or so he thought until he saw light—bright light, moonlight, it looked like—spilling out of another open door, one he had trampled right past during his first charge into the room.

Moonlight? Is that what you think you're seeing? Are you nuts, Normie? I don't know if you remember, but it's foggy outside, son. *Foggy.* And even if this was the night of the fullest full moon of the century, that's a closet. A second-floor closet, in fact.

Maybe it was, but he had come to believe that his sweat-smelling, greasy-haired, crotchgrabbing, cockgobbling poor excuse for a father didn't automatically know everything about everything. Norman knew that moonlight spilling out of a second-floor closet didn't make much sense . . . but that was what he was seeing.

He walked slowly toward the door with the pistol dangling from his hand and stood in the flood of radiance. He looked through the eyeholes of the mask (except now, queerly, it seemed like just one eyehole that both his eyes were looking through) and stared into the closet.

There were hooks sticking out of the room's bare plank sides and empty hangers dangling from the metal bar running down the middle, but the closet's back wall was gone. Where it should have been was a moonlit hillside overgrown with tall grass. He could see fireflies stitching random lines of light in a dark blur of trees. The clouds sliding across the sky looked like lamps when they passed near or in front of the moon, which wasn't full but close to it. At the bottom of the hill was a sort of ruin. To Norman it looked like a busted-down old plantation-house, or perhaps an abandoned church.

I've gone completely crazy, *he thought.* Either that or she's knocked me out somehow and this is all some kind of nutty dream.

No, he didn't accept that. Wouldn't *accept that.*

"COME BACK HERE, ROSE!" he screamed into the closet . . . which was, strictly speaking, no longer a closet at all. "COME BACK, YOU BITCH!"

Nothing. Only that improbable vista . . . and a tiny breath of breeze, fragrant with grass and flowers, to prove it wasn't an eerily perfect optical illusion.

And something else: the sound of crickets.

"You stole my bank card, you bitch," Norman said in a low voice. He reached up and grabbed one of the coathooks jutting out of the board wall, looking like a straphanging commuter in a subway car. Beyond him was a strange, moonlit world, but any fear he might have felt was buried in outrage. "You stole it and I want to talk to you about it. Right . . . up . . . close."

He stepped into the closet and ducked under the bar, knocking a couple of coathangers to the wood floor. He stood where he was for just a moment longer, looking into the other world he could see stretching before him.

Then he went forward.

There was a sense of stepping down a bit, the way you sometimes had to do in old houses where the floors of the various rooms were no longer quite matched, but that was all. One step and he was no longer on boards, no longer in anyone's second-floor room; he was standing on grass and that fragrant breeze was hushing all around him. It slipped into the eyehole (yes, there was only one of them now; he didn't know how that could be, but after the step he'd just taken it didn't seem all that strange), refreshing his bruised and sweaty skin. He grasped the sides of the mask, meaning to slip it up for awhile so he could treat his whole face to a taste of that breeze, but the mask wouldn't budge. It wouldn't budge at all.

IX

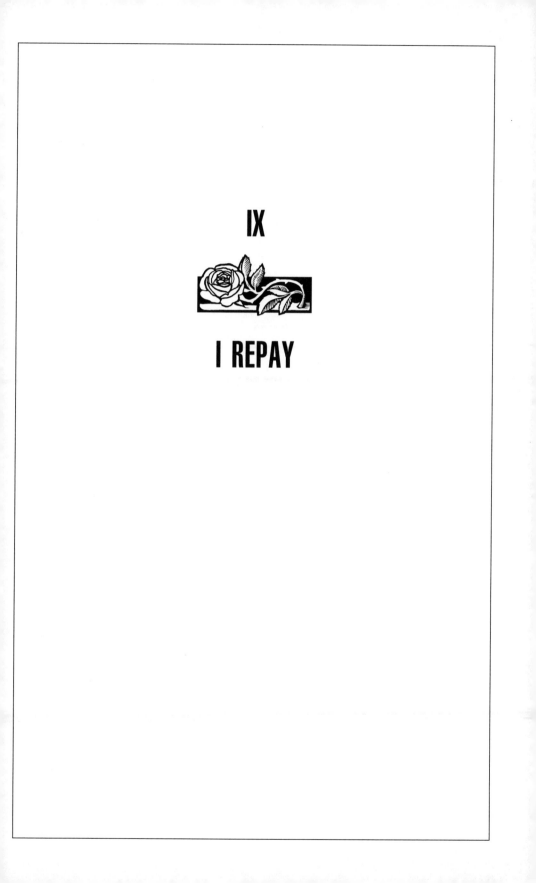

I REPAY

1

Bill looked around the moonwashed hilltop with the careful gaze of one completely unable to credit what he is seeing. One hand went to his swollen throat and began to rub it. Rosie could already see bruises unfolding there like fans.

A night breeze touched her brow like a concerned hand. It was soft and warm and fragrant with summer. There was no foggy dampness in it, no dank tang of the great lake which lay to the east of the city.

"Rosie? Is this really happening?"

Before she could think what sort of answer she might give to that question, an urgent voice—one she knew—intervened.

"Woman! *You*, woman!"

It was the lady in red, except now she was wearing a plain gown— blue, Rosie thought, although it was impossible to be sure in the moonlight. "Wendy Yarrow" was standing halfway down the hill.

"Git him down here! No time to waste! T'other be here in a minute, n you got things to do! Important things!"

Rosie still had Bill by the arm. She tried to lead him forward but he resisted, looking down the hill at "Wendy" with alarm. Behind them— muffled but still horribly close—Norman roared her name. It made Bill jump, but didn't get him moving.

"Who is that, Rosie? Who's that woman?"

"Never mind. Come on!"

She didn't just tug his arm this time; she yanked on it, feeling frantic. He moved with her, but they had only gone a dozen steps or so before he doubled over, coughing so hard his eyes bulged. Rosie took the opportunity to rake down the zipper on the jacket he'd loaned her. She stripped the garment off and dropped it in the grass. The sweater followed. The blouse under it was sleeveless, and she slipped the armlet on. She felt an immediate surge of power, and as far as she was concerned, the question of whether that feeling was real or only in her mind was moot. She grabbed one quick look back over her shoulder, half-expecting to see Norman bearing down on her, but he wasn't, at least not yet. She saw only the pony-cart, the pony itself, untethered and cropping at the moon-silvered grass, and the same easel she had seen before. The picture had changed again. The back-to figure in it was no longer a woman, for one thing—it looked like a horned demon. It *was* a demon, she supposed, but it was also a man. It was Norman, and she remembered seeing the horns jutting up from his head in a brief, bright gunflash.

"Girl, why you so slow? *Move!*"

She slipped her left arm around Bill, whose coughing fit had begun to ease, and assisted him down to where "Wendy" was impatiently waiting. By the time Rosie got him there, she was mostly carrying him.

"Who're . . . you?" Bill asked the black woman when they reached her, and then promptly fell into another coughing fit.

"Wendy" ignored the question and slipped her own arm around him, supporting the side that kept leaning away from Rosie. And when she spoke, it was Rosie she spoke to. "I put her spare *zat* around the side of the temple, so *that's* all right . . . but we got to be quick! There ain't one single moment to waste!"

"I don't know what you're talking about," Rose said, but in some part of her mind she thought that perhaps she did. "What's a *zat?*"

"Never mind your questions now," the black woman said. "We best step lively."

With Bill supported between them, they went down the slope toward the Temple of the Bull (it was really quite amazing how it all came flooding back, Rosie thought). Their shadows walked beside them. The building loomed over them—seemed to loom *toward* them, actually, like something that was alive and hungry. Rose was deeply grateful when "Wendy" turned to the right, leading them around the side.

Behind the temple, dangling from one of the massed thorn-bushes like a garment hanging from a closet hook, was the spare *zat*. Rosie looked at it with dismay but no surprise. It was a rose madder chiton, the twin of the one the woman with the sweet, insane voice had been wearing.

"Put it on," the black woman said.

"No," Rosie said faintly. "No, I'm afraid to."

"COME BACK HERE, ROSE!"

Bill jumped at the sound of that voice and turned his head, his eyes wide, his skin paler than the moonlight could account for, his lips trembling. Rosie was also afraid, but she felt her anger beneath her fear, like a large shark circling under a small boat. She had held onto the desperate hope that Norman wouldn't be able to follow them through, that the picture would snap closed behind them somehow. Now she knew that hadn't happened. He'd found it, and would be with them in this world soon enough, if he wasn't already.

"COME BACK, YOU BITCH!"

"Put it on," the woman repeated.

"Why?" Rose asked, but her hands had already gone to her blouse and pulled it over her head. "Why do I have to?"

"Because it's the way *she* wants it, and what she wants, she gets." The black woman looked at Bill, who was staring at Rosie. "Turn your back," she told him. "You c'n look at her naked in your world til your eyes fall out, for all of me, but not in mine. Turn your back, if you know what's good for you."

"Rosie?" Bill said uncertainly. "It *is* a dream, isn't it?"

"Yes," she said, and there was a coldness in her voice—a sort of spontaneous calculation—she had never heard there before. "Yes, that's right. Do as she says."

He turned so abruptly he looked like a soldier executing an about-face. Now he was looking down the narrow path which led along the back of the building.

"Take off that tit-harness, too," the black woman said, poking an impatient thumb at Rosie's bra. "Can't wear it under a *zat.*"

Rosie unhooked her bra and took it off. Then she pushed off her sneakers, still laced, and removed her jeans. She stood in her plain white underwear and looked a question at "Wendy," who nodded.

"Yep, those too."

Rosie pushed her underpants down, then carefully plucked the gown—the *zat*—from where it hung. The black woman stepped forward to help her.

"I know how to put it on, get out of my way!" Rosie snapped at her, and slipped the chiton over her head like a shirt.

Wendy looked at her with assessing eyes, making no move to step forward again even when Rosie had a brief difficulty with the *zat*'s shoulder-strap. When it was fixed, Rosie's right shoulder was bare and the armlet gleamed above her left elbow. She had become a mirror image of the woman in the picture.

"You can turn around, Bill," Rosie said.

He did. He looked her up and down carefully, his eyes lingering for an extra moment or two on the shapes of her nipples against the finely woven cloth. Rosie didn't mind. "You look like someone else," he said at last. "Someone dangerous."

"That's the way things are in dreams," she said, and once again she heard coldness and calculation in her voice. She hated that sound . . . but she liked it, too.

"Do you need me to tell you what to do?" the black woman asked.

"No, of course not."

Rosie raised her voice then, and the cry that came from her was both musical and savage, not her voice at all, the voice of the other . . . except it *was* her voice, too; it *was*.

"Norman!" she called. *"Norman, I'm down here!"*

"Jesus Christ, Rosie, no!" Bill gasped. "Are you nuts?"

He tried to grasp her shoulder and she shook his hand away impatiently, giving him a warning look. He stepped back from it, much as "Wendy Yarrow" had done.

"This is the only way, and it's the *right* way. Besides . . ." She looked at "Wendy" with a flicker of uncertainty. "I won't really have to *do* anything, will I?"

"No," the woman in the blue gown said. "Mistress gonna do it all. If you tried to get in her way—or if you even tried to help her with her business—she'd mos likely make you sorry. All you got to do is what that bastard up there thinks any woman do, anyway."

"Lead him on," Rosie murmured, and her eyes swam with silver moonlight.

"That's right," the other replied. "Lead him down the path. Down the garden path."

Rosie pulled in breath and called to him again, feeling the armlet burn against her flesh like some strange, deliriously sweet fire, liking the sound of the voice coming out of her throat, so loud, like her old Texas Rangers warcry in the maze, the one she'd used to get the baby crying again. *"Down heee-eeeere, Norman!"*

Bill, staring at her. Frightened. She didn't like seeing that look in his face, but she *wanted* to see it there. She *did*. He was a man, wasn't he? And sometimes men had to learn what it was to be afraid of a woman, didn't they? Sometimes it was a woman's only protection.

"Now go on," the black woman said. "I'll stay here with your man. We'll be safe; the other one'll go through the temple."

"How do you know that?"

"Because they always do," the black woman said simply. "Remember what he is."

"A bull."

"That's right; a bull. And you're the maid who waves the silk hat to draw him on. Just remember that if he catch you, there ain't any *'falias* to distract him off. If he catch you, he kill you. That's flat. There's nothing me or my mistress could do to keep him from it. He wants to fill up his mouth with your blood."

I know that better than you do, Rosie thought. *I've known it for years.*

"Don't go, Rosie," Bill said. "Stay here with us."

"No."

She pushed past him, feeling one of the thorns rake her thigh, and the pain was as sweet to her as her shout had been. Even the sensation of blood slipping down her skin was sweet.

"Little Rosie."

She turned back.

"You have to get ahead of him at the end. Do you know why?"

"Yes, of course I do."

"What did you mean when you said he's a bull?" Bill asked. He sounded worried, pettish . . . and yet Rosie had never loved him more than she did then, and she thought she never would. His face was so pale and seemed so defenseless.

He began to cough again. Rosie put a hand on his arm, terribly afraid he might shrink away from her, but he didn't. Not yet, anyway.

"Stay here," she said. "Stay here and be perfectly still." Then she hurried away. He caught one moonlit flip of the chiton's skirt at the far end of the temple, where the path appeared to open out, and then she was gone.

A moment later her cry rose in the night again, light and yet somehow awful:

"Norman, you look so silly in that mask . . ." A pause, and then: *"I'm not afraid of you anymore, Norman . . ."*

"Christ, he'll kill her," Bill muttered.

"Maybe," the woman in the blue dress replied. *"Somebody* is going to get killed tonight, that's for . . ." She quit, then, her eyes wide and glittering, her head cocked.

"What do you h—"

A brown hand shot out and covered his mouth. It didn't squeeze hard, but Bill sensed it could; it felt full of steel springs. A haunting belief, almost a certainty, rose in his mind as he felt her palm pressing his lips and the pads of her fingers on his cheek: this wasn't a dream. As much as he wanted to believe it was, he simply couldn't do it.

The black woman stood on tiptoe and pressed against him like a lover, still holding his mouth shut.

"Hush," she whispered in his ear. *"He comin."*

He could hear the rustle of grass and foliage now, and then heavy, grunting inhales with a whistle buried deep in each one. It was a sound he would normally have associated with men much heavier than Norman Daniels—men in the three-hundred- to three-hundred-and-fifty-pound range.

Or with a large animal.

The black woman slowly removed her hand from Bill's mouth and they stood there, listening to the creature's approach. Bill put an arm around her, and she one around him. They stood so, and Bill became queerly certain that Norman—or whatever Norman had become—wouldn't go through the building, after all. He—*it*—would come around here, and see them. It would paw the ground for a moment, its hammerhead lowered, and then it would chase them down this narrow, hopeless path, overbear them, trample them, gore them.

"Shhhhh . . ." she breathed.

"Norman, you idiot . . ."

Drifting to them like smoke, like moonlight.

"You're such a fool . . . did you really think you could catch me? Silly old bull!"

There was a burst of high, mocking laughter. The sound made Bill think of spun glass and open wells and empty rooms at midnight. He shuddered and felt gooseflesh ripple his arms.

From in front of the temple there was an interval of quiet (broken only by a puff of breeze that briefly moved the thorn-bushes like a hand combing through tangled hair), and silence from where Rosie had been calling him. Overhead, the bony disk of the moon sailed behind a cloud, fringing its edges with silver. The sky sprawled with stars, but Bill recognized none of the constellations they made. Then:

"Norrr-munnnn . . . don't you want to taaalllk to me?"

"Oh, I'll talk to you," Norman Daniels said, and Bill felt the black woman jerk against him in surprise as his own heart took a large, nasty leap from his chest into his throat. That voice had come from no more than twenty yards away. It was as if Norman had been making those clumsy movements on purpose, allowing them to track his progress, and then, when quiet suited him better, he had become *utterly* quiet. "I'll talk to you up *close*, you cunt."

The black woman's finger was on his lips, admonishing him to be quiet, but Bill didn't need the message. Their eyes locked, and he saw that the black woman was also no longer sure that Norman would go through the building.

The silence spun out, creating what felt like an eternity. Even Rosie seemed to be waiting.

Then, from a little farther away, Norman spoke again. "Boo, you old sonofabitch," he said. "What you doing here?"

Bill looked at the black woman. She shook her head slightly, indicating that she didn't understand, either. He realized a horrible thing: he needed to cough. The throbbing tickle behind his soft palate was almost overpowering. He dropped his mouth into the crook of his arm and tried to keep it back in his throat, aware of the woman's concerned eyes on him.

I can't hold it for long, he thought. *Christ, Norman, why don't you move? You were fast enough before.*

As if in reply to this thought: *"Norr-munnn! You're so fucking* SLOWWW, *Norr-munnn!"*

"Bitch," the thick voice on the other side of the temple said. "Oh you bitch."

Shoes, gritting on crumbled stone. A moment later Bill heard echoing footfalls and realized that Norman was inside the building which the black woman had called a temple. He realized something else as well: the urge to cough had passed, at least for the time being.

He leaned close to the woman in the blue dress and whispered into her ear: "What do we do now?"

Her whispered reply tickled his own ear: "Wait."

2

Discovering *that the mask seemed to have become part of his flesh scared him for a moment or two, and badly, but before fright could escalate into panic, Norman saw something a short distance away that distracted him from the subject of the mask entirely. He hurried down the slope a little way and knelt. He picked up the sweater, looked at it, flung it aside. Then he picked up the jacket. It was the one she had been wearing, all right. A motorcycle jacket. The guy had a scoot and she'd been out riding with him, probably with her crotch pretty well banged into his ass.* Jacket's too big for her, *he thought.* He loaned it to her. *The thought infuriated him, and he spat on it before flinging it aside, leaping to his feet, and looking wildly around.*

"You bitch," he murmured. "You dirty, cheating bitch."

"Norman!" It came drifting out of the darkness, stopping his breath in his throat for a second.

Close, *he thought.* Holy shit, she's close, I think she's in that building.

He stood stock-still, waiting to see if she'd yell again. After a moment, she did. "Norman, I'm down here!"

His hands went to the mask again, but this time they did not pull; they caressed. "Viva ze bool," *Norman said into it, and started down the hill toward the ruins of the building at the bottom. He thought he could see tracks going that way—broken swatches of high grass that might be places where feet had come down, anyway—but the moonlight made it difficult to tell for sure.*

Then, as if to confirm his direction, her maddening, mocking cry came again: "Down heee-eeeere, Norman!" *As if she wasn't afraid of him at all; as if she couldn't wait for him to get there, in fact. Bitch!*

"Stay where you are, Rose," *he said.* "Just stay put, that's the main thing." *He still had the cop's gun stuffed into the waistband of his jeans, but it didn't loom large in his plans. He didn't know if you could fire a gun in a hallucination or not, and he had absolutely no desire to find out. He wanted to talk to his little rambling Rose much more personally than any gun would allow.*

"Norman, you look so silly in that mask . . . I'm not afraid of you anymore, Norman . . ."

You're going to discover that's *a passing fad, you bitch,* he thought.

"Norman, you idiot!"

All right, maybe she wasn't *in the building; she might already have gone through it to the other side. It didn't matter. If she thought she could outrun him on a level playing-field, she was going to get the surprise of her life. The* last *surprise of her life.*

"You're such a fool! . . . did you really think you could catch me? Silly old bull!"

He moved to his right a little, trying to be quiet now, reminding himself that it wouldn't help to behave like, ha-ha, a bull in a china shop. He stopped near the foot of the cracked steps leading up to the temple (that was what it was, he saw that now, a temple like in one of those Greek fairy-tales that guys used to make up back then when they weren't too busy butt-punching each other) and surveyed it. The building was clearly abandoned and falling into ruin, but this place didn't feel spooky; it felt weirdly like home.

"Norrr-munnnn . . . don't you want to taaallllk to me?"

"Oh, I'll talk to you," *he said.* "I'll talk to you right up close, you cunt." *He caught sight of something in the high, tangled grass to the right of the steps: a big stone face in the weeds, staring raptly into the sky. Five paces took Norman to it, and he stared fixedly down at it for ten seconds or more, wanting to make sure he was seeing what he thought he was seeing. He was. The huge tumbled head bore the face of his father, and his empty eyes snarled with idiot moonlight.*

"Boo, you old sonofabitch," he said softly. "What you doing here?"

The stone father made no reply, but his wife did.

"Norrrr-munnnn . . . you're so fucking SLOWWW, Norrr-munnnn!"

Nice language they taught her to use, too, *the bull remarked, only now it was making its remarks from inside Norman's head.* These are great people she's got in with, no doubt about that—they've changed her whole life.

"Bitch," *he said in a thick, trembling voice.* "Oh you bitch."

He wheeled away from the stone face in the grass, resisting an urge to go back and spit on it the way he had on the jacket . . . or to unzip his jeans and take a piss on it. No time for games now. He hurried up the cracked steps toward the black entrance to the temple. Each time his foot came down, it sent agonizing pain up his leg, up his back, into his violated lower jaw. It felt like only the mask was holding his jaw in place now, and it hurt like a mad bastard. He wished he'd brought the Charlie-David cops' aspirin with him.

How could she do that, Normie? *the voice came whispering up from deep inside. It still sounded like his father's voice, but Norman couldn't remember ever hearing his father sound so unsure of himself, so worried.* How could she *dare* do that? What's *happened* to her?

He stopped with his foot on the top step, face aching, his lower jaw feeling as loose as a tire with the lug-nuts working free. I don't know and I don't care, *he told the ghost-voice.* But I'll tell you one thing, Daddy —if that's who you are—when I find her, I'm going to unhappen it in a helluva hurry. That you can take to the bank.

Are you sure you want to try that? *the voice asked, and Norman, in the act of starting forward, stopped again, listening, head cocked.*

You know what might be wiser? *it asked.* It might be wiser to just call it a draw. I know how that sounds, but I'm giving you the benefit of my thinking just the same, Normie. If I was the one with my hands on the controls, I'd turn around and go back the way I came. Because nothing's *right* here. It's all hinky as hell, in fact. I don't know what it is, but I know what it feels like—a trap. And if you walk into it you may have a lot more to worry about than a wiggly jaw or a mask that doesn't want to come off. Why don't you turn around and go back the way you came? See if you can't find your way back into her rented room and maybe wait for her there?

Because they'll come, Daddy, *Norman told the voice. He was shaken by this ghost's insistence and surety, but would not admit it.* The cops will come and they will take me down. They'll take me down before I so much as smell her perfume. And because she said fuck to me. Because she's turned into a whore. I can tell it just by the way she talks now.

Never mind how she talks, you idiot! If she's gone rotten, leave her to spoil on the ground with her friends! Maybe it isn't too late to shut this thing down before it explodes in your face.

He actually considered it . . . and then raised his eyes to the temple and read the words chiselled over the door. SHE WHO STEALS HER HUSBAND'S BANK CARD SHALL NOT BE SUFFERED TO LIVE, *they read.*

Doubt fled. He would listen to his craven, crotchgrabbing father no more. He passed through the yawning doorway and into the damp darkness beyond. Dark . . . but not too dark to see. Powdery shafts of moonlight fell steeply in through the narrow windows, illuminating a ruin that looked spookily like the church where Rose and her folks had worshipped back in Aubreyville. He walked through drifts of fallen leaves, and when a flock of whirling, squealing bats descended through the moonbeams to flutter about his face, he only flapped his arms, waving them away. "Get out, you sons of whores," he muttered.

As he emerged onto a small stone stoop through the door to the right of the altar, he saw a fluff of something hanging from a bush. He leaned over, pulled it free, held it up in front of his eyes. It was hard to be sure in this light, but he thought it was red or pink. Had she been wearing clothes of such a color? He thought she'd had jeans on, but everything was mixed up in his mind. Even if it had *been jeans, she'd taken off the jacket the cocksucker had loaned her, and maybe underneath—*

There was a soft sound behind him, like a pennant rippling in a breeze. Norman turned and a brown bat flew into his face, snapping at him with its whiskery mouth as its wings battered against his cheeks.

His hand had dropped to the butt of the gun. Now he let go of it and seized the bat, crumpling the bones in its wings back against its body like a lunatic concertina player. He twisted it against itself and tore it in two with such force that its rudimentary guts fell out on his shoes. "Shoulda stayed out of my face, asshole," Norman told it, and then flung the pieces back into the temple's shadows.

"You're great at killing bats, Norman."

Jesus Christ, that was close—*that was right behind him! He spun around so fast this time that he almost lost his balance and tumbled off the stone stoop.*

The ground behind the temple sloped toward a stream, and standing there halfway down, in what looked like the world's deadest garden, was his sweet little rambling Rose—just standing there in the moonlight, look-

ing up at him. Three things struck him in rapid succession. The first was that she was no longer wearing jeans, if she ever had been; she was wearing a minidress that looked like it belonged at a frathouse toga-party. The second was that she had changed her hair. It was blonde and pulled back from her face.

The third thing was that she was beautiful.

"Bats and women," she said coldly. "That's about it for you, isn't it? I almost feel sorry for you, Norman. You're a miserable excuse for a man. You're not a man, not really. And that stupid mask you're wearing will never make you into one."

"I'LL KILL YOU, YOU BITCH!" Norman jumped from the stoop and sprinted down the hill toward where she stood, his horned shadow trailing along beside him over the dead grass in the bony moonlight.

3

For a moment she stood where she was, frozen in place, every muscle in her body seemingly locked down as he rushed forward, screaming inside the hideous mask he was wearing. What got her moving was a sudden gruesome image—sent by Practical-Sensible, she had an idea—of the tennis racket he'd used on her, its handle wet with blood.

She turned then, the skirt of the *zat* flaring, and ran for the stream.

The stones, Rosie . . . if you fall in that water . . .

But she wasn't going to. She was really Rosie, she was Rosie Real, and she wasn't going to. Not, that was, unless she let herself think about what would happen if she did. The smell of the water came to her powerfully enough to make her eyes sting . . . and to make her mouth cramp with desire. Rosie reached up with her left hand, pinched her nostrils shut between the knuckles of her second and third fingers, and jumped onto the second stone. From there she leaped to the fourth, and from there to the other bank. Easy. Nothing to it. At least until her feet went out from under her and she went sprawling full-length and started to slide back down on the slippery grass toward the black water.

4

*N*orman saw her fall and laughed. She was going to get wet, it looked like.

Don't worry, Rose, *he thought.* I'll fish you out, and I'll pat you dry. Yes indeed.

Then she was up again, clawing at the bank and casting one terrified glance back over her shoulder . . . except it wasn't him she appeared to be afraid of; she was looking at the water. As she got up, he caught a flash of her butt, as bare as the day she'd been born, and the most amazing thing happened: he started getting hard in his pants.

"Coming, Rose," *he panted. Yes, and maybe soon he'd be coming in another way, as well. Coming as she was going, you might say.*

He hurried down to the stream, trampling the delicate prints of Rose's feet beneath Hump Peterson's square-toed boots, reaching the edge of the running water just as Rosie gained the top of the other bank. She stood there for a moment, looking back, and this time it was clearly him she was looking at. Then she did something that brought him to a dead halt, momentarily too amazed to move.

She gave him the finger.

She did it right, too, kissing the tip of it at him before running for the grove of dead trees ahead.

Did you see that, Norm old buddy? *ze bool asked from its place inside his head.* The bitch just flipped you off. Did you see it?

"Yes," *he breathed.* "I saw it. I'll take care of it, too. I'll take care of everything."

But he had no intention of charging wildly across the stream, and maybe falling in. There was something about the water Rose hadn't liked, and he'd do well to be very careful; to watch his step in the most literal sense. The damned brook might be full of those little South American fish with the big teeth, the ones that could strip a whole cow down to its skeleton on a good day. He didn't know if you could be killed by things in a delusion, but this felt less like make-believe all the time.

She flashed her ass at me, *he thought.* Her *bare* ass. Maybe I've got something to flash at her . . . don't they say turnabout's fair play?

Norman wrinkled his lips back from his teeth, making a grisly expression that wasn't a grin, and put one of Hump's boots on the first white stone. The moon sailed behind a cloud as he did. When it came out again, it caught Norman halfway across the little stream. He looked down at the water, at first just curious, then fascinated and horrified. The moonlight penetrated the water no more than it would have penetrated a flowing stream of mud, but that wasn't what took the breath out of him and brought him to a stop. The moon reflected up at him in that black water wasn't the moon at all. It was a bleached and grinning human skull.

Have a drink of *this* shit, Normie, *the skull on the surface of the water whispered.* Hell, take a goddamned *bath,* if you want. Just forget all this foolishness. Drink and you will. Drink and it will never trouble you again; nothing will.

It sounded so plausible, so right. He looked up, perhaps to see if the moon in the sky looked as much like a skull as the one in the water, and instead saw Rose. She was standing at the place where the path entered a grove of dead trees, beside a statue of a kid with his arms up and his crank hanging out in front of him.

"You're not getting away that easy," he breathed. "I don't—"

The stone boy moved then. Its arms came down and seized Rosie's right wrist. Rosie screamed and beat fruitlessly against its two-handed grip. The stone boy was grinning, and as Norman watched, it stuck out its marble tongue and waggled it at Rosie suggestively.

"Attaboy," Norman whispered. "Hold her—just hold her."

He jumped up on the other bank and ran for his wayward wife, big hands outstretched.

5

"**W**ant to do the dog with me?" the stone boy enquired of her in a grating, uninflected voice. The hands clamping her wrist were all angles and squeezing, bitter weight. She looked over her shoulder and saw Norman leap onto the bank, the horns of the mask he had on digging at the night air. He stumbled on the slick grass but did not fall. For the first time since realizing it was Norman in the police car, she felt close to panic. He was going to get her, and then what? He'd bite her to pieces and she would die screaming, with the smell of his English Leather in her nostrils. He would—

"Want to do the *dog?*" the stone boy spat. "Want to get *down,* Rosie, do some low-ridin, put all *four* on the fl—"

"*No!*" she shrieked, her fury spilling out again, spreading across her thoughts like a red curtain. "*No, leave me alone, quit that high-school bullshit and leave me ALONE!*"

She swung with her left hand, not thinking of how much it was going to hurt to drive her fist into the face of a marble statue . . . and it did not, in fact, hurt at all. It was like hitting something spongy and rotten with a battering ram. She caught just a momentary glimpse of a new expression—astonishment replacing lust—and then the thing's smirking face shattered into a hundred dough-colored fragments. The heavy, pinching pressure of its hands left her wrist, but now there was Norman, Norman almost on top of her, head lowered, breath slobbering in and out through the mask, hands reaching.

Rosie turned, feeling one of his outstretched fingers skate over the *zat*'s single shoulder-strap, and bolted.

Now it would be a footrace.

6

She ran as she had when she was a girl, before her practical, sensible mother had begun the weighty task of teaching Rose Diana McClendon what was ladylike and what was not (running, especially once you were at an age where you had breasts bouncing in front of you when you did it, was definitely not). She went all out, in other words, with her head down and her fisted hands pumping at her sides. She was aware of Norman at her heels to begin with, less aware of his starting to slip back, at first by mere feet, then by yards. She could hear him grunting and blowing even when he had fallen behind a little, and he sounded exactly as Erinyes had sounded in the maze. She was aware of her own lighter breathing, and of the plait bouncing up and down and side to side on her back. Mostly, though, what she was aware of was a mad exhilaration, of blood filling her head until she felt it must burst, but bursting would be ecstasy. She looked up once and saw the moon racing with her, speeding through the starshot sky behind the branches of dead trees that stood here like the hands of giants who had been buried alive and had died struggling to disinter themselves. Once, when Norman growled at her to stop running and quit being such a cunt, she actually laughed. *He thinks I'm playing hard to get,* she thought.

Then she came around a bend in the path and saw the lightning-struck tree blocking her course. There was no time to swerve, and if she tried to put on the brakes she would succeed only in being impaled on one or more of the tree's dead, jutting branches. Even if she avoided that, there was Norman. She had gotten ahead of him a little, but if she stopped, even for a moment, he would be on her like a dog on a rabbit.

All this went through her mind in an instant. Then, screaming—perhaps in terror, perhaps in defiance, probably in both—she leaped forward with her hands out in front of her like Supergirl, going over the tree and landing on her left shoulder. She did a somersault, sprang dizzily up, and saw Norman staring at her over the fallen trunk. His hands were clutched on the fire-blackened stubs of two branches, and he was panting harshly. The breeze puffed and she could smell something besides sweat and English Leather coming from him.

"You started smoking again, didn't you?" she said.

The eyes below the flower-decked rubber horns regarded her with complete unreason. The lower half of the mask was twitching spastically, as if the man buried inside it were trying to smile. "Rose," the bull said. "Stop this."

"I'm not *Rose*," she said, then gave an exasperated little laugh, as if he were really the stupidest creature alive—*el toro dumbo.* "I'm *Rosie.* Rosie Real. But *you're* not real anymore, Norman . . . are you? Not even to yourself. But it doesn't matter now, not to me, because I'm divorced of you."

She turned then, and fled.

7

You're not real anymore, he thought as he went around the top of the tree, where there was plenty of room for easy passage. She had left the far side of the deadfall running full-out, but when he regained the path again, Norman only jogged. It was really all he needed to do. That interior voice, the one that had never let him down, told him that the path ended up ahead, not far from here. This should have delighted him, but he kept hearing what she had said before turning her pretty little tail into his gaze this last time.

I'm Rosie Real, but *you're* not real anymore, not even to yourself . . . I'm divorced of you.

Well, *he thought,* that last part's close, at least. There *is* going to be a divorce, but it's going to be on my terms, Rose.

He jogged on a little while, then stopped, wiping an arm across his forehead, not surprised when it came away sweaty, not even thinking of it, really, although he was still wearing the mask.

"Better come back, Rose!" he called. "Last chance!"

"Come get me," she called in return, and her voice sounded subtly
different now, although just how it was different he could not have said.
"Come get me, Norman, it's not far now."

*No, it wouldn't be. He'd chased her damned near halfway across the
country, and then he'd chased her into another world, or a dream, or some
damned thing, but now she was all out of running room.*

"Nowhere left to go, sweetcakes," Norman said, and began to walk
toward the sound of her voice, his hands rolling into fists as he went.

8

She ran into the circular clearing and saw herself, kneeling by the one
live tree, back turned, head bowed, as if in prayer or deep meditation.

Not *me*, Rosie thought nervously. *That's not really me.*

But it could have been. With her back turned, the woman kneeling
at the base of the "pomegranate tree" could have been her twin. She
was the same height, the same build, possessed of the same long legs
and wide hips. She was wearing the same rose madder chiton—what the
black woman had called a *zat*—and her hair fell down the center of her
back to her waist in a blonde plait identical to Rosie's. The only difference was that both of this woman's arms were bare, because Rosie was
wearing her armlet. That probably wasn't a difference Norman would
notice, though. He'd never seen Rosie wearing such an item, and she
doubted that he would have picked up on it in any case, not the way
he was now. Then she saw something he *might* notice—the dark patches
on the back of Rose Madder's neck and on her upper arms. They
swarmed like hungry shadows.

Rosie came to a halt, looking toward the woman who knelt facing the
tree in the moonlight.

"I've come," she said uncertainly.

"Yes, Rosie," the other said in her sweet, greedy voice. "You've come,
but not yet quite far enough. I want you there." She pointed to the
broad white steps leading downward beneath the word MAZE. "Not
far—a dozen steps should do, if you lie flat on them. Just far
enough so that you won't have to see. You won't want to see this . . .
although you can watch if you decide you *do* want to."

She laughed. The sound was full of genuine amusement, and that,
Rosie thought, was what made it so authentically awful.

"In any case," she resumed, "it may be well that you hear what passes between us. Yes, I think that may be very well."

"He may not think you're me, even in the moonlight."

Again Rose Madder laughed. The sound of it made the hair on the nape of Rosie's neck stir. "Why would he not, little Rosie?"

"You have . . . well . . . blemishes. Even in this light I can see them."

"Yes, *you* can," Rose Madder said, still laughing. "*You* can, but *he* won't. Have you forgotten that Erinyes is blind?"

Rosie thought to say, *You're confused, ma'am, this is my husband we're talking about, not the bull in the maze.* Then she remembered the mask Norman was wearing, and said nothing.

"Go quickly," Rose Madder said. "I hear him coming. Down the steps, little Rosie . . . and pass not too close by me." She paused, then added in her terrible, thoughtful voice: "It's not safe."

9

*N*orman *jogged along the path, listening. There was a moment or two when he thought he heard Rose talking, but that could have been his imagination. It didn't matter in any case. If there was someone with her, he would take that person down, too. If he was lucky, it might be Dirty Gertie—maybe the overgrown diesel-dyke had found her way into this dream, too, and Norman could have the pleasure of putting a .45 slug into her fat left tit.*

The thought of shooting Gertie had gotten him almost running again. He was so close now he thought he could actually smell her—ghostly entwined aromas of Dove soap and Silk shampoo. He came around one final curve.

I'm coming, Rose, he thought. Nowhere left to run, nowhere left to hide. I've come to take you home, dear.

10

*I*t was chilly on the steps leading down to the maze, and Rosie noticed a smell that she had missed on her previous trip—a dank, decayed smell. Mingled in it were odors of feces and rotted meat and wild animal. That disquieting thought

(can bulls climb stairs?)

came to her again, but there was no real fear in it this time. Erinyes was no longer in the maze, unless the wider world—the world of the painting—was also a maze.

Oh yes, that strange voice, the one which was not quite the voice of Practical-Sensible, said calmly. *This world, all worlds. And many bulls in each one. These myths hum with truth, Rosie. That's their power. That's why they survive.*

She sprawled flat on the steps, breathing hard, heart pounding. She was terrified, but she also felt a certain bitter eagerness in herself, and knew it for what it was: just another mask for her rage.

The hands in front of her face were closed into fists.

Do it, she thought. *Do it, kill the bastard, set me free. I want to hear him die.*

Rosie, you don't mean it! That *was* Practical-Sensible, sounding both horrified and sickened. *Say you don't mean it!*

Except she couldn't, because part of her did.

Most of her did.

11

The path he was on emptied into a circular clearing, and here she was. Finally, here she was. His rambling Rose. Kneeling with her back to him, wearing that short red dress (he was almost sure it was red), wearing her whore-dyed hair down her back in a kind of pigtail. He stood where he was at the edge of the clearing, looking at her. It was Rose, all right, no question about that, yet she had nevertheless changed. Her ass was smaller, for one thing, but that wasn't the main thing. Her attitude had changed. And what did that mean? That it was time for a little attitude-adjustment, of course.*

"Why'd you go and dye your goddam hair?" he asked her. *"You look like a fucking slut!"*

"No, you don't understand," Rose said calmly, without turning. *"It was dyed before. It's always been blonde underneath, Norman. I dyed it to fool you."*

He took two big steps into the clearing, his rage rising as it always did when she disagreed with him or contradicted him, when anyone disagreed with him or contradicted him. And the things she had said tonight . . . the things she had said to him . . .

"The fuck you did!" he exclaimed.

"*The fuck I* didn't," *she replied, and then compounded this astoundingly disrespectful statement with a contemptuous little laugh.*

But she did not turn around.

Norman took another two steps toward her, then stopped again. His hands hung in fists at his sides. He scanned the clearing, remembering her murmuring voice as he approached. It was Gert he was looking for, or maybe the little cocksucker boyfriend, ready to shoot him with a popgun of his own, or just chunk a rock at him. He saw no one, which probably meant she'd been talking to herself, something she did at home all the time. Unless someone was crouching behind the tree in the center of the clearing, that was. It appeared to be the only living thing in this still-life, its leaves long and green and narrow, gleaming like the leaves of a freshly oiled avocado plant. Its boughs were weighted down with some weird fruit Norman wouldn't touch even in a peanut-butter-and-jelly sandwich. Lying beyond her folded legs was a wealth of windfalls, and the smell which simmered up from them made Norman think of the water in the stream. Fruit that smelled like that would either kill you or gripe you so bad you'd wish you were dead.

Standing to the left of the tree was something which confirmed his belief that this was a dream. It looked like a goddam New York City subway entrance, one that had been carved in marble. Never mind that, though; never mind the tree and its pissy-smelling fruit, either. Rose was the important thing here, Rose and that little laugh of hers. He imagined it was her crack-snacking friends who had taught her to laugh like that, but it didn't matter. He was here to teach her something that did: *that laughing like that was a very good way to get hurt. He was going to do that in this dream even if he couldn't in reality; he was going to do it even if he was lying on the floor of her room pumped full of police bullets and experiencing a death-delirium.*

"Get up." *He took another step toward her and pulled the gun from the waistband of his jeans.* "We've got some things to talk about."

"Yes, you're certainly right about that," *she said, but she didn't turn and she didn't rise. She only knelt there with moonlight and shadows lying across her back in zebra-stripes.*

"Mind *me, goddam you!*" *He took another step toward her. The nails of the hand not holding the gun were now digging into his palms like white-hot metal shavings. And still she did not turn. Still she did not get up.*

"Erinyes *from the maze!" she said in her soft, melodious voice. "*Ecce taurus! *Behold the bull!" But still she did not rise, still she did not turn to behold him.*

"I'm no bull, you cunt!" he shouted, and tore at the mask with the ends of his fingers. It wouldn't budge. It no longer seemed stuck to his face or melted to his face; it seemed to be *his face.*

How can that be? he asked himself in bewilderment. How can that possibly be? It's just some kid's gimcrack amusement-park prize!

He had no answer to the question, but the mask wouldn't come off no matter how hard he yanked at it, and he knew with sickening surety that if he raked his nails into it, he would feel pain. He would bleed. And yes, there was just the one eyehole, and that one seemed to have moved right into the center of his face. His vision through this eyehole had darkened; the formerly bright moonlight had become cloudy.

"Take it off me!" he bawled at her. "Take it off me, you bitch! You can, can't you? I know you can! Don't you fuck with me anymore, either! Don't you DARE fuck with me!"

He stumbled the rest of the way to where she knelt and clutched her shoulder. The toga's single strap shifted, and what he saw beneath horrified him into a small, strangled gasp. The skin was as black and rotten as the rinds of the fruits decaying into the earth around the base of the tree— the ones so far gone they were now on the verge of liquefying.

"The bull has come from the maze," Rose said, and floated to her feet with a limber grace he had never seen or suspected in her. "And so now Erinyes may die. So it has been written; so shall it be."

"The only one doing any dying here—" he began, and that was as far as he got. She turned, and when the bony light of the moon disclosed her, Norman shrieked. He fired the .45 twice into the ground between his feet without realizing it, then dropped it. He clapped his hands to his head and screamed, backing away, moving jerkily on legs he could now barely command. She answered his cry with one of her own.

Rot swarmed across the upper swell of her bosom; her neck was as purple-black as that of a strangulation victim. The skin had cracked open in places and was oozing thick tears of yellow pus. Yet these signs of some far-advanced and obviously terminal disease weren't what brought the screams raking out of his throat and bolting from his mouth in howling spates; they were not what broke through the eggshell surface of his insanity to let in a more terrible reality, like the unforgiving light of an alien sun.

Her face did that.

It was the face of a bat in which had been set the bright mad eyes of a rabid fox; it was the face of a supernally beautiful goddess seen in an illustration hidden within some old and dusty book like a rare flower in a weedy vacant lot; it was the face of his Rose, whose looks had always

*been lifted just slightly beyond plainness by the timid hope in her eyes
and the slight, wistful curve of her mouth at rest. Like lilies on a dangerous
pond, these differing aspects floated on the face which turned toward him,
and then they blew away and Norman saw what lay beneath. It was a
spider's face, twisted with hunger and crazy intelligence. The mouth that
opened gave upon a repellent blackness afloat with silk tendrils to which
a hundred bugs and beetles stuck fast, some dead and some dying. Its eyes
were great bleeding eggs of rose madder red that pulsed in their sockets
like living mud.*

"Come closer yet, Norman," *the spider in the moonlight whispered to
him, and before his mind broke entirely, Norman saw that its bug-filled,
silk-stuffed mouth was trying to grin.*

*More arms began to cram their way out through the toga's armholes,
and from beneath its short hem, as well, only they were* not *arms,* not
*arms at all, and he screamed, he screamed, he screamed; it was oblivion
he was screaming for, oblivion and an end to knowing and seeing, but
oblivion would not come.*

"Come closer," *it crooned, the not-arms reaching, the maw of a mouth
yawning,* "I want to talk to you." *There were claws at the ends of the
black not-arms, filthy with bristles. The claws settled on his wrists, his
legs, the swollen appendage which still throbbed in his crotch. One wriggled amorously into his mouth; the bristles scraped against his teeth and
the insides of his cheeks. It grasped his tongue, tore it out, flapped it
triumphantly before his one staring, glaring eye.* "I want to talk to you,
and I want to talk to you right . . . up . . . CLOSE!"

*He made one last mad effort to pull free and was instead drawn into
Rose Madder's hungry embrace.*

*Where Norman finally learned what it was like to be the bitten instead
of the biter.*

12

Rosie lay on the stairs with her eyes closed and her fists clenched above
her head, listening to him scream. She tried not even to imagine what
was going on out there, and she tried to remember that it was *Norman*
who was screaming, Norman of the terrible pencil, Norman of the tennis
racket, Norman of the teeth.

Yet these things were overwhelmed by the horror of his screams, his
agonized shrieks as Rose Madder . . .

. . . as she did whatever it was she was doing.

After awhile—a long, *long* while—the screaming stopped.

Rosie lay where she was, fists unrolling slowly but with her eyes still tightly shut, gasping in short, harsh snatches of air. She might have lain there for hours, had not the sweet, mad voice of the woman summoned her:

"Come forth, little Rosie! Come forth and be of good cheer! The bull is no more!"

Slowly, on legs that felt numb and wooden, Rosie got first to her knees and then to her feet. She walked up the steps and stood on the ground. She didn't want to look, but her eyes seemed to have a life of their own; they crossed the clearing while her breath stopped in her throat.

She let it out in a long, quiet sigh of relief. Rose Madder was still kneeling, still back-to. Lying before her was a shadowy bundle of what at first looked like rags. Then a white starfish shape tumbled out of the shadow and into the moonlight. It was a hand, and Rosie saw the rest of him then, like a woman who suddenly sees sense and coherence in a psychiatrist's inkblot. It was Norman. He had been mutilated, and his eyes bulged from their sockets in a terminal expression of terror, but it was Norman, all right.

Rose Madder reached up as Rosie watched and plucked a low-hanging fruit from the tree. She squeezed it in her hand—a very human hand, and quite lovely save for the black and spiritous spots floating just beneath her skin—so that first the juice ran out of her fist in a rose madder stream and then the fruit itself broke open in a wet, dark-red furrow. She plucked a dozen or so seeds out of the rich pulp and began to sow them in Norman Daniels's torn flesh. The last one she poked into his one staring eye. There was a wet popping sound as she drove it home —the sound of someone stepping on a plump grape.

"What are you *doing?*" Rosie asked in spite of herself. She only managed to keep from adding, *Don't turn around, you can tell me without turning around!*

"Seeding him." Then she did something that made Rosie feel as if she had stepped into a "Richard Racine" novel: leaned forward and kissed the corpse's mouth. At last she drew back, took him in her arms, rose, and turned toward the white marble stairway leading into the earth.

Rosie looked away, her heart thumping in her throat.

"Sweet dreams, you son-of-a-bastard," Rose Madder said, and pitched Norman's body down into the dark beneath the single chiselled word reading MAZE.

Where, perchance, the seeds she had planted would take root and grow.

13

"Go back the way you came," Rose Madder said. She was standing by the stairs; Rosie stood on the far side of the clearing, at the head of the path, with her back turned. She didn't want even to risk looking at Rose Madder now, and she had discovered that she could not entirely trust her own eyes to do as she told them. "Go back, find Dorcas and your man. She has something for you, and I would have more talk with you . . . but only a little. Then our time is finished. That will be a relief to you, I think."

"He's gone, isn't he?" Rosie asked, looking steadfastly along the moonlit path. "Really gone."

"I suppose you'll see him in your dreams," Rose Madder said dismissively, "but what of that? The simple truth of things is that bad dreams are far better than bad wakings."

"Yes. That's so simple most people overlook it, I think."

"Go now. I'll come to you. And Rosie?"

"What?"

"Remember the tree."

"The tree? I don't—"

"I know you don't. But you will. Remember the tree. Now go."

Rosie went. And didn't look back.

X

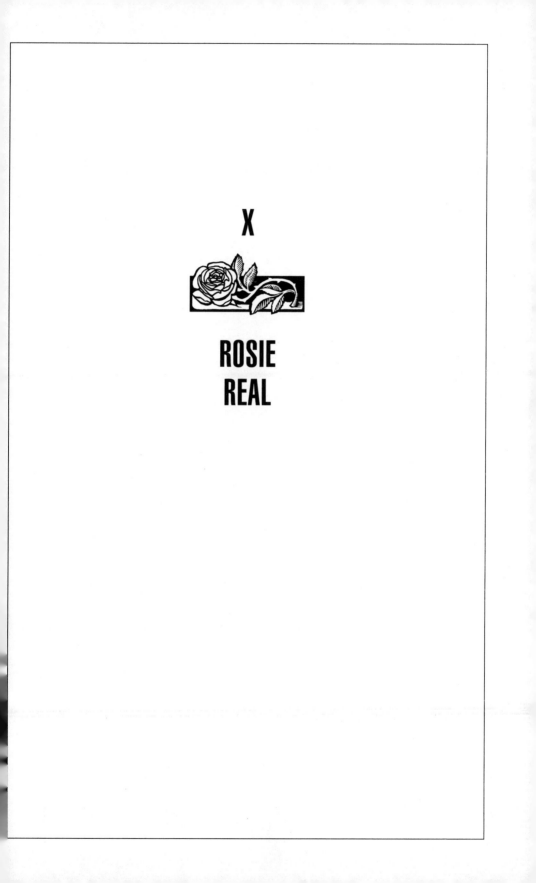

ROSIE
REAL

1

Bill and the black woman—Dorcas, her name was Dorcas, not Wendy after all—were no longer on the narrow path behind the temple, and Rosie's clothes were gone, too. This raised no concern in her mind. She merely trudged around the building, looked up the hill, saw them standing beside the pony-trap, and started toward them.

Bill came to meet her, his pale, distracted face full of concern.

"Rosie? All right?"

"Fine," she said, and put her face against his chest. As his arms went around her, she wondered how much of the human race understood about hugging—how good it was, and how a person could want to do it for hours on end. She supposed some did understand, but doubted that they were in the majority. To fully understand about hugging, maybe you had to have missed a lot of it.

They walked up to where Dorcas stood, stroking the pony's white-streaked nose. The pony raised its head and looked at Rosie sleepily.

"Where's . . ." Rosie began, then stopped. *Caroline,* she'd almost said, *Where's Caroline?* "Where's the baby?" Then, boldly: "*Our* baby?"

Dorcas smiled. "Safe. In a safe place, don't you fret that, Miss Rosie. Your clothes're 'round to the back of the cart. Go on and change, if you like. You be glad to get out of that thing you wearin now, I bet."

"That's a bet you'd win," Rosie said, and went around. She felt an indescribable sense of relief when the *zat* was off her skin. As she was zipping her jeans, she remembered something Rose Madder had told her. "Your mistress says you have something for me."

"*Oh!*" Dorcas sounded startled. "Oh, my! If I went n forgot that, she'd rip the skin right off me!"

Rosie picked up her blouse, and when she pulled it down over her head, Dorcas was holding something out to her. Rosie took it and held it up curiously, tilting it this way and that. It was a cunningly made little ceramic bottle, not much bigger than an eyedropper. Its mouth had been sealed with a tiny sliver of cork.

Dorcas looked around, saw Bill standing some distance away, looking dreamily down the hill at the ruins of the temple, and seemed satisfied. When she turned back to Rosie, she spoke in a voice which was low but emphatic. "One drop. For him. After."

Rosie nodded as if she knew exactly what Dorcas was talking about. It was simpler that way. There were questions she could ask, perhaps *should* ask, but her mind felt too tired to frame them.

"I could have give you less, only he may need another drop later on. But have a care, girl. This is dangerous stuff!"

As if anything in this world is safe, Rosie thought.

"Tuck it away, now," Dorcas said, watching as Rosie slipped the tiny bottle into the watch-pocket of her jeans. "And mind you keep quiet about it to *him.*" She jerked her head in Bill's direction, then looked back at Rosie, her dark face set and grim. Her eyes looked momentarily pupilless in the darkness, like the eyes of a Greek statue. "You know why, too, don't you?"

"Yes," Rosie said. "This is woman's business."

Dorcas nodded. "That's right, that's just what it is."

"Woman's business," Rosie repeated, and in her mind she heard Rose Madder say *Remember the tree.*

She closed her eyes.

2

The three of them sat at the top of the hill for some unknown length of time, Bill and Rosie together with their arms around each other's waist, Dorcas a little off to one side, near to where the pony still grazed sleepily. The pony looked up at the black woman every now and again, as if curious about why so many people were still up at this unaccustomed hour, but Dorcas took no notice, only sat with her arms clasped around her knees, looking wistfully up at the latening moon. To Rosie she looked like a woman mentally counting the choices of a lifetime and discovering that the wrong ones outnumbered the right ones . . . and not by only a few, either. Bill opened his mouth to speak on several occasions, and Rosie looked at him encouragingly, but each time he closed it again without saying a word.

Just as the moon snagged in the trees to the left of the ruined temple, the pony raised its head again, and this time it gave voice to a low, pleased whinny. Rosie looked down the hill and saw Rose Madder coming. Strong, shapely thighs flashed in the pallid light of the fading moon. Her plaited hair swung from side to side like the pendulum in a grandfather clock.

Dorcas gave a little grunt of satisfaction and got to her feet. Rosie herself felt a complex mixture of apprehension and anticipation. She put one hand on Bill's forearm and gazed at him earnestly. "Don't look at her," she said.

"No," Dorcas agreed, "and don't ask no questions, Billy, even if she invites you to."

He looked uncertainly from Dorcas to Rosie, then back to Dorcas again. "Why not? Who is she, anyway? The Queen of the May?"

"She's queen of whatever she wants to be queen of," Dorcas said, "and you better remember it. Don't look at her, and don't do anything to invite her temper. I can't say more'n that; there's no time. Put your hands in your lap, little man, and look at them. Don't you take your eyes off them."

"But—"

"If you look at her, you'll go mad," Rosie said simply. She looked at Dorcas, who nodded.

"It *is* a dream, isn't it?" Bill asked. "I mean . . . I'm not dead, am I? Because if this is the afterlife, I think I'd just as soon skip it." He looked beyond the approaching woman and shivered. "Too noisy. Too much screaming."

"It's a dream," Rosie agreed. Rose Madder was very close now, a slim straight figure walking through jackstraws of light and shadow. The latter turned her dangerous face into the mask of a cat, or perhaps a fox. "It's a dream where you have to do exactly as we say."

"Rosie and Dorcas Says instead of Simon Says."

"Yep. And Dorcas Says put your hands in your lap and look at them until one of us tells you it's all right to stop."

"May I?" he asked, giving her a sly up-from-under-the-lids glance that she thought was really a look of dazed perplexity.

"Yes," Rosie said desperately. "Yes-you-may, just for God's sake *keep your eyes off her!*"

He folded his fingers together and dropped his eyes obediently.

Now Rosie could hear the whicker of approaching footsteps, the silky sound of grass slipping across skin. She dropped her own eyes. A moment later she saw a pair of bare moon-silvery legs come to a stop before her. There was a long silence, broken only by the calling of some insomniac bird in the far distance. Rosie shifted her eyes to the right and saw

Bill sitting perfectly still beside her, looking at his folded hands as assiduously as a Zen student who has been placed next to the master at morning devotions.

At last, shyly, without looking up, she said: "Dorcas gave me what you wanted me to have. It's in my pocket."

"Good," that sweet, slightly husky voice answered. "That's good, Rosie Real." A mottled hand floated into her field of vision, and something dropped into Rosie's lap. It flashed a single glint of gold in the pale late light. "For you," Rose Madder said. "A souvenir, if you like. Do with it as you will."

Rosie plucked it out of her lap and looked at it wonderingly. The words on it—*Service, Loyalty, Community*—made a triangle around the ringstone, which was a circle of obsidian. This was now marked by one bright spot of scarlet. It turned the stone into a baleful watching eye.

The silence spun out, and there was an expectant quality to it. *Does she want to be thanked?* Rosie wondered. She wouldn't do that . . . but she would tell the truth of her feelings. "I'm glad he's dead," she said, softly and unemphatically. "It's a relief."

"Of course you're glad and of course it is. You shall go now, back to your Rosie Real world, with this beast. He's a good one, I judge." A hint of something—Rosie would not let herself believe it could be lust—crept into the voice of the other. "Good hocks. Good flanks." A pause. "Fine loins." Another pause, and then one of her mottled hands came down and caressed Bill's tumbled, sweaty hair. He drew in a breath at her touch, but did not look up. "A good beast. Protect him and he'll protect you."

Rosie looked up then. She was terrified of what she might see, but nevertheless unable to stop herself. "Don't you call him a beast again," she said in a voice that shook with fury. "And get your diseased hand off him."

She saw Dorcas wince in horror, but saw it only in the corner of her eye. The bulk of her attention was focused on Rose Madder. What had she expected from that face? Now that she was looking at it in the waning moonlight, she couldn't exactly say. Medusa, perhaps. A Gorgon. The woman before her was not that. Once (and not so long ago, either, Rosie thought) her face had been one of extraordinary beauty, perhaps a face to rival Helen of Troy's. Now her features were haggard and beginning to blur. One of those dark patches had overspread her left cheek and brushed across her brow like the underwing of a starling. The hot eye glittering out of that shadow seemed both furious and melancholy. It wasn't the face Norman had seen, that much she knew, but she could see that face lurking beneath—in a way it was as if she had put this one on for Rosie's benefit, like makeup—and it made her feel cold and ill. Underneath the beauty was madness . . . but not *just* madness.

Rosie thought: *It's a kind of rabies—she's being eaten up with it, all her shapes and magics and glamours trembling at the outer edge of her control now, soon it's all going to crumble, and if I look away from her now, she's apt to fall on me and do whatever she did to Norman. She might regret it later, but that wouldn't help me, would it?*

Rose Madder reached down again, and this time it was Rosie's head she touched—first her brow, then her hair, which had had a long day and was now coming loose from its plait.

"You're brave, Rosie. You've fought well for your . . . your friend. You're courageous, and you have a good heart. But may I give you one piece of advice before I send you back?"

She smiled, perhaps in an effort to be engaging, but Rosie's heart stopped momentarily before skittering madly onward. When Rose Madder's lips drew back, disclosing a hole in her face that was nothing at all like a mouth, she no longer looked even remotely human. Her mouth was the maw of a spider, something made for eating insects which weren't even dead, but only stung into insensibility.

"Of course." Rosie's lips felt numb and distant.

The mottled hand stroked smoothly along her temple. The spider's mouth grinned. The eyes glittered.

"Wash the dye out of your hair," Rose Madder whispered. "You weren't meant to be a blonde."

Their eyes met and held. Rosie discovered she couldn't drop hers; they were locked on the other woman's face. At one corner of her vision she saw Bill continuing to look grimly down at his hands. His cheeks and brow glimmered with sweat.

It was Rose Madder who looked away. "Dorcas."

"Ma'am?"

"The baby—?"

"Be ready when you are."

"Good," said Rose Madder. "I'm eager to see her, and it's time we went along. Time you went along, too, Rosie Real. You and your *man*. I can call him that, you see. Your *man*, your *man*. But before you go . . ."

Rose Madder held her arms out.

Slowly, feeling almost hypnotized, Rosie got to her feet and entered the offered embrace. The dark patches growing in Rose Madder's flesh were hot and fevery—Rosie fancied she could almost feel them squirming against her own skin. Otherwise, the woman in the chiton—in the *zat*—was as cold as a corpse.

But Rosie was no longer afraid.

Rose Madder kissed her cheke, high up toward the jaw, and whispered, "I love you, little Rosie. I wish we'd met at a better time, when you might have seen me in a better light, but we have done as well as we could. We have been well-met. Just remember the tree."

"What tree?" Rosie asked frantically. "*What* tree?" But Rose Madder shook her head with inarguable finality and stepped back, breaking their embrace. Rosie took one last look into that uneasy, demented face, and thought again of the vixen and her kits.

"Am I you?" she whispered. "Tell me the truth—am I you?"

Rose Madder smiled. It was just a small smile, but for a moment Rosie saw a monster glimmering in it, and she shuddered.

"Never mind, little Rosie. I'm too old and sick to deal with such questions. Philosophy is the province of the well. If you remember the tree, it will never matter, anyway."

"I don't understand—"

"*Shhh!*" She put a finger to her lips. "Turn around, Rosie. Turn around and see me no more. The play has ended."

Rosie turned, bent, put her hands over Bill's hands (they were still clasped, his fingers a tense, woven knot between his thighs), and pulled him to his feet. Once more the easel was gone, and the picture which had been on it—her apartment at night, indifferently rendered in muddy oils—had grown to enormous size. Once more it wasn't really a picture at all, but a window. Rosie started toward it, intent on nothing but getting through it and leaving the mysteries of this world behind for good. Bill stopped her with a tug on the wrist. He turned back to Rose Madder, and spoke without allowing his eyes to rise any higher than her breasts.

"Thank you for helping us," he said.

"You're very welcome," Rose Madder said composedly. "Repay me by treating her well."

I repay, Rosie thought, and shuddered again.

"Come on," she said, tugging Bill's hand. "Please, let's go."

He lingered a moment longer, though. "Yes," he said. "I'll treat her well. I've got a pretty good idea of what happens to people who don't. Better than I want, maybe."

"It's such a pretty man," Rose Madder said thoughtfully, and then her tone changed—it became distraught, almost distracted. "Take him while you still can, Rosie Real! While you still can!"

"Go on!" Dorcas cried. "You two get out of here *right now!*"

"But give me what's mine before you go!" Rose Madder screamed. Her voice was squealing and unearthly. *"Give it to me, you bitch!"* Something—not an arm, something too thin and bristly to be an arm—flailed in the moonlight and slid along the madly shrinking flesh of Rosie McClendon's forearm.

With a scream of her own, Rosie pulled the gold armlet off and flung it at the feet of the looming, writhing shape before her. She was aware of Dorcas throwing her arms around that shape, trying to restrain it, and Rosie waited to see no more. She seized Bill by the arm and yanked him through the window-sized painting.

3

There was no sensation of tripping, but she fell rather than walked out of the painting, just the same. So did Bill. They landed on the closet floor side by side in a long, trapezoidal patch of moonlight. Bill rapped his head against the side of the door, hard enough to hurt, by the sound, but he seemed unaware of it.

"That was no dream," he said. "Jesus, *we were in the picture!* The one you bought on the day I met you!"

"No," she said calmly. "Not at all."

Around them, the moonlight began to simultaneously brighten and contract. At the same time it lost its linear shape and quickly became circular. It was as if a door were slowly irising closed behind them. Rosie felt an urge to turn and see what was happening, but she resisted it. And when Bill started to turn his head, she placed her palms gently against his cheeks and turned his face back to hers.

"Don't," she said. "What good would it do? Whatever happened is over now."

"But—"

The light had contracted to a blindingly bright spotlight around them now, and Rosie had the crazy idea that if Bill took her in his arms and danced her across the room, that bright beam of light would follow them.

"Never mind," she said. "Never mind any of it. Just let it go."

"But where's Norman, Rosie?"

"Gone," she said, and then, as an almost comic afterthought: "My sweater and the jacket you loaned me, too. The sweater wasn't much, but I'm sorry about the jacket."

"Hey," he said, with a kind of numb insouciance, "don't sweat the small stuff."

The pinspot shrank to a cold and furiously blazing matchhead of light, then to a needlepoint, and then it was gone, leaving just a white dot of afterimage floating in front of her eyes. She looked back into the closet. The picture was exactly where she had put it following her first trip to the world inside it, only it had changed again. Now it showed only the hilltop and the temple below by the last rays of the waning moon. The stillness of this scene—and the absence of any human figure—made it look more classical than ever to Rosie.

"Christ," Bill said. He was rubbing his swollen throat. "What happened, Rosie? I just can't figure out what *happened.*"

Not too much time could have passed; down the hall, the tenant Norman had shot was still screaming his head off.

"I ought to go see if I can help that guy," Bill said, struggling to his feet. "Will you call an ambulance? And the cops?"

"Yes. I imagine they're both on the way already, but I'll make the calls."

He went to the door, then looked back doubtfully, still massaging his throat. "What'll you tell the police, Rosie?"

She hesitated a moment, then smiled. "Dunno . . . but I'll think of something. These days invention on short notice is my strong suit. Go on, now. Do your thing."

"I love you, Rosie. That's the only thing I'm sure of anymore."

He went before she could reply. She followed a step or two after him, then stopped. From down the hall she could now see a hesitant, bobbing light that had to be a candle. Someone said: "Holy cow! Is he shot?" Bill's murmured reply was lost in another howl from the injured man. Injured, yes, but probably not too badly. Not if he could produce a noise level that high.

Unkind, she told herself, picking up the handset of her new telephone and punching 911. Perhaps it was, but it might also be simple realism. Rosie didn't think it mattered either way. She'd started to see the world in a new perspective, she supposed, and her thought about the yelling man down the hall was just one sign of that new perspective at work. "It doesn't matter as long as I remember the tree," she said, without even being aware that she had spoken.

The phone on the other end of her call was picked up after a single ring. "Hello, 911, this call is being recorded."

"Yes, I'm sure. My name is Rosie McClendon, and my residence is

897 Trenton Street, second floor. My upstairs neighbor needs an ambulance."

"Ma'am, can you tell me the nature of his—"

She could, she most certainly could, but something else struck her then, something she hadn't understood before but did now, something that needed doing right this second. She dropped the phone back into its cradle and slipped the first two fingers of her right hand into the watch-pocket of her jeans. That little pocket was sometimes convenient, but it was irritating, too—just one more visible sign of the world's half-conscious prejudice against southpaws like her. It was a world made by and for righthanders, as a general rule, and full of similar little inconveniences. But that was all right; if you were a lefty, you just learned to cope, that was all. And it could be done, Rosie thought. As that old Bob Dylan song about Highway 61 said, oh yes, it could be very easily done.

She tweezed out the tiny ceramic bottle Dorcas had given her, looked at it fixedly for two or three seconds, then cocked her head to listen out the door. Someone else had joined the group at the end of the hall, and the man who had been shot (at least Rosie assumed it was he) was speaking to them in a gaspy, weepy little voice. And in the distance, Rosie could hear sirens coming this way.

She went into the kitchenette area and opened her tiny refrigerator. Inside was a package of bologna with three or four slices left, a quart of milk, two cartons of plain yogurt, a pint of juice, and three bottles of Pepsi. She took one of these latter, twisted off the cap, and stood it on the counter. She snatched another quick look over her shoulder, half-expecting to see Bill in the doorway (*What are you doing?* he would ask. *What are you mixing up there?*). The doorway was empty, however, and she could hear him at the end of the hallway, speaking in the calm, considering voice she had already come to love.

Using her nails, she pulled the sliver of cork from the mouth of the tiny bottle. Then she held it up, wafting it back and forth under her nostrils like a woman smelling a bottle of perfume. What she smelled was not perfume, but she knew the scent—bitter, metallic, but oddly attractive, just the same—at once. The little bottle contained water from the stream which ran behind the Temple of the Bull.

Dorcas: *One drop. For him. After.*

Yes, only one; more would be dangerous, but one might be enough. All the questions and all the memories—the moonlight, Norman's terrible shrieks of pain and horror, the woman he had been forbidden to look at—would be gone. So would her fear that those memories might eat away at his sanity and their budding relationship like corroding acid. That might turn out to be a specious worry—the human mind was tougher and more adaptable than most people would ever believe, if fourteen years with Norman had taught her nothing else it had taught her that, but was it a chance she wanted to take? Was it, when things might just as easily go the other way? Which was more dangerous, his memories or this liquid amnesia?

Have a care, girl. This is dangerous stuff!

Rosie's eyes drifted from the tiny ceramic bottle to the sink drain, and then, slowly, back to the bottle again.

Rose Madder: *A good beast. Protect him and he'll protect you.*

Rosie decided that the terminology of that last might be contemptuous and wrong, but the idea was right. Slowly, carefully, she tilted the ceramic bottle over the neck of the Pepsi-Cola bottle, and let a single drop fall from the one to the other.

Plink.

Now dump the rest down the sink, quick.

She started to, then remembered the rest of what Dorcas had said: *I could have give you less, only he may need another drop later on.*

Yes, and what about me? she asked herself, driving the minuscule cork back into the neck of the bottle and returning it to that inconvenient watch-pocket. *What about me? Will I need a drop or two later on, to keep me from going nuts?*

She didn't think she would. And besides . . .

"Those who don't learn from the past are condemned to repeat the bastard," she muttered. She didn't know who had said that, but she knew it was too plausible to ignore. She hurried back to the phone, holding the doctored Pepsi in one hand. She punched 911 again, and got the same operator with the same opening gambit: watch yourself, lady, this call is being recorded.

"It's Rosie McClendon again," she said. "We got cut off." She took a calculated pause, then laughed nervously. "Oh hell, that's not exactly true. I got excited and pulled the phone jack out of the wall. Things are a little crazy here right now."

"Yes, ma'am. An ambulance has been dispatched to 897 Trenton, as per request Rose McClendon. We have a report from the same address of shots fired, ma'am, is your report a gunshot wound?"

"Yes, I think so."

"Do you want me to connect you with a police officer?"

"I want to speak to Lieutenant Hale. He's a detective, so I guess I want DET-DIV, or whatever you call it here."

There was a pause, and when the 911 operator spoke again, he sounded a little less like a machine. "Yes, ma'am, Detective Division is what we call it—DET-DIV. I'll put you through."

"Thanks. Do you want my phone number, or do you trap calls?"

Definite surprise this time. "I've got your number, ma'am."

"I thought you did."

"Hold on, I'm transferring you."

As she waited, she picked up the bottle of Pepsi and wafted it under her nose, as she had the other, much tinier, bottle. She thought she could smell just the slightest tang of bitterness . . . but perhaps that was only her imagination. Not that it mattered. Either he'd drink it or he wouldn't. *Ka,* she thought, and then, *What?*

Before she could go any further with that, the phone was picked up. "Detective Division, Sergeant Williams."

She gave him Hale's name and was put on hold. Outside her room and down the hallway, the murmuring and the groaning replies continued. The sirens were much closer now.

4

"**H**ello, Hale!" a voice barked suddenly into her ear. It didn't sound at all like the laid-back, thoughtful man she had met earlier. "Is that you, Ms. McClendon?"

"Yes—"

"Are you all right?" Still barking, and now he reminded her of all the cops who'd ever sat in their rec room with their shoes off and their feet smelling up the place. He couldn't wait for information she would have given him on her own; no, he was upset, and now he had to dance around her feet, barking like a terrier.

Men, she thought, and rolled her eyes.

"Yes." She spoke slowly, like a playground monitor trying to calm a hysterical child who has taken a tumble from the jungle gym. "Yes, I'm fine. Bill—Mr. Steiner—is fine, too. We're both fine."

"Is it your husband?" He sounded outraged, only a step or two away from outright panic. A bull in an open field, pawing the ground and looking for the red rag which has provoked it. "Was it Daniels?"

"Yes. But he's gone now." She hesitated, then added: "I don't know where." *But I expect it's hot and the air conditioning's broken.*

"We'll find him," Hale said. "I promise you that, Ms. McClendon—we'll find him."

"Good luck, Lieutenant," she said softly, and turned her eyes to the open closet door. She touched her upper left arm, where she could still feel the fading heat of the armlet. "I have to hang up now. Norman shot a man from upstairs, and there may be something I can do for him. Are you coming over here?"

"You're damned right I am."

"Then I'll see you when you get here. Goodbye." She hung up before Hale could say anything else. Bill came in, and as he did, the hall lights came on behind him.

He looked around, surprised. "It must have been a breaker . . . which means he was in the cellar. But if he was going to flip one of them, I wonder why he didn't—" Before he could finish, he began to cough again, and hard. He bent over, grimacing, holding his hands cupped against his bruised and swollen throat.

"Here," she said, hurrying across to him. "Drink some of this. It just came out of the icebox, and it's cold."

He took the Pepsi, drank several swallows, then held the bottle out and looked at it curiously. "Tastes a little funny," he said.

"That's because your throat's all swollen. Probably it's bled a little, too, and you're tasting that. Come on, down the hatch. I hate hearing you cough like that."

He drank the rest, put the bottle on the coffee-table, and when he looked at her again, she saw a dumb blankness in his eyes that frightened her badly.

"Bill? Bill, what is it? What's wrong?"

That blank look held for a moment, then he laughed and shook his head. "You won't believe it. Stress of the day, I guess, but . . ."

"What? Won't believe what?"

"For a couple of seconds there I couldn't remember who you were," he said. "I couldn't remember your *name,* Rosie. But what's even crazier is that for a couple of seconds I couldn't remember *mine,* either."

She laughed and stepped toward him. She could hear a trample of footfalls—EMTs, probably—coming up the stairs, but she didn't care. She wrapped her arms around him and hugged him with all her might. "My name's Rosie," she said. "I'm Rosie. *Really* Rosie."

"Right," he said, kissing her temple. "Rosie, Rosie, Rosie, Rosie. Rosie."

She closed her eyes and pressed her face against his shoulder and in the darkness behind her closed lids she saw the unnatural mouth of the spider and the black eyes of the vixen, eyes too still to give away either madness or sanity. She saw these things and knew she would continue to see them for a long time. And in her head two words rang, tolling like an iron bell:

I repay.

5

Lieutenant Hale lit a cigarette without bothering to ask permission, crossed his legs, and gazed at Rosie McClendon and Bill Steiner, two people suffering a classic case of lovesickness; every time they looked into each other's eyes, Hale could almost read TILT printed across their pupils. It was enough to make him wonder if they hadn't somehow gotten rid of the troublesome Norman themselves . . . except he knew better. They weren't the type. Not these two.

He had dragged a kitchen chair into the living-room area and now sat on it backward, with one arm laid over the back and his chin resting on his arm. Rosie and Bill were crammed onto the loveseat that fancied itself a sofa. A little over an hour had elapsed since Rosie's original 911 call. The wounded upstairs tenant, John Briscoe by name, had been taken to East Side Receiving with what one of the EMTs had described as "a flesh-wound with pretensions."

Now things had finally quieted down a little. Hale liked that. There was only one thing he would like more, and that was to know where the hell Norman Daniels had gotten himself off to.

"One of the instruments is out of tune here," he said, "and it's screwing up the whole band."

Rosie and Bill glanced at each other. Hale was sure of the bewilderment in Bill Steiner's eyes; about Rosie he was a little less sure. There was something there, he was almost sure of it. Something she wasn't telling.

He paged slowly back through his notebook, taking his time, wanting them to fidget a little. Neither of them did. It surprised him that Rosie could be so still—*if,* that was, she was holding back—but he had either forgotten an important thing about her or not fully taken it in to begin with. She had never actually sat in on a police interrogation, but she had listened to thousands of replays and discussions as she silently served Norman and his friends drinks or dumped their ashtrays. She was hip to his technique.

"All right," Hale said when he was sure neither of them was going to give him a string to pull. "Here's where we are now in our thinking. Norman comes here. Norman somehow manages to kill Officers Alvin

Demers and Lee Babcock. Babcock goes into the shotgun seat, Demers into the trunk. Norman knocks out the light in the vestibule, then goes down into the basement and turns off a bunch of circuit breakers, pretty much at random, although they're well marked on the diagrams pasted inside the breaker boxes. Why? We don't know. He's nuts. Then he goes back to the black-and-white and pretends to be Officer Demers. When you and Mr. Steiner show up, he hits you from behind—chokes hell out of Mr. Steiner, chases you guys upstairs, shoots Mr. Briscoe when he tries to crash the party, then breaks in your door. All right so far?"

"Yes, I think so," Rosie said. "It was pretty confusing, but that must be about how it happened."

"But here's the part I don't get. You guys hid in the closet—"

"Yes—"

"—and in comes Norman like Freddy Jason or whatever his name is in those horror pictures—"

"Well, not exactly like—"

"—and he charges around like a bull in the old china shop, stopping in the bathroom long enough to shoot a couple holes in the shower curtain . . . and then he charges out again. Is that what you're telling me he did?"

"That's what happened," she said. "Naturally, we didn't *see* him charging around, because we were in the closet, but we heard it."

"This crazy, sick excuse for a cop goes through hell to find you, gets pissed on, gets his nose pretty much demolished, murders two cops, and then . . . what? Kills a shower curtain and runs? That's what you're telling me?"

"Yes." There was no sense in saying more, she saw. He didn't suspect her of anything illegal—he'd've been cutting her a lot more slack, at least to start with, if he did—but if she tried to amplify her simple agreement, he might go on with his terrier-yapping all night, and it was already giving her a headache.

Hale looked at Bill. "Is that how you remember it?"

Bill shook his head. "I *don't* remember it," he said. "The last thing I'm clear on is pulling up on my Harley in front of that police-car. Lots of fog. And after that, it's *all* fog."

Hale tossed his hands up in disgust. Rose took Bill's hand, put it on her thigh, covered it with both of her own, and smiled sweetly up at him.

"That's okay," she said. "I'm sure it will all come back to you in time."

6

Bill promised her he would stay. He kept his word—and fell asleep almost as soon as his head touched the pillow borrowed from the little sofa. It didn't surprise Rosie. She lay down beside him on the narrow bed, watching the fog billow past the streetlight outside, and waited for her eyelids to grow heavy. When they didn't, she got up, went into the closet, turned on the light, and sat crosslegged in front of the picture.

Silent moonlight informed it. The temple was a pallid sepulchre. The carrion-birds circled overhead. *Will they dine on Norman's flesh tomorrow, when the sun comes up?* she wondered. She didn't think so. Rose Madder had put Norman in a place where birds never went.

She looked at the painting a moment or two longer, then reached out to it, feeling the frozen brush-strokes with her fingers. The touch reassured her. She turned off the light and went back to bed. This time sleep came quickly.

7

She woke up—and woke Bill up—early on the first day of her life without Norman. She was shrieking.

"I repay! I repay! Oh God her eyes! Her black eyes!"

"Rosie," he said, shaking her shoulder. *"Rosie!"*

She looked at him, blankly at first, her face wet with sweat and her nightgown drenched with it, the cotton clinging to the hollows and curves of her body. "Bill?"

He nodded. "You bet it is. You're okay. We both are."

She shuddered and clung to him. Comfort quickly turned to something else. She lay beneath him, right hand locked around her left wrist behind his neck, and as he entered her (she had never experienced such gentleness or felt such confidence with Norman), her eyes went to her jeans, lying close by on the floor. The ceramic bottle was still in the watch-pocket, and she judged there were at least three drops of that bitterly attractive water left in it—maybe more.

I'll take it, she thought, just before her ability to think coherently ceased. *I'll take it, of course I will. I'll forget, and that'll be for the best—who needs dreams like these?*

But there was a deep part of her—much deeper than her old girlfriend Practical-Sensible—that knew the answer to that: *she* needed dreams like those, that was who. *She* did. And although she'd keep the bottle and what was inside it, she wouldn't keep it for herself. Because she who forgets the past is condemned to repeat it.

She looked up at Bill. He was looking down at her, his eyes wide and hazy with pleasure. His, she found, was hers, and she let herself go where he was taking her, and they stayed where they were for quite some time, brave sailors voyaging in the little ship of her bed.

8

Around midmorning, Bill ventured out to get bagels and the Sunday paper. Rosie showered, dressed, then sat on the edge of the bed in her bare feet. She could smell their separate scents and also the one they made together. She thought she had never smelled anything nicer.

Best of all? Easy. No spot of blood on the top sheet. No blood anywhere.

Her jeans had migrated under the bed. She hooked them out with her toes, then retrieved the little bottle from the watch-pocket. She took the jeans into the bathroom, where she kept a plastic clothes basket behind the door. The bottle would go into the medicine cabinet, at least for the time being, where it could hide very easily behind her bottle of Motrin. She fished in the other pockets of the jeans before tossing them in the dirty clothes, a housewifely habit so old she was completely unaware she was doing it . . . until her fingers closed on something deep in the more frequently used left front pocket. She brought it out, held it up, then shivered as Rose Madder spoke inside her head. *A souvenir . . . do with it as you will.*

It was Norman's Police Academy ring.

She slipped it over her thumb, turning it this way and that, letting the light from the frosted glass of the bathroom window shine off the words *Service, Loyalty, Community.* She shivered again, and for a moment or two she fully expected Norman to coalesce around this baleful talisman.

Half a minute later, with Dorcas's bottle safely stowed in the medicine cabinet, she hurried back to the rumpled bed, this time not smelling the fragrance of man and woman that still lingered there. It was the night-table she was thinking about and looking at. It had a drawer. She would put the ring in there for now. Later she would think what to do with it;

for now all she wanted was to get it out of sight. It wouldn't be safe to leave it out, that was for sure. Lieutenant Hale was likely to drop in later, armed with a few new questions and a lot of old ones, and it wouldn't do for him to see Norman's Police Academy ring. It wouldn't do at all.

She opened the drawer, reached forward to drop the ring in . . . and then her hand froze.

There was something else in the drawer already. A scrap of blue cloth, carefully folded over to make a packet. Rose madder stains were scattered across it; they looked to her like drops of half-dried blood.

"Oh my God," Rosie whispered. "The *seeds!*"

She took out the packet that was once part of a cheap cotton nightgown, sat on the bed (her knees suddenly felt too weak to hold her), and laid the packet on her lap. In her mind she heard Dorcas telling her not to taste the fruit, or to even put the hand which touched the seeds into her mouth. A pomegranate tree, she had called it, but Rosie didn't think that was what it was.

She unfolded the sides of the little packet and looked down at the seeds. Her heart was running like a racehorse in her chest.

Dassn't keep them, she thought. *Dassn't, dassn't.*

Leaving her late husband's ring beside the lamp, at least for the time being, Rosie got up and went into the bathroom again, the open cloth held on her palm. She didn't know how long Bill had been gone, she had lost track of time, but it had been quite awhile.

Please, she thought, *let the bagel line at the deli be long.*

She put up the ring of the toilet seat, knelt down, and plucked the first seed off the cloth. It had occurred to her that this world might have robbed the seeds of their magic, but the tips of her fingers went numb immediately, and she knew that was not the case. It wasn't as if her fingers had been cold-numbed; it was more as if the seeds had communicated some strange amnesia to her very flesh. Nevertheless, she held the seed for a moment, looking at it fixedly.

"One for the vixen," she said, and threw it into the bowl. At once the water bloomed a sinister rose madder red. It looked like the residue of a sliced wrist or a cut throat. The smell that drifted up to her wasn't blood, however; it was the bitter, slightly metallic aroma of the stream behind the Temple of the Bull. It was so strong it made her eyes water.

She plucked the second seed off the cloth and held it in front of her eyes.

"One for Dorcas," she said, and threw it into the bowl. The color deepened—it was now not the color of blood but of clots—and the smell was so strong that tears went rolling down her cheeks. Her eyes were as red as the eyes of a woman elbow-deep in chopped onions.

She plucked the last seed off the cloth and held it in front of her eyes.

"And one for me," she said. "One for Rosie."

But when she tried to throw this one into the bowl, her fingers wouldn't let go of it. She tried again, with the same result. Instead, the voice of the madwoman filled her mind, and it spoke with a persuasive sanity: *Remember the tree. Remember the tree, little Rosie. Remember—*

"The tree," Rosie murmured. "Remember the tree, yes, got that, but *what* tree? And what should I do? What in God's name should I do?"

I don't know, Practical-Sensible answered, *but whatever you do, you better do it fast. Bill could come back any minute. Any second.*

She flushed the john, watching as the reddish-purple liquid was replaced by clear water. Then she went back to the bed, sat on it, and stared at the last seed lying on the stained cotton cloth. From the seed she looked to Norman's ring. Then she looked back at the seed.

Why can't I throw this damned thing away? she asked herself. *Never mind the goddam tree, just tell me why in God's name I can't throw this last seed from it away, and be done with it.*

No answer came. What did was the excited pop and burble of an approaching motorcycle, drifting in through the open window. She already recognized the sound of Bill's Harley. Quickly, asking no more questions of herself, Rosie put the ring in the soft blue swatch of cloth along with the seed. Then she refolded it, hurried across to the bureau, and took her purse off the top. It was scuffed and dowdy, this purse, but it meant a lot to her—it was the one she had brought out of Egypt with her that spring. She opened it and put the little blue packet inside, stuffing it all the way to the bottom, where it would lie even more securely hidden than the ceramic bottle in the medicine cabinet. With that done, she went over to the open window and began breathing in great lungfuls of fresh air.

When Bill came in with a fat Sunday paper and an outrageous number of bagels stuffed into a paper bag, Rosie turned to him with a brilliant smile. "What kept you?" she asked, and thought to herself: *What a fox you are, little Rosie. What a f—*

The smile on his face, the answer to hers, suddenly faltered. "Rosie? Are you all right?"

Her smile brightened again. "Fine. I guess a goose just walked over my grave."

Except it hadn't been a goose.

9

*M*ay *I give you one piece of advice before I send you back?* Rose Madder had asked, and late that afternoon, after Lieutenant Hale had brought them the shocking news about Anna Stevenson (who hadn't been discovered until that morning, due to her oft-expressed dislike of unauthorized visitors in her office) and then departed, Rosie took that advice. It was Sunday, but Hair 2000 at the Skyview Mall was open. The hairdresser to whom she was assigned understood what Rosie wanted, but protested briefly.

"It looks so pretty this way!" she said.

"Yes, I guess it does," Rosie replied, "but I hate it anyway."

So the beautician did her thing, and the surprised protests she expected from Bill when she saw him that evening did not come.

"Your hair's shorter, but otherwise you look the way you did when you first came into the shop," he said. "I think I like that."

She hugged him. "Good."

"Want Chinese for supper?"

"Only if you promise to stay over again."

"All promises should be so easy to keep," he said, smiling.

10

*M*onday's *headline:* ROGUE COP SPOTTED IN WISCONSIN

Tuesday's headline: POLICE MUM ON KILLER COP DANIELS

Wednesday's headline: ANNA STEVENSON CREMATED; 2,000 IN SILENT MEMORIAL MARCH

Thursday's headline: DANIELS MAY BE DEAD BY OWN HAND, INSIDERS SPECULATE

On Friday, Norman moved to page two.

By the following Friday, he was gone.

11

Shortly after July 4th, Robbie Lefferts put Rosie to work reading a novel about as far from the works of "Richard Racine" as it was possible to get: *A Thousand Acres,* by Jane Smiley. It was the story of an Iowa farm family, except that wasn't what it *really* was; Rosie had been costume designer in the high-school drama society for three years, and although she had never trod a single step in front of the footlights, she still recognized Shakespeare's mad king when she encountered him. Smiley had put Lear in biballs, but crazy is still crazy.

She had also turned him into a creature that reminded Rosie fearfully of Norman. On the day she finished the book ("Your best job so far," Rhoda told her, "and one of the best readings I've ever heard"), Rosie went back to her room and took the old frameless oil painting out of the closet where it had been ever since the night of Norman's . . . well, disappearance. It was the first time she had looked at it since that night.

What she saw didn't surprise her that much. It was daylight in the picture again. The hillside was the same, overgrown and rather ragged, and the temple down below was the same (or *about* the same; Rosie had a sense that the temple's queerly skewed perspective had somehow changed, become normal), and the women were still gone. Rosie had an idea that Dorcas had taken the madwoman to see her baby one last time . . . and then Rose Madder would be going on alone, to whatever place creatures like her went when the hour of their deaths had at last rolled around.

She took the picture down the hall to the incinerator chute, holding it carefully by the sides as she had held it before—holding it as if she feared her hand would slide right through into that other world, if she should be careless. In truth, she did fear something like that.

At the incinerator shaft she paused again, looking fixedly one last time at the picture which had called to her from its dusty pawnshop shelf, called with a tongueless, imperative voice that could have belonged to Rose Madder herself. *And probably did,* Rosie thought. She lifted one hand toward the door of the incinerator chute, then paused, her eye caught by something she'd missed before: two shapes in the tall grass a little way down the hill. She ran a finger lightly over the painted surface of those shapes, frowning, trying to think what they might be. After a few moments it came to her. The little blob of clover-pink was her sweater. The black blob beside it was the jacket Bill had loaned her for the motorcycle ride out Route 27 that day. She didn't care about the sweater, it was just a cheap Orlon thing, but she was sorry about the jacket. It wasn't new, but there had been good years left in it, just the same. Besides, she liked to return the things people loaned her.

She had even used Norman's bank card just that once.

She looked at the painting, then sighed. No sense keeping it; she would be leaving the little room Anna had found for her soon, and she had no intention of dragging any more of the past with her than necessary. She supposed she was stuck with the part of it that was lodged in her head like bullet-fragments, but—

Remember the tree, Rosie, a voice said, and this time it sounded like Anna's voice—Anna who had helped her when she had needed help, when she'd had no one else to turn to, Anna for whom she hadn't been able to mourn as she'd wanted to . . . although she had cried rivers for sweet Pam, with her pretty blue eyes always trained for "someone interesting." Yet now she felt a sting of sorrow that made her lips quiver and her nose prickle.

"Anna, I'm sorry," she said.

Never mind. That voice, dry and slightly arrogant. *You didn't make me, you didn't make Norman, and you don't have to accept responsibility for either of us. You're Rosie McClendon, not Typhoid Mary, and you'd do well to remember that when storms of melodrama threaten to engulf you. But you have to remember—*

"No, I don't," she said, and slammed the painting together on itself, like someone closing a book with authority. The old wood upon which the canvas had been stretched snapped. The canvas itself did not so much tear as explode into strips which hung like rags. The paint on these rags was dim and meaningless. "No, I don't. Not *anything,* if I don't want to, and I *don't.*"

Those who forget the past—

"*Fuck* the past!" Rosie cried.

I repay, a voice answered. It whispered; it cajoled. It warned.

"I don't hear you," Rose said. She pulled the flap of the incinerator open, felt warmth, smelled soot. "I don't hear you, I'm not listening, it's over."

She shoved the torn and folded picture through the door, mailing it like a letter intended for someone in hell, then stood on tiptoe to watch it fall toward the flames far below.

Epilogue

THE
FOX-WOMAN

1

In October, Bill takes her out to the Shoreland picnic area again. This time they go in his car; it's a pretty fall day, but too chilly for the motorcycle. Once they're there, with a picnic spread before them and the woods around them flaming with fall color, he asks her what she has known for some time that he means to ask her.

"Yes," she says. "As soon as the decree comes through."

He hugs her, kisses her, and as she tightens her arms around his neck and closes her eyes, she hears the voice of Rose Madder deep in her head: *All accounts now balance . . . and if you remember the tree, it will never matter, anyway.*

What tree, though?

Tree of Life?

Tree of Death?

Tree of Knowledge?

Tree of Good and Evil?

Rosie shudders and hugs her husband-to-be even tighter, and when he cups her left breast in his hand, he marvels at the feel of her heart pounding away so rapidly beneath it.

What tree?

2

They're married in a civil ceremony which takes place midway between Thanksgiving and Christmas, ten days after Rosie's decree of non-responsive divorce from Norman Daniels becomes final. On her first night as Rosie Steiner, she wakes to her husband's screams.

"I can't look at her!" he screams in his sleep. *"She doesn't care who she kills! She doesn't care who she kills! Oh please, can't you make him stop SCREAMING?"* And then, in a lower voice, trailing off: "What's in your mouth? What are those threads?"

They are in a New York hotel, staying over on their way to St. Thomas, where they will honeymoon for two weeks, but although she left the little blue packet behind, still at the bottom of the purse she carried with her out of Egypt, she has brought the ceramic bottle. Some instinct—woman's intuition will do as well as any other name in this case, she reckons—has told her to. She has used it on two other occasions following nightmares like this one, and the next morning, while Bill is shaving, she tips the last drop into his coffee.

It'll have to do, she thinks later as she tosses the tiny bottle into the toilet and flushes it down. *And if it doesn't, it'll have to do, anyway.*

The honeymoon is perfect—lots of sun, lots of good sex, and no bad dreams for either of them.

3

In January, on a day when billows of wind-driven snow come driving across the plains and over the city, Rosie Steiner's home pregnancy kit tells her what she already knows, that she is going to have a baby. She knows something more, something the kit can't tell her: it will be a girl.

Caroline is finally coming.

All accounts balance, she thinks in a voice not her own as she stands at the window of their new apartment, looking out at the snow. It reminds her of the fog that night in Bryant Park, when they came home to discover Norman waiting.

Yeah, yeah, yeah, she thinks, almost bored with this idea by now; it comes almost with the frequency of a nagging tune that won't quite leave your head. *They balance as long as I remember the tree, right?*

No, the madwoman replies, in a voice so deadly clear that Rosie whirls on her heels, heart thudding sickly all the way up in the middle of her forehead, momentarily convinced that Rose Madder is in this room with her. But although the voice is still there, the room is empty. *No . . . as long as you keep your temper. As long as you can do that. But both things come to the same, don't they?*

"Get out," she tells the empty room, and her hoarse voice trembles. "Get out, you bitch. Stay away from me. Stay out of my life."

4

Her baby girl weighs in at eight pounds, nine ounces. And although Caroline is and always will be her secret name, the one that goes on the birth certificate is Pamela Gertrude. At first Rosie objects, saying that, with their last name added to the second, the child's name becomes a kind of literary pun. She holds out, with no great enthusiasm, for Pamela Anna.

"Oh, please," Bill says, "that sounds like a fruit dessert in a snooty California restaurant."

"But—"

"And don't worry about Pamela Gertrude. First of all, she's never going to let even her best friend know that her middle name is Gert. You can count on it. And second, the writer you're talking about is the one who said a rose is a rose is a rose. I can't think of a better reason to stick with a name."

So they do.

5

Not long before Pammy turns two, her parents decide to buy a home in the suburbs. By then they can well afford it; both have prospered in their jobs. They begin with stacks of brochures, and slowly winnow them down to a dozen possibles, then six, then four, then two. And this is where they run into trouble. Rose wants one; Bill prefers the other. Discussion becomes debate as their positions polarize, and debate escalates into argument—unfortunate, but hardly unheard-of; even the sweetest and most harmonious marriage is not immune from a tiff every now and then . . . or the occasional shouting-match, for that matter.

At the end of this one, Rosie stalks out into the kitchen and begins to put supper together, first sticking a chicken in the oven and then putting water on for the corn on the cob she has picked up fresh at a roadside stand. A little while later, while she is scrubbing a couple of potatoes at the counter beside the stove, Bill comes out of the living room, where he has been looking at photographs of the two houses which have caused this unaccustomed dissension between them . . . except what he has really been doing is brooding over the argument.

She does not turn at his approaching step as she usually does, nor does she when he bends and kisses the nape of her neck.

"I'm sorry I yelled at you about the house," he said quietly. "I still think the one in Windsor is better for us, but I'm truly sorry I raised my voice."

He waits for her reply, and when she makes none, he turns and trudges sorrowfully out, probably thinking she is still angry. She is not, however; anger in no way describes her current state of mind. She is in a black rage, almost a killing rage, and her silence has not been something as childish as "giving him the cold shoulder," but rather an almost frantic effort to

(remember the tree)

keep from seizing the pot of boiling water on the stove, turning with it in her hands, and throwing it into his face. The vivid picture she sees in her mind is both sickening and blackly compelling: Bill staggering back, screaming, as his skin goes a color she still sometimes sees in her dreams. Bill, clawing at his cheeks as the first blisters begin to push out of his smoking skin.

Her left hand has actually twitched toward the handle of the pot, and that night, as she lies sleepless in her bed, two words play themselves over and over in her mind: *I repay.*

6

In the days which follow, she begins to look obsessively at her hands and her arms and her face . . . but mostly at her hands, because that is where it will start.

Where what will start? She doesn't know, exactly . . . but she knows she will recognize

(the tree)

it when she sees it.

She discovers a place called Elmo's Batting Cages on the west side of the city and begins to go there regularly. Most of the clientele are men in early middle age trying to keep their college figures or high-school boys willing to spend five dollars or so for the privilege of pretending for a little while that they are Ken Griffey, Jr., or the Big Hurt. Every now and then a girlfriend will hit a few, but mostly they are ornamental, standing outside the batting cages or the slightly more expensive Major League Batting Tunnel and watching. There are few women in their mid-thirties stroking grounders and line drives. Few? None, really, except for this lady with the short brown hair and the pale, solemn face. So the boys joke and snigger and elbow each other and turn their caps around backward to show how bad they are, and she ignores them completely, both their laughter and their careful inventory of her body, which has bounced back nicely from the baby. Nicely? For a chick who is clearly getting up there (they tell each other), she is a knockout, a stone fox.

And after awhile, they stop laughing. They stop because the lady in the sleeveless tee-shirts and loose gray pants, after her initial clumsiness and foul ticks (several times she is even hit by the dense rubber balls the machine serves up), begins to make first good contact and then *great* contact.

"She drivin that beauty," one of them says one day after Rosie, panting and flushed, her hair drawn back against her head in a damp helmet, screams three line drives, one after the other, the length of the mesh-walled batting tunnel. Each time she connects she voices a high, un-earthly cry, like Monica Seles serving an ace. It sounds as if the ball has done something to offend her.

"Got that machine cranked, too," says a second as the pitching ma-chine hulking in the center of the tunnel coughs out an eighty-mile-an-hour fastball. Rosie gives her indrawn cry of effort, her head down almost against her shoulder, and pops her hips. The ball goes the other way, fast. It hits the mesh two hundred feet away down the tunnel, still rising, making the green fabric bell out before dropping to join the oth-ers which she has already hit.

"Aw, she ain't hittin that hard," scoffs a third. He takes out a cigarette, pokes it in his mouth, takes out a book of matches, and strikes one. "She just gettin some—"

This time Rosie *does* scream—a cry like the shriek of some hungry bird—and the ball streaks back down the tunnel in a flat white line. It hits the mesh . . . and goes through. The hole it leaves behind looks like something which might have been made by a shotgun fired at close range.

Cigarette Boy stands as if frozen, the lit match burning down in his fingers.

"You were sayin, bro?" the first boy asks softly.

7

A month later, just after the batting cages close for the season, Rhoda Simons suddenly breaks into Rosie's reading of the new Gloria Naylor and tells her to call it a day. Rosie protests that it's early. Rhoda agrees, but tells her she is losing her expression; better to give it a rest until tomorrow, she says.

"Yeah, well, I want to finish today," Rosie says. "It's only another twenty pages. I want to *finish* the damned thing, Rho."

"Anything you do now will just have to be done over," Rhoda says with finality. "I don't know how late Pamelacita kept you up last night, but you just don't have it anymore today."

8

*R*osie *gets up and goes through the door, yanking it so hard she nearly tears it off its fat silent hinges. Then, in the control room, she seizes the suddenly terrified Rhoda Simons by the collar of her goddamned Norma Kamali blouse, and slams her facedown into the control board. A toggle switch impales her patrician nose like the tine of a barbecue fork. Blood sprays everywhere, beading on the glass of the studio window and running down it in ugly rose madder streaks.*

"Rosie, no!" Curt Hamilton shrieks. "My God, what are you doing?"

Rosie hooks her nails into Rhoda's throbbing throat and tears it open, shoving her face into the hot spew of blood, wanting to bathe in it, wanting to baptize this new life which she has been so stupidly struggling against. And there is no need to answer Curt; she knows perfectly well what she is doing, she is repaying, *that's what,* repaying, *and God help anyone on the wrong side of her account books. God help—*

9

"*R*osie?" Rhoda calls through the intercom, rousing her from this horrid yet deeply compelling daydream. "Are you okay?"

Keep your temper, little Rosie.

Keep your temper and remember the tree.

She looks down and sees the pencil she has been holding is now in two pieces. She stares at them for several seconds, breathing deeply, trying to get her racing heart under control. When she feels she can speak in a more or less even tone of voice, she says: "Yeah, I'm okay. But you're right, the kiddo kept me up late and I'm tired. Let's rack it in."

"Smart girl," Rhoda says, and the woman on the other side of the glass—the woman who is taking off the headphones with hands that only shake a little—thinks, *No. Not smart. Angry.* Angry *girl.*

I repay, a voice deep in her mind whispers. *Sooner or later, little Rosie, I repay. Whether you want it or not, I repay.*

10

She expects to lie awake all that night, but she sleeps briefly after midnight and dreams. It is a tree she dreams of, *the* tree, and when she wakes she thinks: *No wonder it's been so hard for me to understand. No wonder. All this time I was thinking of the wrong one.*

She lies back next to Bill, looking up at the ceiling and thinking of the dream. In it she heard the sound of gulls over the lake, crying and crying, and Bill's voice. *They'll be all right if they keep normal,* Bill was saying. *If they keep normal and remember the tree.*

She knows what she must do.

11

The next day she calls Rhoda and says she won't be in. A touch of the flu, she says. Then she goes back out Route 27 to Shoreland, this time by herself. On the seat next to her is her old purse, the one she carried out of Egypt. She has the picnic area to herself at this time of the day and year. She takes her shoes off, puts them under a picnic table, and walks north through the shallow water at the edge of the lake, as she did with Bill when he brought her out here the first time. She thinks she may have trouble finding the overgrown path leading up the bank, but she does not. As she goes up it, digging into the gritty sand with her bare toes, she wonders how many unremembered dreams have taken her out here since the rages started. There is no way of telling, of course, nor does it really matter.

At the top of the path is the ragged clearing, and in the clearing is the fallen tree—the one she has finally remembered. She has never forgotten the things which happened to her in the world of the picture, and she sees now, with no iota of surprise, that this tree and the one which had fallen across the path leading to Dorcas's "pomegranate tree" are identical.

She can see the foxes' earth beneath the dusty bouquet of roots at the far left end of the tree, but it is empty, and looks old. She walks to it anyway, then kneels—she is not sure her trembling legs would have supported her much farther, anyway. She opens her old purse and pours out the remains of her old life on the leafy, mulchy ground. Among crumpled laundry lists and receipts years out of date, below a shopping list with the words

PORK CHOPS!

at the top, underlined, capitalized, and exclamation-pointed (pork chops were always Norman's favorite), is the blue packet with the spatter of red-purple drops running across it.

Trembling, beginning to cry—partly because the scraps of her old, hurt life make her so sad and partly because she is so afraid that the new one is in danger—she scoops a hole in the earth at the base of the fallen tree. When it is about eight inches deep, she puts the packet down beside it and opens it. The seed is still there, surrounded by the gold circle of her first husband's ring.

She puts the seed in the hole (and the seed has kept its magic; her fingers go numb the instant they touch it) and then places the ring around it again.

"Please," she says, not knowing if she prays, or for whom the prayer is intended if she does. In any case, she is answered, after a fashion. There is a short, sharp bark. There's no pity in it, no compassion, no gentleness. It is impatient. *Don't fuck with me,* it says.

Rosie looks up and sees the vixen on the far side of the clearing, standing motionless and looking at her. Her brush is up. It flames like a torch against the dull gray sky overhead.

"Please," she says again in a low, troubled voice. "Please don't let me be what I'm afraid of. Please . . . just please help me keep my temper and remember the tree."

There is nothing she can interpret as an answer, not even another of those impatient barks. The vixen only stands there. Its tongue is out now, and it is panting. To Rosie it appears to be grinning.

She looks down once more at the ring circling the seed, then she covers it over with the fragrant, mulchy dirt.

One for my mistress, she thinks, *and one for my dame, and one for the little girl who lives down the lane. One for Rosie.*

She backs to the edge of the clearing, to the head of the path which will take her back down to the lakeshore. When she is there, the vixen trots quickly to the fallen tree, sniffs the spot where Rosie buried the ring and the seed, and then lies down there. Still she pants, and still she grins (Rosie is now sure she is grinning), still she looks at Rosie with her black eyes. *The kits are gone,* those eyes say, *and the dog that got them on me is gone, as well. But I, Rosie . . . I bide. And, if needs must, I repay.*

Rosie looks for madness or sanity in those eyes . . . and sees both.

Then the vixen lowers her pretty snout to her pretty bush, closes her eyes, and appears to go to sleep.

"Please," Rosie whispers, one final time, and then she leaves. And as she drives the Skyway, on her way back to what she hopes is her life, she throws the last piece of her old life—the purse she brought with her out of Egypt—out the driver's-side window and into Coori Bay.

12

The rages have departed.

The child, Pamela, is far from grown, but she is old enough to have her own friends, to have developed applebud breasts, to have begun her monthly courses. Old enough so she and her mother have started to argue about clothes and nights out and nights in and what she may do and whom she may see and for how long. The hurricane season of Pam's adolescence has not fully started yet, but Rosie knows it is coming. She views it with equanimity, however, because the rages have departed.

Bill's hair has gone mostly gray and started to recede.

Rosie's is still brown. She wears it simply, around her shoulders. She sometimes puts it up, but never plaits it.

It is years since they have picnicked out at Shoreland, on State Highway 27; Bill seems to have forgotten about it when he sold his Harley-Davidson, and he sold the Harley because, he said, "My reflexes are too slow, Rosie. When your pleasures become risks, it's time to cut them out." She doesn't argue this idea, but it seems to her that Bill has sold a huge batch of memories along with his scoot, and she mourns these. It is as if much of his youth was tucked into its saddlebags, and he forgot to check and take it out before the nice young man from Evanston drove the motorcycle away.

They don't picnic there anymore, but once a year, always in the spring, Rosie goes out by herself. She has watched the new tree grow in the shadow of the old fallen one from a sprig to a twig to a sturdy young growth with a smooth, straight trunk and confident branches. She has watched it raise itself, year by year, in the clearing where no fox-kits now gambol. She sits before it silently, sometimes for as long as an hour, with her hands folded neatly in her lap. She does not come here to worship or to pray, but she has a sense of rightness and ritual about being here, a sense of duty fulfilled, of some unstated covenant's renewal. And if being here helps keep her from hurting anyone—Bill, Pammy, Rhoda, Curt (Rob Lefferts is not a worry; the year Pammy turned five, he died quietly of a heart attack)—then it is time well-spent.

How perfectly this tree grows! Already its young branches are densely dressed in narrow leaves of a dark green hue, and in the last two years she has seen hard flashes of color deep within those leaves—blossoms which will, in this tree's later years, become fruit. If someone were to happen by this clearing and eat of that fruit, Rosie is sure the result would be death, and a hideous death, at that. She worries about it, from time to time, but until she sees signs that other people have been here, she doesn't worry overmuch. So far she has seen no such sign, not so much as a single beercan, cigarette pack, or gum wrapper. Now it is enough simply to come here, and to fold her clear, unblemished hands in her lap, and look at the tree of her rage and the hard splashes of rose madder that will become, in later years, the numb-sweet fruit of death.

Sometimes as she sits before this little tree, she sings. *"I'm really Rosie,"* she sings, *"and I'm Rosie Real . . . you better believe me . . . I'm a great big deal . . ."*

She isn't a big deal, of course, except to the people who matter in her life, but since these are the only ones she cares about, that's fine. All accounts balance, as the woman in the *zat* might have said. She has reached safe harbor, and on these spring mornings near the lake, sitting in the overgrown, silent clearing which has never changed over all the years (it is very like a picture, that way—the sort of humdrum painting one might find in an old curio shop, or a pawn-and-loan), her legs folded beneath her, she sometimes feels a gratitude so full that she thinks her heart can hold no more, ever. It is this gratitude that makes her sing. She must sing. There is no other choice.

And sometimes the vixen—old now, her own years of bearing long behind her, her brilliant bush streaked with wiry threads of gray—comes to the edge of the clearing, and stands, and seems to listen to Rosie sing. Her black eyes as she stands there communicate no clear thought to Rosie, but it is impossible to mistake the essential sanity of the old and clever brain behind them.

June 10, 1993–November 17, 1994